REYNARD THE FOX

2012 Calliope Press Trade Paperback Edition

Manufactured in the United States of America.

REYNARD THE FOX
ISBN 978-0-578-08777-1

REYNARD THE FOX

by

David R. Witanowski

CALLIOPE PRESS

FOR MY MOTHER AND FATHER

REYNARD THE FOX

I

The fiddler was late.

One of the great bells of the temple of Fenix was tolling over the wet slosh of the Vinus, a sound that normally would have signaled nothing more than the coming of dusk, when the priest-smiths of the Firebird would congregate for their evening prayer. But on this particular night it also marked the hour that had been appointed for Lord Chanticleer's masked ball, and the dull worry that churned within the guts of his chief steward doubled in intensity as he anticipated the explosive anger of his master.

Lord Chanticleer was the head of the powerful Butcher's Guild, and incredibly rich. Indeed, it was commonly said that Chanticleer was so wealthy that if he dropped a bar of gold in the street it would be beneath him to bend over and pick it back up. A man so rich expects to get what he wants, and woe to the servant who fails to deliver.

And save for gold, there was nothing that Lord Chanticleer loved so much as music. He was a self-proclaimed connoisseur of the art, and much of his manor was given over to his collection of rare instruments. His salon was a virtual concert hall, replete with its own pipe organ (a monstrously expensive thing that had likely cost as much as the construction of the wing that housed it), and hardly a month passed between the lavish spectacles mounted there by the guild master.

But of all Chanticleer's contrived amusements none pleased the city's elite better than the masked ball held in honor of the festival of Summer's End, which superstitious peasants call Wulf's Night. And though common folk might spend that night with doors locked and bolted, it was considered fashionable amongst the rich to dress in the manner of the Watcher's servants, and to invite his dour priests to play mournful songs of bloody murder as they quaffed heady wine and danced and howled under the pale light of the skull moon until either drink or exhaustion brought their revelry to an end- it being hard to fear the ravening warg when one lives safe behind high walls, and is accustomed to well-lit streets patrolled by the city watch.

All through Redmonth Lord Chanticleer's chief steward had been anxiously preparing for the festival's raucous festivities, all of which had to be personally overseen so as to ensure that nothing went amiss. Stacks of invitations written on expensive paper and sealed with Lord Chanticleer's personal signet ring had to be properly delivered, a task that had involved a small army of uniformed guild messengers. Case after case of fine wine, shipped to the manor by river barge, needed to be hand counted before being packed in fresh ice. And as the house's kitchen staff had trebled in size to accommodate the prodigious and finicky appetites of Chanticleer's guests, the chief steward had been required to ensure that each new member of the staff was reasonably clean, and that their faces and hands were free of any unsightly blemishes.

Chanticleer had also hired the city's finest decorators, and the steward had been run ragged trying to fulfill their mounting demands as they transformed Lord Chanticleer's estate into a suitably grim place, hung with great swathes of black cloth inlaid with blood red stitching and specially commissioned lanterns that had been fashioned to project the images of ravenous wolves, swarms of night flutterers, and gruesome scenes of the walking dead. Meanwhile the artisans of the Tailor's Guild were put to work sewing ornate costumes for the ball, and it was up to the chief steward to navigate a complex web of spies and informants from rival houses to learn what designs would be in fashion this year, and which would draw the scorn of good society.

Yet of all of these many tasks, the one that the steward found most egregious was that of dealing with the grim priesthood of the Watcher, who were few and far between in the city. They had no formal temples, had to be contacted at the taverns where they played for their suppers, and most of them routinely refused to entertain the rich on Summer's End, for it was one of the holiest nights of their master. But still, Lord Chanticleer had ordered that four of these priests should be present every year at his ball, in order that they might form a morbid string quartet, and the chief steward had taken great pains to ensure that this year was no different.

And now Copee, the fiddler, was late.

She was a young woman, but already renowned as a great virtuoso with her instrument. She played at The Slaughter Prince, one of the busiest taverns of River Quarter, and it had taken much flattery, and more gold, to procure her services.

At first, the chief steward had not found her absence unusual, for the servants of the Watcher were often late, maintaining that they came and went as they pleased, beholden to no one but the Winter King himself. So, as in the past, the steward had made adequate provision for the tardiness of the followers of Wulf.

After an hour had passed, and Copee had still failed to appear at the front gates, the steward grew angry. Surely, he thought, he would never again hire on such an irresponsible woman, talented or not; what a bother her lateness would cause amongst the other priests of the Watcher, who had no fiddle player with whom to rehearse!

But when it became obvious that Copee might not make her appearance until shortly before the fall of darkness, the steward began to worry. A poor showing on her part would reflect poorly on him, and he had no wish to go back to the life of a common domestic servant, which is surely where he would end up if Lord Chanticleer dismissed him from his service.

So now he stood beneath the grand entrance to his master's estate, visions of cleaning boots and emptying chamber pots filling his addled head as his eyes frantically scanned the street that led down to River Quarter. All the while a steady stream of servants came and went, forced to trek to the front of the house to keep him abreast of the situation inside the manor. He silently thanked the Firebird that Lord Chanticleer was currently engaged with his tailors, who were even now applying the finishing touches to his elaborate costume.

Then the last ringing temple bell grew hush, and the steward could see the first guests coming up the promenade towards him: Lord and Lady Roxat, each of them carried in a silk-bedecked litter, preceded by the great banner of the Carpenter's Guild. Very soon the wide avenue before him would be crowded with the servants and followers of the rich and powerful, and the masked revel would begin.

And as the retinue of the Roxats drew closer, it finally dawned on the steward that Copee might not show up at all, and his fear of being released from employment was quickly replaced by a desperate concern for his own personal safety. Such a gaffe at the ball would prove incredibly embarrassing for Lord Chanticleer, who had never been known for his forgiving nature. By the end of the night the steward imagined that he might share the fate of the clumsy maid who had once dropped one of Lord Chanticleer's prized mandolins: namely, his throat would be slit by one of Chanticleer's knifemen, and his body would be weighed down with rocks before being dumped into the river under cover of darkness.

Briefly, the chief steward considered flight. He could, for example, secure a place onboard a boat that would take him far away, but he suspected that even if he made it as far as Tyris one of his master's hired killers would eventually find him and drag him back to be tortured as a further punishment for attempting to escape his master's wrath. And likely, the steward thought, it would be that tattooed Glyconese demon, Ghul, whom Lord Chanticleer retained for his most heinous knife work. He'd never seen the man at his business, but he'd heard the cries that occasionally echoed up from the sub-cellars, and watched as the dead were removed from the estate. Their bodies often looked remarkably unharmed, save for the delicate puncture wounds that the steward personally found more disturbing than if they'd been torn limb from limb.

Would it be better to hang himself now, he wondered, and get it over and done with?

The steward was in the middle of pondering where he might find the rope necessary for such an endeavor when his eyes fell on a strange figure across the street that he could have sworn he had not seen just a moment before. It was a man, and he was clothed in a weathered scarlet doublet with a matching pair of breeches, high red leather boots, and over one shoulder was slung a fashionable sort of cape, the kind that the nobility were fond of wearing. Over his face he wore a mask crafted so that it resembled that of a common fox.

And he had a fiddle in his gloved hands.

As the steward watched, all of his attention now bent on the stranger, the fox-headed man set down a wooden bowl on the pavement, and began to scratch out a lively tune with his instrument. He was no master of his trade, certainly, but he played well, and with a natural sense of style and flair.

It took the steward a great deal of restraint to stop himself from dashing across the street right then and there- but then, restraint was a required part of his job, and so he paused for a moment, and considered his scant options.

On the one hand, this man was no more than a common street minstrel, and there would be no way to pass him off as Copee, for everyone knew that the best fiddler of River Quarter was a woman. It was also likely that he was not even a trained musician, and the other priests of the Watcher would surely pierce any claim of the steward's to the contrary.

But on the other hand, the chief steward knew that despite all of the wealth and influence his master wielded, and the long hours he spent training with some of the city's finest music masters, Lord Chanticleer had a terrible ear for music. Even the lowest, most uncultured servant could tell that their lord and master had no talent, that his voice was dull and toneless, and that he could little tell the difference between a virtuoso and a hack.

The steward dashed down the stairs hurriedly, feeling dreadfully exposed as he trod over the manicured lawn that separated his master's estate from the well-worked stones of the street.

"You there," the steward called out as he approached the stranger, "Fiddler! What is your name?"

"You may call me Fox, your Lordship," the stranger replied in a resonant voice as he continued to play his fiddle. The steward could see that underneath his brightly colored mask he appeared to be quite handsome, with a strong jaw line and a well-formed mouth. Most striking were his eyes: almond, flecked with slivers the color of polished tin.

"Fox, eh?" the steward said as he looked the man's costume over. "A very appropriate name."

"Yes, your Lordship," the man called Fox said, playing a complex flourish as a passing couple dropped a copper bit into the wooden bowl set out beside him. "And easy to remember as well."

"Tell me, then, Master Fox, are you interested in making a great deal of coin?"

The man called Fox stopped playing momentarily and bowed, gracefully, his fiddle held carefully behind his back. "Lordship! Your words cleave so skillfully to the very heart of my desire!"

"Good. Now, do you know whose house this is?" the steward asked, gesturing at the grand estate behind him.

"Why, no your Lordship, I must confess that I do not."

"It is the house of Lord Chanticleer and, as luck would have it, he has need of another fiddler for his grand ball this evening."

Fox's face blanched at the mention of the powerful guild master's name.

"You honor me sir," Fox said, "but I fear you overestimate my ability! I am but a mere street musician. Surely one as noble and wealthy as Lord Chanticleer could afford a far better fiddler than I."

"Yes, well, be that as it may, he has need of one of your kind tonight, and if you perform well I will see to it that you will be amply rewarded for your services. Let us say . . . two silver nobles?"

"Sir!" the minstrel replied, his tone suddenly indignant, "I might make as much on the street after a good night! If Lord Chanticleer desires my services, you will have to make me a better offer than that."

Nonsense, the steward grumbled inwardly. No common street musician made more than a handful of copper bits an evening, if that. And, if circumstances were different, the steward would have had the man thrown into the gutter for having the impudence to reject his more than generous offer.

But as each passing moment brought the Roxats closer he realized that there was no time to haggle with the man, much as he would have liked to.

"Five then," the steward muttered under his breath.

"Done, sir!" The minstrel bowed once again, and scooped up his wooden bowl as he rose, the single copper bit disappearing under his stylish cloak.

"Come along then," the steward urged, now that the deal was struck. "We must get you inside, and quickly."

The man named Fox nodded sagely, as if sympathetic, and followed the steward across the lawn and up marbled steps before passing through the arched doorway that led to the manor's lavish receiving hall.

Already a number of lesser servants had noticed the steward's momentary absence, and now they converged on him en masse with concerns and questions. With a series of threatening gestures and harsh words he pressed his way through the throng, until they were given enough room to push onwards into the manor.

The steward led the fiddler through room after room, until they came at last to the rear of the estate. A lush garden grew there, whose stone pathways and white marble benches were situated to overlook the Vinus as it wound its way through the heart of the city. A wall of mortared stone crowned with sharpened iron barbs separated the green from the canal, broken only by a wide gate that led to the wooden dock that housed Lord Chanticleer's personal barge.

In the midst of the garden stood a wooden gazebo painted brilliantly in colors of crimson and emerald, within which lounged the hired priests of the Watcher, who were chatting with each other as they tuned their instruments and sipped out of bottles of wine that had been provided for them. The chief steward nodded to himself in silent approval of their ceremonial dress, which his master had expressly ordered. Each priest was clothed in sewn up animal pelts, and wore masks fashioned to resemble the fearsome wargs of the forest. Only their taloned gloves were missing, for they would have need of their fingers to play.

"You aren't, by any chance, a servant of the Watcher?" the steward asked the minstrel in a nonchalant manner, so as to not give up his desperate situation. "I only ask because you play the fiddle."

"No, Lordship," Fox responded. "I took some lessons with one, years ago, but I think the Winter King's got more than his fair share of fiddlers to satisfy him."

"Ah," the steward sighed. "Then you don't tell stories, I take it."

"Oh, I can wind a good bit of yarn. But not proper ones like that lot can," Fox said, nodding towards the priests of Wulf. "Never been good at telling dreadfuls either, if that's what you're getting at. Don't have the right voice for it."

"Yes, I see, but I suppose that will have to be acceptable. You can just keep your mouth shut and play. I'll have some words with the priests about it. Of course," the steward proceeded with his next words carefully, "should anyone ask you if you were-"

"I'll just give them the old smile and play them a bit of Princess Virago's Lament. Is that what you had in mind?"

"Quite so."

"And it will only cost you another five nobles."

"What's that you say?"

"Ten silver nobles. Up front," the man called Fox said casually, "Or I tell your great lord and master that not only am I *not* a priest of the Watcher, but that you got me straight off the street."

The steward's face turned white, then red.

"This is blackmail," the steward managed at last.

"Just business, Lordship, I assure you. But, say, I just had an idea: maybe, after you get tossed out on your duff, we might form a duo. Do you know how to play the deep crier? It would so compliment my own-"

"Be silent!" the steward barked, and then clapped a hand to his mouth when he realized that his shout might be heard from inside the house.

"Do we have a deal, then?" Fox asked.

The steward's hands curled into fists, and his breathing came harsh and loud.

"Seven nobles."

"Ten," Fox rejoined, forcefully. The man obviously knew that he had the steward over a barrel. "We can just call it one gold crown if you like, Lordship, if that will make it easier."

The steward glared at the man's smile, fuming, but his hand fumbled into his own coin purse and doled out the ten silver coins into the minstrel's hands.

"There," Fox said softly as the coins vanished under his cloak. "Not so painful, was it now? And I do promise you a good show."

"At this price, your playing had better be as sharp as Hydra's Teeth. Now come with me, and keep your mouth shut."

Fox just nodded happily and smiled under his leering mask, revealing that his teeth were surprisingly good for a man of such low class.

The steward led him down a winding path to the foot of the gazebo, and waited as patiently as he might for one of the priests to acknowledge his presence.

Eventually Malvoisin, who was the eldest of the trio, lazily stepped down to see what the nervous little man wanted.

"Who's this?" the gaunt priest said with a nod towards the stranger, resplendent in his red outfit.

"Master Fox," the minstrel said, bowing very low, "At your service."

"He's no servant of Wulf," one of the other priests sneered.

"No," the steward began to sputter, "But I'm afraid that Mistress Copee appears to be, ah, indisposed for the evening. But, I am sure you will find Master Fox here to be more than capable-"

"Boy," Malvoisin's voice cut the steward off neatly. "Can you play Lady of Diamonds?"

Fox took but a moment to think before bringing his worn instrument up to his neck and, placing his bow upon its taut strings, he coaxed from the instrument the mournful opening chords of a popular peasant song that concerned a pair of particularly ill-fated lovers.

Even the angered steward had to admit: the man was quite good, though not polished. Some of the servants inside the house peeked out to see who was playing, but the priest merely listened impassively, his arms folded before him.

"How about," said Malvoisin, "Magpie's Delight?"

Without stopping, Fox changed his tune to the lilting strains of the new song, his notes surer and stronger than they had been before. He began to dance lightly around the gazebo as he did so, his feet just brushing the ground as he spun.

"The Four Sisters!" one of the other priests cried out, smiling now and readying his own instrument, a finely lacquered zither.

There were a few delighted claps from the household staff as Fox leapt onto one of the steps of the gazebo and held out a long, harmonious note. It was the traditional beginning of the song, which represented an argument between the four daughters of a widower- each of whom wished to replace their mother as the head of the household. Soon, the zitherist priest joined in, followed by a female priestess on the deep crier.

Last to play was Malvoisin himself, who was a master of the mandolin. He began to pluck his instrument, and soon the air was full of the delightful nattering and complaining of the four sisters.

"He'll do," Malvoisin said to the steward, a rare smile on his face.

The steward, relieved, turned to go, but before he could he found his path blocked by Fox who, still fiddling madly, smiled at him toothily.

"While you are in the house, your Lordship," Fox said then, "Would you pick me up a bottle of wine to take some of the chill out of the air?"

"I'll see what I can do," the steward replied icily, and pushed roughly past him.

"On second thought," Fox called after him as he retreated into the house, "Make it four bottles. We've all got to keep our spirits up, don't we?"

The steward's brow burned as he stalked back through the manor, and when one of the pages dared to approach him with the news that Lord

Chanticleer had need of his presence, he struck the boy to the floor with a backhanded swipe of his hand.

* * * * * *

"Maxon," Lord Chanticleer said in a low voice that could scarcely be heard over the din of the masked men and women all around them, "Whatever became of that other fiddle player? Coppen was her name, I believe?"

"Copee, Lord," the steward corrected, suddenly tense. Lord Chanticleer never called him by his proper name unless he was very pleased or very angry, and he hoped for his sake that it was the former and not the latter. "She was- forced to call off her engagement with us this evening."

"Well," Lord Chanticleer said darkly. "See that you speak to the owner of The Slaughter Prince about it. Mistress Copee shall just have to content herself with playing in some Old Quarter dive for the rest of her days."

The steward smiled. Lord Chanticleer had swallowed his lie concerning the missing fiddler, the woman would be punished for causing him so much undue distress, and excluding the matter with Fox the night had progressed without a single hitch.

Once all of the guests had arrived they had been herded into the salon, where the lanterns of the house were, one by one, dimmed and covered, until the room was so dark that the guests could scarcely see a foot in front of them. Then, in a puff of explosive powder that the Temple of Fenix had provided, the host of the revel appeared- his bejeweled and stylishly slashed doublet and breeches cunningly tailored to suggest the emblem of the Butcher's Guild: a vibrantly feathered rooster. To complete the effect, his gloved hand held the handle of a beautiful lacquered mask with the beaked face of a cock, and a garish and resplendent comb the color of blood.

Chanticleer's grand entrance had drawn cries of awe and applause from the crowd assembled below. Of course, these reactions had been carefully rehearsed in advance, since every guest at the ball who was worth anything had long since learned of Lord Chanticleer's plans and had come dressed in similar fashion: each guild master adorned in costumes which resembled the animals that symbolized their guilds. Lord Belin of the

Weaver's Guild, for instance, carried a mask of a horned ram's head, and his costume was constructed out of heavily bleached wool, while Lord and Lady Roxat's silvery gray outfits were each equipped with a long tail made of expensive fur, so that they resembled a mated pair of squirrels.

As the priests of Wulf and Master Fox moved indoors to play for the vibrant sea of costumed merchant lords and ladies, the servants uncorked the wine, and the masked ball had begun in earnest.

"Tell me, Maxon," Lord Chanticleer went on, gulping down a mouthful of wine out of a fluted glass, "Wherever did you find this Fox fellow? He has made a very good impression on my guests."

"He is a new man to the city, sir," the steward said, trying desperately to conceal his inner anxiety. He could not have Lord Chanticleer asking too many questions about the stranger.

Fortunately, he had thought of just the right lie to put his master off of the scent.

"A talented man," the steward went on, lowering his voice, "But a Luxian, if I guess correctly, my Lord."

"A Luxian priest of the Watcher? In Arcas?"

The rebel county of Luxia had once been a southern province of the Duchy of Arcas, before their defection had sparked over a hundred years of warfare. Racially, there was little difference between the two peoples, but any self-respecting Arcasian would tell you that Luxians were of considerably lower stock, before adding that they were dirty, uneducated, and crude.

"An exile, I believe. He hides it well, under that mask, but you can see it in the cut of his jaw, and the coarseness of his hair."

"Ah, yes- I see," Lord Chanticleer said, and laughed, his already flushed face turning red. "How delightfully scandalous, Maxon! Just think of the uproar it will cause when I let slip that my guests have been entertained by a common Luxian!"

"Indeed, my Lord," Maxon replied, and breathed a sigh of relief.

"Still, it would best to keep this quiet, until after the ball. I trust that you will be discreet?"

"But of course."

"One can't help but feel almost sorry for the boy," Chanticleer said with mock pity. "He'll certainly not find work ever again, not in any place of quality."

"I would hope not, my Lord," the steward said, his thin mouth curling into a tight smile.

"Chanticleer!" a voice boomed over the din of the ball. Its owner, an obviously drunk man with a long-eared hare mask over his face, was pressing through the crowd towards them. With his spare hand he was dragging along a trio of giggling young women in similar attire, though their bodices were certainly cut much lower than that of most of the women present.

"A splendid party!" the hare said as he and his companions at last came to a halt in front of Lord Chanticleer. He lifted up his mask, revealing the florid face of Baron Gallopin, grand master of the Royal Guild of Messengers.

"I am glad that you enjoy it, Baron Gallopin," Lord Chanticleer said as he handed his half empty glass to the steward and leaned in a polite half-bow. "I see you have been enjoying the wine."

"Excellent stuff," Gallopin said, returning the bow sloppily. "But, then, what else is to be expected of the great Lord Chanticleer!"

"Indeed," Chanticleer replied, stiffly. The steward knew that Chanticleer despised Baron Gallopin, and he didn't blame him. The man's manners were certainly lacking, and his taste in clothing and company were vulgar in the extreme. Still, Gallopin was of the nobility, and he would be a powerful enemy if insulted. For that reason alone Chanticleer tolerated him.

"The girls like it anyway, don't you girls?" Gallopin laughed and passed his glass to the nearest of his companions, who lifted up her own mask to reveal a fresh faced young woman, probably not much older than sixteen or seventeen summers. Her cheeks were red and flushed, and she gulped the wine down greedily.

"A new set of mistresses, Baron?" Chanticleer asked, coolly. The steward smirked at his master's rare restraint, thinking it more likely that these were mere servant girls in fancy dress.

"The more the merrier, eh, Chanticleer?"

Gallopin grabbed hold of one of the girls from behind and gave her chest a vigorous squeeze, sending her into a fit of mock cries of distress. Her companions then proceeded to shriek as they struck the Baron lightly with their masks, until he released the girl from his grip.

"And what does the Baroness Gallopin have to say about these lovelies you keep at your side?"

"Why, nothing!" Gallopin replied with joy. "Nothing at all! She has her own amusement these days, if you take my meaning, sir."

"Oh?" Chanticleer asked, genuinely surprised. The Baroness was a rather mousy woman, hardly the type to have taken on a lover. "I was not aware."

"Yes, some young man- Balanz, or Malanche or something like that- never met him myself, but when I do I'll be sure to shake his hand! He's kept her wonderfully occupied lately." Gallopin's female escorts laughed as he took another playful swipe at one of them.

"Then she did not bring her own . . . companion, then?"

"Oh, I'm afraid not. She told me she had grown too weary of public functions to attend this evening's festivities, so I suspect she's got the poor man shut up with her somewhere private."

"Another time then, perhaps."

"Of course," Gallopin shouted, "Why, you must promise to come hunting with me Chanticleer! That is, if you can ever drag yourself out of your quaint little music hall." Gallopin laughed uproariously, and the steward could feel his master's ire rise considerably.

"I will have to check with my chief steward, and see if I can spare an afternoon."

"Ah, but Chanticleer- all this talk about my wife reminds me!" Gallopin stepped closer to the master of the Butcher's Guild, and the chief steward could smell the sweat as it rolled off of the man's face. "She tells me that you have recently purchased a new instrument. I can't remember its name but she said it was something very valuable. Do I miss my guess?"

"Ah, yes," Chanticleer said, as he took a step away from the drunken noble, his foul mood brightening considerably now that he had an opportunity to brag. "A very rare violin, and very old. It is one of the few made by the famed Master Kasha of Arioch. It is truly a one of a kind piece."

"And which one of these is it?" Gallopin asked, pointing to one of the hundreds of instruments securely hung from the walls.

Chanticleer laughed softly. "My good Baron, you do not think that I would keep such an item out in plain sight? No, my lord, the Kasha I keep in a private display case, safely out of the reach of my own staff. Only myself and my chief steward here have the keys that allow access to it."

"And might I see it?" Gallopin asked thickly, his attention already wandering towards the posterior of one of his escorts.

"Perhaps I may host a private showing, in a month or two," Chanticleer said, obviously ready to be rid of the boorish noble. "I do not like it to be touched unnecessarily."

"Oh, do come along, my lord," one of the Baron's escorts whined adorably. "This talk of instruments is so boring!"

"Yes," another added, grabbing hold of the drunken Gallopin. "You promised us you would take us dancing!"

"Well," Gallopin said as the trio began to drag him away, "I suppose I must bid you good evening, Chanticleer! I will tell my wife that you give her your best!"

"That is most generous of you," Chanticleer said, bowing as the man disappeared into the throng of dancers, his three escorts stumbling along with him.

"Steward," Chanticleer said, turning a now stern face towards the man.

"Yes, my lord?"

"Make certain that the staff keeps Baron Gallopin well clear of the private display rooms. I wouldn't want any of them to lose their positions due to that man's clumsiness."

"It will be done as you say, my lord," the steward said, and rushed to comply with his master's orders.

* * * * * * *

The skull moon had nearly sunk below the horizon when the last group of drunken Lords and Ladies finally left the manor, still clinging to bottles of liquor and filling the dark streets with their shrill laughter. Their burly house guards followed at a respectful distance, their hands ready on their swords in case any fool should choose this moment to molest their employers.

The steward watched them go, and breathed more easily now that the party was over. The first to leave had been the more genteel of the guild masters, who no doubt grew tired of the night's exuberant decadence. Next had gone those who had passed out from inebriation, along with those who wished to consummate a romantic assignation. Last went the priests of the Watcher, leading the majority of the remaining guests to terrorize the city with them.

Lord Chanticleer himself had long since retired for the night, excusing himself so that he might meet more privately with the Lady Pertelote, who was currently his favorite mistress.

So the house was left to the servants, who were expected to clear away the considerable mess of the ball by morning. It would be exhausting work, but one of the many benefits Maxon enjoyed as chief steward was the freedom to delegate hard physical labor to the lesser staff.

His bed awaited him, and perhaps, he thought smugly to himself as he began to loosen his silk cravat, he would call for one of the maids to help warm it.

He had just begun to close the front door to the manor when he suddenly found himself on the floor, having been bowled over by a besotted guest wearing an enormous plumed hat. Now he, the guest, and the ridiculous hat lay in a heap on the marble floor.

"I say," the potbellied man complained in a thick but cultured voice as he struggled to rise, his hands rudely pushing against the steward. "Do watch where you are going, idiot!"

The man had apparently lost his mask, and his young face was streaked with makeup that he had obviously sweated off during the ball. The steward did not recognize the guest, who must have collapsed during the party somewhere out of sight, perhaps underneath a table in one of the house's drawing rooms, but Maxon bit his tongue anyway. There was no telling what great house this foolish bravo belonged to, and he was still a mere servant.

"Pardon me, my lord," the steward managed as he struggled to lift himself up, lowering his eyes as a symbol of respect. "I did not see you."

"See to it that you are more careful, then, or it will be a whipping for you!" the guest said, stumbling as he knelt to retrieve his hat.

The steward's teeth ground against each other as he kept his head lowered, bending into a formal bow as the man firmly put the hat on his head and strode out into the night, singing a bawdy drinking song as he went. When he had staggered out of earshot, the steward shut the door angrily, and locked home the numerous bolts.

"Fool," he said to himself, quietly, and began to pat down his now rumpled uniform.

Then Maxon noticed the dull gleam of metal winking at him from the floor, and saw that in the scuffle with the guest he had dropped the key to his master's private quarters. He scooped it up and returned it carefully to his pocket, silently thanking the gods for his good fortune in seeing it in time. He couldn't imagine what trouble he might get in if one of the other servants discovered it- all of the money he had spent hiring the obnoxious minstrel might have been for naught.

The minstrel.

When, Maxon thought worriedly, had the minstrel left the party? He hadn't seen him with Malvoisin and the priests. Had he left early, having already been paid? Or was he in one of the storerooms, pilfering his master's larder?

With such fearful thoughts running through his head, Maxon put off retiring until he had checked the house and grounds, and could ensure that the odd man was not up to further mischief.

He promptly summoned the house guard to accompany him as he went from door to door, and room to room, and made certain that all outside doors were securely shut, and that each member of the staff was about their proper duties.

Near dawn both the search and the cleaning were complete, and no sign of the Fox could be found. Maxon, exhausted, changed into his nightshirt and climbed into his bed, placing his right arm over his tired eyes, and resolving to catch a few hours of sleep before his master had need of him again.

A sharp rapping at his door woke him with a start, and he bashed his knee on his bedpost as he raced to answer the door, his heart pounding. What time was it? Had the servant boys let him oversleep? Who was it pounding so harshly on his door?

He opened it, and saw the page that he had struck the night before. The boy had a strange expression on his face. It looked almost like a smile.

"What is it?" Maxon snapped.

"Lord Chanticleer requests your immediate presence," the page said.

"Already? But I am not yet dressed! Why didn't the servants wake me?"

"It is still early, sir," the page replied, rudely.

"You will address me with respect, boy," Maxon said and struck the lad again. "I am chief steward, and if I wanted to, I could have you thrown into the river!"

"Yes, sir," the page said, his freshly bloodied lips curling again into a smirk.

Shaken, Maxon threw on his outfit, and made his way through the winding corridors of the servant's quarters, his knee throbbing, and his mind reeling as he wondered what his master could possibly want so early in the morning. Had the cook overdone his breakfast? Had the maids moved too slowly as they had put away his master's clothes? Perhaps the master was sick, and had need of the priestesses of Sphinx . . .

A crowd of servants was huddled around the door that led to Chanticleer's private quarters and as Maxon passed them he noticed that more than a few of them shared the smug expression of the page.

"My lord," the steward said as he entered the room that displayed his master's musical treasures, "How may I assist you this morning?"

"Ah, Maxon," Lord Chanticleer replied, "I suppose you might start the day by explaining *this* to me."

Lord Chanticleer drew the steward's attention to the glass display case that sat at the center of the room. Within it were a number of expensive instruments, but near the top of the case was a place reserved for Chanticleer's latest, and most prized possession: the Kasha violin.

Of course, the violin was no longer there. In its place sat a weathered fiddle, of the simple sort that unskilled craftsmen make. And from its neck hung a mask that had been carved to resemble the face of a smiling fox.

And Maxon knew then, as sure as he knew that he would find himself beneath Ghul's cruel knives before the day was out, that the man who had called himself Fox had been no minstrel, as his appearance had suggested.

He was a thief.

II

Calyx, the marbled capital of the once mighty nation of Arcasia, is home to many varieties of thieves.

The slums, called Old Quarter by the wealthy merchants and nobles of the upper city, and the Anthill by its own residents, were thick with lowly cutpurses, gangs of club-wielding muggers, and petty confidence men who sold foul chemicals as medicine to those unfortunates stupid enough to buy them.

But one could find just as many thieves in Royal Quarter, too, and most of them just as bad as the predators of the Anthill. There were the merchants whose ability to shortchange was nothing less than an art form, the petty scribes and clerks whose greased fingers stole every tenth copper bit from their master's tills, and those men or women who would enter a shop wearing a great cloak before stuffing all manner of articles into hidden pockets.

The greatest thieves, of course, were at the highest levels of society. The greedy guild merchants, the crooked captains of the city watch, and the pickpocket who fears no watchmen: the tax collector.

As for Fox, he was of a rare breed of thief, all but extinct in the city: the cat burglar. And, unlike his fellow thieves, he preyed only on the rich and powerful.

Fox was not his proper name, of course. His mother had called him that, when he was still stealing scraps of food for her. It was one of many names that she had given to her son, when she had still been alive. Pup she called him when she had been in a humorous mood, and Lambkin when he was sick and she held him in her arms. He was Scrap when she was angry and could not find him, and Runt when she finally did, and she used her gnarled punishment rod on him.

But for all the names she used, she rarely ever called him by the name that his father had given him:

Reynard.

* * * * * *

Shortly after he had passed out of sight of the great house of Chanticleer, Reynard's drunken, stumbling walk had straightened and his pace had quickened considerably. He veered from the main thoroughfare, plunging into the claustrophobic alleys that crisscrossed the city, until he was far from the walled manors of the guild masters and petty nobles.

Once he was certain that he was alone he removed his fine doublet and with few sharp snaps of his arm he turned it inside out. Then he pulled up his styled trousers to reveal tall leather boots, and unfastened the padded leather gut that he had worn in order to conceal his newly won plunder. Carefully, so as not to damage what lay inside, he unwrapped the Kasha violin from the folds of his crumpled up cape. Then he retied the gut's straps so that it resembled little more than a common traveler's pack.

When he exited the alley he was Fox the minstrel again, though he still wore the bravo's outrageous hat to draw attention away from the fine violin that he carried in his hands.

Of course, Reynard might have passed completely unnoticed through the streets, if he so wished. But it was important that a few of those about on Wulf's Night see him. He had left the Fox mask to sign his work, after all, and it was now important that he leave a false trail for the fat Lord Chanticleer to follow. He made certain that he walked down streets that clearly led to River Quarter, and the city's docks.

By this manner he came to the harbor, where great ships lay at anchor. The vessels were moored so close to each other that the slender masts seemed a forest of leafless trees. Across the river the stacked tenements of the Anthill loomed, the pale ruined spires of the old citadel at its apex thrusting towards the sky like those of a broken crown.

From here Reynard would change course, and turn towards home. But first, he noted with a rueful smile, Fox would have to die.

He approached one of the larger jetties, on which were stored a hundred or so barrels stamped with the crest of the Vintners: a hind crying tears of blood, a black arrow lodged in one of its flanks. These barrels were empty, waiting to be loaded in the morning onto a nearby barge before being sent down river to the wine-growing country near Barca.

A trio of watchmen from the Vintner's Guild sat on the deck of the barge, hunched over the weathered cards of a Spoils game. None of them made any sign that they could see the dark shape moving carefully amongst the barrels.

Earlier in the day Reynard had come here in the rough guise of Rovel, well known within the taverns of River Quarter as a hardened dock laborer with a blistering, sun-scorched face: an effect that Reynard created by allowing rough soap to dry on his skin before pouring vinegar over it to let it blister into something that the casual observer would take for sores. Reynard often became Rovel when he needed to travel to the Anthill to deal with Porchaz, his primary fence, or for when he wanted to move through River Quarter unmolested.

It had been Rovel who had spiked Copee's ale with a potent sleeping draught, so that she would miss her engagement at Lord Chanticleer's ball. And it had been Rovel who had rolled a barrel identical to those belonging to the Vintner's Guild up the jetty, set it upright, and made note of where it lay in relation to the barge before disappearing back into the press of dock workers.

Now, he relocated his barrel, which he had purposely left well out of sight of the barge. It took him several moments to find it, but at last he saw the jagged rune carved into the lid that marked it as his own.

The lap of waves against the moored ships served to mask the dull pop that the barrel made as Reynard pried open its lid, and the stink of the fishmonger's stalls covered the sickly sweet scent that filled the air as he tipped it on its side.

Inside the barrel was the corpse of a man, stripped bare of all but a simple loincloth.

Procuring a fresh corpse had not been easy, since the worshippers of the Firebird always burned their dead, and Reynard tried to avoid killing when he could. In fact, he had nearly given up finding one, when he remembered a rumor about a small island on the outskirts of the city, where the strange folk of the south went to bury their dead beneath the cold earth. These rumors soon proved to be true, and under the dark of twilight he'd dug up the body that would serve as his double.

This particular corpse had been from the southern kingdom of Glycon, which was fortuitous for Reynard, for the Glyconese believe that the spirits of the dead remain trapped within their own bodies, and that their corpses must be treated with herbs and chemicals to preserve them until the day that Hydra rises from the sea to destroy the world. As such, this mere shell of a man had not yet begun to decay, and even now he looked as though he might only be sleeping.

As he required his proxy to rot, Reynard had slashed the dead man's throat and hung him upside down from a tree, draining him as best as he could. But the stench of the thick fluid that had flowed out of the dead man still hung heavy about him, and Reynard had to suppress the urge to gag as he stripped off his garments and dressed the corpse in Fox's clothes. He decided to keep the hat, for Fox had never worn it.

When Reynard was done dressing the Glyconese, one could no longer see the curling tattoos that covered his arms and legs. In fact, the dead man's sallow face was so nondescript that he might have resembled anyone. Besides, Reynard mused, there was no reason that the man who had dared to rob Lord Chanticleer could not have been a Glyconese. After all, some of Chanticleer's best knifemen were from that serpent-filled country, were they not?

Satisfied, Reynard whispered a final apology to the man, and stuffed him back into the barrel before resealing the lid.

When he was certain that the guards were still fully engrossed in their game Reynard gave the barrel a good shove with his foot, sending it off the dock and into the sluggish pull of the Vinus. Predictably, the loud splash startled the men aboard the boat, but by the time they had roused themselves from their cards to investigate, Reynard too had vanished.

The false 'Fox' would be found, a day or two from that evening, by some fishing boat or merchant caravel. And when the crew opened the barrel there would be the pale corpse of a man whose clothes fit the description of the bandit who had dared to steal the Kasha violin, his throat slashed. Then they would conclude that Lord Chanticleer's killers had dealt justice to him, and they would burn the body and say no more concerning the matter.

As for the fat guild master, Reynard knew that he would believe that the man called Fox had been slain to cover the tracks of a rival collector, possibly even one of the other guild masters of the city.

And no one would be the wiser.

Reynard decided that he would miss Fox as he walked along the docks, dressed now in the simple garments of a sailor. The minstrel had reminded him of younger days- for, though he had never worked as a street musician, he hadn't lied to Maxon about the time he spent studying with one of the Wulf's priests. That had been back when he thought that the life of a servant of the Winter King might suit him, and it had made him smile to play the songs with the Watcher's servants one last time.

"Fare thee well, Fox," he sighed, and tossed his ridiculous hat into the stream below, sending it floating after the dead man in the barrel.

* * * * * *

Just south of the wide bridge that led to the Anthill gaped one of the entrances to the city's storm sewer, which was said to be nearly as expansive as Calyx itself. Climbing down a set of steps Reynard entered the yawning tunnel, needing no light to find his way to the locked gate that was intended to keep out vagrants. He had his own copy of the key that the miserable sewer workers of the city used to allow them access to this subterranean realm, so he generally came and went as he pleased.

He could walk quite quickly through the darkness, his right hand held against the wall to count the side passages and openings, and making the turns that would bring him home. He had learned the way by heart over the years, and no longer required light. He seldom saw the sewer workers, but he could always tell when they were nearby by the gleam of their own lanterns. He certainly didn't want to afford them the same advantage.

When he had gone a considerable distance along a route that would have confounded all but the best tracker, he stopped, his fingers having brushed against the familiar section of lead piping that marked his destination. He then placed a hand against the low ceiling and, once he had located the appropriate stone tile, gave it a firm push.

The tile swung upwards until its hinge met a catch with a click. Reynard, who had been forced to crouch in the low tunnel, needed only to straighten to reach the bottom rung of the iron ladder that would lead him home, the well-oiled trapdoor closing shut behind him as he began to climb.

When he was not about his larcenous business, Reynard lived in a modest River Quarter warehouse, which he owned through a series of aliases. He had purchased the building with stolen gold, and then he had hired dozens of artisans to renovate the interior to suit his need for secrecy and security. Each of these men had been responsible for the construction of a different section of the place, so that only Reynard himself knew the complete layout.

A passerby on the street might think the warehouse to be somewhat neglected, or recently abandoned, but he would also find the building's main door securely locked, and the shuttered windows barred.

Inside there was a large storage chamber stacked high with crates, most of which were full of packing straw, and a tiny corner office with a locked door that led up to the second story. The trapdoor that led down to the sewer (which could be locked from within when not in use) was normally kept hidden by a stack of heavier crates, and as Reynard clambered into the room he shifted these back into place.

Reynard picked up an oil lamp from the table and lit it with a flint and steel lighter shaped like the Firebird, a handy thing he had picked up on an earlier job. Lamp in hand, he entered the office and unlocked the door to the second story, relocking and bolting the door behind him.

Once upstairs, Reynard entered the modest apartment of Master Percehaie, the most public of his many guises. Percehaie was a Frisian spice merchant, one of the few trades that the guilds of the city did not control, and it was in his name that this building had been purchased. He was a likeable fellow who did very little business, just enough to get by, and he rarely hired on employees for very long. Those who knew of him were generally of the impression that he was the second son of a rich merchant family from Belnor, and that he had been sent here to run another branch of the family trade in the capital of Arcasia.

It was a good cover, for Reynard might have been a great merchant, if he had wanted to be one. He had a quick mind, a witty tongue, and a great memory for names, places, and dates. He loved to organize things, and there was little that he did that he had not planned out in advance.

But then there were a great many things that Reynard might have been, if he'd not been born into poverty.

Should an intruder manage to infiltrate Master Percehaie's quarters he would find a few minor baubles, a set of practical clothes and boots, and a coffer with just enough silver to satisfy him- but he would likely miss the inconspicuous catch that opened the hidden portal that led up to

Reynard's personal quarters, where a persistent intruder would face yet another locked iron door, which Reynard kept tightly bolted when he was at home. Reynard had long since grown accustomed to not feeling entirely secure unless he slept behind at least three locked doors.

Once through this last defense, Reynard casually walked up the steps to his real apartment.

A wooden canopy bed dominated the room, under which lay an exotic Irkallan carpet: an enormous thing that stretched almost to the corners of the hardwood floor. Flanking the bed were a pair of finely carved night tables that had been inlaid with hundreds of enamel tiles, and laden with dozens of rare and unusual volumes from around the world. The thick walls, which housed only the smallest of windows, were decorated with fine tapestries of a pastoral nature, and from the high gabled ceiling hung two onion-shaped lamps made of bronze and colored glass, so that they resembled flowers just beginning to bloom.

With his lamp Reynard lit one of the slender wooden sticks that he kept in a cylindrical tin by his bedside, and used it to ignite the lamps above. Then he opened the clasps of the great chest that sat at the foot of his bed.

Inside this trunk Reynard kept a few personal effects, and the main part of his treasury. Beneath his nightshirt and morning robe sat row after row of leather pouches containing gold crowns, silver nobles, copper bits, and precious gems. Should this impressive hoard be plundered, Reynard could release a catch on either side of the chest to reveal a false bottom, which held a reserve supply of coin that could last him for half a year comfortably.

Into this cache Reynard deposited the nobles that Chanticleer's steward had paid him and, after he had taken out his nightly attire, he shut the chest and placed on its top the assorted rings, necklaces, brooches and earrings that he had lifted so dexterously from the drunken guests of the party. These fancies and baubles he sold to the city's many fences, always in small enough increments throughout the year so as not to generate too much suspicion. As for the pieces that were too recognizable to be sold, these Reynard would harvest for their gems, or melt down into untraceable ingots that Master Percehaie could then sell to the Royal Mint itself.

Placed at intervals along the walls of the apartment were a dozen wooden mannequins, all but one of them dressed in a complete set of clothing. Reynard hummed to himself as he stripped off his sailor's clothes and laid them over the shoulder of the figure that had worn Fox's outlandish garb for the last couple of months, then paused to regard his other personas, whose blank faces stared at him as if inquiring which of them would be used on the morrow.

It would have to be Master Cuwart, Reynard decided as he settled on the dummy dressed in the smart powder blue uniform of the Royal Guild of Messengers. There was a delicate farewell letter that needed to be delivered to the Baroness Gallopin, and Reynard didn't want another messenger boy to know from whom the letter had come.

"Poor woman," Reynard said, picking up the letter from his tidy writing desk. The Baroness had fallen quite hard for the handsome young rake named Malbranche, a card shark and seducer of women whose well-cut clothes and fashionable rapier hung amongst Reynard's assembled throng of aliases, and it had taken Reynard several drafts before he could settle on the farewell words of a cad who has finally decided to put the needs of his imperiled country above that of the mad love that both he and she had shared, promising always to carry a memory of her in his heart. Reynard also thought it prudent that Malebranche should continue to compose letters to his love, promising one day to return, until he would at last die in a grand act of heroism on some remote battlefield, his last recorded words being those of the Baroness Gallopin's name.

It was trite, and overly dramatic, but the Baroness would be certain to eat it up like fine pastry. Satisfied, he sealed the letter with wax, marked it with Malbranche's signet ring, and placed it in the messenger's pouch that lay near Cuwart's wooden feet.

Directly across from Reynard's sleeping space was a grand wardrobe, which he opened to reveal shelves thick with polished lock picks, sealed vials of corrosive liquid, flasks of oil, tiny jars filled with makeup with which he could coat his face black, small chisels and hammers, lengths of wire, pins, hooks, wedges and the other sundry accoutrements of his profession. He had also installed a large mirror inside the wardrobe, so that he might see himself clearly as he disguised his true face to the world outside. Under the mirror sat a silver washbasin that Reynard had earlier filled. He dipped his hands into it now and washed his face clean of the grime and makeup that he had worn to subtly change both his complexion and facial structure.

When he was done Reynard unwrapped the Kasha violin from the false gut, and set it on a finely carved shelf, next to his other trophies. There were only a dozen or so items that he had felt compelled to keep in such a fashion, either as a point of personal pride or because they would be impossible to fence.

Newly enshrined, the Kasha violin seemed quite at home nestled between the royal signet ring which once rode on the finger of Baron Gallopin, and the bejeweled ceremonial hammer of Petipas, the city's high priest of Fenix.

* * * * * * *

"What are you thinking about?" Hermeline asked as she massaged cleansing oil into Reynard's thick hair. "You are very quiet today."

Reynard let out a noncommittal hum from the back of his throat, but opened his eyes and stared up at the woman who was leaning over the great copper tub he sat in so that she could wash and rinse his hair.

"Just daydreaming," he said, and smiled up at her.

"Very well," she said, gently scratching his scalp, "You may keep your secrets if you like."

Hermeline was a priestess of Sphinx, the Lioness, and she was Reynard's favorite of the Temple. She was a mature woman, perhaps a good five years older than he, but her age had not diminished her beauty. She had a very friendly face, a rich complexion, proud lips, and kept her hair in luxuriant curls that dangled down to her muscular shoulders. She still danced with the other girls at the Crowning festival, and her legs and rear were strong from regular use.

"I'm sorry, I'm just a little tired," he said, stretching out his arms and repositioning so as to be more comfortable.

"A late evening, perhaps?" Hermeline poured a little more oil into her hands. "You should get more sleep you know. You always come here with those awful bags under your eyes."

"I will try to get more, I promise."

"You make many promises, my sweet Percehaie," Hermeline said, one of her hands wandering down to pinch his ear, "But you seldom keep them."

"Tonight, then," Reynard said, "For your sake, I will sleep long and well tonight."

"Good," Hermeline said, and Reynard closed his eyes again as she continued to wash him, focusing only on the strong fingers running slowly through his hair. Soon she was rinsing it with hot water from the tub, and then she was trimming it with a fine pair of scissors.

He often visited the Temple of the Lioness after a successful job, to celebrate his victories over the merchant lords and petty nobles of the city, and it was one of the few institutions that Reynard had forbidden himself from targeting. After all, the priestesses who worked here had dedicated their lives to treating the ill, rich or poor, and stealing from them would be as low as stealing from a sick beggar. Besides, the servants of Sphinx kept few material possessions beyond the tools of their trade—unlike their brothers, the wealthy smith-priests of Fenix, whose forges supplied the city with all of its glass and metal goods.

"You are eating well, I trust?"

Hermeline's voice awoke Reynard with a start. He hadn't realized that he had fallen asleep. She laughed and ran her hand over his chest.

"My, you are tired, my poor little man."

"I was up late."

"Oh," she said, a tinge of jealousy entering her voice. "Do you have a new lover that keeps you up?"

"No, no. Just business."

"Ah, you men and your business. It couldn't have waited until morning I suppose?"

Reynard fabricated a story about a late shipment, and made the usual noises of a merchant who is worried about his financial future. He had heard enough of this talk to become quite good at it, but it hardly mattered because Hermeline was only half paying attention anyway. The details of men's banal prattle must soon become irrelevant to the women of Sphinx's Temple, but as he suspected that they liked to hear the noise as they worked, he indulged her.

"Well," Hermeline interrupted him as she made a few last snips with her scissors. "I'm certain that everything will be fine. Your hair is done, by the by. Would you like to see?"

"I trust you," Reynard said without turning. "You always do a good job."

"Thank you," she said, warmly, and finished drying his hair with a towel. When she was done combing it neatly she began to push him up, and she climbed into the tub herself, pressing the fullness of her body against his back.

"Now turn around," she said huskily, "and we'll do your face."

Reynard obliged, and she repositioned herself so that they sat facing each other. As usual, she wore a gauzy light chemise, and the water made it cling to her beautiful skin fetchingly. Reynard gave her his customary half smile, and her face beamed with pleasure.

"So, you have no new lover, then?" she said, a hand stroking his leg absently.

"No."

"Then perhaps you'd like to play for a bit, before your shave?"

Her hand traced a circuitous path up his thigh, but Reynard reached down and stopped it before it could make its way to his quick. He looked into her face, on which was now etched a slight pout.

"I'm tired," he said, and brought her hand up to his lips.

Hermeline's own lips smoothed themselves into a perfect line. "Very well," she said archly, "Just the shave then."

She reached over the side of the tub and retrieved some of her instruments from the table that sat nearby. From an ewer she poured a little water into a bowl and coated a brush with a thick lather of shaving soap that she applied to Reynard's face. Finally she reached for her long razor with its tortoise shell handle, and smoothly, very smoothly, began to shave him.

"Is there something wrong with me?" she said, as she ran the blade up his neck slowly. "Do you think I have become old and ugly?"

"Of course not," Reynard replied. "You are very beautiful. But I am not in the mood today."

"I could call for one of the other girls, if you'd like. There's a new one you haven't met that I think you'd enjoy. She'd enjoy you too, I think. Would you like me to fetch her?"

"No, Hermeline, I don't want some skinny little girl. I want you."

"So," she said, her razor coming to a halt at the base of his throat. "I am fat, then? Is that it? The new girl, she is skinny, and I am fat?"

Reynard looked into her eyes, but they showed no mercy.

"Yes," he said at last, and he grinned.

"You are a terrible, horrible man," Hermeline said and nicked him very gently with the razor. "You are lucky that you make me laugh, or I would have slit your throat years ago."

"Is that all you keep me around for?" he said with a coy smile. "You do not love me?"

"Yes, you ass, though I swear by the Watcher that I don't know why. You always stink of the sewer, you are always cruel to me, and you have a small dick."

"You wound me, madam," Reynard protested, clutching his heart dramatically. "You cut me to the quick!"

"Just be happy that I do not cut your quick off," she grumbled as she guided her razor over one of his cheeks. "It is quicker than most anyhow . . ."

"Put that down," he said firmly, pushing aside her razor. "And kiss me."

"But you are not done with your shave."

"I don't care."

He pulled her forward then and they kissed. He could feel her smile as he wrapped his hands around her full waist.

"My," he said, as they parted, "It seems as though I may need to shave you as well. You've grown quite a handsome goatee. It's a little white, though."

Hermeline giggled girlishly and wiped the lather from her chin.

"A sign of old age perhaps?" he said as she clambered onto his lap.

"Shut your mouth," she said, her hand coming to rest on the back of his neck.

"As you wish," he said, and pressed his lips to hers.

* * * * * * *

"Hermeline," Reynard said, after they had been lying still for a while.

"Yes, my love?"

"Are you happy?"

"Yes, you silly man," she said, reaching over to his side of the bed and teasing his freshly mussed hair. "You know that I am."

"Your life, I mean." Reynard searched for the right words. "Serving the Lioness. Does it make you happy?"

"Ah," she said, and straightened somewhat. "Am I content to mother horrible men like you for the rest of my life? Is that what you mean?"

"Not just that, of course, but all of it- to be a priestess. To serve one of the gods."

"You know that it is a great honor to serve the Lioness. I have a good life here, and good friends."

"But were you chosen, or did you decide to become a priestess?"

"So, first you are silent as a stone and now the questions come pouring out of you. Perhaps I had best check your head to see if my Percehaie has a fever of the brain!" She laughed and sat up, reaching for a jug near her bedside. "Would you like some water?"

"Please," Reynard said and drank a few gulps that felt refreshingly cool to his parched mouth.

"If you would really like to know," Hermeline said then. "I chose the life of a temple priestess. I did not think that they would take me! I was so awkward when I was young, I could hardly walk straight. Everyone thought that I was a fool. But the old high priestess, Fiere, ah, she has been dead for many years now- she was very kind to me. She asked me all sorts of questions, and made me dance for her. At the time it was very frightening, but I was so happy when they chose me. And a good thing it was, too, that I did not listen to my fears! For I might have spent my days as a laundress, or a servant, or one of those weaver girls that the guildsmen keep locked up day and night at the loom. You would not see me smiling then."

"And the men," Reynard asked. "You do not mind sleeping with them?"

"I am a priestess," she said without further explanation.

"Surely though, they are not all as good looking as me."

"No, Percehaie," she answered, and stroked his arm gently. "They are not. But they are polite. And you need not be jealous! You will always get my best treatment. Which is more than I can say about how you treat me."

"Has anyone ever-" again Reynard tried to be delicate, "Hurt you?"

"Once," she said, and turned away. "Long ago."

Reynard asked no more. Harming a priestess was a crime punishable by death, often at the hands of the priestesses of Sphinx themselves, for it is generally unwise to cross the woman who shaves your face.

"I think that is enough for today," she said, reaching for her diaphanous robe. "It is growing late, and I have other appointments to keep."

"My dear," he said, slipping out of bed and embracing her gently from behind. "I hope that I haven't upset you."

"No, my love," she said, turning to him. "You could never do that."

She kissed him lightly on the mouth, then pulled away from his arms and opened the door to the next room, where the junior girls of the temple were already cleaning out the inside of the copper tub. They giggled a bit at the sight of Reynard's naked body, but Hermeline shushed them with a glance. As for Reynard, he reached down and retrieved a handful of his clothes from the floor, and proceeded to dress.

"Where do you go now, my dear Percehaie? Back to some dreary office, or the dockside that stinks of fish?"

"Eventually," he said, buttoning up his breeches. "I have some other business to attend to first at the Royal Mint."

"Ah, money, money, money! Is that all you think about besides sex?"

"Sometimes I find myself growing fond of food," he replied with mock gravity, "But it always passes in the end."

Hermeline groaned and, snatching up one of the wax tablets that hung by the door to the bath, she began to work out the details of Reynard's bill with a stylus.

"Don't trouble yourself with that," Reynard said, placing a pair of gold crowns onto the tablet.

"Oh, my love, this is far too much," she complained half-heartedly. Reynard always overpaid her.

"Keep it. Perhaps you could buy yourself a new dress?"

"You know I'm not allowed."

"Then buy one for the Lioness," he said, and threw on his cloak. "And do be sure to let her know it is from me."

She clucked her tongue. "You shouldn't speak of the gods so lightly."

"Why? They don't seem to mind."

"Oh, my dear, what will I ever do with you?" she sighed.

"That's funny," he said, "You seemed to know exactly what to do with me just a little while ago."

The younger priestesses tried to stifle their laughter at Reynard's cheek, and Hermeline's face flushed. She took hold of him and began to escort him to the door.

"Will you get out of here, you brute? The next customer is waiting for me."

"I could buy him off, perhaps- spend another couple of hours with you."

"And miss your *important* work at the Royal Bank?" she teased.

"I had almost forgot," he said, looking appropriately sheepish.

"Money, money, money," she said again as he walked into the cool antechamber, where a balding merchant sat waiting on a thickly-cushioned divan, a cup of the temple's wine in his clammy-looking hands. "I suppose that is what keeps you happy, right, my love?"

"Yes," he lied.

* * * * * *

Outside, the air was quite cool. The first few days of Coldmonth had passed, and the temperature was beginning to drop. Soon the vibrant red leaves of the city's trees, which were thickest in the temple district, would fall and leave the branches as bare as skeletons.

As Reynard walked the wide lonely streets of the upper city he heard his false words to Hermeline echoing in his mind. The weight of the gold bar he carried in his satchel serving only to remind him of how tiresome the mere acquisition of wealth had become.

I should be happy, he thought to himself bitterly. He'd made a small fortune from one night's work, and he'd made a fool of an arrogant braggart. But already the sweet taste of victory over Lord Chanticleer had turned to ashes in his mouth. Already he felt restless again, in need of something new to revitalize him, some pretext within which he could find a reason to go on.

When he had started in his trade, just a boy really, he had stolen to survive. He needed only to eat and keep a roof over his head to be content. But as he'd grown older, and began to feel the rush that came after a successful theft, he realized that the life of a thief agreed with him. He began to target wealthier prey, and the thrill had increased exponentially.

And he'd begun to feel something else, too, as time went on. It was a kind of pride, he supposed, his own secret knowledge that he had dared to accomplish something that other men could not- but the more experienced he became, and the greater his victories, the less he cared. It was no challenge for him, anymore, to simply lift a man's purse from his belt, or to raid the house of a rich merchant. And it was not enough either to merely steal from those who saw themselves as his betters. No, now his pleasure came from the game itself and the manner in which he stole, sometimes right from under his victims' noses.

Now, even that was beginning to bore him. He had hoped that by signing his work, by letting the mighty Lord Chanticleer know just how he had been cheated, he might prolong his moment of triumph, and feel whole . . . but instead he only felt more depressed than he had before the job had begun. His sweet Hermeline had only managed to cheer him for an afternoon and, now that he was back on the city streets, he felt empty and alone.

"A new job," he muttered under his breath as he passed underneath the arched entrance to the Royal Quarter, briefly drawing the attention of the armed soldiers of the Duke that were stationed there. He smiled at them with a slight shake of his head, as if dismissing something, and touched his index finger and thumb to the brim of his hat before quickening his pace.

Yes, he thought, *a new job.* True, it was only a few days since the affair at Lord Chanticleer's, and the houses of the merchants and petty nobles would be watched closely now that news of the Fox had spread throughout the city, corpse or no corpse.

Still, he thought that would only make the job that much more challenging.

But from whom should he steal, and what, he wondered as he went through the routine business of depositing the gold at the Royal Mint. Lord Ferran of the Wheel and Wainwright's Guild, whose collection of erotica was second to none? Or perhaps from the Baron Cherax, personal treasurer of Duke Nobel and master of the Royal Mint itself . . .

Reynard was so lost in these thoughts that, as he was making his way down the royal avenue, he nearly collided into a small crowd that was blocking the road.

Composing himself, he saw that both men and women were quickly filling the street, and were staring down it expectantly. At first Reynard wondered if an obscure religious festival had been scheduled for the day, but he heard no distant cry of song, and the crowd made no sound beyond a hushed collection of whispers. Then he heard the somber beat of drums, and the clatter of hooves on the street's cobblestones, and the crowd grew silent.

A pair of horsemen, resplendent in their azure coats and polished cuirasses, rode into Reynard's view. They wielded lances adorned with swallow-tailed pennons, with which they forced the gathering throng to make way. Carts and wagons were steered onto the flagstones of the pavement, and even the wealthiest looking men made haste to comply.

When the street was clear Reynard could see that there was a column of figures making its way up the road, and at its head was a mounted man wearing the ornate armor of the Arcasian military, replete with the classical avian designs that the priest-smiths of Fenix added to all of their best work. Behind the rider a mounted attendant held aloft a great blue and white banner, on which an ivory white lion reared menacingly.

It was the royal standard of the Lord of Arcas, and Reynard realized that the rider at the vanguard of the procession was none other than Duke Nobel.

He'd never seen the Duke at so close a distance and now, unlike most of the other men and women who went down to their knees as a sign of respect, he glanced up at Calyx's ruler as he passed.

Nobel wore no helmet, so Reynard could clearly see his face. He was an imposing-looking man, for he had a strong jaw, high cheekbones, and an imperious aquiline nose. There was, however, a delicacy about the way he carried himself in his lavishly engraved armor that betrayed that he was more accustomed to the soft life of a courtier than to that of a real warrior.

At a respectful distance behind the Duke and his standard bearer rode several squadrons of Arcasian cavalry in full battle dress. Then came a company of military drummers, marching in step as they beat out what sounded like the dirges that the priests of the Watcher played at public funerals and executions.

Behind the musicians there was a curious sight. A full company of Arcasian pikemen, their faces concealed by helmets, surrounded what appeared to be a horse drawn carriage. The carriage had only a light silk canopy for its cover, and inside it were seated two women.

The first of the two that Reynard saw, for she was sitting on the side of the carriage nearest to him, was an angularly featured woman of middle age with an incredibly distant look in her eyes. Her graying hair was held in a tight bun, and kept rigidly in place with a slender pin. She wore a very austere auburn dress, and in her elegant hands was clutched a silk fan, which she was using to cool herself despite the crispness of the air.

This woman, whomever she was, was sitting very stiffly and upright, but as the carriage drew closer it went over a slight bump in the road and she leaned back- and then Reynard caught sight of her companion.

The first thing that Reynard noticed about her was the way that her immaculately parted hair, which was black as ebony and decorated with pearls, framed her delicate face so that it resembled a heart. Then she turned, very slightly, and he could see the smooth line of her neck, and the simple perfection of her profile. She was obviously nobility, for she was clothed in a purple dress that had been embroidered with silver stitching, and at her neck she wore a matching silver necklace in which was set a large violet ruby.

"Who," he found himself asking no one in particular as the procession, and the woman in the carriage, passed him by, "Who is that?"

"Who's that?" an incredulous voice responded. It belonged to a lanky-looking man, a guild baker if Reynard had to guess from the man's flour stained apron. "You 'ent heard the news?"

"I'm afraid I'm not from here, friend," Reynard said lamely, playing the part of the visiting petty merchant.

"Why, that was the Countess Persephone of Luxia herself, Duke Nobel's prisoner!"

"Prisoner?" Reynard balked. All around them the crowd was breaking up, and he had to raise his voice to be heard over the din.

"There's been a truce called, don't you know, by those southern dogs! They need time to lick their wounds, so they've sent her as a sign of good faith that they won't break the treaty. Course, you can't trust a Luxian."

"Of course, but-"

"We all know they'll break the peace when it's convenient," the baker said, cutting Reynard off. "And then we'll put her filthy head up on a pole outside the palace!"

"But," Reynard said more forcefully, "Why would they abandon their own Countess?"

"Hur hur hur," the baker laughed, "She's not the Countess yet- not really- just the dead Count's oldest daughter, his- heir I think it's called. Her uncle's the real one in charge, though, even if he isn't really the Count. They got a name for that too I think."

"Regent?" Reynard offered.

"Yer- but if you ask me," the baker went on, drawing closer and shoving his finger into Reynard's chest, "I bet she's got a bit of chimera blood in her veins. I hear most of 'em do, down there, those Luxian nobles. Spend too much time in them deep forests, if you catch my meaning."

Reynard nodded compliantly, and slipped the man's coin purse into one of his pockets.

"Yer," the baker said, making his way back to his little shop. "It'll be good riddance when they do 'er in! Her and all of them Luxian scum."

Reynard wasn't listening anymore to the baker's words, however. Instead he was gazing up the street, towards the graceful minarets and high walls of the Duke's palace, thinking about the beautiful woman in the carriage and the valuable ruby that lay against her graceful neck.

Reynard's lips turned upwards into a sly smile. *Why not?* he thought. *I have stolen from guild masters and barons . . .*

Why not a countess?

III

It was just past dusk when it began to rain. Reynard cursed under his breath and sank back into the shadows of the trees.

He hated rain.

A lot of younger, less experienced thieves think that bad weather is good for the kind of work that he intended to do tonight, under the false assumption that rain will hide what one is doing in the dark, and provide cover for one's trespasses. Fools, Reynard thought them, and lazy fools at that. He'd long since learned how to be quiet, and how to move without being seen, no matter the weather. Rain only served to make roof tiles slippery, and it could drench the lightweight clothes of a cat burglar until they were heavy with water.

On a normal job Reynard would have used one of his aliases to gain entry to a wealthy man's home, but Nobel was no mere guild master or petty noble. It would be impossible for Reynard to pose as a member of the staff, for the servants of the Duke were almost a species of royalty themselves, the scions of families that had served the Dukes of Arcas for generation upon generation; they would soon spot an outsider amongst them, and then the game would be over.

Reynard had considered trying to enter the Duke's palace in the guise of Cuwart, and had in fact already delivered a forged missive from the Royal Mint in the hopes of getting an idea of the layout of the place. But even the uniform and baton of a guild messenger had only gotten him as far as the interior of the outer gatehouse, where the bound scroll he carried had been transferred to a clerk in the Duke's service before he was promptly ushered over the bridge that led back to the city.

So, Reynard figured that he would just have to break into the palace the old-fashioned way: through stealth.

The palace had been built on an island that sat in the absolute center of the Vinus. A high limestone wall ringed it, whose crenellated battlements and towers were manned by regular patrols, and Reynard quickly put out of his head the idea of slinking his way past the dozen or so watchmen stationed at the outer gatehouse. That way would inevitably lead to capture, and almost certain death.

But the outer wall did have a weakness: a smaller postern gate, set at the rear of the structure, from which a stone jetty jutted. The Duke's servants used this entrance to receive deliveries of foodstuffs, barrels of wine, and other sundries, and its iron portcullis was often left open while a single pair of soldiers stood watch.

Reynard knew that this gate was the best way of bypassing the palace's outer defenses. As for what lay beyond, he could only guess, but his instincts were rarely wrong, and he trusted that he would be able to locate the apartments where the Countess was kept.

Now he leaned against one of the manicured trees that the wealthy maintained along the avenues of their quarter of the city. His clothing was light and loose, and had been dyed dark hues so that he could more effectively find refuge in the shadows. He had his tools carefully strapped underneath a voluminous hooded cloak, and wore his rapier in case he encountered any real trouble.

Movement across the river caught his attention. A uniformed servant had come through the postern gate with a long-handled torch held in his hands, stopped briefly to chat with the watchmen, and then went about the business of lighting the lanterns that hung on either side of the entrance.

As Reynard watched, a dozen or so servants appeared and stood at patient attention. Soon a number of wide-bottomed boats could be seen coming up and down the canal, converging on the dock.

The servants watched impassively as the boatmen unloaded their goods onto the dock. When they were finished they cast off, and the servants collected the numerous sacks, casks and crates before disappearing back into the depths of the palace.

The night's darkness was almost total by the time this laborious process was done. Reynard moved from his perch and made his way through the trees so as to be closer to the water, the storm clouds above shielding him from the Watcher's light.

Drawing his cloak tighter over himself, as if against the night's chill, he began to affect the hurried walk of one who is late for an appointment.

By doing so he managed to catch up to the last boat that had disembarked from the postern gate's dock, and was now heading back downriver.

"Boatman," he called out, and the solitary man on the water turned his head to face him.

"What do you want?" the man replied harshly.

"Where are you headed?"

"To River Quarter, not that it's any of your business."

"Good," Reynard said. "I'm going that way myself. Why don't you pull over here, and let me board?"

"You have some cheek! Does this look like a ferry to you, sir?"

"I'll pay. Five bits."

"Forget it," the boatman said, and he increased the pace of his paddling. "Could lose my license if I take on a passenger. It's against the rules."

"A noble, then."

The boatman steered his boat so that it came to rest alongside the walkway where Reynard stood.

"Where's my silver?" the boatman said, holding out his palm.

Reynard dropped a coin into it.

"You keep your hood up and your head down," the man said as he helped Reynard into the boat. "And don't talk or I'll drop you into the river and you can swim the rest of the way."

Reynard nodded, and the man bent over to move a coiled up rope out of the way. As he did, a leather sap appeared in Reynard's right hand, and he raised it sharply to strike.

"Now then, you sit here where I can see-"

The boatman's words were cut off abruptly, and he slumped over in the boat, unconscious.

"I suppose this could be the reason for those harsh guild rules, friend," Reynard said as he quickly took hold of the oars, and rowed out into the center of the Vinus before turning back upriver.

As he rowed he glanced towards the battlement above him. Burning lamps hung in iron cages at various points along it, and occasionally he could make out the dark form of an armored watchmen going about his rounds. When he had come to a place directly between two of the lamps, he steered the boat so close to the wall that no watchmen above could see it, and resumed his course.

He took his time, so that when he had returned to the place where the jetty thrust out into the river, the servants were long gone. So were the two guards, who regularly ended their shift during the dinner hour, leaving only the river and the portcullis to guard the palace's rear entrance.

He rowed smoothly up to the edge of the dock, still concealed from the sight of any guards who might be above, and disembarked, pushing the boat back into the channel with his foot. The boat and its slumbering cargo disappeared into the gloom.

Wasting no time, he slipped on a pair of fingerless leather gloves that had a series of claw-like protuberances embedded into their palms, and began to scale the wall.

The masonry of the wall had been coated with lime, so that it would appear as if carved from a single block of stone, and this made for a slow ascent. Reynard hoped that a passerby on the other side of the river would not chance to see the dark form that crawled spider-like against the stone.

When he had reached a point just above the keystone of the arch, he set his feet down on the narrow ledge and very carefully turned himself around. He removed his climbing claws, and drew his gray cloak about him tightly.

Reynard stood there for a long while, very still. A casual observer might have thought him a decorative bit of statue. As he stood he used his hands to balance against the wall behind him, ignoring the growing cramps in his arms and legs.

Finally Reynard heard the rumble of the portcullis opening, and the steady tread of hobnailed boots as the first of the relief watchmen took their fixed positions below him.

"You see the way that Columbine kept looking over at us?" one of the watchmen asked the other as Reynard crouched as low as he could without falling. "I think she fancies you."

"That chambermaid?" the other watchman replied, yawning. "I didn't notice."

"What's not to notice about her? She's got a beautiful set on 'er. And those legs- phew! You should take her up on it, friend."

"Eh, I don't fancy her."

The first watchman shook his head, and slapped his fist on his leg. The jingle of mail covered the dull sound of Reynard's boots as he landed smoothly behind the two men.

"You're crazy," Reynard heard the first watchmen exclaim behind him as he slipped through the gate and entered a torch lit hallway. "If I had a woman like that after me I'd leap on her in a flash."

"Why don't you go after her then," the second watchman drawled, his voice echoing weirdly off of the walls of the passage, "If you're so eager?"

"Well, for one thing there's that rotten twist, Arlequin. He'd be rather sore about it, if'n he found out . . . "

The watchmen's voices faded as Reynard reached an intersection. The passage to his right slanted upwards until it met another bend, while the one on his left was marked by a series of open archways. In the flickering torchlight he could just make out the shape of stacked grain bags beyond the nearest arch.

Reynard was pleased. He had hoped that the palace storerooms would be located near the postern gate, and now he only needed to find an out-of-the-way vault in which he might hide until the inhabitants of the palace retired for the night, making it much safer for him to move about.

Hugging the wall, Reynard entered the third chamber he came upon. As his eyes adjusted to the dimness he could see that it was a wine cellar, and generously stocked at that. Finding a good dark corner of the room he settled into it, stepping between two tall racks of bottles and getting as comfortable as he could against the cool stones behind him.

To pass the time he mentally reviewed his strategy, and when he had grown tired of that he tried to recapture the image of the woman in the carriage, who had become mere bits and pieces of memory to him. He clung to what he remembered: the flash of the stone at her neck, the pearls in her hair, her sad hazel eyes.

His long reverie was only interrupted once, when a single white-haired servant entered the cellar and pulled a pair of bottles from off of the shelf nearest to the door. He didn't even take a single glance into the corner where Reynard stood before disappearing back into the corridor.

Finally he could hear the dull tramp of boots in the hallway, and knew that it was midnight. The night guards had come to relieve the ones stationed at the postern gate. The noise rose and faded, and before long he heard another set of footsteps coming back up the hall, and the familiar voices of the watchmen he had already passed.

" . . . so why don't we play some cards?" Reynard heard the second guard ask the first.

"Guess I'm up for a game," his companion responded. "Too early to sleep just yet."

"Spoils or Queens?"

"Queens."

"Guess we'll need two more then."

"Bertrand will play," the first watchman offered, his voice beginning to trail off.

"Ask him, and I'll see if Turlupin is willing."

"You do that," the first watchman guffawed. "That fool never has any luck! Remember when he lost all of his wages on . . ."

For a little while Reynard could still hear the sounds of the guards' cheerful voices, and then they were gone and it was silent.

He took a few steps into the middle of the wine cellar and stretched his limbs.

Now, he thought, *the real fun can start.*

* * * * * * *

The slanting corridor led him up to a storage level much like the one where he had been hiding, only these seemed to be pantries from the way that they were stuffed with smoked and salted meat, fresh game, butter, and all manner of fresh provender. The kitchen would be near, Reynard guessed, and that would likely connect to the rear of the palace somehow.

At the end of the hallway there was a reinforced wooden door with a lock. Next to it a guard slumbered peacefully in a wooden chair, an empty cup of beer still clutched in one of his hands.

I hope they can do better than this, Reynard thought as he slipped a key from the man's belt.

The now unlocked door led to the rear of a great kitchen, where there were hearths so enormous that they could have been used to roast oxen. The embers of the cooking fires were still smoldering, and huddled on a cot beside them was a dozing scullery maid whose garments had been stained black with soot. The earlier rainstorm must have passed, Reynard noted, for the cold light of the Watcher streamed into the room through high soot covered windows, casting an eerie light over the girl's slack face.

Stepping lightly and carefully so as not to disturb the hanging gauntlet of fine copper kettles, saucepans, and cooking utensils, Reynard crossed to the other end of the kitchen, where an open stairwell likely led up to the living quarters of the palace's servants, and came to a set of unlocked doors.

The doors opened onto a carpeted corridor, whose wooden floor had been fashioned out of skilled parquetry, and whose painted plaster walls were hung with expensive cerulean drapery. The hallway's sconces were unlit, but the light of the skull-moon filtered through a series of tall windows, beyond which Reynard could make out the contours of an extensive garden. Fountains gurgled there, surrounded by formally manicured hedges, and between the boughs of a ring of ash trees he could make out a graceful bronze statue that had been fashioned to resemble Chloris the Serene.

A series of carved steps led from this enclosure to a terrace of the palace itself: an imposing stone structure riddled with high arched windows and circular towers capped with lance-like spires. From his vantage point Reynard could see that he was moving through a connecting corridor between two wings of the palace, and from the finery around him, he could guess that he was leaving the servants' wing behind.

Reynard had almost reached the midpoint of the corridor when he heard the tell-tale click of a door opening. Without pause he nestled next to one of the hanging drapes as a shaft of light burst into the hallway, throwing wild shadows across the walls.

The light bobbed forward, and in its dull gleam Reynard could make out the grim face of a helmeted sentry carrying a hooded lantern. The guard turned to close the door behind him, and then began to tread heavily down the hallway, whistling tunelessly as he went.

Reynard dipped his hand into a pouch at his side and when he lifted it out there was a small but smooth stone pinched between his thumb and forefinger.

When the man was almost upon him Reynard flicked the stone off of his thumb, sending it skittering across the opposite side of the hallway.

"Who goes there?" the sentry called out, taking a few tentative steps towards the disturbance and providing Reynard with all the time he needed to creep around the man unseen.

"Cursed rats," the man said as he returned to his patrol. "I told 'em them traps was worthless."

Reynard had reached the end of the hall by then. He waited until the guard was at the doorway to the kitchen before turning the latch of the door at his end of the corridor. He didn't care to see if the route of the watchman's patrol would take him through the servants' quarters or not, and he moved on.

Reynard was not surprised to discover that the corridor connected to a lavish dining hall. A long wooden table ran down the length of the room, its surface festooned with silver cutlery and ornate candelabras. High above the table there was a wooden gallery where musicians could accompany Duke Nobel's meals without the inconvenience of being seen.

A pair of fireplaces flanked the hall, above each of which hung the stuffed heads of hunting trophies: boar, bear, and even the antlered head of a faun chimera. Reynard felt its glass eyes staring lifelessly at him from its all too human face as he passed, and he shuddered slightly.

Also displayed here were the painted likenesses of the nobility of Arcasia. On his right Reynard recognized the stern face of the former Duke, Leo, now rumored to be a helpless cripple confined to his bed and waited on by maids. To his left Nobel stared imperiously from his own portrait, a sculpted ivory scepter clutched in his left hand.

Smug, aren't you? Reynard thought to himself. *That's fine- I'll cut you down to size before the night is through.*

Reynard glanced into the chambers that connected to the dining hall, and dismissed them one by one. They were nothing but formal drawing rooms, or lavish studies that had been decorated with the kind of ostentatious curiosities that only the incredibly wealthy could afford: cabinets crammed full of exotic sea shells, the sculpted busts of kings and queens of Aquilia long since dead, and suits of ceremonial armor which held ancient weapons in their lifeless grips.

What Reynard really needed was a way up; he doubted very much that the Countess would be kept in some miserable oubliette, or barren cell, even if she were a hostage. Rather, he imagined that Nobel might keep her near his own quarters, and those would doubtlessly not be located on the ground floor.

At the end of the dining hall there was another lavish archway, blocked by a thick set of embroidered portieres. Slowly, Reynard created a small opening at the place where the curtains naturally parted, and peered into the room beyond.

What he saw was a room whose vaulted ceiling rose as high as the palace itself, the glow of its numerous lamps reflecting off the mirror-like polish of its smooth marble floor. A pair of curved staircases wound their way up to a balcony, beyond which Reynard saw a pair of immense iron doors, and the set of disciplined looking watchmen that were stationed beside them.

Reynard found himself grudgingly impressed by the sight, which had been designed to awe, as he let the portiere fall back into place. He was certain that those stairs would lead to the Duke's apartments, but he also knew that it would prove almost impossible to get to them without being noticed by the watchful eyes of the house guard.

There must be another way up . . .

He studied the recessed balcony above the dining table, and thought for a few moments before slipping into the nearest of the adjoining chambers.

This particular study's cabinets were stocked with decanters containing numerous varieties of liquor, and it smelled strongly of tobacco-it being likely the room to which the Duke retired after a meal to sip on brandy and smoke with whatever count or baron might have dined with him that evening.

A centuries old map of the unified Duchy of Arcasia hung from one of the walls, and hanging next to it was a woven textile cord that disappeared into a discreet opening in the room's woodworked ceiling. Reynard gave this cord a single tug, and though he could hear nothing, he knew that somewhere in the palace a servant's bell was ringing.

He didn't have to wait very long before someone responded to the call for service, and Reynard smiled to himself when a carved wooden panel swung silently into the room, revealing a passage by which the palace's servants could move about without disturbing their masters.

A young footman entered the drawing room through this opening, a lit candle held out before him. A perplexed look passed over the servant's boyish face as he quickly realized that the room did not appear to be in use.

"My lord?" the footman said to the darkness.

When he received no reply the servant crossed the room to inspect the bell pull. When he was satisfied that there was nothing faulty with its mechanism, he entered the dining hall, walking so close to the place where Reynard stood hidden behind a drape that the thief could have reached out and tapped him on the shoulder.

After a cursory inspection of all adjoining rooms, the footman reentered the service corridor, and resealed the hidden door that led to it.

A moment or two later, Reynard was admiring the skill of the craftsman who had installed the secret portal. It blended so perfectly into the wall that it would have been impossible for anyone to detect normally, and it took even him some time to locate the bit of decorated woodwork that, when turned counter clockwise, sprung the door open.

He pulled the panel shut behind him. The service corridor was very low and narrow, and it was unlit. Reynard would have to move along by touch alone, and he would have to be fast, for there was no place to hide if a servant came across him.

Orienting himself, he turned to his left and ran his hands along the walls as he walked. He passed two doors on his left and then his right hand lost contact with the wall.

He took a few more steps, gropingly, and when his hand again found the wall he was able to determine that he had reached a fork in the corridor.

After taking a moment to consider, he took the rightward passage, hopefully assuming that this honeycomb of service corridors would have a central nexus of some sort where, he reasoned, he might find the servants' stairway to the upper level.

Before long Reynard could hear the distant sound of voices. As they grew louder Reynard realized that they were not coming from the corridor that he was in, but through the wall itself. He pressed his ear against the wooden panels, straining to hear, but could make nothing distinct out of it.

As he came to a sharp left turn in the passage, the voices immediately grew louder. Further, he could see a faint light outlining a door at the end of a dead end corridor.

When he pressed his ear against this concealed door, Reynard could just make out what was being said. He heard something else as well: a strange twittering sound, like the chirp of a songbird.

A man with a high resonant voice was speaking heatedly.

" . . . It is too much to bear! Arcasia *must* stand united, or forever be enslaved!"

"I understand your fervor," an aged voice responded. "When I was a young man, I too had dreams like yours: dreams of glory, and of freedom for our people. And, there too was a time when I thought that I might achieve them, when I sent an army to retake Larsa. Then the Calvarians landed at Kloss, and thirty thousand men died trying to stop them."

"I am familiar with history."

"Then you should know that to defy Calvaria is nothing but a young man's vanity, and we need speak no more on the matter."

"Would you have our own people starve, then, Father?"

"I would have peace," the old voice said wearily, "And have my son live to be as tired as I am of war."

"Your grace," a third voice interjected, deeper than the others. "Perhaps it is time that we retired for the night? You have taxed yourself enough for one evening."

"You are right as ever, Lord Bricemer," the old man replied. "Paquette, you may take me back to my quarters now."

Reynard had never seen Bricemer, the Count of Lothier, but he knew him by reputation. He was the seneschal of Arcas, and a close advisor to the Duke.

A fourth voice, probably one of the old Duke's maids, murmured something too quiet to be heard through the panel.

"Goodnight, my son," the old Duke said, his voice receding.

"Goodnight, Father," came the formal reply as Leo was doubtlessly wheeled back to his bed.

A door opened and shut, and for a while there was quiet in the room beyond.

"Coward!"

Nobel's voice cut through the silence, and something metallic clattered across the floor. Whatever strange bird was housed in the chamber squawked angrily at the disruption.

"He is only doing what he feels is best for the people, my lord," Count Bricemer said in a soothing tone.

"What he is doing, Bricemer, is allowing himself to be blinded by the failures of the past! The Calvarians are not demons. We could drive them from this country, and need never pay tribute to them again!"

"They may not be demons, your grace, but you cannot deny that they will not easily be dealt with."

"I did not say that it would be easy," Nobel said, calming somewhat. "But nothing is impossible. Was it not I who brought Luxia to its knees? With enough men at my back I might do the same to the 'terror of the north.'"

"And how do you intend to raise such a mighty army, my lord?"

"I think," Nobel's voice dropped very low, and Reynard strained to make out his last words, "That this is not the time or place to discuss this particular matter. Shall we meet on the morrow, at the appointed hour?"

"As you wish, your grace," Bricemer replied. "As ever, I am at your complete disposal."

"Goodnight then, Bricemer," Duke Nobel said curtly. "And see to it that this mess is cleaned."

Again, Reynard heard the dull sound of a door being closed. Then there was only the clicking of the Count's heels as he walked from one side of the room to the other. The light gleaming through the door dimmed, and then went out entirely. Then Bricemer was gone, and the room was silent.

The talk of Calvaria intrigued Reynard. Almost a half a century had passed since the last invasion of the dreaded inhabitants of the north- so long, in fact, that most children considered the Calvarians to be the invention of reproachful parents. But real the Northerners were; the siege-blackened stones of the citadel that sat atop the Anthill were a grim reminder of what became of those that took them lightly.

What is Nobel planning?

Suddenly, Reynard heard another door open somewhere in the corridor behind him, and when he turned he could see the rapidly approaching glow of a bobbing handheld light. Bricemer must have rung for a servant, and in a few moments the man would round the corner and see him!

Frantically, Reynard glanced upwards, but the ceiling of the service corridor was too low to use as a hiding spot, even if he could clamber up there in time. Disappointed, Reynard's hand went to the leather sap hanging from his belt. He hated to rely on the thing, and it would be hard to gauge how long the servant he struck down would remain unconscious, but it was better than being discovered and he readied himself to strike a solid blow as the man came around the bend.

A long musical trill wafted through the panel behind him.

Of course, Reynard thought, lowering the sap. *How could I be so stupid?*

He returned to the panel, and finding the catch that opened it, slipped into the chamber beyond.

Immediately Reynard relaxed somewhat. The octagonal room he now found himself in was a domed conservatory, and it was strewn with all manner of rare and delicate plants from around the world- in short, it would provide him with ample places to hide. He ducked behind the fronds of a Tyrisian jungle plant, and crouched down low.

The panel reopened and the footman (Reynard saw that it was the same one that he had summoned earlier) stepped gingerly into the room, his eyes glancing about nervously.

Reynard chuckled to himself.

The poor boy. I didn't mean to spook him so badly. I've probably got him seeing phantoms in every shadow now.

From somewhere above him, there came the twittering chirp of some large bird, and the servant stopped in his tracks, frozen. Reynard followed the boy's frightened gaze upwards, and then he too felt his heart skip a beat.

Perched on a thick iron rod above them was a female shrike: a particularly stunning specimen of its kind, with iridescent emerald plumage, and a long train of tail feathers that hung like a bustle from its rear. It had probably come from the depths of Vulp Vora, or been bred in captivity, for the thing's upper torso was more human than any of the chimera he had ever seen in his lifetime, and its pale, cruel-looking face had a weird beauty to it that was ruined only by its pupil-less red eyes.

And, Reynard realized, those eyes were gazing straight at him.

The shrike sidled back and forth on its perch, repositioning itself and twittering as it did so. Reynard guessed that it was probably quite tame, a songbird for the enjoyment of the Duke, but its sharp-clawed talons still looked as though they could rip a man open without much effort.

After much hesitation the footman bent to pick up the filigreed goblet that Nobel had earlier thrown to the floor, and produced a cleaning rag from the folds of his uniform to sop up the spilled wine. He worked quickly, and never took his eyes off of the chimera above for longer than a moment or two.

Suddenly the shrike spread its spectacular wings and leapt from its perch, gliding smoothly down to the tiled courtyard. It landed alarmingly near Reynard's hiding spot. The startled footman back peddled wildly, dropping the goblet as he did so.

Reynard's hand slowly went to the hilt of his rapier. The chimera tilted its head at the action and, whistling sharply from the back of its throat, hopped towards him, bursting through the foliage faster than any human could advance. He had only half drawn his sword when the thing's taloned feet struck him, pinning his arms against his sides.

Reynard silently began to struggle, but the shrike shook its head at him slowly, like a reproachful mother.

"Shhh," the shrike hushed him in a soothing tone, its musical voice weirdly human.

As the shrike's grip on him was too powerful to break, Reynard obeyed and lay still.

Underneath the feathered bulk of the chimera, Reynard could no longer see the footman, but he heard his voice call out with trepidation from across the room.

"What's that you've got there, girl? Another rat?"

The shrike smiled, and now Reynard could see that its teeth were as sharp and pointed as thorns. It lowered its neck so that its face hovered directly above his. Its long emerald colored hair hung like curtains around him, and its rank breath beat against his face in hot blasts.

Then it leaned forward and nipped at his face. Reynard had hardly known that it had happened until he felt warm blood running down his cheek. Then, the shrike began to lap at the wound, until its lips and chin were besmeared with gore. All the while it made a cooing noise that Reynard could feel reverberating inside his chest.

Seemingly content, the thing leapt off of him, and took a few leisurely steps away from his hiding place. Immediately, Reynard pressed his hand against his cheek to staunch the flow of blood.

When the footman saw the shrike's blood-smeared mouth, he quickly returned to his business, rushing now to be out of there. The shrike leapt onto the edge of a low fountain at the center of the room, and began cleaning itself the way that Reynard had sometimes seen small birds do in the city's parks.

His job done, the footman exited the room the way he had come, and firmly shut the door.

Once Reynard's eyes had grown accustomed to the dim illumination filtering through the dome above he picked himself up and walked over to the fountain. The shrike went on preening, as if unconcerned with his presence.

Dipping his hand into basin of the fountain, he wetted a spare cloth and cleaned his wound, which appeared to be only superficial. The cool water felt good, and he washed his face clean of sweat.

Reynard stepped cautiously away from the chimera and made his way to the only visible door. It was unlocked, and it led to a moonlit room whose high walls were lined with books: the palace library, he guessed. More important however, was the cast iron spiral staircase that led up to a long gallery, where Reynard could just make out a door that would grant him access to the second story.

He turned towards the shrike, who had ceased its cleaning and was gazing at him, its thin lips stretched into a odd smile.

"Thank you," he said, with a polite bow.

"Welcome," the shrike croaked at him, and fluttered back to its perch.

* * * * * * *

The second story of the palace was even less well guarded than the ground floor had been. Perhaps, Reynard speculated, the Duke thought his outer defenses secure enough to bar all entry to this point. Reynard soon found that he had only to occasionally avoid a pair of guardsmen on patrol to have his run of the place.

All of the hallways on this level connected to a central point: an airy chamber where the Duke likely held court, receiving supplicants and emissaries while comfortably seated on a raised and canopied throne. Further, each hall led to a separate wing of the palace.

The first wing he explored appeared to be a communal office of some sort, its pigeonholed walls stuffed full of rolled up parchments, and its half dozen or so desks bulging with missives and writing tools. Reynard moved on, doubting that the foreign Countess would be kept in what was clearly the administrative wing of the palace.

The next wing consisted of a set of apparently neglected rooms. What little furniture there was lay under great white cloths that had been draped over them to protect them from dust. Perhaps these chambers had once housed the young Duke, or some other scion of the royal family long since dead, but whatever the case they could safely be dismissed.

The third wing, however, proved far more promising.

For one thing, it was guarded, though Reynard again found himself sighing at the sight of dozing sentries leaning on their pikes for support.

Secondly, the first room he came upon was locked.

Once Reynard had sprung the last tumbler and opened the door he saw what appeared to be an audience chamber, a sort of miniature version of the room where the Duke held court. Carefully drawing the drapes open, he saw that the room was decorated in the same hue of burgundy that was used by the nobility of Luxia.

Satisfied that he had found his mark, Reynard moved on to the next chamber: a less formal drawing room where the Countess might receive more intimate visitors. This luxury must be a mere formality, Reynard assumed, for as a prisoner he imagined that she would not be allowed much real privacy.

The next door opened onto a dressing room. Several logs were burning on a cast iron firedog in a quaint fireplace, and in their glow Reynard could make out a series of immense dressers, a copper bath inlaid with gold, and a small daybed that had been set up in the room's corner. Sleeping on this cot was the still form of the gray haired woman Reynard had seen riding with the Countess. She wore a silk sleeping mask over her eyes, and was snoring so loudly that Reynard barely needed to soften his footsteps as he crossed the room.

Surprisingly, the door to the Countess' private room was not locked, and it took Reynard only a gentle push to open the door.

Far from the grand bedchamber he had been expecting to find while planning his entry, Reynard found the room to be quite intimate. Like the previous room, it had been provided with a fireplace, but other than a number of trunks it contained only a comfortable-looking bed and a marble topped vanity.

And there, lying snuggly on the cushioned velvet interior of an ivory casket, Reynard could see the lustrous gleam of the ruby necklace that he had come to steal.

He crept across the floor and wrapped his fingers around the silver chain that clutched the violet pendant. He lifted it up and stared into its brilliance, admiring the fine cut of the gem.

All he had to do now was slip the necklace into a pouch at his side, and then retrace his steps. When morning came he would use the chaos of the theft's discovery to make his escape, perhaps in the stolen garb of one of the very soldiers who would be hunting the grounds for him.

And then, he thought to himself, his grip on the necklace loosening, *what will I have but a cold, worthless rock?*

An odd sound came then from the thick coverlets of the bed- a soft cry, pained and low. Reynard returned the necklace to its casket, and moved softly to the Countess' beside.

She lay there sleeping restlessly, her brow furrowed and dewy with sweat and her body twitching slightly as she cried out in her sleep. Reynard could see that she was far younger than she had looked from the street, and she seemed almost a child to him then, lost inside of a nightmare.

He reached out to her, almost thoughtlessly, certainly not thinking anymore of the necklace, or of the great danger, and began to brush her head with the tips of his fingers to soothe her. Soon, she quieted somewhat, and after awhile she grew silent, her breathing more regular.

Then her eyes opened.

Reynard took a wild step back, and in a single motion he drew his rapier- but the Countess did not scream, to Reynard's great surprise. Instead, her eyes merely narrowed somewhat, and when she spoke her voice was calm.

"I had been wondering when my uncle would send someone to kill me," she said rather petulantly, "But I thought it would be someone with more sense than to wake his victim before he's done his work."

"Your uncle didn't send me," Reynard said, trying to hide his shock at the girl's apparent lack of concern for her own life.

"One of his ministers then? That venomous little toad, Dendra?" she asked. "Or perhaps you are an Arcasian patriot, who'd see your entire country burn before treating with a Luxian? Is that it?"

"Be quiet," Reynard said in harsh whisper, reluctantly bringing the point of his sword against the nape of the Countess' neck. He could still tie and gag her, but only if she would cooperate.

"Now," he said, borrowing a bit of Rovel's ragged bark, "Still your wagging tongue, girl, or your life is forfeit!"

"I'll take no orders from you," she said defiantly.

"Do you not fear me, woman?"

"I'm not afraid of the likes of you. So kill me if you must, else I will scream for the house guard, and have you cut into mincemeat!"

With a sigh, Reynard lowered his weapon.

"So! You've lost your nerve, have you?" the Countess taunted. "You aren't a very brave assassin. I hope whoever hired you isn't paying very much."

"I . . . didn't come here to kill you," Reynard said, using his own voice.

"You didn't . . ." The Countess' voice trailed off, her proud tone fading. "Who are you, then? What is the meaning of this intrusion?"

"If you must know," Reynard replied, "I am a burglar by trade, and I came here to steal from you."

"A thief?" the Countess said, and she began to laugh. "You are nothing but a common thief?"

"Not so common," he said, his pride hurt. "I made it this far without being discovered."

"You aren't by any chance that man I've heard so much about since I came here? That daring rogue that they call 'The Fox?'"

"I am," Reynard said, hoping that this at least might impress her.

"Well," she said, sitting up in her bed to get a better view of him, "I cannot imagine how you got your reputation, Master Fox. You are apparently as bad a thief as you are an assassin."

"And you are very bold," Reynard rejoined, "For an unarmed woman alone with a stranger."

As she stared at him, Reynard's eyes flicked downward, and he could see that she wore nothing but a gauzy silk night robe the color of lavender. The Countess saw his gaze wander, and drew her comforter modestly over her chest.

"Why were you touching me?" she asked accusingly, her tone suggesting that she thought him a very low sort of man.

"You were- making noises," Reynard explained. "In your sleep."

"Was I?" she asked. "I didn't realize."

"I thought that you were having a nightmare."

"I must say, you are very considerate for a thief."

"It's only that you-" He hesitated, and turned from her.

"Yes?" she prompted.

"You reminded me of someone."

"Someone close to you?"

"A long time ago, yes."

"A woman, I suppose?"

"Yes."

"And what happened to her, this woman?"

"She died."

Reynard had gone over to the fireplace, and as he stared into the dancing flames he could almost hear the burning timbers as they had come crashing down around him, and smell the sickly sweet stench of burning flesh.

"Well," the Countess said, bringing him back from that night, "I have to admit that you were right."

"About what?"

"The nightmare," she answered. "I thought that I was back in Engadlin, riding to meet Duke Nobel. Have you ever been there?"

"No," Reynard said. "But I've heard stories."

"They say its soil is the richest in the world, but most of its farmlands lie fallow now, and its people starve. Our armies pillage and loot whatever food they can find, and what is left falls into the hands of the brigands that infest the countryside. We came upon a farmstead one day, during a storm. There was a man sitting on the front porch, cooking. One of the escorts rode up to see if he could offer our mounts shelter, and that is when he saw-" Her voice cracked somewhat and Reynard saw that her eyes were tearing up at the memory she had dredged up.

She composed herself and went on. "He was boiling pieces of a child. A little boy. It might even have been his own."

"It sounds like a charming place."

"You would not make light of it," the Countess said sternly, "If you had seen it with your own eyes."

"You are probably right, though I'm no stranger to hunger. You'll find that you won't have to make the journey south to Engadlin if you want to see starvation. We have our own breed of it right here in Calyx."

"So you are an Arcasian then?"

"Oh, yes. I was born here, just across the river. I'd escort you to the grand apartments where I was raised, but I'm afraid that they burned down years ago."

"I could not accompany you even if you owned the finest mansion in Calyx," the Countess said, and sighed. "Madam Corte would not approve."

"Madam Corte?"

"My chaperone," she explained. "When I was younger she was my governess, and before that she was my nanny. You must have seen her if you came through my dressing room." A tinge of fear crept over her face. "You haven't *done* anything to her, have you?"

"So," Reynard said, leaning on the hilt of his sword, "There is something that frightens you after all!"

"If you have harmed her, I swear I will have you drawn and-"

"Don't worry," Reynard said. "She's perfectly safe."

"Good. She is very dear to me, you know, even if she does still treat me like I'm a child."

"You're certainly no child," he said with a half smile.

"How do you mean?"

"A sword at your throat, and you didn't cry out for mercy. I'm not sure I'd be able to do the same, if I were in your shoes."

"I have grown accustomed to attempts on my life over the years. There have been several others."

"But why would your uncle want you dead?" The question had been gnawing at him since she had blurted out the accusation.

"Chiefly it is because he is not really my uncle. He married my father's sister, and after my father died he was named Regent of Luxia. Now he wants his own children to inherit my father's lands and title, and that's why he offered me up like a prize to the Duke."

"I see. And, how did your father die?"

"He was killed in battle."

"I am sorry."

"It is alright- I was very young, and I do not remember him very well."

"And, what do you make of him?" Reynard asked, changing the subject. "Nobel, I mean."

"He has treated me with more courtesy than I thought to receive from an Arcasian, and he seems to want peace between our countries."

"On his own terms, I would expect."

"You don't think much of your Duke, then?"

"He is no Duke of mine," Reynard snapped. "I bow to no man, and especially not to one of his kind: born rich and self-satisfied, expecting deference from the ants down below as he parades himself through the streets!"

"Well," she huffed. "At least he has the courage to do so under the light of day, instead of skulking about in the shadows like a rat!"

"I imagine it is easy to be brave with a regiment of soldiers at one's beck and call, to do your fighting for you."

"Oh? What would you know about it, you lowborn brigand?"

"More than you ever will, you pampered trophy! You remind me a little of that shrike that the Duke keeps: safe and comfortable behind the bars of a gilded cage!"

"I grow weary of this conversation," the Countess said tersely. "And I think I've had more than enough of you, Master Fox! Now, remove yourself from my chambers before I ring for the guards."

The Countess reached for the bell pull that hung near her bed, but Reynard's sword flashed through the air, severing the rope high above her hand.

"Madam Corte!" she managed to scream before he forced a gloved hand over her mouth to muffle her cries. She lashed out at him with her arms, and he climbed on top of her to force her to be still.

"Will you be quiet?" he fumed. "I told you that I wouldn't hurt you!"

"Then unhand me," she managed to say from beneath his glove.

"First you must promise to let me take what I want from you, and then I will leave you in peace."

"And what is it that you want?"

"Promise me first," he said. "And I'll tell you."

"Very well," she said. "You may take any gem or jewel of mine that you desire. They mean little to me."

"Swear on it then."

"By Sphinx I swear on it," she blurted. "Now take what you want! Take them all if you like, but let me go!"

Reynard looked over at the vanity, and the fortune of jewelry that sat there, but he did not get up.

"What is it?" she asked testily. "Is it not enough for you?"

"No," Reynard replied. "It's not that."

"What then?"

"Well, you see," he said, "I came here to steal that lovely ruby you wear. But now that I've looked at it up close, I don't think its worth as much to me as a kiss from a Countess' lips. Even one as stubborn as you."

"You cannot be serious," she said, her brows upraised. "I could not possibly-"

"Ah," Reynard said, clucking his tongue. "But you made me a promise, did you not? And swore by the Lioness too. Would you offend the gods?"

The Countess stared up at him, her eyes narrowed.

"No," she said.

"Kiss me then," he said and leaned closer to her.

She pulled back, hesitating. "At least put away your weapon. Or are you the kind of man who uses a sword to get what he wants from a woman?"

Carefully, Reynard sheathed his rapier.

"There," he said, "No sword."

"And what about your boots?" she asked as he leaned in again.

"My boots?"

"You might keep a dagger there, hidden."

Reynard laughed. "I don't know what kind of nonsense stories you've been reading, Countess, but I don't usually go about with daggers stuck in my boots. What prattle!"

"You know something, Master Fox?" the Countess sniffed. "You are a bastard."

"Too true," he replied, pulling her close to him, so that their faces nearly touched. He could feel the flutter of her heart against his, and realized with surprise that he too was nervous.

"Wait," she said in a soft voice.

"What is it?"

"I don't even know your real name."

He looked into her deep hazel eyes, so kind yet sad, and they were more beautiful to him than any stolen jewel.

"It's Reynard."

"Persephone-" she said and their lips met.

The door slammed open behind him, and Reynard's head whipped around to see a quartet of watchmen standing in the door, their swords drawn.

"Assassin!" the first guard said, charging into the room.

Hydra's Teeth! Reynard cursed to himself. *The chaperone has called out the house guard!*

"Don't kill him!" the Countess shouted, but the guardsmen showed no intention of listening to her plea.

He tossed the Countess aside and rolled off the side of the bed. He immediately went into a low crouch and pulled out the throwing dagger that he had concealed in his right boot. As the watchman came around the poster he flicked his wrist and buried the weapon into the man's sword arm.

The guard's weapon clattered to the ground as he clutched at his arm and howled in pain.

"Why, you liar!" Persephone cried out with indignation at the sight of the dagger.

"I believe I did say 'usually,'" Reynard said with an apologetic grin as he kicked the wounded guardsman back into his fellows.

Wasting no time, Reynard lifted up the cushioned chair that stood in front of the vanity and swung it heavily at the nearest window.

The chair shattered in his hands as it connected against the thick pane of glass. Reynard stared dumbfounded at the broken headrest in his hands, only then noticing that all of the Countess' windows had been fitted with strong iron bars.

"You really are a prisoner, aren't you?" he said, throwing the remains of the chair at the head of the next guardsman. The man ducked, giving him time to redraw his sword.

"They are supposed to be for my protection," she said, pulling a large pillow towards her and covering her body with it.

With a twist of his sword Reynard disarmed his closest foe, and as the man stared at his now empty hand he smashed the butt of his weapon into the man's face. His broken nose gushing blood, the sentry collapsed.

The two remaining guards came at him together, probably hoping to surround him, but in a single whirling slash Reynard managed to nick the two of them across the forehead. The wounds were not very serious, but they bled terribly, and soon both of the men were blinded by the flow of scarlet running down their faces. Reynard kicked one in the crotch, and the other he stabbed in the shoulder.

All four men lay moaning on the floor.

"You are very good," Persephone said, obviously impressed.

"I practice," he said with a flourish of his sword. He knew he couldn't stay long, however. He could already hear the tramp of more guards approaching.

Something heavy crashed over his skull as he rushed into the next room. The world whirled before his eyes, and then the floor began to swim up to meet him. He lost hold of his sword as he fell, and both he and it slammed hard against the wooden slats.

Above him hovered Madam Corte, a silver candlestick gripped in her bony hands and her hair a wild tangle. She was screaming something at him, but his mind was slipping into unconsciousness and he couldn't make it out.

"Typical," he said up at her as blackness overtook him.

IV

"You have a visitor, Rat."

The sound of the jailor's voice woke Reynard with a start. He groaned as he realized that he was still in the dungeon cell that the Duke's men had thrown him into.

When was that? He wondered to himself. *A day ago? More?*

Reynard opened his eyes as wide as he was able. They were still swollen from the terrific beating that he had received from the guards he had injured trying to escape. Gingerly he touched a finger to his broken nose, and his head reeled with pain.

The least that they could do, he thought, *would be to let it heal before they break it again.*

"Back for more, eh?" he slurred as he slowly got to his feet. "Let's make this quick, I have a very important appointment I have to keep."

"Shut your mouth," the jailor said, tossing a bundle of cloth at him.

"What is this?" he asked, picking up a surprisingly clean linen shirt.

"You'll put it on," the other man grumbled, "If you know what's good for you."

"Well," Reynard said, slipping his head into the shirt, "I've never gotten dressed for a beating before, but I suppose there's a first time for everything."

"Ah, Master Fox," a familiar voice drawled, "I see your stay here hasn't done anything to dampen your spirits. And, speaking of dampening, will you do the honors Mezzetin?"

The jailor snickered under his breath, and proceeded to douse Reynard with a bucket of cold water.

Reynard squinted at the blurry shape that stood on the other side of the bars, and rubbed at his bleary eyes. When his vision cleared he could see that it was none other than Duke Nobel. A thick crowd of bodyguards and attendants accompanied him.

"Come to gloat?" Reynard asked, slumping against one of the cold walls of his prison.

"Perhaps a little," the Duke replied, "But also to see what kind of man has been terrorizing my city. Frankly, I am disappointed. You are so much bigger in the stories they tell about you."

"I didn't eat enough as a child."

"I am sure. But it was not hunger that drove you to break into my house, was it Master Fox? If what I hear is true, you have acquired quite the fortune by now."

"And," the Duke went on calmly, "Perhaps you might tell me where you have been hiding all of this wealth?"

"Why should I tell you when you're only going to kill me anyway?"

"No," the Duke sighed, "I suppose I did not expect that you would answer me willingly. Mezzetin, if you would."

The jailor undid the iron lock with one of his keys, and opened the door. Ten of the Duke's soldiers entered the cell then, swords drawn, two of which lifted Reynard's limp form up off of the floor.

"I would like to show you something," the Duke said, and he beckoned to a uniformed valet who stood near the door to the prison. The man stepped forward, a long dark wooden box in his hands.

Opening the box the Duke produced a strange looking metal instrument shaped like a pear that was ringed with sharp ridges. This device was attached to a rod tipped with something that resembled a key.

"Have you ever seen one of these?" the Duke asked.

"I can't say I have."

"It is a Glyconese invention. They call it the 'pear-of-anguish.' They are a very barbaric people, the Glyconese- I have heard tell that they worship snakes and lizards, if you can imagine- but I must admit that they are so very clever when it comes to devising new and interesting ways to cause suffering. Hold his mouth open, will you?"

The guards holding Reynard forced open his jaw as the Duke approached. Reynard spat and bit, but they were too strong, and in his present condition he was far too weak. He gagged somewhat as the metallic pear slipped past his teeth and into his mouth.

"You see," the Duke said casually, "The way that it works is simple. You merely turn the key on this end . . ."

The Duke gave the key a single twist, and Reynard felt the sharp iron ridges expand, pressing painfully against his tongue and the roof of his mouth.

" . . . And springs inside the pear cause it to grow. Eventually it will shatter teeth, and it is strong enough to break a man's jaw."

The Duke gave the device another twist, and Reynard strained to open his mouth as wide as he was able. Tears ran freely down his cheeks from the pain, and he could taste his own coppery blood running down the back of his throat.

Just when he thought that he could no longer take the pressure, the Duke twisted the key the opposite way, and the pear shrank to its original shape. Then he pulled it from his mouth, and handed it back to the servant, who began cleaning it carefully with an oiled rag.

"Once you are done with the mouth," the Duke said, lifting up Reynard's face so that he could stare coldly into it, "It can be used in . . . other places."

"Looking forward to it," Reynard said, and spat a thick gout of blood into the Duke's face.

One of the guards struck Reynard hard across the face, and he likely would have continued to beat him if the Duke's voice hadn't called out for him to stop.

"You are stubborn," the Duke said, wiping his face with a silk handkerchief. "And I admire that in a man. But, what if I told you that I did not intend to use this lovely device on you?"

Reynard did not answer, but Nobel could tell that he had his complete attention.

"You see, when you were captured news spread fairly rapidly that the reign of the infamous 'Fox' had come to an end. It was not long before my clerks were overwhelmed by messages from one guild master or another, howling for your blood- it seems that you have made a lot of enemies in my city over the years, Master Fox! Lord Chanticleer of the Butcher's Guild in particular made me a very generous offer to turn you over to his care."

The Duke laughed, and handed his dirty handkerchief to an attendant. "But the strangest request of all came from a certain priestess of Sphinx, who apparently recognized your description. Her name was Hermeline."

"Never heard of her," Reynard said, desperately trying to sound callous.

"Well, she apparently knows you, Master Fox. Or," he raised an eyebrow. "Should I call you Master Percehaie? She was able to describe you quite easily, down to the most intimate detail."

Some of the Duke's guards chuckled.

"In any case, this Hermeline requested that she be allowed to care for you before your execution. Very touching, don't you think? It would be a shame should anything untoward happen to such a kind and selfless woman, would it not?"

"She's a priestess," Reynard hissed. "You wouldn't dare touch her."

"Oh, I myself certainly wouldn't hurt her, no," Nobel said, leaning down to whisper into his ear. "Whatever would the common folk say if they knew I had ordered the torture and execution of a servant of the Lioness? But accidents do happen, Master Fox, even to the servants of the gods."

Reynard looked up into Nobel's cold eyes. He might be bluffing, true, but what good were his riches to him now?

"You've found my apartments, I take it?" Reynard asked with resignation.

"Yes, and the gold you have kept stored in my Mint- but my agents have not found any of the finer items you have stolen. Tell me, where is it that you keep them?"

"The warehouse, in the bedroom- a hidden catch behind the wardrobe will open the way to a third story. Your goons should be able to take it from there."

"Ah, very clever," the Duke purred. "And I trust my men will not find themselves poisoned by hidden needles, or tumbling down into dead falls while they search?"

"It's not trapped, if that's what you mean," Reynard replied tiredly. "Now if you are quite done threatening me, I think that I've had quite enough of this visit. It's getting late, and I need my sleep."

"Yes, Master Fox. By all means," Nobel said, and bent in a mock bow. "Do catch some rest. Tomorrow will likely prove to be something of an ordeal for you, and I would hate for you to face it without proper sleep."

With that Nobel exited, his soldiers following close behind.

"It was a pleasure to have met you, Master Fox," the Duke said as the jailor sealed the cell door shut. "Tell me, do you have any final requests?"

"Will you let Hermeline see me?"

"Oh, I am afraid I cannot allow that," Duke Nobel said with a hint of pity in his voice. "But I can assure you that I will have an excellent seat set aside for her at your hanging."

* * * * * * *

Reynard's cell had no windows, so it was impossible to tell how much longer he had until the morning. The only way he could measure time was by the changing of the guards that stood watch over him.

He decided that he was not in Westgate, the city's official prison, as he had been inside that dreadful place once before, and his cell was far too dry and clean by comparison. The constant presence of the Duke's personal guard, and the occasional glimpse of a servant soon had him convinced that he was still being held somewhere within the palace grounds.

The Duke's men were true professionals, and they took no chances with Reynard. At least four of them stood watch over his cell at all times, and they were relieved often enough that they never seemed to grow tired or bored with their duty. They did not play dice or cards, drink, or even speak as they watched him, and he quickly grew tired of trying to engage them in conversation.

On the other hand, he soon found that his principal jailor, Mezzetin, had a penchant for singing- and he actually wasn't that bad. If Reynard had been allowed a fiddle, and if his present circumstances had been different, he might have enjoyed accompanying him.

He'd had a pretty good run, he supposed. And even if he had managed to escape the palace he would most likely have been forced to flee Calyx, perhaps even Arcasia altogether. He'd always thought that maybe he'd retire to some balmy Frisian isle, and use his amassed wealth to live out the rest of his days in luxury. But then he also knew that such a life would bore him dreadfully, and it wouldn't be long before he'd be at his old game.

Better maybe to get it over with now, he tried to reason with himself, though he found it difficult to cease searching for an opportunity to make his escape.

After the tenth change of the guard, he gave up looking and closed his eyes. If he got enough rest he imagined that he might manage a bit of a scuffle when they came to take him.

He wondered what Hermeline thought of him, now that she knew he was a thief, and found himself wishing that he'd given her more money before being caught- and, though he was not normally religious, he found himself asking the Lioness to watch over the closest friend he had ever known, and prayed that she would not weep too long over him.

When his prayer was done he scraped up a bit of grime from the floor and smeared it on his forehead with his thumb.

It was perhaps because of his mind's preoccupation with the priestess that he thought he heard her voice calling for the guards to open the door to his cellblock.

"Hermeline?" he called out weakly from the floor as Mezzetin admitted his visitors.

"Who is this Hermeline?" a woman's voice asked him, and he gazed up to see the Countess staring down at him through the bars of his cell. Madam Corte stood at her side, her face twisted into a barely concealed grimace at the sight of his wounds.

"Just a friend," Reynard said, pushing himself off of the floor slowly. "I thought maybe Nobel had changed his mind about letting me see her."

"Your face," Persephone said, her own features softening with worry. "Did the Duke's men do this?"

Reynard nodded.

"How dreadful," she replied, turning an accusing eye on Reynard's keepers. None of them could meet her gaze for long, Reynard noted.

"It is less than this low creature deserves, mistress." Madame Corte's voice was far louder than her slight frame would suggest. "It is only right that he be beaten, if you ask me."

"When I wish your council, Madam Corte" the Countess said archly, "I will ask for it."

"Yes, Mistress," the chaperone acquiesced and bowed her head. Still, Reynard could see the contempt that radiated from the woman's eyes.

"Are you in great pain?" the Countess asked, her voice lowering.

"Only when I breathe," Reynard said, only half joking.

The Countess turned to Mezzetin. "You. Fetch someone to see to this man's wounds."

"But, my lady," the man whined, "He is to be hanged in a matter of hours. I don't quite see the point."

"My mistress had given you an order, wretch," Madame Corte said, advancing on the man. "Who are you to question her commands?"

"The Duke's orders-" Mezzetin sputtered.

"Duke Nobel himself has given me permission to visit this man," Persephone said, "And to see to his care if I so wish. Now, run and find me a priestess of the Lioness, or you shall have to answer to him."

The jailor nodded and left, his keys jangling as he jogged out of the room.

"Not that I'm ungrateful," Reynard said, "but why are you helping me?"

"I suppose that it is because I feel partly responsible for what is happening to you."

"And that's all?" Reynard asked, his bloodied lips curling into a smile.

"What other reason could I have?" she said, trying to appear nonchalant.

He'd made an impression on her, he could tell, and it cheered him greatly.

"None, I suppose," he said, and slowly got to his feet. "Will you be attending the hanging?"

"No," she said quietly.

"Then perhaps you can do me a favor?"

Madam Corte snorted with derision, but kept her mouth shut.

"I may," Persephone said, "But I will need to know what it is before I agree to it."

She smiled then, only for a moment. It was a lovely sight.

"My friend, Hermeline," he began, "I have a message I'd like to deliver to her."

"That may prove difficult," Persephone said, "But I will try. Where might one find this friend?"

"She is a priestess, at the temple of Sphinx."

"A temple whore," Corte muttered darkly, but a cutting glance from her mistress silenced her.

"And the message?"

"Tell her that I am sorry for having lied to her," he said. "And . . . tell her that I loved her."

The Countess nodded slowly, turning away from him slightly as she brought a hand up to her eye.

Mezzentin returned then with an old priestess wearing a dusky gown- one of the old Duke's personal physicians Reynard guessed. She clutched a surgical kit under one arm, and was admitted into Reynard's cell under close watch. The Countess watched silently as the woman cleaned and dressed Reynard's wounds, even as she reset his broken nose.

When the woman was done Reynard's face ached, but the unguent that she had spread over his cuts soothed him considerably.

"Thank you," he said to the woman. She merely nodded, repacked her tools, and promptly left.

A quartet of guards entered the room then. One of them held a tray with a steaming bowl of stew on it.

"My lady," Mezzetin said as firmly as one could without sounding disrespectful, "It is time for this prisoner's final meal. I'm afraid I'm going to have to ask you to leave."

The Countess nodded, and turned back to Reynard.

"I am not sure what to say," she said, her hands curling around the bars.

"Goodbye might be appropriate."

He stepped towards her, in order to take her hands, but the guards immediately dragged the Countess away from the bars. Madam Corte took great offense to this and beat the men with her fan until they released her near the door.

"Goodbye, Master Fox," the Countess said, trying rather unsuccessfully to speak without crying. "I will deliver your message for you."

He nodded in thanks, and then she and her chaperone were gone. For a while afterwards he could hear the rustle of Madam Corte's skirts, and then he was alone again with his captors.

"Alright now, Rat," Mezzetin said as he took the tray from one of the guards. "Eat up! The Duke doesn't want you collapsing before the time comes for you to dance."

The jailor slid the tray through a slot underneath the bars, spilling liberal amounts of the stew as he did so.

Reynard considered refusing to eat, but it was the first food he'd been offered since he'd been imprisoned. And it smelt quite good.

"No spoon?" Reynard asked.

"Don't push it," the jailor snarled. "You don't have that Luxian bitch here to protect you anymore."

The man had a point.

Reynard scooped up the bowl and used his hands to shovel food down his throat. His nostrils had not deceived him: it tasted fantastic.

He was halfway through his meal when he noticed that there was something odd going on. He felt nearly as drunk as if he'd been on a three day bender. The bowl slipped from his fingers, and he stumbled. The guards didn't laugh either, but watched him coolly as he staggered to the bars.

"Bastards," he slurred. "What is this?"

They didn't answer. He tried to use the bars of his cell to keep himself on his feet, but his arms were as useless as wet noodles. He slid down to the floor, trying to stay awake, but his eyes were already closing on their own accord.

The last thing he heard was the cell door opening, and a distant voice saying, "Grab his legs."

* * * * * *

At first it seemed to Reynard that he was traveling down a very long, dark tunnel, with only a mere pinprick of light at its end. As the light grew he could begin to hear the garbled sound of conversation, the creak of wheels and the steady clip of horses' hooves on pavement.

"Poisoned," he murmured, suddenly finding himself staring at a pair of booted feet.

"No, Master Fox, not poisoned." He recognized the voice. It belonged to Count Bricemer.

Reynard forced his head up. He was inside of a comfortable coach, squeezed between two rough looking soldiers. A pair of manacles bound his wrists together.

Someone had dressed him while he had been unconscious, and he was surprised to see that the garments he wore were his own, and that they'd been cleaned.

It was dim. The coach's heavy curtains had been drawn, so that only a few cracks of light illuminated the interior.

Across from him sat two men. The one on the right had to be Bricemer: a long limbed man with a carefully trimmed moustache. His clothing was immaculate. But despite Bricemer's height, the Count was dwarfed by the strange figure who sat at his side.

He was a Calvarian. That much was obvious due to his pale skin and his piercingly blue eyes. His hair, cut short and lightly greased, was so white that Reynard might have taken him for an old man were it not for his hale physique. The fairness of his complexion was offset by his somber dress: a black uniform that had red accents around the cuffs and collar. A fine looking sword hung from his belt.

The man met his curious stare coolly. He had a killer's eyes, Reynard decided: they betrayed nothing.

"Where are you taking me?" Reynard asked at last.

"To an execution," Count Bricemer replied. "Yours in fact."

Something odd was definitely going on. He'd never heard of a criminal arriving at the execution grounds at Harbor Square by coach, and certainly not in the company of nobility.

"Who's this?" Reynard asked, with a nod towards the Calvarian. "Another of the Duke's pets? Or is he one of your own?"

"You'll find out soon enough," Bricemer said softly, "For now, be silent. We are almost there."

Indeed, Reynard could already hear the loud murmur of a crowd rising in intensity as they approached Harbor Square. Above the general babble he could also make out the call of street vendors who must have set up shop in the early morning hours, hoping to pull in some extra trade from the crowd. Then the murmur became a roar. From the sound of it, the entire city had turned out to see him swing.

He found that fact surprisingly touching.

They slowed to a crawl, and then rattled to a stop, the driver striking his whip against the side of the coach to signal that they had reached their destination.

Bricemer lifted a gloved hand and parted one of the curtains just enough so that Reynard could see through the polished glass.

The carriage was parked quite near the scaffold, and they had a fairly clear view of the proceedings. A pair of hooded executioners was making their final preparations, checking that the rope had been tied properly, and that the trapdoor mechanism would fall when triggered.

Directly in front of the scaffold were seated the cream of the city's gentry, their servants standing nearby with umbrellas in case it began to rain. The guild masters and priests had the second best seats along either side. Behind them stood the mass of Calyx's lower class. The din was incredible.

Reynard searched the crowd with his eyes, but nowhere could he find Hermeline. He was glad she hadn't come. He didn't want her to see him like this.

Reynard prepared himself for the moment when one of the guards would open the door and drag him out of the coach. He anticipated the jeers' of the crowd, the stones and filth that would be hurled at him. The wait was agony.

Then he heard the sound of a fiddle playing high and joyous. A great roar went up from the crowd. Something was happening, just out of view. Reynard leaned forward to see what, but the guards at his side pulled him back firmly.

"Sit still," the one to his right grunted.

"What are they cheering for?" Reynard asked Bricemer. "Is it the Duke?"

"No," Bricemer said. "Just a priestess of the Watcher that the Fox made a fool of. Duke Nobel has granted her the right to play at his death."

"Copee," Reynard said, catching sight of the wild-haired woman as the crowd parted for her. She capered merrily, and played a song that Reynard did not recognize. He wondered idly if it was one that Lord Chanticleer had commissioned for the occasion.

Then Reynard noticed something odd. The cries of the crowd were intensifying wildly. A knot of soldiers appeared, and at their center walked a diminutive figure, his clothes ragged and torn, and his face a mass of bruises and fresh injuries.

"Who is that?" Reynard asked, flummoxed.

"Why, that is the infamous Fox of course," Bricemer said, plucking a nearly invisible piece of dirt from his sleeve.

Reynard blinked, but didn't argue.

The imposter was led up the scaffold, and Copee danced circles around him as she played. At the sight of the noose he hesitated, and one of the soldiers struck him in the gut with the butt of his spear, sending him wheezing to the ground. As he knelt there, Copee produced the Fox mask that Reynard had worn to Lord Chanticleer's ball and strapped it over the man's face. When he lifted his hands to remove it, he received another blow for his efforts.

Mercifully the executioners stepped in, one of them gently guiding the condemned man over to the trap as the other fitted the noose around his neck. The man's mouth opened in a cry that Reynard couldn't hear over the crowd. Copee played madly. A figure rose from the crowd of nobles: the Duke. The crowd went silent. Copee stopped her fiddling. The condemned man's mouth formed words: I'm not the Fox.

The Duke lifted a handkerchief into the air and then let it drop. The trap opened. The man fell, the noose pulled taut, he danced spasmodically, and then was still. The crowd erupted into the anthem of Arcasia.

Bricemer closed the curtain.

"Now, then," the Count said. "You are dead, Master Fox. It would have been better if you'd shown more decorum in the end, but I suppose that a man raised in Low Quarter cannot be expected to have the same strength of character as a nobleman's son."

Bricemer rapped the ceiling with his cane. The driver whipped his reins and the coach began to laboriously make its way back through the crowd.

"Then," Reynard said slowly, "You aren't going to kill me?"

"Kill you?" Bricemer laughed. "My friend, I was told you were clever. Perhaps the stories about you have been blown out of proportion."

Bricemer continued to chuckle as the coach picked up speed.

"My dear Master Fox, we want to hire you."

* * * * * * *

Count Bricemer would not say a word more as the coach rumbled on. He merely smiled thinly, something that worried Reynard more than the knowledge of his impending death had. What in the world could they need him for so badly that they'd go to such lengths?

He couldn't help but admire the skill with which the Duke had played his hand. The abuse heaped on him in prison had served to make him unrecognizable to anyone, so that any man of similar build and complexion could then be sacrificed to slake the public's lust for blood, and his wealthy victims' thirst for revenge.

It was a scheme that he might have come up with himself, if he'd had the power that Nobel wielded.

He gazed at the Calvarian sitting across from him and remembered the conversation that he'd overheard in the palace. The Duke was planning something against the old terror of the North, that much was evident, but what?

Whatever it was, it was big- big enough that the Duke had spared his life, and was running the risk that his subterfuge would be discovered. Nobel would make a lot of rich enemies if word got out that he'd faked the Fox's death.

And how could they even ensure his cooperation? He'd already lifted the key to his bonds from the guard sitting to his left, using a heavy bump in the road to mask his sleight of hand. At the first opportunity he could break from his captors and escape. He wondered how fast the Calvarian could run.

Then he remembered the Duke's torture device, and the threat that had forced him to submit to Nobel's will.

"Where is Hermeline?" he asked suddenly.

"She is safe," Bricemer said simply, as if he'd been expecting the question. "But if you run, she dies."

Reynard nodded ruefully. The only way out for him would be to sacrifice Hermeline. And they already knew that he would do no such thing.

"And the man?" Reynard asked. "The one on the scaffold. Who was he, really?"

"Does it really matter?" Bricemer replied.

"It does to me."

Bricemer regarded him for a moment, and Reynard could almost hear the whir and click of the man's mind working like one of the temple of Fenix's automatons. A lifetime of caution had likely taught the Count to weigh every decision carefully.

He answered:

"If you are asking if he deserved his fate, then I'm not certain if I can give you a satisfactory answer- but I can tell you that he would have spent a lifetime of misery inside of Westgate prison. Perhaps this was more merciful?"

Bricemer let the question hang in the air. When Reynard did not reply, he turned back to the window, and they rode in silence.

Some time later the coach came to a halt, and again the driver gave the signal that they had arrived at their new destination. Bricemer smiled at Reynard faintly before shooting a glance at the Calvarian that the tall man seemed to understand.

The Northerner reached behind his head and pulled a dark hood over his face.

The door to the coach opened, and Reynard shielded his eyes from the sudden influx of light. He heard gulls crying, and could smell the dull fish-like stink of the river, so when his eyes adjusted he was not surprised to see that they had come to a stop at the end of a long pier. A single ship was moored there: a slender caravel that was almost entirely covered with tarps.

The Count exited the coach first, before letting the guards roughly escort Reynard out. Last came the Calvarian, who was even taller than Reynard had guessed. Were all Calvarians this large, he wondered, or was this one a giant amongst his kind?

The lanky man stretched his long limbs, and tugged at his cloak so that it concealed as much of his pale skin as possible.

"Release him," Bricemer commanded the men holding Reynard, who promptly let go of him. "And undo his manacles."

"No need," Reynard said, slipping the things from his wrists. He tossed them at the Calvarian, who caught them with a gesture so effortless that it suggested that he would be as deadly in a fight as he looked.

"Hold on to those, will you?" Reynard quipped to the man, and followed the Count down the pier and up a gangplank. He was certain that the Northerner's icy gaze was boring into him as he walked, and he did not turn around to find out.

There were a few leathery skinned men lounging about on the deck, dressed in loose clothing that might have once been colorful. They seemed to know Bricemer, and ignored him as he descended into the hold below. Reynard they stared at, their squinting sailor's eyes looking uniformly unimpressed.

Reynard avoided eye contact, and followed Bricemer down into the darkness.

Once his eyes had adjusted to the dim light, Reynard could see that the main hold had been cleared to make room for a long table that was covered with books, maps, and rolled up charts. Arrayed around it sat a dozen or so men- a rough looking crew, if Reynard had ever seen one. He felt their eyes sizing him up as he walked down the last few steps.

Count Bricemer motioned for Reynard to sit in a nearby chair. He nodded and did so, finding himself uncomfortably close to an armored man with a great bushy beard streaked gloriously with white. The man smiled at him darkly, revealing a gleaming silver tooth.

As the Calvarian entered he closed the door to the hold behind him, plunging the room into almost total darkness.

"May we have more light, Captain Roenel?" Bricemer's calm voice asked politely.

Reynard heard movement from the other end of the table, and then the soft glow of a set of oil lamps flared into life. When it was light enough to see, Bricemer nodded and took a place at the head of the table. The Calvarian stood behind him, the light barely penetrating the dark folds of his cloak.

"I apologize, gentlemen, for having kept you waiting this long," Count Bricemer began, "But I felt it best that all of the partners of this . . . expedition were accounted for before we began."

Expedition? Reynard thought to himself, keeping his face a blank mask. He noticed that some of the other men around the table were also surprised.

"Furthermore," Bricemer went on, "I would like to remind you all that, regardless of your individual circumstances, what you hear today is a state secret of the highest importance. For those of you who have agreed to take the Duke's pay, you already know the consequences of attempting to renege on your contracts. As for the rest of you," Bricemer took this moment to glance at Reynard, his moustache curling as he smiled, "I remind you that you can easily be returned to the circumstances from which you were plucked."

The message was clear: join, or die.

"I've had enough of all this big talk and mystery, Bricemer," a dark-eyed man wearing a hardened leather breastplate said harshly. "Stop wasting our time and get to the point."

"Patience, Tybalt," the Count replied softly. "Or would you prefer we return you to your cell in Westgate? I'm sure there are all manner of things there to occupy your time."

The man named Tybalt's face paled, and he shook his head. Another prisoner of the Duke, Reynard guessed. How many condemned men were present?

"Didn't mean no offense," Tybalt said quietly, and began to casually clean his nails with a sharp knife, flicking away the dirt underneath as he did so.

"Then if we are all agreed?" Bricemer said, and scanned the table for any sign of dissension. There was none. "Good. We may proceed then."

Bricemer reached forward and picked up a particularly ancient looking tome from the table. He opened it carefully, so as not to crack the brittle pages. Reynard could see that it was written in Aquilian, the language of the old kingdom.

"Tell me, gentlemen," Bricemer said as he thumbed slowly through the book. "How many of you know the story of the three great treasures of the kingdom of Aquilia?"

There was a murmur around the table as some of the men shot each other skeptical glances.

"That old children's story about the Demon King, and the seven heroes?" the bearded man seated to Reynard's right asked the Count.

"The very one," Bricemer responded.

"Yeah, I know it. Don't imagine there's a youth within a hundred thousand miles who hasn't heard that nonsense."

"I have not heard it," said a man sitting at the far end of the table. Glyconese, Reynard noted. There was something very unnerving about the man that took Reynard a second to register: his eyes did not match. The right was a vibrant brown, the left hazel.

"Then I will tell you as truncated a version of the story as I know," the Count said, still thumbing through the book. "At the end of the Age of Demons, the dark rulers of the world fought a great battle between each other. We do not know its cause, but it tore their empire apart. Millions of their slaves died to satisfy their lust for domination as they unleashed the terrible sorceries that created the Plain of Glass, and the Waste . . . and, in the end, only one of them remained standing: Stormbringer, the Demon King."

"Immortal he was, and his reign might have lasted until the end of all things, but the war between the Demons had sapped the strength of his newly won empire, and it was in that time that a hero rose from the ranks of his slaves. His name was Aquilia, and together with the Faun Queen Zosia he forged an alliance with the mighty princes of the chimera, and fought the beast in his dark fortress- there fell Florfax the Swift-Wing, fierce Prince Orthus, and Stheno the Wily. At last the mighty Aquilia, Zosia the Beautiful, and Chiron the Wise each dealt the Demon King a mortal blow, wiping his race from the world forever."

Bricemer apparently found what he was looking for: a faded plate set into the book that depicted the three treasures of Aquilia: sword, mirror and jewel. He turned the tome around and lifted it slightly so the men could see the images as he spoke.

"And when the battle was done each of the three surviving heroes took a trophy, so that great day would be remembered long afterwards. Aquilia took a shard from Stormbringer's soul crushing blade, and from it was forged the great sword, Thunderclap, that could not again be broken. For his prize Chiron lay claim to a great mirror carved from obsidian, and it was said that within its smoky depths one could see visions of both past and future. But to Zosia went the greatest of the treasures: a great gem the size of a man's heart that the Demon King had worn in his iron crown. And it was said that the compassion of the Faun Queen went into it, and that whoever bore the gem would rule justly, and with love. And when Chiron and Zosia died, they passed on their gifts to their old companion, and when his time came as well he gifted the three treasures to his own son, and he to his son, and so on throughout the generations of the old Kings of Aquilia."

"Nonsense," the bearded man sitting to Reynard's right repeated when Bricemer was done.

"Most likely," Bricemer said. "But that is the story as it has been passed down through our most ancient legends. And, even if one does not believe these stories, one cannot deny the existence of the treasures."

Bricemer set down the book.

"And where are these 'great treasures' now, Count Bricemer?" Tybalt asked sarcastically. Reynard found himself disliking the man immensely. He had known many men like this back when he lived in the Anthill: all smoke and hardly a lick of flame to back it up.

The Count cleared his throat, and drew the assembled men's attention to the largest of the maps in front of them. It was of the known world, and excellently drawn. As he spoke his gloved hand brushed the countries that he named.

"We know the location of only two of the regalia, as the Mirror of Truth was said to have sunk into the depths of the seas west of Lorn, along with the last child Queen of Aquilia, a thousand years past."

"As for the supposedly unbreakable sword, Thunderclap, it now lies in thirteen pieces, each sliver of it held by one of the petty princes of Frisia."

"And the gem?" Reynard prompted, though he could already see where this was heading.

"For generations it was held by the Dukes of Arcas, a treasured symbol of the unity of their realm. Then the Calvarians landed in the North, and forced the Duke who ruled then to swear fealty to them. As a symbol of his submission the Calvarians stripped him of Zosia's jewel, and carried it with them when they finally returned to their own cruel land. Two years later the whole of Southern Arcasia broke from the Duke's rule, and we have known civil war ever since."

"Sad story," said a veritable bear of a man wearing a stained Arcasian uniform. "But where do we fit in?"

"I should think that would be obvious by now, Master Bruin," Bricemer said, his fingers drumming the table. "You are going to sail to Dis, the capital of Calvaria, and steal back our gem."

V

As the men seated around him reacted with understandable incredulity Reynard was interested to note that, besides himself, only three others appeared unfazed by the Count's words: the Calvarian, the Glyconese with the mismatched eyes, and a nautical-looking fellow whose coat had been so well crusted with salt that it was nearly chalk white.

The Calvarian is the Count's creature, he mused, *but what of the other two?*

As the uproar began to die down, Bricemer raised his gloved hand for silence and said, "I admit, that it is a difficult task you are about to undertake-"

"Difficult?" Tybalt snorted. "It's suicidal! Better to spend the rest of my days in Westgate than risk getting killed in some frozen wasteland."

A few of the other men agreed.

"Now hold on," the bearded man seated to Reynard's right said over the din. "I for one would like to hear the Count's plan- or don't any of you remember that we won't be around for much longer if we refuse?"

"Thank you Master Grymbart," Bricemer said with a nod to the man. "I'm glad that, unlike some of your fellows here, you at least possess some common sense."

"Oh, just get on with it," Tybalt growled.

Bricemer cleared his throat. "As I was saying, retrieving the gem will be difficult, but not impossible."

Bricemer produced another map and rolled it open. This one was of Calvaria. Curious, Reynard leaned forward, as did most of the men assembled. He guessed that they too had never seen such a detailed map of the dreaded Northern country.

"Where did you get this?" asked a man whose hair was as black as the raven that perched on his shoulder.

Reynard knew the answer, and glanced up at the pale skinned man looming over the Count.

"To answer that question," Bricemer said, "I think that it is time that I introduced you to the gentleman whose participation in this little endeavor will make possible both your success and survival."

The Calvarian stepped forward, and removed his hood.

"Hydra's Teeth," Tybalt said, speaking for the room.

"Gentlemen, this is Master Isengrim. He is an exile from Calvaria, and completely dedicated to our cause. It was he who produced these maps for us."

"An exile?" the big man that Bricemer had called Bruin slurred. "I thought that the Calvarians were supposed to be merciless."

"They are," the Northerner said in a deep voice, devoid of any accent. "But only with those that they consider to be . . . inferior."

"What was your crime?" Reynard asked.

"That," Isengrim answered with an icy glance, "Is none of your concern."

"Alright," Tybalt said, his arms crossed in front of him. "We've got some fine looking maps, but I still don't see how this is going to get us past the Calvarian fleet- not to mention the thousands of miles of hostile territory we'd have to cross to get to Dis."

"You won't be marching anywhere, loudmouth," the man in the salt-encrusted coat said. "If you recall, the Count said we would be sailing to Dis, not marching there."

"Captain Roenel is correct," Bricemer said. "In fact, Master Tybalt, you will not be leaving the Quicksilver at all if everything goes well."

"The Quicksilver?" Bruin said, his stumbled words leading Reynard to suspect that he was a little slow.

"The Quicksilver is my ship," Captain Roenel said. "And while you are on her you'll follow my rules, or I'll be the first to throw you over her side."

The last comment had been directed at Tybalt, who scowled and continued to play with his knife.

"I hate to agree with loudmouth here," Grymbart said, stroking his moustache, "But we'll be sailing through waters that are under the direct control of the Calvarian navy. We might be able to outrun a few of their galleys, but they've got ships just as fast as this one. No offense to the Quicksilver, of course."

"None taken," Roenel replied. "And, you're right- it would take a miracle for us to escape detection completely if we were taking the long route around the northern coast."

"*If?*" Grymbart raised an eyebrow. "I can tell we're about to discover another wrinkle in this plan of yours, Count Bricemer, and I already don't like it."

"I don't imagine that you will, Master Grymbart, but it is the only way we've found to effectively circumvent the Calvarian navy."

Grymbart motioned for the Count to continue.

"As you can see from this map, Greater Calvaria is a peninsula. But, fortunately for us, its capital is located on Thule," Bricemer tapped a point on the map with the tip of his cane, "A large island that lies just off of the eastern coast."

"I don't quite see how that makes any difference," Tybalt said.

"That is because you, much like the Calvarians themselves, are completely unaware that there is a river several hundred miles to the southeast of their capital that, if followed correctly, connects to a similar river here, at the eastern border of Solothurn."

Bricemer traced a jagged line across the map.

"But that would take us-" Tybalt said, and stopped, truly stunned.

"Yes," Bricemer said in the silence. "It will take you through the heart of Vulp Vora."

Vulp Vora: home to fierce chimeras, twisted mutants and other monsters that defied easy description. Its once great cities rotted slowly beneath toxic jungles. And then there was the Waste, which still burned with the invisible fire of the Demon's ancient sorcery. Even the Calvarians had failed to tame it.

Reynard swallowed, hard.

"How do we know that such a passage even exists?" said the man with the raven. "Few are the men who have gone into Vulp Vora and returned to tell of it."

"Doom!" the raven croaked, as if echoing the man's sentiment.

"It's real enough," Captain Roenel said.

"You've taken the trip yourself?" Reynard asked.

"Not entirely," the Captain admitted. "But I have been as far as Lake Hali before, and have spoken to captains that have made the complete voyage. It's not safe by any means, but they say it can be done. That is, if you watch your back."

"And that, gentlemen," Bricemer added, "Is what *most* of you have been hired for: to defend this ship as it makes the passage through Vulp Vora. Once you reach Calvaria, Isengrim will take over the operation. Fail to protect him, or this man," Bricemer singled out Reynard, "And you can consider the mission to be a complete failure."

"Oh? And what's so special about him?" Tybalt asked, staring at Reynard darkly.

"He is the one who will accompany Isengrim into Dis to retrieve the gem. Consider his safety as you would consider your own."

The men looked Reynard over again, eyebrows raised. He didn't blame them- he couldn't look like much, particularly with a face covered in fresh bandages.

"Not that I don't enjoy a challenge," Reynard addressed the Count, "But how will a dark-skinned fellow such as myself avoid being chopped to pieces once we're in Calvaria?"

"Isengrim will fill you in on the details," Bricemer replied. "And to protect the secrecy of the mission I think it would be best if you kept such plans from the crew, in the event that any of them are captured."

"And once we have the gem?" Reynard asked.

"Captain Roenel has been fully briefed on how to proceed from there," Bricemer replied, rising from his seat as he did so. "For now I suggest that all of you focus on the task at hand: keeping this ship safe and retrieving the gem. Do your job well, and there will be pardons and rewards for the survivors. I suppose that I need not tell you the reward for failure?"

The silence of the men spoke volumes.

"Then may Fenix guide you, gentleman," Bricemer said, stepping away from the table and mounting the first step out of the hold.

Tybalt flicked his wrist, and his dagger plunged into a wooden crossbeam just above Bricemer's head.

"Sorry," Tybalt said, smiling toothily. "It's just that you never told us when we were leaving on this pleasure cruise."

The Count turned, seemingly unfazed. Reynard had to admire the man's calm.

"Winter will soon be upon us. You will have to make quick progress to make the trip before the Northern seas turn to ice, which will also serve to slow any Calvarian pursuit. What say you, Captain Roenel? Is the Quicksilver ready to sail?"

"She will be within the hour, your Excellency," Roenel said, removing his hat and bowing courteously.

"Then I suggest you do so."

* * * * * * *

Shortly afterwards, Reynard was shown to a small cabin at the rear of the main hold- his home, he supposed, until this business was done. He was pleasantly surprised to find that someone had stowed his extensive thieves' kit, rapier, dagger, and several fresh changes of clothing, along with several things that had been seized from his warehouse: his avian flint and tinder lighter, his own set of toiletries, and even the old fiddle that he'd learned to play on. He silently thanked whichever of the Duke's minions had done so, for it made him feel a little less like he had lost everything.

Less pleasing to him, however, was the sight of the items laid out on the cabin's only other cot: a whet stone, a small tinderbox, a set of ivory handled eating utensils, a shaving razor, various bottles of ointment, a jar of boot polish, and a neatly folded Calvarian uniform.

Isengrim was his bunkmate.

At least the man travels light, Reynard mused as the Northerner entered the cramped room.

"You are wanted on deck," Isengrim said without further elaboration.

Reynard excused himself and, finding that all of the other hired muscle had been assembled as well, he was swiftly put to work. He didn't mind- he'd done his fair share of naval duty in the guise of Rovel, and the old sailor's knots came as easy to him as they would to a true salt.

He could also tell that most of the others were unused to such work. Captain Roenel's first mate, a gruff man named Pelez, made certain that the new men understood how slow and clumsy he thought them.

At the very least, the hard labor kept Reynard's mind occupied as the Quicksilver sailed farther and farther away from Calyx. He looked up from his work briefly as they rounded a wide bend in the river, and the city that he both loved and hated disappeared behind a dense copse of trees.

"Homesick already?" a voice asked him.

It belonged to Grymbart, who had been helping him tack one of the sails. The man had stripped off his armor, revealing that his stout body was covered with scars. His muscles were well defined from years of physical labor, excepting his gut, which had broadened into a considerable paunch.

Reynard shook his head. "Just never been this far from Calyx."

"A city man born and bred, eh?"

"Something like that."

"Guess I felt a little strange too, first time I left home. Don't worry, you'll get used to it soon enough. Might even get to like it, if you're not careful."

"Where are you from?" Reynard asked.

"Mandross. Guess I've been gone so long that you can't even hear the accent."

"You a mercenary then?" Mandross was renowned for both its neutrality, and its willingness to supply troops to whoever had the most gold to spend.

"Since I was young. Come from a long line of sellswords. Figured I shouldn't buck tradition."

Reynard smiled. He liked the man.

"Name's Grymbart," the man said, offering his hand.

"Fox," he replied.

"Fox?" Grymbart repeated, "You're not *the* Fox, are you?"

"He's dead," Reynard said, smiling sardonically.

"Well," Grymbart sighed, obviously impressed, "It's quite the crew Duke Nobel has assembled here."

"Oh?" Reynard hadn't recognized anyone else, but then he moved through different circles than a Mandrossian mercenary.

"You see that man over there? The one with the raven?"

Reynard nodded. He found it odd that the man's pet bird stayed so close to him, even as he strained to hoist a sail.

"That's Tiecelin. Used to be a Luxian scout. I doubt there's a better tracker on the continent, and he's deadly with a bow in his hands.

Saw him shoot down a whole scouting party back when my company was fighting for the Arcasians."

"Bruin," Grymbart indicated the huge man who Reynard had found slow, "Was a sergeant in Nobel's army, before he was condemned to death. Sweet guy, actually, when he's not drunk."

"What did he do?"

"Killed a man over a game of cards. The way I hear it, he did it with his bare hands."

"Not hard to believe," Reynard replied, noting that Bruin's hands were nearly as big as his own head.

Pelez's voice ripped across the deck. His target was Tybalt, who had obviously done something improperly, and the two men proceeded to engage in a shouting match that only ended when the first mate threatened to get out his scourge.

"Loudmouth over there, Tybalt, he's a bandit. Sort of a prince of his kind, back in Engadlin."

"I have a hard time imagining him in charge of anything."

"He's smarter than he looks. Ruthless too. Killed his own brother to become chief, they say. I'd try and keep clear of him, if I were you."

Reynard nodded. He had no intention of being baited into a fight.

"What about the Glyconese?" he asked. The odd-eyed man was working mechanically, his bare chest revealing an intricate tattoo of a dragon swallowing its own tail.

"Him?" Grymbart replied. "He showed up just last night. Don't know much about him, apart from his name- I heard Bricemer call him Ghul."

* * * * * * *

The first morning out was exhausting. To Reynard it seemed an eternity before the Firebird had reached her peak- at which point Captain Roenel ordered the removal of the heavy tarps that covered the Quicksilver's fore and aft. This revealed the ship's figurehead, a youth holding aloft a messenger's rod that had been gilded with silver, and the regular crewmen let out a cheer at the sight of it.

Shortly afterwards they were allowed a short break to sup. Their meal, a sort of unidentifiable porridge that was doled out by a piggy-eyed sailor, left much to be desired. But Reynard had to admit that it felt good to have hot food in his belly, and he slurped it down.

He'd almost finished his meal when a shadow appeared over his shoulder. He knew it was Tybalt, and went on eating as if ignorant.

"Hey, you!" Tybalt growled, trying to startle him.

Reynard rose, slowly and deliberately. He saw that the other men had formed a loose circle around them, already expecting a confrontation.

"Hey, I'm talking to you!" Tybalt said, giving him a shove that sent him half-stumbling forward. He held onto his bowl.

"Can I help you with something?" he said calmly as he turned to face the former brigand.

"You could say that," Tybalt sneered. "Grymbart here says you're the Fox- some master thief that no one could catch . . . only I guess he got caught, huh?"

Reynard shrugged. "Could be."

"Well, I think you're full of shit. I mean, how do we even know you're really the Fox? I bet you told Bricemer a lot of tall tales to get your ass out of the noose, and when it comes time for you to do the deed you'll foul it up like some piss pants amateur!"

Tybalt's face was mere inches from his now, the man's spittle spraying freely into Reynard's eyes.

"And suppose I prove my skills," Reynard said smoothly. "Will that put your mind at ease?"

Tybalt crossed his arms, and laughed. "Sure, why not? Why don't you show us what the famous Fox is capable of! Can you disappear for us, like they say that you can?"

"If you like," Reynard said.

"Well, let's see it then," Tybalt snorted with derision. A few of the others looked skeptical as well.

"You'll have to turn around."

"Oh, very good! A man who can disappear when you're not looking at him."

Bruin guffawed at that.

"Only for a moment," Reynard explained. "Then you may look for me wherever you like."

Tybalt sighed and proceeded to perform for the others, snapping his head around as he turned as if to catch him in the act, until he had shown Reynard his back.

"Can I turn around now?" Tybalt asked. When he got no response he turned.

Reynard was gone.

Tybalt twisted around, but nowhere could he see the man who had been standing before him just moments ago.

The other men began to snicker.

Tybalt walked over to the side of the ship and glanced towards the rigging, to see if his quarry was dangling somewhere above. No sign.

As he turned to look at a pile of crates something fell off of his shoulder and clattered to the deck below. It was a spoon- the one that Reynard had been using.

The snickering of the crew began to turn to laughter.

"Where are you, you twist?" Tybalt shouted, his face reddening with anger. "Show yourself!"

"As you wish," Reynard said, and dumped the remaining contents of his porridge bowl onto Tybalt's head.

The men roared with laughter. All the while Reynard had been standing directly behind the man, following his movements so perfectly that he could not be seen.

"You move very quietly," Tiecelin said to Reynard. Considering what Grymbart had told him earlier, Reynard took it as an extreme compliment.

"Curse you!" Tybalt said as he wiped the porridge out of his eyes. "I'll show you what happens when someone tries to make a fool out of me!"

Tybalt reached for the knife he kept at his belt, only to find that it wasn't there. His head snapped back up to see Reynard held it in his left hand.

"I think you dropped this," he said, and flung it into the deck at Tybalt's feet.

His face twisted with fury, the former bandit stooped over to retrieve his weapon, but before he could free it a pair of rough hands grabbed him around the middle and lifted him effortlessly into the air.

"That's enough," Bruin said, his grip tightening.

"Let me go!" Tybalt snarled, kicking at Bruin's chest with little effect.

"He's proven himself, Tybalt," Grymbart said, still laughing. "And remember what Bricemer said? You kill him and this whole thing's over before it began. That is, of course, if you could even manage it."

"Alright ladies!" Pelez's voice cracked through the air like a whip. "Fun's over!"

"Ah, leave 'em be, Bald!" said one of the sailors, a pure Telchine whose skin was almost as golden as the choker he wore round his neck. "It was just getting interesting!"

Pelez scowled at sailor's use of the nickname. Reynard could tell it was a source of contention between the two.

"You heard me," Pelez grunted. "Get back to work!"

Bruin gently put down Tybalt, who immediately retrieved his knife- and for a moment Reynard thought the man might ignore the consequences and fling it into his chest. At this range he wasn't sure if he could dodge it in time.

"Drop it," the first mate said, his hand fingering the hilt of his cutlass.

A wild stream of obscenities erupted from Tybalt's lips as he walked away and returned to his work.

"He curses like a sailor at least," Pelez groused as he stamped off.

Reynard noticed that he swept a hand under his hat as he did so, adjusting an extremely realistic wig.

* * * * * *

Over the next couple of days Reynard learned the names of all of the Quicksilver's crew, as well as where they stood in the pecking order.

After Pelez, the highest-ranking member of the vessel was a woman named Moire, that all the men called Lady. Reynard assumed that the title was ironic, for she was a tough old salt who looked as though she'd been around the world several times. If she'd been beautiful when she was younger, there was no trace of it now.

The rest of the crew were generally considered equals, but some were obviously liked or disliked more than others. Foinez, who sat in the crow's nest above, and whom everyone called "Spy" (it seemed that just about all of the crew had private nicknames for each other) had apparently not gained this position because his eyes were any sharper than the others. Rather, it was because he stank terribly, even when he bathed, and putting him in the nest kept him far from the crew's nostrils.

If there was one member of the crew that everyone liked, it would have had to be the nimble deckhand called Cointereau. He was probably only fifteen or sixteen summers old, Reynard guessed, and he smiled often. He could clamber up and down the rigging with such ease that he'd earned the name "Monkey." Even Pelez went easy on him, and let him tell jokes or play on a painted set of tom-toms that the boy obviously treasured greatly.

The rest of the men were a mixed lot. The gold-skinned Telchine's name was Odon, which apparently meant Dolphin in his native language, and most of the men called him that anyway. Espinarz, a rather prickly fellow who drank and gambled whenever he was not on duty, was the ship's helmsman- he and Bruin were soon fast friends. The others- Baucent the cook, and the four regular deckhands Condylure, Frobert, Musard, and Tardis- were from the various petty island kingdoms of Frisia, and Reynard got the impression that they were all pirates of one sort or another.

But unlike his men, Roenel (whom the crew only ever called the Captain, and the gods help you if you didn't do the same) was Arcasian. He had the bearing of someone who had once been groomed for greater things than to be the captain of a sea-raider's vessel, but had fallen somewhere along the way. Perhaps he too was an exile, like the brooding Northerner.

Twelve men, Reynard counted, *one woman*. If he included himself and the other mercenaries that Nobel had coerced into joining the expedition, that brought the crew's number up to just under twenty, a far smaller complement than was normal for a ship of the Quicksilver's size- but then he reasoned that a smaller crew could be fed with fewer supplies. Sure enough, every available nook and cranny of the lower hold had been packed with crates of salted pork, hardtack, limes, and dozens upon dozens of stout barrels of beer- for there would be no certainty that the ship could re-supply once they entered Vulp Vora.

But Vulp Vora, and what lay beyond, seemed far away at this point. The weather was mild, and as the boat glided smoothly downstream it seemed that they were on a holiday of sorts.

When the ship reached Barca, the small city that marked the halfway point between the capital and the port of Larsa, they moored to take on fresh supplies. And, though the crew had been forbidden to leave the Quicksilver, Pelez returned that evening with a crate of wine, and in the company of nearly two dozen priestesses of Sphinx. He even offered his own services to the Lady Moire, but she just laughed and said she would be content with the wine.

The rest of the crew drank and made love like men who know that they may not live to do such things again. Reynard found that he had no taste for the business, and tried to make peace with Tybalt by offering him the use of the girl that Pelez had brought for him, so that he might have two women to warm him for the evening. Tybalt made some half-hearted slurs about Reynard's manhood, and then descended into the hold with a priestess under each of his arms, telling them a far-fetched tale about his band of thieves in Engadlin.

Reynard leaned against the mast and played his fiddle. After a while Cointereau, flushed from both wine and the afterglow of sex, joined in with his tom-tom.

Ah, Reynard sighed to himself, *to be young, and naïve.*

They played a bit of the lay of Virago: the princess who had gone blind from staring too long into the setting sun, waiting for her lover to return to her. Every time he played this piece Reynard envisioned her standing on the beach, her long dark hair wafting behind her in the wind that came off the ocean. Her face had always been something of a blur, an amalgam of every beautiful woman he had lusted after as a youth. But now, as he closed his eyes, he thought he could almost make out the details of her face: proud but fragile, her hair laden with pearls, and her lovely hazel eyes full of sorrow.

He knew whose face it was, and his playing faltered slightly, though Cointereau didn't seem to notice. When the song was over Reynard launched into "The Slippers of Rose," and tried to put the Countess' face out of his mind.

As he played he saw Isengrim rise out of the hold, his hood still worn over his face despite the fact that it was night and the Watcher was hidden behind a thick blanket of clouds.

He'd seen little of the man since the voyage had begun, for Isengrim had not been made to work with the rest of the crew, and he rarely left their shared cabin until after night had fallen.

The Calvarian crossed the deck, his long legs taking huge strides. Cointereau stopped beating his drums and scampered away as the man approached.

"I must speak with you," he addressed Reynard. "Alone."

Reynard considered a jest, but thought the better of it. He doubted that Isengrim would be as easy to best as Tybalt had been.

He ceased his playing and stood up. The Calvarian strode back to the entrance to the hold, obviously expecting Reynard to follow.

The evening's festivities were still in full swing as Reynard climbed down into the hold. One of the temple girls beckoned to him from the shadows, her fingers brushing against his leg as she whispered sweet promises.

"Another time, darling," Reynard begged off politely, wondering absently how much Pelez must have paid these women to make them so tractable.

Isengrim led him to their shared quarters, and locked the door.

"Sit," he said, taking a seat himself.

"I'd prefer to stand," Reynard replied, shifting his weight slightly.

"That was not a request," Isengrim said, his eyes staring up at Reynard coldly.

"Very well," Reynard said and sat on the footlocker he'd been provided. "If you insist."

"There is much I must teach you," the pale-skinned man said, "And I will have no time for your insolence. So, from now on, when I give you a command, you will obey it. Do you understand?"

"I do," Reynard replied. "And it seems as though you've mistaken me for a trained dog. I am not one, I assure you, and I bow to no man's will but my own."

"We will see," Isengrim replied. "For when we arrive in Calvaria you must act as my servant."

"Ah. And that is how I will be able to move about Dis so freely, so to speak?"

"Yes."

"Well, *Master* Isengrim, I think I've played enough servants in my lifetime to know how to bow and scrape appropriately."

"Show me then," the Calvarian said. "Serve me a cup of water."

Reynard adopted the dignified posture of a valet, and reached for a canteen that hung on the wall over the man's bunk.

There was a whistling noise, and then Reynard felt a sharp pain as something hit him in the back. His head snapped towards Isengrim, who now held a vicious-looking leather switch in his hand.

"Not that one, fool," Isengrim glowered, "I like my water fresh."

"Shall I fetch it from the river, my lord?"

"Do not speak," Isengrim replied, and whipped the switch viciously against Reynard's ribs. When he clutched at the injury Isengrim struck the back of his palm.

"That hurt," Reynard said. In response Isengrim sent the switch whistling towards his face.

Reynard caught the switch in his hand.

A moment later the heel of the Northerner's boot connected with Reynard's chest, the force of the blow throwing him against the side of the cabin before sending him crashing to the floor.

"You are fast," Reynard said once he'd regained some of his breath.

"As are you," Isengrim admitted, "But if we were in Calvaria I would be forced to kill you now. Even then I'm not certain that I would be able save myself by doing so. For understand that while I can teach you how to look, sound, and act as a proper Calvarian servant would, I can do nothing to conceal the contempt that I can see hidden behind your eyes. So, Master Fox, swallow what you consider to be your pride, or I might as well kill you now- for if you do not learn how to behave properly both our lives will be forfeit."

"So," Reynard said, getting to his feet, "If I understand you correctly, you need me just as much as I need you?"

The Calvarian paused, but answered: "Yes."

"You might have said so from the start," Reynard groused. "Very well- I will play the part of your servant- but if I do as you ask, then you must also agree to my conditions."

"And what might those be?"

"First," Reynard said, "You will teach me how to speak Calvarian."

"I had already planned to teach you enough so that you might answer appropriately when spoken to, but-"

"You will teach me as much as you can before we reach Dis, or you can forget the whole thing."

"I doubt a Southerner would be able to master it."

"Expect to be surprised."

"As you wish," Isengrim consented. "What else do you ask?"

"When I must act as your servant, we will speak in your tongue. Then- and only then- will I do as you ask without hesitation."

"Very well," Isengrim replied. "It shall be as you say- though do not expect me to show you any leniency should you fail to carry out my commands."

"You may hit me as much as you like," Reynard replied. "As long as you realize that I will one day hit you back."

"You may try," the Northerner said darkly. "Now then, shall we begin?"

"Oh," Reynard interjected, "I nearly forgot- just one last thing."

"What is it?"

"Say, 'please.' Didn't your mother ever teach you good manners?"

The Northerner's brow twitched slightly. Reynard smiled to himself secretly. He'd struck a nerve.

"*Please*," the man said at last.

"Master Isengrim," Reynard said. "I think we have ourselves a deal."

VI

The next morning the Quicksilver reached the point where the Vinus emptied into the sea. There, straddling the river, was the once great port of Larsa, a jewel in the crown of old Arcasia that had been shattered by war. Its thick limestone walls had long since been stained emerald with slime, and Reynard could see the great rents where the Calvarians had broken them apart with their siege engines, over a century past.

The city itself was dismal; its buildings were little more than shells that had been devoured by the fires of war, and tottering within their broken husks were the cramped tenements that housed those unfortunate enough to live under Calvarian rule.

There was only one place, Reynard noted cynically, where the city's general decay was absent, and that was undoubtedly the quarter of the Calvarians. There the older structures had been leveled to make room for their garrison, and even now Reynard could see that the pale-skinned Northerners were in the process of demolishing an ancient temple of Fenix, their engineers plundering its walls for paving stones, and smashing its façade to harvest the precious gems inlaid there.

As they passed underneath the city's river gate, Reynard saw that a hulking Calvarian war galley was moored amongst the trading vessels and barges of his own people. Captain Roenel ordered Espinarz to give the galley a wide berth, but as the Quicksilver glided across the harbor another ship moved to intercept them. Its sails were marked with a proud antlered stag, the emblem of the Count of Lothier.

"Ahoy!" a scruffy looking man shouted at them as the vessel approached. He was one of several shabby looking marines visible on the ship's deck. "Who sails there?"

The Captain stepped to the nearest gunwale and replied in a bellow that Reynard was sure could be heard clear across the bay. "Roenel, Captain of the Quicksilver, seeking passage through your port!"

"Where are you bound?" the other man asked lazily. He and his men looked terrifically bored.

"Kloss!" Roenel called. "And then further, all the way to Vassa."

"Cargo?" As the other boat came alongside theirs several of the marines tossed grappling hooks over the Quicksilver's side in order to board.

"Liquor and some other small luxuries to trade for furs," the Captain said, frowning at the gouges that the hooks were cutting into his ship's beautifully polished timbers. "And, here, now! What's the meaning of this?"

"Sorry," the man grunted. "We need to board you. New orders from the Grays."

Reynard assumed that the man referred to the Calvarians.

"What new orders?"

"There's a tax now on liquor. You know how the Grays are about that stuff. 'Fraid we'll have to collect now if you're not coming into port."

Roenel made all the usual complaints about the strangling Calvarian taxes, apparently trying to appeal to the man's sense of patriotism, but the tariff officer retorted that he was only doing his job and emphasized how much trouble he would be in if he let their ship pass without being checked. Roenel replied that it hardly seemed worth the effort that the tariff officer's men would have to go through just to collect a handful of silver nobles- nobles that wouldn't even be going into their pockets, anyhow.

"Can we just settle this thing without a search?" Captain Roenel asked, adding: "I'll pay a little extra just for your trouble."

"How much extra?" the tariff officer asked casually.

"Five crowns?"

"Ten."

"Seven."

"Done."

Roenel dropped the coins into a leather purse and tossed it onto the deck of the other vessel. The officer picked it up and, after examining a few of the coins, motioned for his men to release the hooks. The Quicksilver's crew flung the tools back to the other sailors, and then the tariff vessel cruised to intercept another victim.

"Traitors," Roenel growled after them, and gave the order to loosen the main sails.

"Were those not Count Bricemer's men?" Reynard asked Grymbart as the ship maneuvered around the city's sea wall. "He is the Count of Lothier, and lord of Larsa, is he not?"

"Aye," the grizzled mercenary replied, chewing on a piece of salted beef. "But it has been many years since these lands have seen their lord and master. The Calvarian governors are the real power here. They only use locals so they don't have to get their own hands dirty."

"Lucky for us then," Tybalt said. "I doubt the Captain could have bribed those pale-skinned demons so easily."

"No," Isengrim agreed, "And they may board us yet, before we reach Falx."

* * * * * * *

They did not land at Kloss, as the Captain had told the corrupt tariff officer they would. That city the Calvarians had razed in retaliation for the old duke's defiance, and in its place they had constructed an ominous towered fortress ringed with thick walls. Beneath its cruel parapets a dismal shanty town had grown, sprouting up like mushrooms on a long dead corpse.

Instead, the ship kept its course, hugging the coast as closely as Roenel dared, for fear of being spotted by a patrolling Calvarian warship.

And as they sailed, Isengrim taught Reynard how to behave as his servant.

"Let us start," Isengrim began, "With a word used often by Calvarian children: *laruwa*."

"*Laruwa*," Reynard repeated.

"You have a good ear, Master Fox."

"Two, even," Reynard quipped. "*Laruwa*. It means 'master' I take it?"

"It does- but it also has another meaning."

"And that is?"

"Teacher."

Reynard soon learned that the servant of a Calvarian was held to a standard higher than any of the great noble houses of Arcasia. In poise, speech, grooming and dress he was expected to conform to an ideal of perfection that he doubted many man were capable of- not even the fastidious Count Bricemer would have been spared the switch that his cruel mentor wielded.

Somewhat mercifully, Isengrim abstained from striking Reynard's face and hands, excepting, of course, the blows that he had received during their first session together. Isengrim explained that marks on a servant's skin were often a clear sign that they had not been born into servitude or that they had been improperly trained, and that such a thing would reflect poorly on their master. On the other hand, a handsome servant would be admired, the way one might recognize a well-bred hound, or a fine steed.

Reynard was interested to learn that Calvarians did not normally keep servants, save for officers who had spent considerable time in what the Northerners called the 'Southern Kingdoms,' where manpower was apparently short. When their duties were completed, such men would sometimes bring their Southern thralls back to their homeland. It reminded Reynard of the way that a trader who had journeyed to Lazaward Tor might return to his wife bearing a necklace inlaid with the lustrous blue stones of that island.

To that end, Isengrim saw to it that Dolphin, who acted as the ship's surgeon whenever they were out of port, carefully tended to the various injuries Reynard had sustained during his imprisonment, and that his broken nose healed properly.

When the last of his bandages were removed, Reynard was given a splendid-looking dun colored uniform that Isengrim informed him he should wear at all times- at least until they had entered Vulp Vora. Any stain on his outfit, Reynard soon learned, would be cause for swift and immediate punishment.

During the now rare moments he spent on deck, Reynard saw that the trees were changing. The great forests of Lothier and Carabas, their leaves vibrant in the face of winter, were giving way to the pines and firs of Solothurn. These dense forests had a lonely look about them, for there were few signs that men had ever been there, except perhaps for the occasional glimpse of worked stone lurking amongst the trees.

"Do the men of Solothurn so fear the coast?" Reynard asked Lady Moire when day after day passed without any sign of habitation. "Or is the ground here too barren to till?"

"There were many great cities here once, they say, in the days of old Aquilia," Moire replied grimly, "Alkonost there was, and Sirin the Magnificent. But then the Calvarians decreed that this forest should feel the bite of no axe but their own. Year after year they would raid, slaying all who refused to leave, until those great cities were nothing but a memory."

"What right do they have?" blurted Cointereau, who had been listening to Moire's words from the rigging with growing agitation. "What right to say where men may live?"

"The oldest right of all," Reynard said, answering the young man wearily. "That of the strong over the weak."

"It is they who should be wiped from the world!" Cointereau shouted, his handsome face twisted into the unclouded hatred that only the young are truly capable of. "As the Firebird did the children of Pestis, in the beginning of days!"

"Would you become as they are, then?" Reynard asked, and the young man was quiet for a time. Then he clambered down onto the deck and began to beat on his tom-tom, his voice raised in a fierce song that seemed to fill the great silence of the abandoned coast.

Reynard watched Cointereau as he sang, and the sight reminded him of another young man, this one still learning how to play his master's weathered fiddle, his fingers aching, playing as if he might rid himself of his anger, his sorrow, and his lust for revenge.

Something in the corner of Reynard's eye caught his attention. It was Isengrim. Had he heard the boy's hate filled words? And, if he had, what was going on behind those cold blue eyes of his? Reynard wondered what had happened to turn this man against his own people, and how much of his disgust for his dark-skinned companions was just for show.

Once the Quicksilver had left Arcasian waters, Isengrim began to conduct Reynard's lessons on the main deck, a sight that often drew the crew's attention away from their own duties. Tybalt in particular found great sport watching as the Northerner administered a well-placed blow on Reynard as punishment for some minor infraction, but even he had to admit that he'd not once seen Reynard wince.

The reason for this change in his training became clear to Reynard when, their sixth morning out from Calyx, he heard Foinez ringing the bell that served as the ship's general alarm.

"Captain," the lookout hollered, "Ship off of our stern!"

"Calvarian?" Roenel asked.

"It has black sails!"

"We must have passed them in the night," Grymbart mused, loosening his sword from its scabbard.

"Quiet on deck!" Pelez snapped.

Reynard watched as Captain Roenel pulled a spyglass from his coat and squinted into it. Apparently unsatisfied, he called Tiecelin onto the poop deck and let him have a look through the instrument.

"Definitely Calvarian," the former scout said, leaning farther over the gunwale. His pet raven hopped across his back as he did so, in order to perch on his other shoulder. "Not one of their galleys . . . no oars. Most likely it's a scouting vessel on coastal patrol. They've seen us, too."

"Are you certain?" Roenel asked, squinting at the dark speck.

"They're coming about, Captain!" Foinez shouted from the crow's nest.

"Yes," Tiecelin replied, and handed Roenel back his spyglass.

"Doom!" Tiecelin's pet raven squawked. It was apparently the only word the bird knew, and the crew had taken to calling it Prophet.

"Can we outrun them, Captain?" Pelez asked Roenel, sweating despite the cold.

"We can always try," Roenel replied.

The Calvarian vessel gained on them rapidly. Soon Reynard could see the crimson wolf that had been emblazoned on its mainsail, its yawning jaws revealing a row of dripping fangs.

"Full sails, Captain?" Pelez said, and Reynard could hear that a hint of panic had crept into his bluster.

Roenel hesitated, then said: "What say you, Master Isengrim?"

The Northerner had hardly moved from Reynard's side since the Calvarian ship had been spotted, and he was now staring off into the middle distance, as if he were someplace else.

At last, he said, "If we do, they will know that we are running- and when they catch us they will kill us."

"Aye," Roenel replied in a tone that suggested that he had been thinking the same thing.

"Come about, very slowly, and lower the sails," Isengrim said. "We must allow them to board us."

"Orders, Captain?" Pelez asked, obviously irritated by the Northerner's presumption.

"Do as he says, Pelez."

"Aye, sir," Pelez grumbled, "Well, you heard the man, come about full!"

Before long the Quicksilver was sitting dead in the water, only the swell of the sea causing it to drift as they waited for the warship to come within boarding range.

"Something isn't right about this," Tybalt whispered harshly as they stood watching the Calvarian vessel loom closer. "I can smell a double cross a mile off."

"Don't you think that if he had wanted to betray us, he would have done so back at Larsa?" Reynard shot back.

"Still- that doesn't mean that he hasn't lost his nerve, now that we're in the wolves' jaws, so to speak."

"No," Ghul said, surprising Reynard and Tybalt both by uttering his first words since their meeting with Count Bricemer. "I sense no fear in that one."

Tybalt did not argue the point further.

"We are all petty traders, and I am your Captain!" Isengrim shouted then from the stern. Pelez started to protest but Isengrim shot him a look that might have quieted a giant. "If you value your lives, then do not speak, do not smile, and do not laugh! And be certain that you do not look any of them in the eyes, for they will almost certainly kill you for it! Show them only that you are afraid. That they will expect."

"What if we are spoken to?" Grymbart asked.

"They will not bother to speak with you," Isengrim replied.

"Shouldn't we keep our weapons handy?" Bruin asked. "In case there's a fight?"

"If it comes to that, Master Bruin, then we are dead already. Now then, Master Fox!"

Reynard stepped forward, his heart beating wildly in his chest. Was he ready?

"Get yourself below and prepare yourself as I have taught you," Isengrim said. "When you are needed, I will call for you. Do you understand?"

"Gea, laruwa," he replied and darted below deck to effect his transformation.

Reynard's years of experience in rapidly changing his appearance served him well now. Even without the aid of a mirror he was able to artfully trim his facial hair into what the Calvarians considered proper, using some of the Northerner's own reserve of grease in order to shape it before tending to his uniform with a heavy brush.

As he whisked away the dirt from his boots something weighted and heavy struck the ship with a metallic clang, and then Reynard could hear the unmistakable tread of booted men stamping onto the deck as the Quicksilver was boarded.

There was silence for a moment, and then he heard two voices speaking to each other in Calvarian. One of them belonged to Isengrim. He could barely understand a word of what was being said, having only learned rudimentary bits and pieces of the Northern tongue, but he found himself surprised by the calm, polite tone that both men used, as if they were old friends chatting over a quiet dinner.

"Fox!" he heard Isengrim call out, no hint of anger in his voice. It was the tone of one who is used to being obeyed without question.

He gave his uniform a final brush and climbed up out of the hold, wishing only that he'd had more time to prepare for this moment.

The Calvarian vessel, which was actually much smaller than the Quicksilver, was moored to theirs by means of a wide bridge whose underside was equipped with iron claws.

There was a company of Calvarian marines standing on the main deck, some fifty men in number. Their uniforms were very similar to the one Isengrim kept in their shared cabin. Each man wore a pair of gray woolen coats, the larger of the two slung over one shoulder like a half cape, and matching trousers that they had stuffed into black knee length boots. Thick bear fur, silvered buttons, and lacing interspersed with crimson accents completed the look. Each man wore a longsword at his belt, and carried in his hands a spear whose point had been forged out of Calvarian steel. And though they appeared to be standing at ease, there was a uniformity among them that made Reynard shudder. They reminded him of the way that a cat looks when it has seen a bird, and has just begun to coil its spine to pounce.

The crew of the Quicksilver was clustered on the fore and aft of the ship, their attention wholly occupied by two figures: Isengrim and another Calvarian, an officer Reynard guessed by the extra embellishments on his uniform and the fact that he alone did not carry a spear. He was younger than Isengrim, his hair the color of the orange fruits that grow in Frisia.

Isengrim did not turn his head to look at Reynard as he approached, but continued to speak to the Calvarian officer in the language of their kind.

Reynard kept his eyes trained on the deck as he approached, and bent into the formal bow that Isengrim had taught him.

The officer asked Isengrim a question then, and while Reynard didn't understand the meaning of what was said, he could tell that it concerned him. He swallowed his fear and kept still.

"Fox," Isengrim said, reverting to the common tongue, "Go below and fetch me a bottle of whiskey from the cargo hold."

Out of the corner of his eye, Reynard could see the Calvarian officer regarding Isengrim with suspicion, and inwardly cursed the Northerner for not trusting him.

"Gea, laruwa," he said with a formal nod, and retraced his steps with as much precision as he could muster.

In the hold below, Reynard found a set of crates marked with the seal of the Prince of Sakartvelo, and surmised that Count Bricemer had provided Roenel with cheap whiskey so as to complete the illusion that the Quicksilver was a merchant vessel headed for Solothurn.

As he picked up a crowbar in order to break open the seal, he noticed he that one of the crates had already been opened, and that a number of the bottles were missing. Filing this information away for later use, he pulled out one of the remaining bottles and returned to the deck.

The Calvarian officer frowned at him as he approached, and again Reynard felt a tight knot of fear rush through his body as he approached. Outwardly, he kept his composure and presented Isengrim the bottle.

Reynard offered the bottle by the neck, and Isengrim reached out to take it.

Isengrim's fingers had just begun to curl around the glass when Reynard let go.

The bottle dropped from his hands, and shattered across the deck.

The Calvarian soldiers, startled by the noise, immediately brought their spear points to bear on the crew, and on Isengrim himself. The officer's sword had appeared in his hand, readied so that he could cut Isengrim down with a single thrust.

Muttering apologies, Reynard knelt down and began to pick up the broken shards of glass.

"Awyrigung!" Isengrim grunted and kicked Reynard in the face.

The force of the blow threw Reynard backwards. He looked up just in time to see Isengrim deliver another kick to his ribs. He rolled over and received another for his efforts. Then Isengrim began to strike him without mercy, roaring out in his own language as he did so.

Reynard did not fight back, but took blow after blow without complaint. He knew both of their lives depended on it.

Suddenly, the assault ceased. Reynard heard the sound of a blade being drawn from its sheath. Blearily he glanced up and saw that Isengrim had drawn his own sword. It was a fine looking weapon, graceful and elegant- the level of craftsmanship that gone into its making was evident. Even the steel weapon that the Calvarian officer held seemed a mere tool by comparison.

"Bend your neck," Isengrim ordered through gritted teeth.

Reynard complied, and felt the cool edge of the blade tickle the hairs on the back of his neck as Isengrim positioned himself to hack off his head.

The Calvarian officer spoke softly then, and guided Isengrim's sword with his own until both of their points came to rest harmlessly on the deck. The man said a few more words, and then Isengrim re-sheathed his sword and went into a bow of his own.

"Get up," he said to Reynard. "And fetch me another bottle."

"Gea, laruwa," Reynard said and struggled to stand. Every part of his body protested, but at last he managed to regain his feet and began to make his way back to the entrance to the hold.

"Stop," the officer said, using the common tongue for the first time.

Reynard halted, and turned. Isengrim had told him to always obey the commands of other Calvarians, as long as they did not contradict those of his true master.

The officer sheathed his own sword. He made a gesture and his soldiers raised their spears and brought them back to attention. Another gesture caused them to turn mechanically and then they marched back across the bridge to their own vessel.

The officer spoke several more words to Isengrim and then strode over to Reynard.

The man lifted up his chin, and stared balefully into his eyes for a moment. Reynard avoided his gaze as best he could.

He spoke again so that Reynard could understand:

"You should be grateful, dog, that your master chose to spare your life. He may not be so merciful the next time you are so careless with his property. Do you understand?"

"*Gea* . . . Lord," Reynard said. He had not yet been trained how to address those who were not technically his master, but to not answer a direct question would have been fatal.

The officer squinted at him, and for a moment Reynard thought that he could see through his disguise, but then he let go of his chin and turned back to Isengrim. He spoke a few more words, and bowed politely before scaling the bridge and returning to his own ship.

The others were very still as the Calvarian vessel released its hold on the Quicksilver and retracted the bridge. Isengrim ordered Reynard to clean up the mess on the deck before delivering a final salute to his kinsman as they sailed back towards whatever cove they had been lurking in.

"Are you injured?" the tall man asked Reynard once the Calvarians were well out of earshot.

"Nothing broken I think," he replied, rubbing his side. "I thought you were really going to kill me for a moment there."

"I would have, Master Fox," Isengrim replied, "If their *heafodcarl* had not intervened. Why did you drop the bottle?"

"Simple misdirection- I could tell that they weren't buying your act, so I gave them something else to look at- something I figured they would understand."

"Your plan was that simple?"

"The simplest plans are usually best," Reynard replied. "Lend me a hand?"

Isengrim nodded and, taking Reynard by the arm, hauled him to his feet. Reynard adjusted his uniform, and then held out his hands in front of him.

"If you plan on stealing a man's coin purse with your right hand," Reynard said, curling his hands into fists, "Only let him see your left."

Reynard opened his right palm. In it was the pair of the decorative pins that normally adorned the front of Isengrim's coat.

"You dropped these, I believe," Reynard said, returning the pins with a smile.

A flicker of surprise passed fleetingly across the Northerner's face, and then the moment passed and the rest of the crew was crowding around them.

"The ship is yours, Captain," Isengrim addressed Roenel. "May you do with it as you will."

"What did you tell them?" the Captain asked Isengrim.

"The truth."

Roenel cocked an eyebrow. "And that is?"

"That I am an exile," Isengrim explained as he reattached his pins to his uniform. "They saw one who was once great amongst them reduced to selling liquor to the mindless brutes that infest these lands. They had great pity for me."

"Why did their Captain stop you from killing Fox?" Tybalt asked. "He didn't care whether he lived or died."

"No," Isengrim answered icily, "But he did manage to convince me that I would regret killing the only half competent servant I had amongst you scum. My people do not usually treat our possessions with such disregard."

* * * * * * *

Isengrim grew distant in the days following their encounter with the Calvarians. He rarely struck Reynard now, and his attention would often wander as he corrected his poise and bearing. He would sometimes stop speaking in mid-sentence, his attention drawn somewhere else: the past, if Reynard didn't miss his guess.

It was after one of these silences that the Northerner came out of his reverie with an odd gleam in his eyes. He stood, studied Reynard for a moment, and then began to stretch his long limbs.

"I have had more than enough of this cramped cabin," he said, for they had been practicing grammar apart from the others. "Follow me- I believe that it is time that I taught you more than I would a servant."

Reynard complied without comment, curious as to what the Northerner had in mind.

Most of the crew was relaxing as they climbed out of the hold. Baucent was doling out the midday meal, another one of his mediocre concoctions throwing great clouds of steam into the chilly air.

Isengrim led him to a generally clear area of the main deck, just below the crow's nest. Ghul was there, sitting cross-legged on a woven prayer mat- seemingly the Glyconese man's only possession beyond the clothes he wore on his back. His palms were joined, his eyes closed, and from his open mouth spilled a sibilant chant that reminded Reynard of the whispering tongue of a snake.

Isengrim ignored the Glyconese and said, "Fox, it may happen that we may be discovered during our foray into Dis, and we will be forced to kill in order to defend ourselves. Should it come to that, I would like to know that the man standing at my side could be relied upon. Do you understand?"

"*Gea, laruwa,*" Reynard said, but Isengrim waved the honorific away with his hand.

"You may drop the act. If we are to fight together, we must be as equals."

"I agree," Reynard replied, and wondered if he'd made a bigger impression on the man than he'd intended.

"Then begin," Isengrim said, his stance subtly changing. "Fight me."

"But, I don't have my weapons," Reynard said, glancing at the beautiful sword that hung from the Northerner's belt.

"Your body is a weapon," Isengrim replied. "And if you think that Calvarians allow their servants to wear swords then you are greatly mistaken. Now, begin!"

Reynard had been in dozens of fights in his life, from the dirty scuffles of the Anthill to the flashy duels of High Quarter, but he'd never fought anyone like Isengrim. He honestly wasn't sure if he could beat the man.

At least, not without cheating.

Reynard clenched his fists and lowered his stance.

"C'mon, Fox!" Grymbart shouted. "Show this pale-skin how us Southerners fight!"

The others cheered, happy to have some entertainment while they ate.

Reynard waded in, and made a few careful swings to gauge his opponent's speed. Isengrim dodged each of them, and then swept his feet out from under him with a single kick.

Tybalt began to laugh uproariously. Reynard resolved to slip several extra doses of Hivan pepper into the man's next meal.

Regaining his feet, he came at Isengrim again, more carefully this time. The Northerner caught him by the wrist and threw him to the ground, tossing him aside as easily as he might a child.

"Your blows are sloppy," Isengrim said as Reynard picked himself back up.

"Yours hurt," Reynard rejoined, rubbing his posterior.

"I am being as gentle as I can," Isengrim replied with a rare hint of mockery in his voice.

"Hydra's Teeth!" Reynard growled, feigning embarrassment as he launched himself into a hopeless counterattack. Sure enough, Isengrim sent him crashing to the deck with yet another well-placed blow.

"You use far too much force," Isengrim chided. "Your own momentum defeats you. You must be like the blade of a well-made sword: strong but flexible."

"A well-made sword, eh? Like this one?"

In his hands, Reynard now wielded the Calvarian's own double-edged blade.

"That's got him!" Grymbart roared. "Fox wins!"

"Yes," Reynard repeated. "I win."

"I told you that you will not be allowed a sword in Calvaria," was all that Isengrim said in response.

"But you never said that I couldn't borrow one. After all, things that don't belong to me have a habit of turning up in my hands."

"And do you truly believe," Isengrim replied quietly, "That the outcome of this fight will be different because you have a sword and I do not?"

"In my experience," Reynard answered, "Yes."

"Prove it, then."

"As you wish," Reynard answered, executing a few practice swings to loosen his arm. Isengrim's sword was incredibly well balanced. It was longer than his own, but it felt right in his hands, and its greater reach should even the odds between him and the tall Northerner.

"To first blood?" said Reynard.

"If you wish."

"You are certain that you do not want a blade of your own?" Reynard offered.

"I will not need one."

Reynard shrugged and assumed a duelist's stance, his sword held at eye level, and then came at Isengrim with a series of cuts and thrusts, every one designed to inflict a merely superficial wound.

There were audible gasps from the crew as Isengrim deflected each of Reynard's best strokes with only one of his gloved hands.

Reynard steadily quickened his blows, changing dueling styles freely in an attempt to confuse his opponent, but Isengrim never lost his calm demeanor or his perfect economy of motion.

"You fight well," Isengrim said as he weaved. "But you hold back. Why?"

"I don't want to kill you," Reynard managed as he dodged one of Isengrim's kicks.

"When you fight," Isengrim shot back, "Fight to win."

"Very well," Reynard replied, and drew his dagger from out of his coat.

Now he came in fast, feinting and counter-feinting with both sword and dagger. At last he saw an opening, and he brought his blade whistling in, intending to slash the Calvarian's cheek.

Before Reynard could understand what had happened, Isengrim had caught the sword with one hand, and then used his other to disarm him. A second later the Calvarian held his blade at Reynard's throat.

"First blood was it?" Isengrim said, and then he nicked Reynard's throat very lightly- the faintest hint of a scratch.

The crew was silent.

"You may rest now," Isengrim said as he sheathed his sword. "I am hungry."

"How?" It was all that Reynard could think to say.

"Do not be ashamed," the Northerner said, accepting a bowl of slop from a shaking Baucent. "I have been trained to fight since I was old enough to walk."

"I suppose you were wrestling with wargs when you were still at your mother's teat!" Tybalt laughed.

"I never knew my mother," Isengrim said, his face plainly showing that he did not find the matter amusing.

"Isengrim," Reynard said as Baucent filled his own bowl. "May I ask you a question?"

"Speak your mind," the Northerner said.

"You told us that you were a great man among your people. Were you a nobleman? Some prince forced from your throne by rivals?"

"Calvaria has no princes. It does not have nobility of any kind. All are born as equals there."

"Who rules then, if you have no lords? Who keeps the peace?"

"The Judges maintain the order of Calvaria," Isengrim said, and Reynard could hear a tinge of anger in the tall man's usually calm voice. "They hold authority absolute. Beneath them are the officers of the law. I was one of them, long ago."

Reynard laughed.

"You find the idea amusing, Master Fox?"

"I have to admit that I have a hard time picturing you as a mere watchman, breaking up a tavern brawl."

"You would do well not to mistake me for one of your corrupt constables," Isengrim frowned. "I was once of a high and noble order, my entire life dedicated to upholding Calvarian law and preserving the purity of our race."

As he said the word 'purity' Isengrim sneered, as if at an ill jest.

"Besides," the Northerner went on, his brief swell of anger draining as he spoke, "You will find no taverns in Dis- nor will see any drunks."

"Do your people not drink?" Lady Moire asked, and when Isengrim shook his head she whistled in astonishment. "An entire country without a single drop of wine! Now that is frightening."

"But why not?" Bruin asked, his mouth full of porridge. "There must be some land you could use to grow grapes, or at least some barley beer."

"Liquor clouds the mind and weakens the body, Master Bruin. Therefore, it is forbidden."

"My people too seek to cleanse ourselves of impurity," Ghul said. He had apparently ended his midday ritual and had rolled up his prayer mat. "So that the desires of the flesh may be shaken off and cast aside. Only then can the spirit be truly free."

"Horseshit," Tybalt muttered, but shut his mouth when Ghul's odd eyes turned to face him.

"I suppose there may be some similarities between the ways of my people and yours," Isengrim said to Ghul, breaking the tension of the moment somewhat. "But we do not concern ourselves with otherworldly hopes, or with empty rituals."

"Then," Cointereau asked before the Glyconese man could respond, "You have no priests?"

"No. Calvaria has no priests. It has no gods, no altars, no holy days. A Calvarian considers nothing sacred- except for the laws that govern them."

"Then they are a cursed race," Ghul said with a conviction that Reynard found unsettling. "And when The Destroyer rises from her slumber she will cast down their towers, and her venom will rot their flesh. And when their spirits come begging to be accepted into the bliss of her coils- into the bliss of oblivion- then she will deny them, and they will be doomed to linger on in a dead world, where they will drink dust and long for an end that will never come."

Ghul's fingers had been tracing the tattoos on his arms and chest as he had talked, and when he had finished he turned brusquely and went to return his prayer mat to the cargo hold.

Reynard stood aside as he passed, knowing full well that the words he had spoken had been directed at all of them.

"Touchy fellow, isn't he?" Tybalt said when the Glyconese man was gone.

"Almost as bad as you are, Tybalt." Grymbart replied, and laughed. "Still, best to watch one's tongue around that one. He is dangerous."

"Crazy is more like it," Tybalt said, scowling. "Just like the rest of his race."

"Do not judge our kind by him," Dolphin snapped. He seemed so like the other crewmen that Reynard often forgot he was a Telchine. "The minds of the Glyconese are as twisted as the wretched serpent they worship."

"No offense meant," Tybalt said. It seemed the closest thing to an apology that the man was capable of.

"Forgive me, Isengrim," Grymbart said, "But I had always thought that the Calvarians worshipped the Watcher. Is that not why they bear the wolf as their emblem?"

"It is true that my people once worshipped Wulf, long ago," Isengrim answered. "And before that we shared the veneration of your other gods, though we called them by different names than yours."

"What changed your people?" Reynard asked.

"It is written that, like the men of the South, our forefathers broke free of the rule of the creatures that you call demons- but while your ancestors colonized the hot lands, mine were drawn to the high mountains and forests of the North. The land was warmer then, much as Arcasia is now, and our people prospered there."

"But as the centuries passed, our winters began to grow harsher, and our summers shorter. The Hyperborean peninsula could no longer support our numbers, and our people starved. The priests of the Watcher declared that Fenix had abandoned us, and so the followers of the Firebird were driven from our lands, and brother slaughtered brother in order to sate the Winter King's thirst for blood. Raiders sailed from our shores, bent on slaughter in the name of Wulf, and hauled back food to feed our young- but no amount of bloodshed could halt the advance of the ice upon the land, and my people edged closer and closer to extinction."

"After almost five hundred years of this chaos, the lawgiver Vanargand No-Father- who was then nothing but a vagabond- came to understand the truth: when they are left to their own devices, men will breed and multiply until the land they inhabit can no longer sustain them. Therefore, he reasoned, men must be forced to restrict their numbers, lest they destroy themselves. Thus was born the first law of Calvaria: that man and woman may bear one child, and no more."

"That is foolish," Lady Moire said. "Children may die, even after they have grown. Who would care for you in your old age if you had no children?"

"Aye," Grymbart said. "I've got a half dozen wives myself- each of 'em in a different country of course. That way I'll have some options when I decide to retire."

"And if this Vanargand was only one man," Reynard said, reasoning it out, "Or even if he had followers, I don't see how his people could ever have outnumbered those of your race who did not wish to live under his law."

"Vanargand No-Father realized this as well," Isengrim said, nodding to Reynard. "So in the days of his conquests he enacted the great exception to the first law, which is that a Calvarian may have half as many children as enemies that he or she has personally slain in combat."

"That is monstrous," Moire said.

"Is it as monstrous as letting your children starve because there is not enough for them to eat?" Isengrim rejoined.

"But it is not for us to make that decision. Only the gods can-"

"The gods, if they exist, do not seem to care whether we live or die, if we do not help ourselves."

"I've heard enough," Lady Moire spat, kissing her thumb and rubbing it on her forehead in order to ward off the anger of Sphinx before stalking off.

"I think I can guess what happened to your people," Reynard said when she'd gone.

"Yes?" Isengrim said, regarding him with a skeptical look.

"It just follows that, if only the best warriors were allowed to have more children, then eventually *all* of your people would be fit to be warriors- even the women, maybe. Strength of body and of mind must have become your highest virtues."

"Very astute, Master Fox," Isengrim said, nodding. "Yes, even though the warlike years of unification are now behind them, my people strive to attain perfection by breeding only the best of our kind. And that is why, when the descendants of Vanargand No-Father and his followers met to codify Calvarian law, they created amongst my people a high order sworn to protect the purity of our race."

"And you were one of these?" Reynard asked.

"Yes. I was of the-" Isengrim stopped and thought for a moment. "Forgive me, there is no word in your language for its proper name, but perhaps 'guard of the blood,' or 'blood-guard' might be the closest approximation- for it is their task to maintain the record of our people's bloodlines, and to judge whether or not two lovers should be allowed to breed, or whether or not a sickly child should be allowed to live."

"And to make it impossible for anyone to ever overthrow the Judges," Reynard added.

"Yes," Isengrim replied quietly, and Reynard could tell that he had touched upon something deep within him.

"And how does one become one of these . . . blood-guards?" Grymbart asked.

"There is only one requirement," Isengrim answered flatly. "You must be an unwanted child."

VII

Two days later Reynard heard Foinez call out that land had been sighted to the north. By that afternoon he could make out the jagged coastline of the Hyperborean peninsula, a land of forlorn snow-capped mountains and vast stretches of coniferous forest.

Rising from somewhere inland, far from the coast, was a great plume of gray smoke.

"What is that?" Cointereau asked Isengrim as the rest of the crew stared at the distant conflagration. The young deckhand's previous resentment towards the Northerner had apparently turned to curiosity, Reynard noted.

I probably had a hand in that, Reynard thought, and leaned against the gunwale, his entire body aching from his latest bout with Isengrim. He had to admit that he was a little jealous of the young man's change of heart.

"Those are the fires of the city of Erebus," Isengrim replied. "They burn all day and night, for the forges there are never allowed to grow cold."

"Who works them if you have no servants of the Firebird?" Cointereau asked, baffled.

"My people are great smiths, more than a match for Southern priests who hoard the knowledge of their craft so that none but they can master the art of working metal."

"Do they make singing birds, like our priests do? Or wolves made of iron that can walk on their own?"

Isengrim shook his head. "What use is there in making such things? No, our artisans create only what is necessary for our survival, though they do consider everything that they make to be a work of art."

"Like your sword?" the young man asked.

"You admire it, do you?"

"It is beautiful," Cointereau said breathily. "I bet it would be a match for Thunderclap itself, if it were whole again."

"Would you care to hold it?"

"Could I?"

"If you are careful." The Northerner unsheathed his weapon and handed it to the deckhand. Cointereau merely stared at it, too awed to even wave it about. After a few moments he handed it back and thanked the Northerner.

"It must have been a master smith that forged that sword," Reynard said as Isengrim sheathed the blade.

"I do not like to think of myself as a master," Isengrim said with a faint smile, "But I thank you for your praise, Fox."

"You forged it?"

"It is the last test of a member of the blood-guard, to forge his own sword. He must trust his blade as he trusts his own body. This sword is a part of me, just as my hand is a part of my arm."

"What do you call it?" Cointereau asked excitedly.

"It has no name. Do we name our hands? It is a part of me, an extension of my will. Let that be enough."

Lady Moire, who had been listening to this talk from the forecastle, laughed bawdily and said: "I've known many men who have names for the 'extensions of their will!' Ain't that right, Espinarz?"

"I calls mine 'Spike!'" Espinarz called out from the helm and the men laughed.

"Yeah, I named me own girls as well;" here Lady Moire cupped her chest with her hands and patted her sagging bosom. "This one's 'Milk' and this one's 'Honey.'"

"That well went dry years ago, Lady!" shouted Foinez.

"You're lucky you are all the way up in that crow's nest, Spy!" Moire shouted back. "Or I'd beat you so hard the stink might come off you!"

Foinez chuckled and thrust up two of his fingers in a rude gesture that Moire did not see, for now she had a corner of Cointereau's shirt gripped tightly in her fist, and was in the process of dragging him away.

"These decks aren't going to clean themselves, Monkey," she said. "Now get back to work or I'll give you a spanking."

"She loves him," Isengrim said, watching as the young man escaped Moire's grip and led her on a good chase around the deck.

"Yes," Reynard replied, puzzled by the Northerner's comment.

"Like a mother loves a son?"

Reynard did not answer.

"I remember a nurse," the Calvarian went on, "When I was very young, she was kind to me. I cannot remember her name or face, but sometimes I think I see her, when I am asleep. In my dreams."

"It is a good thing," Reynard said, "To be loved."

"Did you know your own mother?" Isengrim asked.

Reynard paused.

"I did."

"Then you were lucky, Master Fox."

"No," Reynard said, and turned to go. "I wasn't."

* * * * * * *

That evening, as Isengrim reviewed some of the finer points of Calvarian grammar with Reynard, Captain Roenel brought the ship around and Pelez had the deckhands ready the ship's oars as they sailed towards a dismal-looking estuary. It was the mouth of the river Vodyanoy, Reynard knew- the first part of the route that would take them through Vulp Vora- and though it looked no different to him than any other waterway he had seen during their voyage along the coast, the knowledge of where it would lead them lent its dark waters a sinister hue.

But despite his apprehension, Reynard was relieved to leave the sea behind him- for every hour the coastline of Calvaria had been drawing closer, until he reckoned that one might be able to swim the distance between Solothurn and that feared land. Now he would not see it again until they came out of Vulp Vora and passed into whatever sea lay beyond.

"Take up an oar, Master Fox," Pelez rumbled, breaking him from his dark thoughts. "That is, if you don't have anything better to do?"

Reynard nodded and paired up with his tutor; they could always run over Calvarian vocabulary as they rowed.

The ship's progress was slow, for they traveled upriver, and no longer had the wind at their backs. The forest was even thicker here than it had been along the coast, and Reynard could not see very far through its dark boughs. He began to have the strange impression that the wood itself was aware of their presence, and that he was watched by unseen eyes.

Even Cointereau, he noticed, did not sing, for fear of disturbing whatever lurked in the dark.

"*Niedling,*" Reynard said as he pulled on the oar, reviewing the different words that Calvarians had for servant with each stroke. "*Niedpeow. Nydpewetling. Ltyle. Inbrydling.*"

"Will you shut up?" Tybalt groused.

"Sorry," Reynard apologized. "But it helps to say the words out loud."

"Well keep it down, at least."

"And watch your syllables," Isengrim added.

They rowed well into the night, and most of the next day as well, until they at last came within sight of the trading outpost of Falx. It was a wretched-looking place, Reynard decided, little more than a tight cluster of gable-roofed buildings huddled around a motte-and-bailey that had been constructed out of logs. Still, it was something of a relief to see human habitation after so many days of staring at lonely forested hills.

As the Quicksilver moored at one of the town's long docks, Captain Roenel addressed the crew.

"We will be spending a single night here," he began, "Which should be more than enough time to unload this Frisian whiskey and take on fresh supplies. To that end, I must meet with what passes for a lord here to negotiate a good price- and I want you, Master Isengrim, to accompany me."

"Is that necessary, Captain?" Isengrim asked, glancing towards Reynard.

"I don't have time to dicker with these rustics," Roenel answered, "And nothing will keep them more honest than the presence of a Calvarian. Besides, it will be good to have someone with your skill watching my back."

"Very well," Isengrim said, "Though I do not like the thought of leaving Master Fox alone."

"Very touching," Reynard said, "But have no fear, *laruwa*, I can take care of myself."

"That," Isengrim said, "Is what worries me."

Roenel coughed loudly and went on:

"Pelez, put the crew to work, but see to it that the Count's men- *all* of the Count's men- remain onboard. I don't want anyone jumping ship now."

"Aye, Captain," the first mate said, shooting Tybalt a nasty look.

"If I was going to jump ship," Tybalt said, picking at his nails as ever with his knife, "Do you really think I'd wait until we were in this shit-hole?"

Reynard had to agree with Tybalt. Falx didn't look as though it had anything of much interest to someone who had grown up in one of Arcasia's largest cities. Besides, the Solothurnians themselves were a dour looking lot, their bodies covered in heavy fur coats, and their hair unkempt and dangling over their faces, so that Reynard had to peer carefully to see the sullen eyes of the men. There seemed to be very few women here, and those that he did see appeared just as haggard and unfriendly as their male counterparts.

"You have your orders," Roenel said as he walked down the gangplank. Isengrim followed, pulling his dark cloak over his face to avoid startling the locals.

While daylight lasted Reynard helped the deckhands haul crate after crate out of the hold- and he could not help but notice that the one he had recently found unsealed was no longer among them.

After supper, Reynard decided to turn in early, figuring that he might not get another chance to relax once they'd entered Vulp Vora. As he passed through the hold he saw that Espinarz, Dolphin, Tybalt, and Bruin were engaged in a game of Spoils- but instead of coins they appeared to be using the bottles of rotgut liquor that would be sold to the inhabitants of Falx as wager.

"Last card," Tybalt said, flicking the Seven of Skulls onto the table and grabbing Bruin's bottle. "I win again."

"Well, that's one mystery solved," Reynard said as he approached the men. "I'd been wondering who'd got into that crate."

Tybalt took a slug from the bottle, and said, "While the sea-rats are away this cat will play."

"Who are you calling a rat?" Espinarz slurred as he dealt out a fresh hand.

"Don't worry," Dolphin told Reynard. "The Captain lets us get away with a little mischief now and then, as long as we keep it under control. Want to join?"

"I don't have anything to wager."

"Take my bottle," the Telchine said, wobbling to his feet so as to make room. "I'm halfway to Domdaniel already."

"Sit you down, Master Fox!" Bruin burbled darkly, his cheeks ruddy and his eyes small with drink. "Play a couple of hands with us."

Reynard glanced at Bruin, a tingle of worry rushing down his spine as he recalled what Grymbart had told him about the former soldier.

"Deal me in," Reynard said, and took a seat between Tybalt and Espinarz. "What are the stakes?"

"A dram a hand," Espinarz answered as Tybalt began to deal. "Winner chooses whose bottle he drinks from. Double dram for Spoils."

"Watcher is wild?"

"Aye."

Tybalt finished dealing and flipped the top of the stock over to reveal the Emerald Maiden. Bruin hummed with disappointment.

Reynard drew a card: the ten of Stars.

"Lance through nine," he said, laying down his match.

"No help," Espinarz muttered as he squinted at his own cards.

"Hit," Bruin breathed, adding the Firebird and the High Priest to Reynard's pile. Reynard discarded the two of Skulls.

Tybalt drew, and grinned widely.

"Spoils," he guffawed as he slammed down all of his cards: he had a straight of Serpents.

"That was fast," Bruin grumbled as Tybalt took two hits off of his bottle.

"Just lucky I guess," Tybalt chuckled, reshuffling.

Too lucky, Reynard thought to himself as he watched the former bandit's hands work. He'd done it enough times himself to know that Tybalt was stacking the deck.

Tybalt dealt.

"Spoils!" Bruin said, revealing a full hand of high cards.

"Not so fast," Tybalt said as Bruin reached for his bottle, and laid out his own hand. He had dealt himself a flush of Goddesses.

"Draw?" Bruin said hopefully.

"Naw," Espinarz said, tossing his cards towards Tybalt. "Goddesses are high, remember?"

"Hydra's Teeth!" Bruin seethed, his face growing redder as Tybalt drank up more of his dwindling booze.

"Hey," Tybalt said, "It's not my fault you can't count."

"My deal?" Reynard asked hopefully, reaching for the cards.

"What do you think I am, stupid?" Tybalt spat, plunging one of his knives into the table between Reynard's hand and the weathered deck. "Winner deals, end of story!"

Tybalt, you idiot, I'm trying to save your life! Reynard cursed inwardly. *Luckily, you're not the only one who knows how to cheat at cards . . .*

Tybalt dealt. Reynard's hand was one of the worst he'd ever seen: nothing but mismatched lows. He drew the Skull.

"Pass."

Espinarz drew, and laid down three twos, and the Watcher with them. "Hand of twins."

"No help," Bruin snapped. "You going to deal me a good hand or what?"

"Eclipse over nine," Tybalt smirked in response.

Reynard drew the Warg.

"Hit," he said and flipped it on top of the Eclipse.

"You hit on one card?" Tybalt chortled. "Maybe you're not as clever as I thought."

Tybalt discarded the Dragon.

"Spoils," Reynard said, throwing a handful of high cards on top of the discarded serpent.

Tybalt looked down at Reynard's hand in disbelief.

"But- But I-" he stammered.

"What?" Reynard asked with mock innocence.

"Forget it- your deal."

"Bottle?" Reynard said, scooping up the cards.

"Choke on it," Tybalt replied as Reynard took a few judicious sips of the foul stuff.

Reynard shuffled, and dealt.

"Spoils!" Bruin shouted with glee. "Gimme that bottle!"

Reynard surrendered Tybalt's bottle, then watched as the big man took two enormous swigs of whiskey out of it.

"Wulf, Bruin!" the former bandit whined. "That's far more than two drams!"

"It's not my fault you can't drink," the big man replied mockingly. "Just deal the cards."

Bruin dealt.

"Three of a kind," Tybalt grumbled as he laid down the four of Stars, Serpents, and Skulls.

Reynard drew. "No help."

"Same here," Espinarz said, leaning wearily against the bulkhead.

Bruin drew, and laid out four cards. "Lioness over ten."

"Hit," Tybalt said, adding the nine, eight, and seven of Seeds to Bruin's pile. The helmsman discarded the Sickener.

"Hit," Reynard said, throwing the six and five of Seeds onto the pile. Bruin laughed and discarded the Star- his last card.

"Last card!" the big man said, draining the last of Tybalt's liquor. "You should pay more attention next time Master Fox!"

Reynard shrugged. "Guess I'm a little rusty at this."

"Who invited you to play anyway?" Tybalt spat as he attempted to gain his feet. He failed and sat back down heavily.

"Not much whiskey left," Reynard said as Bruin's clumsy hands began to shuffle the deck. "Why not make it interesting- let's say, a dram a hand?"

"Fine by me," Espinarz said.

"Yer," Bruin said, his head lolling as he spoke. "Dramma hand."

Bruin dealt, slowly.

"Three of a kind," Reynard said, and took a swig out of the helmsman's bottle.

"Twins," Espinarz said, taking Bruin's.

"Firebird over Lance." Bruin snatched his bottle back from Espinarz and drained it. The helmsman seemed too inebriated to care.

"No help," Reynard said, ignoring the winning cards in his hand.

"Three of a kind," Espinarz said, drinking the last of Reynard's bottle.

"Hit," Bruin said and took the last bottle in hand.

Pass out, Reynard begged as Bruin greedily sucked down a quarter of a bottle. *Pass out for pity's sake!*

"Seeds in a row," he said out loud. "Spoils."

"Here ya are, Master Fox" Bruin said, handing him the bottle.

"Why don't you do the honors?"

"Yer," Bruin said, "Good idea."

The big man emptied the bottle, and Reynard waited for him to topple.

He didn't.

"Another hand?" Bruin asked.

"There's no more booze," Tybalt pointed out.

"Praise Wulf," Espinarz added.

Bruin stood up, his stool toppling over as he did so.

"Just gotta get some more then."

"Where from?" Tybalt asked.

"Falx- gotta be a tavern or something." Bruin took a few unsteady steps forward. He was obviously very inebriated, but unfortunately not enough to stop him from moving.

"Can't," the helmsman said blearily. "Can't leave the ship, remember?"

"Who says?" Bruin asked.

"Captain."

"Captain," Bruin repeated mockingly and began to make for the exit to the hold. "Captain ain't here, is he? Piss on 'im."

"Here now," Espinarz said, angry now, "That's the Captain you're talking about."

"Yer," Bruin said, "What of it?"

"Why don't you just both calm down?" Reynard said.

"I said, what of it?" Bruin repeated, pushing Reynard aside with a drunken sweep of his enormous right arm.

Dolphin, who'd been lounging in a hammock since Reynard had joined the game, slipped out of the sling to stand at the helmsman's side.

"Captain says no one leaves."

"Who's gonna stop me? You?"

"Yeah," Espinarz said, taking a threatening step forward.

In response, Bruin floored the sailor with a punch to the jaw.

"Spike!" Dolphin cried, reaching for his knife.

Bruin laughed at the sight of the weapon, and smashed one of the empty bottles over the Telchine's head. Blinded by blood, Dolphin dropped his blade and staggered away.

By now Bruin's outburst had caught the attention of the rest of the crew, who were storming down into the hold, their swords drawn.

"Listen, you big idiot," Tybalt said, taking Bruin by the arm. "You're going to get yourself killed!"

"Keep yer hands off me," Bruin rumbled, wrenching his forearm out of Tybalt's grip with enough force to throw the smaller man headfirst into the bulkhead.

"See, now you're endangering *my* life," Tybalt mumbled as he slid to the floor.

"Gods," Grymbart said, surveying the carnage. "What happened?"

"Get out of my way, Grymbart," Bruin said, his voice rumbling in the back of his throat.

"Be careful," Reynard urged. "He's drunk."

"I'm not that drunk!" the big man roared. "Now get out of my way!"

"Guess there's no way I'm going to stop you," the mercenary said, and stepped aside.

"One of you," Pelez ordered as Bruin approached. "Stop Bruin."

"You stop him," Espinarz groaned from where he lay.

None of the other men seemed keen to tackle the giant either, and made way.

When they parted, Reynard could see that Isengrim was standing at the entrance to the hold.

"Where are you going, Master Bruin?" Isengrim asked.

"Gonna get me some more whiskey," the big man replied, squinting at the Northerner.

"I believe you have already had more than enough."

"What would you know about it, pale-face?" Bruin spat.

Isengrim's stance changed, and Reynard knew that he was readying himself to fight- perhaps even kill.

"Enough!" Reynard yelled, stepping between the two. "Bruin, if you want more drink, you should have just asked me."

"What're ya talking about?"

"I mean, it's a bit of a walk to town, and I've got more whiskey in my cabin."

"Thought you said you didn't have any," Bruin said, his eyes narrowing.

Reynard thought fast. "I've got it hidden in my cabin, so the others couldn't find it. But I tell you what: I'll get it for you, and you can have some beer while you wait? Cointereau, get this man a mug."

"Don't want none of that piss," Bruin grumbled, but sat down all the same.

Reynard rushed into his cabin. It didn't take him long to find what he was looking for: a small bottle that was nestled amongst his acids and oils. He pulled out the cork and poured the contents of the flask into a wooden cup.

Bruin had already downed the mug that the young deckhand had brought for him.

"Now this is strong stuff," Reynard said as he handed Bruin the cup. "So you might want to take it slow. Chase it with some more beer maybe?"

"Yeah," Bruin said before downing the entire contents of the mug. "Get me another one, boy."

Cointereau had hardly taken two steps before Bruin collapsed face first into the table.

"What was in that stuff?" Grymbart asked.

"Sleeping draught," Reynard said. "I had some left over from my last job."

"When will he wake up?"

Reynard grimaced. "Hard to say, seeing as he drank the whole thing- but you can bet that when he does, he's going to feel like someone danced the Chozo on his head."

* * * * * * *

"I am impressed," Isengrim said later, as they stood watch on deck together. "With how you dealt with Bruin."

Reynard shrugged. "Wits often serve better than force. A sword may win a battle, but the right words can win a battle before it even starts."

"Wise council."

"Just something I learned when I was young," Reynard replied. "Tell me, would you have killed Bruin?"

"If he had forced me to, yes, I would have killed him. I would kill any of the men on this ship to preserve our mission."

"Is it so important to you, this task we do for the Duke?"

"It is," Isengrim answered. "For ten summers I have prepared for this journey."

"And afterwards," Reynard asked. "When the deed is done- what will you do then?"

Isengrim was silent for a time.

"Should we return," he said at last, "I will do as Count Bricemer commands me."

He's hiding something, Reynard noted as the Northerner moved to the other end of the ship. *But what?*

* * * * * * *

Captain Roenel, who was not amused by the evening's festivities, made certain that Bruin was roused from sleep as soon as he could stand up on his own, as well as Tybalt, Espinarz, and Dolphin, who then were forced to do the bulk of the heavy lifting as the crew refilled the Quicksilver's hold with fresh supplies. Reynard watched as the big man, his face ashen and beaded with sweat, loaded crate after crate onto the ship. At last he staggered over to the edge of the dock and vomited noisily into the river.

"I am sorry that I drugged you," Reynard said when Bruin had finally ceased his heaving, and offered him a steaming bowl of broth. Bruin pushed it away, his gorge obviously threatening to rise again as he clutched at his skull.

"Don't apologize, Fox," Bruin said, kneading his forehead with a massive thumb. "If you hadn't I would probably be dead now. I don't know what I was thinking."

"Grymbart told me that you can be a pretty mean drunk."

"Yeah," Bruin said glumly. "Shouldn't touch the stuff, really, but people expect a big guy like me to be able to hold his liquor. And, problem is, once I get started it's hard for me to stop."

"Perhaps you should give it up," Reynard said. "I've seen more than enough men die from drink in my day."

"Guess I won't have a choice now- suppose there'll be no stills in Vulp Vora."

"No," Reynard said. "And no taverns either."

＊ ＊ ＊ ＊ ＊ ＊ ＊

Two days passed without incident, and Reynard resumed his training with Isengrim. Though his vocabulary was still limited he could speak Calvarian freely now, and he felt he had nearly mastered the grace required of him as a servant. But if the Northerner was impressed with the speed of his student's progress, he rarely showed it, and continued to push Reynard harder, both mentally and physically, so that by the end of each day his body ached as it never had before.

On the third day out from Falx the river branched. A great number of wooden totems and carven fetishes were arrayed haphazardly around the mouth of the eastern tributary, and it came as no surprise to Reynard when the Captain ordered Espinarz to steer the ship towards this forbidding channel.

As they drew closer, Reynard saw that there were bone-carved amulets hanging from almost every branch, and that some of the trees had more macabre decorations: human corpses that had been hanged by the neck swayed gently in the wind.

"They must hang criminals here," Grymbart said to no one in particular. "An' leave the bodies to appease whatever lurks in these woods."

"Let's hope they're contented then," Lady Moire said, and pressed her thumb to her forehead as she mumbled a prayer.

As the day went on the river narrowed, until the boughs of the biggest trees brushed against the rigging. Grymbart and Bruin took up positions on either side of the ship, trading their jerkins for breastplates and shields, while Tybalt fastened on his bandolier of knives. Tiecelin replaced Foinez in the crow's nest, and kept his bow and a pair of quivers handy. Ghul slipped into a beautiful suit of mail of Glyconese make- each of its scale-like plates had been engraved with curling prayers to Hydra.

Isengrim eschewed armor, but to Reynard he lent a brigandine coat, as well as a set of plate for his exposed arms and legs. Reynard felt rather uncomfortable in it, preferring the full range of motion that lighter clothes afforded him, but he was glad to have more than a uniform between him and the claws of some Vulp Voran beast.

Several days passed, and then the Quicksilver came upon another branch in the river, and the crew dropped anchor while the Captain consulted his charts.

"Would you like to play some cards?" Reynard asked Isengrim as they waited for the Captain to give the order to sail on. "It might pass the time."

"I do not play cards," Isengrim replied.

"No, I don't suppose you Northerners do anything just for fun."

"If I had a proper board, and all of the pieces, I might teach you how to play *campraeden*. It is a very popular game among Calvarians."

"War?" Reynard translated. "How is it played?"

"The board is a replica map of Calvaria as it was in the days before Vanargand No-Father. Each player is given a random starting position, and a number of pieces to represent different kinds of warriors: horsemen, infantry, archers, and so on."

"And I imagine that the object is to eliminate the others players?"

"Precisely. One may ally with other players, but eventually there can be only one winner."

"So even your games train you how to fight," Reynard said and chuckled darkly. "Yours is indeed a cruel land."

"Cruel, yes," Isengrim replied, apparently taking no insult at Reynard's remark. "But also beautiful- I have seen nothing in the Southern Kingdoms that rivals it."

"And your women?" Reynard asked, as curious as he was joking. "Are they as lovely as the priestesses of Sphinx? Or do you find even our most fetching girls no better than dogs?"

"I am certain that there are some Calvarians who might find your women handsome, but not I. They are too soft, both in form and manner. The beauty of our women is like the beauty of our land: they are both pure and strong."

"And are they as cold?" Reynard asked.

"Some of them- but not all."

Roenel ordered Espinarz to take the passage to the right, and they lifted anchor.

* * * * * *

Gradually the woods gave way to a chilly wetland, and as it deepened Reynard began to hear the cries of marsh birds, and he found himself pestered by noisome insects- odd things that were much larger than the roaches and beetles of the city, some of them as large as a child's hand. At dusk they sang together, and at times it seemed as if there were words amongst their drone.

Other noises came with the night, from the shrieking of owls to the eerie lingering cries of animals that no one could place.

When the marshland again turned to forest Reynard noted that the foliage was similar to that which grew in and around Calyx, though the trees had a sickly look to them, their leaves a bizarre combination of indigo and violet and, though it was late fall, grotesquely shaped fruit hung from their boughs.

Cointereau, hanging from the rigging, reached out and snatched one of these growths from a nearby branch. He soon dropped it with a cry, and when it splattered against the deck Reynard saw a long yellowish insect crawl from the pulpy ruin, a thing with too many legs and feelers that seemed to swim across the deck with incredible speed. Tybalt cut the thing in half with an expertly thrown dagger, and for a while both ends of it sped about on their own before curling up and dying.

"Do not eat anything that grows here," Lady Moire chided Cointereau after the men had tossed the insect's remains over the side of the ship. "This land is cursed."

Cointereau nodded and climbed higher in the rigging, so that he was far from the reach of the trees.

Later that day, Pelez came down to the hold and shouted for everyone to assemble on deck.

"Trouble?" Reynard asked the first mate as he came out of his cabin. He'd been practicing his bows while Isengrim stood watch.

"Could be," Pelez replied, itching nervously at the bare scalp underneath his wig.

Once he was on deck, Reynard immediately understood the first mate's worry: the river ahead was clogged by a number of fallen trees, which formed a crude dam of sorts. If the ship was to continue they'd have to cut their way through the obstacle.

"Perfect place for an ambush," Tybalt said, eyeing both sides of the riverbank.

"I agree," the Captain said. "Someone, or something, did this deliberately."

"Is there another way around, Captain?" Espinarz, who was manning the helm, asked hopefully.

"No. This is the only river that will lead us directly to Lake Hali, and then back North to the coast."

"Hydra's Teeth," Espinarz swore, quietly, so as not to rile Ghul.

"Well, it's not going to get any lighter," Captain Roenel said, scanning the sky above. "Pelez, break out the axes and have the men start clearing the way."

Soon the crew was being ferried down to the western shore of the river, utilizing one of the two skiffs that had been lashed to the deck. Roenel insisted on leading the first party, leaving Lady Moire in charge of the skeleton crew, which included Cointereau, the cook Baucent, Foinez, Tardis, and Musard. Ghul and Tiecelin remained on board as well, in the event that the ship itself came under attack.

"Where do you think you are going?" Isengrim asked Reynard as he was preparing to shimmy down one of the ropes to the skiff below.

"I can cut wood as well as any other man," Reynard sniffed.

"I cannot replace you. If anything happens-"

"The same is true of you, isn't it? And you are going."

"Very well," Isengrim conceded. "But stay close to me."

As Reynard splashed onto the riverbank he realized that he had been living on the Quicksilver long enough to turn standing on solid ground into a novel experience. He tried his best not to be distracted by it, and instead kept his eyes on the shadows beneath the trees.

Isengrim established a perimeter of watchmen, and then the men took turns chopping through the overturned trunks. It was grueling work, Reynard found. The wood was soggy, and the bank itself was nothing but thick clay that made his footing difficult. As if the toil were not enough, it soon began to drizzle, and before long it was pouring rain.

"Lovely country, Vulp Vora" he said as he gave up his axe to the deckhand named Condylure. "Charming weather, beautiful scenery, insects as long as your arm . . ."

The deckhand laughed and began to chop while Reynard kept watch.

By dusk they had managed to hack their way through most of the obstacle, and began hauling the split trunks onto the riverbank.

"Fetch some pitch from the ship and have some fires lit," Roenel ordered Pelez, "It's starting to get too dark to work."

"Not sure if it'll catch in this rain, Captain," Pelez groused. "And I'm not too keen on letting whatever set this snare know that they've caught some juicy game."

"If the sound of our axes hasn't got their attention, then I doubt a little fire is going to make much of a difference- and if we're going to have company, I'd at least like to be able to see ten feet in front of my face."

"Yes, sir," Pelez said, and had the men on deck lower a barrel of pitch and some torches down to the skiff.

None of the men complained as they continued working past nightfall, and Reynard wasn't surprised. He too believed that spending the night here would be an unwise decision.

"Almost through boys!" Pelez said as he and Espinarz threw another chopped up log into the stream. "I think we can drag this last big one onto the shore. Tie some ropes around it!"

As the men rushed to comply with Pelez's command, Reynard heard something rustle somewhere in the trees above him. He had hardly glanced upwards when there came the unmistakable 'swoosh' of an arrow flying through the air. Something screeched and fell from a low hanging bough, landing only a few feet from where Reynard stood. The feathered thing tried to regain its feet, and then died with a shudder.

At first he thought that it was a bird, albeit some odd kind that inhabited Vulp Vora, but even though it had a hooked bill Reynard could see that it was a wild shrike, much smaller than the one he had encountered in the Duke's conservatory.

The red fletching along the arrow's shaft marked it as one of Tiecelin's, whom Reynard could not even see through the thick rain. How he'd made the shot was mystifying.

"Chimera!" Reynard cried out, and as he did so the forest erupted into a chorus of hoots and calls that burbled from alien throats.

Another shrike dove at him, this one gray with a great ruff of moss green feathers around its bulbous neck. It shrieked as it came, reminding Reynard of the remorseless cry of a hunting falcon.

He slashed the thing's throat with his sword, and then dove to one side in order to avoid being bowled over by the momentum of the shrike's body as it crashed to the ground.

Another one had landed on Condylure's shoulders, its sharp claws rending at the man's flesh, and with a thrust of his sword he impaled the thing. As he flung its corpse to the bank he caught a glimpse of Tybalt flicking his daggers, his hands almost too fast for the human eye to follow. Then he saw that there not just shrikes amongst their attackers, but two-legged faun as well: Bruin was busy hacking down one with the horned head of a goat, and Grymbart was trading blows with another such creature.

But despite their fearsome appearance, none of the chimera seemed to be match for the well-trained killers in the Duke's employ. Before long only a handful of shrikes were left circling above them, the few grotesque faun that had come with them having either been killed or sent screaming back into the woods.

Reynard was wondering why Tiecelin was not still shooting down the remaining shrikes when he heard the horrible screams wafting from the Quicksilver.

He raced over to the skiff, and found himself climbing into the boat beside the Captain, along with Dolphin, and Pelez. As the sailors manned the oars, Reynard could see that the ship's deck was thick with a crowd of faun, at whom Tiecelin was firing arrow after arrow from the crow's nest. Ghul appeared to be holding his ground at the helm, his blades flashing as he whirled and kicked at the brutes clambering towards him.

No sooner had they reached the side of the ship before Roenel and Dolphin caught onto the ropes and began hauling themselves up them like monkeys on vines. Reynard and Pelez followed suit, and as they reached the top they drew their weapons and leapt over the gunwale.

There were over a dozen of the wild faun left on the deck. Three were busy with Ghul, and another pair was climbing clumsily up the rigging to get at Tiecelin, but the others threw themselves towards the newly arrived foes with what seemed to Reynard to be a complete disregard for their own lives.

They were unarmored, their weirdly proportioned bodies decorated with vibrantly painted violet tattoos, and as weapons they wielded crude axes, clubs and spears that had been chipped out of flint. A few wore flimsy loincloths, but most were entirely naked, and Reynard could clearly see that they were all male. There was no uniformity to their features. Some possessed horns, while others' legs bent in reverse and were capped with cloven hooves. Almost all of them had the strangely elongated irises common amongst goats and sheep, except for one that sported a toothless knobbed beak and the pure black eyes of a bird.

This bizarre faun-shrike was the first to die, stabbed through the chest by Dolphin. Another hacked at Pelez as he cut it down, its stone axe shearing into the first mate's leg before he could free his sword from the dying chimera. As for Reynard, he dodged a thrown spear as another one of the vile things fell upon him, impaling itself on his dagger. The creature bleated noisily and clawed at him with filthy nails as it died on top of him, its loathsome death throes filling him with revulsion.

By the time he had pushed the dead faun off of him the other chimera were dead, felled by sword and arrow shaft. Ghul was going from body to body, methodically slicing open each of the things' necks to ensure that none would live.

There were two human corpses amongst the faun. Near the bow lay Tardis, his throat torn open. Foinez lay sprawled over one of the gunwales, a broken spear protruding from his back.

There was no sign of the rest of the crew.

Above, Tiecelin was still firing arrows over the port side of the Quicksilver. Reynard scrambled to the gunwale in time to witness a large number of chimera crossing the river in crude canoes carved out of logs.

"Where are Lady Moire, and the others?" Reynard called up to the archer.

"The chimera took them!" Tiecelin shouted as he launched another arrow at one of the fleeing faun.

"Doom!" Prophet cried as he circled above the Luxian. Reynard wished that the thing would learn to keep its mouth shut.

"Help me unhitch this boat!" Roenel shouted then, gesturing to the other skiff. "Ghul! Round up Grymbart, Bruin, and Tybalt and meet us on the other shore as fast as you can! And tell Isengrim and the others to stay put!"

The odd-eyed man wasted no time. He was over the gunwale and belaying his way down to the first skiff within seconds.

By now the faun had reached the eastern shore of the river and had disappeared into the forest. Tiecelin climbed down from the rigging and busied himself retrieving his arrows from the corpses on the deck.

"Are we going after them, Captain Roenel?" the archer asked once he had replenished his quiver.

"Yes," the Captain replied. "Can you track them?"

"Shouldn't be hard. I doubt they bothered to cover their trail."

"Good," the Captain said and turned to his first mate. "Pelez, I want you to stay here with the crew and get this last tree out of our way. If we're not back by dawn you sail on with Isengrim and Master Fox here."

"But, Captain, you should be the one to stay. I can lead the party-"

"That's an order, Pelez!"

"Excuse me for saying so, Captain," Reynard interrupted. "But I'd like to go with you."

"Out of the question," the Captain said. "You stay here with Isengrim and help move those logs."

"Well, I hate to point this out, but isn't that Isengrim with Grymbart and the others?" Reynard pointed to the first skiff, which was making its way across the bow of the Quicksilver.

"Curse him, I gave him an order!" Roenel spat, and looked back at Reynard. "Alright, you come along, but only because I need someone else to help row that Calvarian twist back to the others! Thinks he can ignore me, does he?"

The Captain kept up an impressive stream of curses as he, Reynard, and Tiecelin lowered themselves into the second skiff and rowed swiftly to the eastern shore.

"What do you think you're about, Isengrim?" Roenel barked as soon as they had landed.

"I should be asking the same of you, Captain Roenel," Isengrim replied. "This is a lot of men to send after four non-essential crewmen."

"Non-essential?" Roenel repeated the Northerners words furiously. "They are members of my crew, and I'm not going to abandon them!"

"Who is missing?"

"Moire, Baucent, Musard, and Cointereau!"

"Then you would risk our entire mission on the lives of a boatswain, a cook and a pair of deck hands?"

- 133 -

"I've got to agree with the pale-face, Captain," Tybalt said. "We've no idea what's out there, and for all we know they all could be dead already."

"I am going," Roenel said with grim finality. "Whether you like it or not!"

"I'll go with you," Grymbart said then. "But Count Bricemer better double my pay when we get back to Calyx."

Bruin grunted reluctantly and stepped over to stand with Grymbart.

"I'm going too," Reynard said. He had grown very fond of Cointereau. The thought of him in the hands of the twisted things that had come out of the dark made him sick.

"You are so determined to go?" Isengrim asked.

"I am."

"Then I have no choice but to accompany you," Isengrim went on, adding: "It's the only way I can ensure that you come back alive."

"We're wasting time Captain," Tiecelin said before Roenel could argue the point. "Every moment we wait here they gain more ground on us.

"Then lead the way, Tiecelin."

The Luxian nodded and plunged into the underbrush at a quickstep, his raven flitting from branch to branch as he pushed into the rain-shrouded woods. Grymbart and Roenel went next, followed by Bruin, Isengrim, Reynard, and Ghul.

"Idiots!" Tybalt yelled after them. "You're all going to get yourselves killed!"

When Tybalt realized that the skiffs were too large for him to row effectively, and that he was standing alone on the dark Eastern bank, he cursed and raced to catch up with the others.

VIII

Tiecelin kept a brisk pace as he tracked the chimera war party, stopping only briefly to ensure that the marauders had not split their number. The trail was not particularly hard to follow, for the creatures had trampled much of the strange undergrowth of the forest floor flat, and had kept a nearly straight course through the choking foliage. Reynard could think of only two reasons that this might be: the chimera either did not expect to be followed, or they were lying in wait somewhere ahead.

He hoped that it was the first one.

The rain clouds overhead drifted as they marched, and soon the dank woods were full of the strange night sounds that until now Reynard had heard only from the relative safety of the ship: screeching birds, lolling cries, and the insane hum of insect wings.

The stench of the forest was sickeningly intense: vanilla, lavender, and what Reynard took to be some kind of potent animal musk. As the rain cleared, night flowers began to unfurl their petals, revealing blooms that shone with a weak luminescence that he found beautiful yet unsettling.

Suddenly, they came to a halt. Ahead of him Reynard saw that Tiecelin was holding up a flattened palm.

The forest had gone silent around them.

No, Reynard noted. *Not silent.* There was something crashing through the trees ahead of them, something large.

And it was coming straight towards them.

Tiecelin raised his bow and fired just as some dark shape burst from the underbrush. His arrow flew home into the great dark eye of a monstrous thing that appeared to be a combination of horned elk, hunting cat, and crustacean. It let out a deep moan and collapsed mere yards from the Luxian scout.

"Gods," Tybalt swore as he gazed at the creature's bulbous head, its lithe body, and its two segmented forelegs. "What is it?"

"It's ugly, whatever it is," Bruin said, burying his axe in the thing's forehead to ensure that it was dead.

"Keep moving," Tiecelin said. "We are getting close."

"How can you tell?" Reynard asked.

"Their pace slowed here- and there is music in the wind."

Reynard tilted his head and then he too could hear the faint piping of flutes and the steady beat of drums wafting from the forest ahead of them. Then the insects resumed their chirping, and drowned out the sound completely.

Another mile they marched, and then the path suddenly descended into a small dell, where Reynard saw something that he would not soon forget.

A number of roaring bonfires illuminated a ghastly throng of chimeras, most of which were dancing wildly around a strange megalith. There was something about the black stone's perfectly carved angles and polished surface that seemed utterly wrong to Reynard, as if it were not a thing of this world.

Atop this bizarre menhir sat an idol of a winged creature. Like many of the things cavorting below its gaze it had a goat-like head and legs, but its body was that of a seductively curved woman, its belly grossly distended. Cradled in the statues shapely claw-tipped hands were a pair of chimera cubs, both of them insanely bizarre things with multiple heads, tails that ended in fanged mouths, and the gossamer wings of insects.

"Demon worshippers," Ghul whispered, his voice filled with what Reynard guessed was a sort of perverse glee at the sight of so many throats worth cutting.

As they drew closer, Reynard could see that there was more than just dancing going on beneath the statue's lascivious gaze- faun, shrike, and gods knew what else were copulating freely on the grass, while others feasted upon raw meat and drank from bowls of what looked like fermented milk. He watched with growing disgust as a male faun that had collapsed from exhaustion was torn apart by its brethren, its eyes plucked from their sockets by the curved bill of a female shrike.

On the opposite side of the dell, reclining on a slab of granite that formed the top of a low dolmen, Reynard saw what he assumed was the chieftain of these creatures: a male faun with the head of a bull. Its body was riddled with piercings made of bone and metal, and its enormously muscled arms and chest were painted with curling glyphs and runes. It was clearly some sort of mutant, for its hands were blessed with extra digits, and a third arm tipped with a crushing claw, like that of a lobster or crab, sprouted from its left armpit. Around this beastly lord lounged a harem of female chimera, dressed in ragged remains of silks and linens- it was they who played both drum and pipe, in between servicing whatever creature ventured within their reach.

"There," Tiecelin said then, drawing Reynard's attention to a trio of wooden cages on the other side of the dell, within which could be seen several humans.

"They are still alive," Captain Roenel said, shooting a hard look towards Isengrim.

"Some of them, at least," the Northerner replied.

"I should be able to get over there unnoticed," Reynard offered. "It doesn't seem as if there's anyone keeping watch."

"Too risky," Isengrim said. "Better to split into two parties and attack from opposite ends of the dell."

"Attack?" Tybalt balked. "Do you see how many of those things are down there?"

"I do, but most of them appear to be unarmed, and they are clearly not expecting a fight. If we cut down as many as we can in the first few moments they will be kept off balance."

"One of the groups should free the prisoners," Roenel said. "They might help even the odds."

"Agreed," Isengrim said. "I will lead that party."

Roenel nodded his approval, adding, "Then I will lead the other."

"Who goes with who?" Grymbart asked the Northerner.

"You, Bruin, Tybalt, and Tiecelin will stay with the Captain," Isengrim answered. "I will take Fox and Ghul. Be prepared to attack on my signal."

"And what will that be?"

"You will know when you see it," Isengrim replied, and began to creep along the edge of the dell.

Reynard followed the Northerner, as did Ghul, whom Reynard noticed was rather quiet for a man wearing jingling mail.

So . . . perhaps our Glyconese friend here has had some assassin's training. A curious sort of man to send on a mission like this.

They went slowly so as not to draw attention to themselves, though Reynard wasn't sure that the inebriated faun would have noticed a trio of giants stomping through the wood. Taking a glance behind him he saw that Roenel and the others were spreading back out, forming a sort of skirmish line that would funnel enemies towards their center.

They had nearly circumnavigated the dell when Reynard noticed that the cages held only three of their companions. In one sat Musard and Baucent, and in the other was Lady Moire. All looked ill-used: Moire sat hugging her knees as she rocked back and forth in the cage, while the men were staring with haunted eyes at the horrific sights below them.

Several pairs of male and female chimera were guarding the cages, though they seemed far more occupied with each other's company than in keeping a close eye on their captives.

"Ghul," Isengrim said in a hushed voice, and the Glyconese nodded.

Ghul leapt out of the underbrush, his twin swords whirling as he slew two of the creatures before they could make a sound. Startled, the other chimera awkwardly began to disengage themselves from each other, but then Isengrim was among them, his deadly steel blade carving through flesh and bone as if they were butter.

"Glad I could help," Reynard said as Isengrim administered the coup de grace to the last pair of monsters, their gurgling death cries drowned out by the obscene moans drifting up from the dell below.

"Get those cages open," Isengrim ordered. "Ghul and I will keep watch."

Reynard made short work of the simple mechanisms that kept both cages closed, and immediately both Musard and Baucent scurried out of their enclosure, not needing to be told to be quiet.

Moire, on the other hand, would not budge.

"Come on," he urged the woman, and reached out to take her hand.

As he did so Lady Moire began to scream.

"Keep her quiet!" Isengrim hissed. "Gag her if necessary!"

"Lady," Baucent said, gently pushing Reynard to one side. "Lady it's only me. Piggy, remember?"

Moire's howling abruptly stopped, and seeming to recognize Baucent she clutched onto him as a frightened child might.

As the cook helped Moire to her feet, Reynard turned to the other deckhand and asked, "Where is Cointereau?"

"Below," Musard replied, glancing down at the throng.

Reynard scanned the crowd, hoping desperately to catch sight of the young man. "Is he alive?"

Musard did not answer, but merely pointed to one of the bonfires.

There, spiked on a wooden spit like a suckling pig, were the cooked remains of the cheery boy who had once played his tom-tom and sung with Reynard under the stars. His arms and legs were gone, and then Reynard knew what kind of meat it was that the chimera feasted on.

"When do we give the signal?" Reynard asked, his hands tightening around the pommels of his sword and dagger.

"Now," the Northerner replied and hurled his knife straight at one of the flute-playing females. The blade sunk home in the chimera's neck, and as she clutched at it Isengrim charged down the embankment, cutting down any creature that had the misfortune of standing in his path.

Reynard raced after him, his blood pumping wildly as he slashed at goat-headed faun and strangely feathered shrikes alike. He was faintly aware of Ghul racing past him to rampage amongst a thick knot of still copulating monstrosities.

By now the chimera's cries of pleasure had turned to those of alarm. Those that were able grabbed hold of weapons, or merely charged at the invaders with tooth, horn and claw. But as the chimera turned to face them, Roenel's band hit them from behind. Several of the shrikes began to rise groggily into the air only to be brought low by Tiecelin's arrows and Tybalt's throwing knives. Bruin, roaring out a wild battle cry as he advanced, split open a four-legged faun with a single stoke of his axe. The Captain and Grymbart guarded the big man's flanks, bashing their foes aside with shield and buckler as they hacked their way through the crowd.

Reynard had just slain a female chimera armed with a rusty sickle when there was a deafening roar behind him. He turned, and found himself staring into the murderous eyes of the chimera's bull-headed chieftain. The beast had armed itself with a double-headed axe that was nearly the size of Reynard, and as it advanced its chitinous claw snapped viciously in the air before it.

"Figures," Reynard said, and dove to one side as the head of the chieftain's axe buried itself into the patch of ground he had just been occupying.

As the chieftain readied its axe for another swing a pair of chimera rushed out of the crowd to engage Reynard, who promptly slashed open the first one's throat and danced around the second, delivering a kick to its backside that sent it hurtling directly into the deadly arc of the giant faun's axe.

As the chieftain freed its weapon from the quivering form of the unlucky chimera, Reynard lunged forward and plunged his rapier into the thing's left breast- a stroke that would have killed, or at the very least slowed down, a normal opponent.

But not this one.

The chieftain struck Reynard with the back of its hand, a blow that sent him sailing several feet backwards until the topmost part of the dolmen broke his fall.

"Wulf! My sword," he mumbled as he realized that the weapon had been knocked out of his hands, and began to stagger to his feet.

"Fox!" someone shouted.

Isengrim.

Reynard looked up, and saw that the former blood-guard was now standing between him and the chieftain, who paused only for a moment before raising its axe and charging.

Isengrim dodged neatly to one side as the thing's weapon whistled downwards, and with a single stroke he sheared off the beast's right hand. Its eyes rolling, the thing struck out wildly with its crab-like appendage, but the crushing pincers caught only a bit of the Northerner's cloak as he spun away.

Seemingly undeterred, the giant lowered its horned head and charged, rolling its head as it came. Again Isengrim dodged, severing the creature's spine as it crashed past him with a single cut. The faun collapsed, gasping, and crushed several of its brethren as it did so.

At the sight of the death of their chieftain the fight went out of the remaining chimera, and they began to flee into the woods. Within moments the dell was empty of the vile things, save for those that littered the clearing.

"Thank you," Reynard said as he walked up to Isengrim, "Though I think I could have handled that thing on my own."

"Even without your sword?" Isengrim replied, kicking up Reynard's lost rapier with one foot and offering it to him by the hilt.

"I had a plan," Reynard said nonchalantly as he took the weapon. "But that's alright- your way worked too."

Isengrim sighed. "Must you always be so flippant?"

"Must you always be so serious?" Reynard replied.

The Northerner stared at him for a moment, and then he joined Ghul in the task of ensuring that each chimera was truly dead by plunging their swords into their hearts.

"Should I take that as a yes?" Reynard called after him.

* * * * * * *

Roenel and Musard removed what was left of Cointereau from the spit, and wrapped his remains in the Captain's own cloak. Lady Moire, meanwhile, had resumed her rocking. She had not yet spoken a word.

"What is the matter with her?" Grymbart asked.

"They- used her," Reynard replied, hoping that the distraught woman was out of earshot.

"Gods," the mercenary spat, and kicked at one of the inert faun. "This is a land of monsters."

"One day it will be wiped clean," Ghul said, and for once Reynard found the Glyconese fanatic's words to be comforting.

The odd-eyed man hurled a fist-sized stone through the air that toppled the demonic statue from its perch. It hit the ground with a dull thud, and they took turns smashing it beyond recognition.

"Where is Tiecelin?" The Captain asked shakily when they'd finished venting their rage. "We're going to need him to get back to the Quicksilver."

"I saw him over by the tree line," Grymbart said, pointing. "Think he's looking for his bird."

"Doom," Tybalt croaked, and chuckled.

"Well someone get him back here," the Captain said. "I'm not keen on waiting around."

"I'll go," Reynard said, anxious as well to be gone. The forest had been silent for some time now, and it was only a matter of time before the chimera, or some other twisted thing, would get up the courage to attack them again.

"Alright, Master Fox," Roenel said, adding, "But take Tybalt and Bruin with you- and be swift."

Reynard nodded, and made his way across the clearing with his reluctant guardians in tow.

He found Tiecelin kneeling next to a small cairn that he had constructed out of twigs, a piece of flint and a fire striker in his shaking hands. As they got closer Reynard could see that Prophet was lying on top of it, dead.

"Tiecelin?" Reynard said, and at the sound of his voice the Luxian turned- he had tears in his eyes. "Captain says we're going."

"They killed my bird," Tiecelin said simply.

"You giving him a funeral?" Bruin asked.

"Yes."

"We don't have time for this," Tybalt began to groan, but Reynard shushed him.

"Don't worry," he said. "I have something that should move things along."

Reynard reached into his pocket, and quickly found what he was looking for.

"Here," he said, offering his bird-shaped lighter to the scout. "Use this. It'll light easier."

"I- thank you," Tiecelin said quietly, and bent back over the fire.

"You're pretty resourceful, aren't you, Master Fox?" Tybalt said grudgingly as the kindling caught. "Maybe I was wrong about you."

Reynard was about to thank the man when Tybalt's hand flicked a dagger in his direction. The thing sailed past his head, and lodged itself into the breast of an azure and scarlet-feathered shrike that had been about to pounce on Reynard from a nearby tree branch.

"Then again, maybe not," the former bandit said, and grinned wickedly. "I guess it's a good thing us real men are here to watch out for you."

All four of them gazed down at the dying chimera at their feet. Unlike many of the others, this one was practically human. Nearly its entire torso was free of plumage, and it looked as it if might be able to stand erect on its clawed avian legs.

"Pretty one, this," Bruin said. "Makes you wonder what it'd be like . . . with one of them."

"Why don't you ask Lady Moire," Tybalt sneered. "I'm sure she'll have some stories for you."

"Just put it out of its misery, Tybalt," Reynard said, his feelings of gratitude towards the crass man evaporating rapidly.

"Yeah, yeah," Tybalt said, and readied his sword to strike.

The shrike looked up at them with obvious contempt, and then in a stilted tongue it was able to form a single word that it screeched at her killer:

"Bas-tard!"

Tybalt shot the others an amused look and then hacked through the shrike's neck.

"I have never heard of a shrike that could speak," Tiecelin said, his voice hushed. "Except in the old stories."

"The Duke had one like this," Reynard said. "It could speak too."

"Here now," Tybalt said, "Look at this."

Tybalt directed their attention to what Reynard had at first thought was a bulbous growth on the side of the tree in which the shrike had been lurking. Upon closer inspection he realized that it was a woven collection of fibers and vines.

"A shrike nest," Tybalt said and hopped up onto a low hanging branch. He climbed higher until he could look into the tangle of twigs and brambles that formed the majority of the nest.

"What do you see?" Tiecelin asked. Reynard had never heard the man sound so engaged.

"See for yourself," Tybalt replied and, using the flat of his sword, flipped an oval object out of the nest: a speckled shrike egg. It cracked open when it hit the ground, revealing a half-formed chick. Reynard's stomach turned at the sight of the pathetic thing, all the more because it was almost as human as its mother had been.

"That was- a cruel thing to do," Tiecelin said.

"I'm just doing 'em a favor," Tybalt said and flicked another egg out of the nest. "They've got no mother now. Probably just get eaten by some of their own kind if it weren't for me."

"Stop," Tiecelin said.

"What's this, Tiecelin? Pity? Even after what those things did to Cointereau?"

"I said stop," Tiecelin repeated, raising his bow ever so slightly.

"Or your precious bird, eh? Course, there's more where that one came from!" Tybalt tossed another egg, this one towards the Luxian scout, and when it broke open the man's boots were splattered with fluid.

Tiecelin drew, and let fly. His arrow knocked Tybalt's sword out of his hands, sending it clattering off of the branches to the ground below.

"You rotten twist," Tybalt spat, going for his knives as the Luxian drew a second shaft.

"That's enough, Tybalt!" Reynard said, stepping between the two men. "Get down and leave him be!"

"What- you're taking *his* side?" Tybalt sneered. "I just saved your life!"

"Then consider us even," Reynard replied.

Tybalt looked down at him hatefully, the fingers on his left hand twitching. Then he began to climb down from the tree.

"Waste of time anyway," he said, retrieving his sword and pushing past Reynard. "Let's just get out of this place."

"Are you coming?" Reynard asked Tiecelin as he went to join the others on the far side of the clearing.

"I would like a moment alone," the scout replied. "I won't be long."

Reynard nodded, and then he and Bruin began to make their way back towards the others. When he turned back he saw that the man was still standing over the corpse of the dead shrike, and her murdered young.

* * * * * * *

The Watcher had set by the time they returned to the river. The last of the dam had been cleared, and Reynard saw that the crew had built a pyre out of the debris.

They laid Cointereau's remains beside those of Foinez and Tardis, and doused them with pitch to aid their journey.

"Fenix," Roenel said, "Accept these men, and so that you will know them I will name them: Foinez, Tardis, and Cointereau- Cointereau, who was the youngest of us . . . "

Roenel's voice choked somewhat, and he rubbed at his eyes.

"I cannot say if they were good men, or bad, but I knew them to be loyal and true- and so let them become one with your flame, and feel no pain or fear, and be at peace."

As he spoke these words Pelez lit the pyre, and they watched as the flames engulfed the bodies of their companions.

"Let us be away from this place," Roenel said wearily.

The fires were still burning as the Quicksilver sailed on into the twilight before dawn.

* * * * * * *

The loss of three deckhands, four if one counted Lady Moire, whom Reynard did not expect to recover anytime soon- if at all- meant that there was more than enough work to go round on deck. Isengrim temporarily suspended his lessons so that both of them could take turns watching the dark forest that clung to either side of the river.

Captain Roenel was consulting his maps and charts almost constantly now, for their route through Vulp Vora led through a dense maze of crisscrossing rivers and streams- but even amongst these chimera haunted woods Reynard saw signs of habitation, human or otherwise. Some appeared to be mere outposts nestled by the riverbank, many of which appeared to have been abandoned. In the ruins of one of these forlorn places Reynard caught a glimpse of a scorched pole topped by an image of the Firebird. Likely it had been the home of a missionary of Fenix, but what had brought such a man to this desperate land he could not begin to guess.

Reynard watched with morbid fascination as the landscape changed, the trees growing paler and sickly-looking. Here and there great white rocks split the mantle of the earth, and he found himself fancying that they were the broken bones of some fallen behemoth, forgotten by time itself.

The temperature too was changing- each day strangely hotter than the last, despite the lateness of the year, until Reynard found even his nightclothes stifling. The air went dense with humidity, and the foliage grew wilder, the riverbank receding at last into the depths of a mangrove-choked swamp. Baucent informed them that insects had spoiled most of the supplies, and they were forced to subsist primarily on little more than limes, weevil-infested hard tack, and beer.

"Lovely country," Reynard mumbled one fog-shrouded afternoon as he picked some of the wormy larvae out of his midday meal, his sense of humor having been considerably dulled by the last week of travel. "Friendly natives, excellent food . . ."

"Gods it's hot," Bruin interrupted, tugging aimlessly at his sweat drenched undershirt.

"You don't see him sweating," Grymbart chuckled, tossing his head towards Isengrim, who was standing watch by the prow of the ship.

"That's because he's not human," Reynard said. "At night, when the Watcher is full, he turns his skin inside out and becomes a warg."

"How do you survive the night?" Grymbart asked.

"Well, after every meal I save little bits of bacon . . ."

"We haven't had bacon in days," Bruin pointed out.

"I know," Reynard answered. "And I'm scared."

"I'd kill a man for some meat myself," Grymbart said, laughing.

Reynard offered the mercenary a wriggling grub. "You can have mine if you like."

"No thanks," the man declined. "Not that I haven't eaten maggots before, but I don't trust these local critters."

"You ate maggots?" Reynard asked, flicking his own specimen over the side of the ship. He'd been desperately hungry before, but not that hungry.

"More than a few times when I was fighting in Engadlin. They're not half bad boiled, either."

Reynard was about to respond when Tiecelin rang the alarm. He'd replaced Foinez as the ship's lookout, and since the attack he had spent almost all his time perched above- even to sleep, Reynard had noted.

"There's something in the water," the Luxian shouted down at them. "Moving."

Reynard stood, his meal forgotten as he readied his weapons.

No sooner had he done so, than the whispering began.

If there were words within the hushed voices that were echoing out of the fog, they were not in any tongue that Reynard could recognize, but all the same, there was something . . . intriguing about them.

"Beautiful," Bruin said beside him, and lowered his axe.

"Yes," Reynard agreed, shaking his head as the whispering took on a more seductive tone, full of sultry coos and sighs, like those of a lover only half-forgotten.

He was moving towards the edge of the ship when Isengrim clapped a firm hand on his shoulder.

"They are naga!" Isengrim shouted. "Do not follow their voices, or they will drag you under and drown you!"

The naga, if naga they were, giggled at the Northerner's harsh tone, and their song grew more powerful. For a moment Reynard could hear Hermeline- or was it the Countess - beckoning to him, pleading for his company, and despite himself he took yet another step towards the gunwale.

Isengrim dragged him backwards, and struck him across the face.

"Clear your minds!" Isengrim shouted. "All of you!"

By now one of the deckhands, Frobert, had climbed onto the gunwale, his face blissful. Before anyone could stop him he leapt, and as he hit the water the voices went silent, and whatever spell they had all been under was momentarily broken.

"Frobert!" Espinarz screamed and ran to the place where the deckhand had jumped overboard. Reynard rushed over to stop the man from leaping after him.

"Let me go!" Espinarz protested. "We can still save him!"

"It is too late!" Reynard said, holding the man firmly. "You will just be drowned too!"

As the helmsman ceased struggling Reynard glanced over the side of the ship. For a moment he saw the Frisian sailor, scaly arms caressing him as he was dragged beneath the thick roots that choked the swamp. Then a set of ophidian yellow eyes was staring up at him from the still rippling water.

With some effort he turned from that gaze, and backed away from the gunwale.

"Man the oars!" Captain Roenel shouted. "Row!"

As the men scrambled to obey the Captain's command, Reynard ran towards the helm and began to cut great swaths out of the tarp that covered one of the skiffs.

"What in the world do you think you are doing, Master Fox?" Pelez snarled at him. "Didn't you hear the Captain's orders?"

"I need it," he replied, and began wrapping a thick strip of it around his head. "It will-"

"Drown out the naga!" Captain Roenel finished Reynard's thought. "Master Pelez- all of you- do as Fox says! Strip the other skiff if need be, but cover your ears!"

The rest of the crew had hardly finished wrapping their heads with sailcloth when the naga resumed beckoning them to their deaths- but whatever spell the things could weave with their song had lost much of its potency, and the partially deafened men redoubled the speed of their strokes as they rowed out of the fog.

As the air cleared, Reynard was amazed to see that Ghul was sitting near the prow of the boat, his head uncovered and his eyes closed in rapture- and as the voices faded into nothingness, the Glyconese man went back to his duties with a beatific look in his mismatched eyes.

"I told you that one was crazy," Tybalt said once they'd all felt secure enough to unwrap the cloth from their heads.

"It is his people's way," Dolphin explained. "They believe that the naga are the heralds of the Destroyer."

"The bastard," Pelez spat. "Didn't even bat an eye for Frobert."

"I doubt he cares much for any of us," Reynard said. "We're all just heretics and pagans to him."

"Aye," Grymbart agreed, "I wonder what Count Bricemer is paying him?"

The more important question, Reynard mused, *is what is Count Bricemer paying him to do?*

"You have encountered naga before?" Reynard asked Isengrim, changing the subject.

"In the early days of my exile," the Northerner replied. "There is a great colony of them along the southeastern coast of Calvaria."

"That surprises me," Reynard said. "I wouldn't think that your people would tolerate the presence of chimeras so close to your homeland."

"My people, though great, have not yet learned how to breathe underwater," Isengrim quipped, and Reynard smiled for the first time since the night that Cointereau died.

So. There is a sense of humor under all that thick skin after all.

"And besides," Isengrim went on "It is a good thing that my people have not yet wiped them out, for their presence has, in part, made our mission possible."

"How so?" Grymbart asked.

"You will see."

* * * * * *

Gradually the mangroves gave way to open water, and Reynard realized that they had entered the fabled waters of Lake Hali.

For several days they sailed, until one night Reynard thought that he could make out a string of lights on the distant horizon.

"Are those the lights of a city?" he asked Captain Roenel, who was one of the few men still on watch.

"Yes," the Captain replied. "You see the lights of lost Carcosa, dust choked and ancient, last remaining city built by the demons."

"You have been there before?"

Roenel rubbed his eyes.

"Once," Roenel answered. "In younger days, when I served onboard another ship."

"Do men live there?"

"Men and chimera, and other things. You will see, for the river we must take passes through the city."

"And they will not attack us?"

"They may, if desperate enough, but they would be putting themselves in great danger by doing so."

"What kind of danger?"

"There are- things in the city. Some say that they are the old servants of the demons. They keep the peace, in their own fashion."

"What are they?"

"I do not know," Roenel said. "But you will know them when you see them."

When his watch was over Reynard managed to catch a few hours of sleep before Isengrim roused him.

"We approach the demon city," he said, and led him up to the deck where, through the haze of early morning, Reynard caught his first glimpse of Carcosa.

It was truly ancient, its streets choked with dust and its great domes and spires crumbling under the weight of time. No human had built this place, and no hand, chimera or otherwise, appeared to have touched it since. Whatever dwelt here, Reynard decided, was lurking within the ruins.

As they neared what might have once been the city's harbor he saw that they were sailing over a graveyard of other ships and vessels, their masts and prows coated with a pale slime. Dim shapes swam within that gloomy aquatic forest, but whether they were fish, naga, or some other horror Reynard could not say.

As the ship came alongside a stone pier, Reynard scanned the city for any sign of life- but contrary to the Captain's earlier words, the streets were completely deserted.

Nothing stirred.

"Espinarz," Roenel said. "Bring the ship alongside the dock. We will moor here."

"Captain?" Pelez said, his face blanching. "We've got food and water enough to last us through several months- certainly there's no reason to stop here."

"Nonetheless, I have orders from Count Bricemer to do so," Roenel said. "There is a bit of . . . business that I must attend to. But do not worry overmuch, Pelez, we will be gone before it grows dark."

The first mate nodded, obviously unsatisfied but unwilling to argue with the Captain further.

"What could anyone possibly want from this accursed place?" Tybalt commented as they secured the Quicksilver to a set of sun-baked mooring posts.

"They say that there is a strange flower that only grows near the edge of the Waste," Dolphin replied. "Its seeds, when eaten, brings waking dreams. And the sap of its seeds can be smoked or boiled and ingested."

"Do you mean Ambrosia?" Reynard asked, his throat tightening. "Demon's Blood?"

Dolphin nodded. "Yes, it has many names, depending on the way in which it is taken. Ambrosia I have heard it called, and Soma, but among my people it is Lotos, the flower that brings sleep."

" . . . And death," Reynard added, his voice hard.

"Is that so?" Tybalt asked the Telchine. "It can kill you?"

"Yes," Dolphin answered. "If too much is taken, or if it is taken over too long a time, the dreams begin to affect the waking mind. Eventually the Lotos eater loses interest in anything but ingesting more and more of the plant, until finally the mind itself dies. Then the body wastes away."

Reynard continued to silently tie his own mooring line. His cheeks were flush with anger, more than he had felt for many years. And though Tybalt and Dolphin continued to banter, he was no longer listening to their words.

"Does something trouble you?"

Isengrim had come up behind him without his noticing.

" No," he lied as he softened his expression into that of the raffish Master Fox. "Just got a bit dizzy for a moment- I'm alright now."

Isengrim studied him for a moment, but if he could see beneath Reynard's easy smile he did not say.

Instead, he said: "Captain Roenel has ordered me to escort him a short ways into the city, and as I must go, so will you. Do you find that arrangement acceptable?"

"*Gea, laruwa,*" he answered, ignoring the Northerner's lingering gaze as they made their way towards the gangplank, where Roenel waited for them- as did Grymbart, Bruin and Tybalt. The latter two were carrying a metal strongbox between them.

"Ah," the Captain said as they approached. "We are all assembled then."

"What's in the box?" Tybalt asked. "Gold?"

"Stay close together at all times," the Captain said, ignoring Tybalt's question. "And no matter what occurs, do no violence here."

"Where are we going?" Reynard asked.

"This way," Roenel answered, and began to lead them down one of the city's gloomy avenues.

There was an overbearing sense of abandonment that hung over the place that Reynard found quite disturbing given the great number of lights he had sighted from the deck of the Quicksilver the night before. Where were the men, or half-men, that had lit those fires?

The answer to this riddle was at least partially answered when, after having traveled through several desolate city blocks, one of the arcane-looking lamps that lined the street suddenly flared to life. The pale light that it cast flickered maddeningly, and was accompanied by a low hum, like the thrumming of a giant insect's wings.

"Sorcery," Bruin hissed, backing away from the strange thing.

"Ignore it," Roenel said, "And keep moving."

The lamp continued to flicker long after they had left it behind.

As they penetrated the city the oppressive silence was occasionally broken by the echoing clatter of a disturbed stone or pebble, and then Reynard began to notice that there were figures lurking in the shadows of the ruins: dusty shapes clothed from head to toe in rags, whose eyes he could not make out. They did not attack, but Reynard was beginning to get the distinct impression that they were being followed.

The Captain's route soon brought them to a vast square. Now Reynard could see up close some of the inhabitants of Carcosa, withered and gaunt-looking creatures whose bodies were a canvas on which a multitude of deformities had been painted. Here scurried children who had been born without eyes, men scratched idly at the molting scales that were splayed across their skin, and more besides that went about without various arms and legs.

Many of these pitiable things chewed on the dull purple seeds of the Lotos flower, and their blank faces told Reynard that these were addicts whose minds were on the brink of oblivion. Many sat huddled together, if only for warmth, and amongst these clusters he could see the withered skeletons of those that the waking dreams had already claimed.

In the middle of the square squatted a sort of low domed cell. It was large enough to hold more than a dozen men, but in the dense shadows behind the bars Reynard could make out only a great heap of scaly coils, one pale as ivory, the other was black as pitch, as if a pair of great serpents lay within the cage, the one looped around the other.

Around the cage an ominous-looking bazaar had been set up, and it was towards this point that Roenel now led them.

"Remember," Roenel said as they crossed the square, "No violence."

Reynard nodded, but he kept his hand near his sword anyway, as did the rest of the company he noticed.

Roenel approached the largest of the stalls, an herbalist's tent stuffed with all manner of botanicals. The place stank of human waste, sweat, and the pungent odor from the bundles of plants that hung from the stall's beams. Dozens of Lotos addicts lurked nearby.

The proprietor of this place seemed to be kin to the rag shrouded figures that they had seen earlier in the alleyways along the main avenue. It seemed to possess a vaguely human shape beneath its yellow robes, but there the similarity ended. Its hands were artificial things carved from wood and given the illusion of life by an intricate series of strings and pulleys, and over its face it wore a mask, pallid and expressionless.

As Roenel approached, the robed figure shifted slightly to regard the group of newcomers to Carcosa, and whatever was behind the mask chattered and clicked for a moment before speaking.

"Welcome," it said in a hollow voice that was not entirely male or female. "You are strangers to Carcosa, are you not?"

"I- I have been here before," Roenel answered shakily. "But that was many years ago."

"Why have you returned here?" the thing asked, one of its unnatural hands dipping into one of the clay jars arrayed before it. Then it held out, pinched between forefinger and thumb, a Lotos seed. "For this, perhaps?"

"Yes," Roenel answered. "We seek to purchase the seeds of the flower that grows along the eastern shores of Lake Hali. The ones that bring visions."

The thing . . . laughed? It wasn't quite the right word to describe the tinny sound that rattled from behind its emotionless visage.

"And what have you brought here that you can offer in payment?" it asked.

Roenel motioned for Bruin and Grymbart to bring forward the strong box. Once they'd set it down Roenel motioned them to step back and only then did he open it so that the robed figure could see what lay inside.

"This is satisfactory," the hollow voice said at last.

"Then we have a deal?" Roenel asked, shutting the crate shakily. Reynard was relieved that he had not been able to see what was inside of it.

"Correct," the thing said and, after measuring out a large number of seeds on a balance, it poured them into a roughly woven bag and held it out for Roenel to take, which he did after some hesitation.

Immediately the men and women that surrounded them began to plead for the Captain to share some of his newly acquired goods. Whatever fear they had of the strange merchant obviously did not apply to outsiders, Reynard guessed, and now they whined and begged for the drug that would release them from their pain.

Many of the beggars could barely walk, and so they shambled and crawled forward, clutching onto whomever was nearest. They were not very strong, but their grip was tenacious, and soon there was not a man among them that did not have at least one of the pitiful creatures hanging off of them.

"Get back to the ship!" Roenel bellowed over the din.

Reynard had just extricated himself from one of the beggars when he felt another pair of bony fingers wrapping around his leg. He looked down and saw an ancient crone staring up at him with sunken eyes.

"Please, son," the woman wheezed. "Please, don't leave me."

Reynard recoiled at the words and backed away, dragging the old woman across one of the dust covered slabs that made up the floor of the marketplace.

"Just a little more, just to keep me warm," the old woman said, ignoring the fresh cuts and scrapes across her bony arms. "You can do that for me, son? Can't you?"

"Get off of me!" Reynard screamed.

He tugged his leg violently to escape the old woman's grip, but succeeded only in tripping himself. When he landed the crone began to crawl on top of him, her pleading whine so familiar to him that suddenly he was a boy again, living in a filthy garret that boiled in summer and froze in winter, his only companion a woman whose mind was gone, but whose body refused to die.

"Fox!" Isengrim shouted. "Stay calm!"

"No, son, don't leave me," the crone pleaded as she clutched at him, "Don't leave me here-"

"Shut up!" Reynard screamed and struck the old woman mercilessly with clenched fists. She howled and rolled off of him, going limp, but even then he did not stop. "Leave me alone! You're dead! You're dead! You're dead!"

"No, Fox!" Roenel shouted, dragging Reynard off of the old woman, but it was too late.

The old woman was still.

The beggars' assault on the men ceased as quickly as it had begun, and those that had been able to walk now did so- as fast as their legs could carry them- away from the center of the square. Those that remained looked around with wild eyes, and moaned piteously.

"Shall we run, Captain?" Grymbart asked, eyeing each of the streets that emptied into the market square.

"Can't run," one of the beggars moaned. "Can't run from the puppets!"

"Puppets?" Tybalt said, obviously panicked, "What does he mean 'puppets?'"

"Why did you do that, Fox?" Roenel demanded, wrenching Reynard around to face him. "Answer me, curse you!"

"I- I'm sorry," he choked, backing away from the lifeless body at his feet. "I didn't mean to . . ."

A gloved hand clapped Reynard on the shoulder. He turned, and for the first time found that he could not meet Isengrim's gaze.

"I should not have come," he said, his calm restored. "I am- sorry."

"We may speak of it later," Isengrim said as he released him. "If we live."

"All of you- form on me," Roenel ordered as calmly as he could. "Right now."

They formed a tight circle around the Captain, but still they did not draw their swords.

"There!" Tybalt said, pointing to one of the entrances to the square. "Look!"

A strange procession had appeared, moving with great rapidity towards them. It was made up of a dozen or so slender man-like figures, entirely encased in armor that must have been as old as the city itself- whatever color it had once been had long since turned to rust. Their faceplates were similar to the mask that the yellow robed figure wore, blank and expressionless, and they wielded long metal staves with cruel looking blades set at the end of them.

Then Reynard noticed that one of them wore no mask.

"They're- they're empty," he exclaimed.

The hollow suits of armor surrounded both the men from the Quicksilver and the Lotos addicts that had accosted them, but they did not yet move to attack. Instead a series of chirps and clicks that no human mouth could have produced emanated from them- a message that was answered by a similar series of sounds from the masked figure at the stall.

Whatever had been said, the rust choked things erupted again into life and went about the task of gathering up the Lotos addicts, who cried out for mercy as they were dragged off to whatever fate awaited them.

As for the old woman, her corpse was hacked apart by the sentinels' polearms, and the bits of her mangled corpse were tossed into the cage at the center of the market. Immediately the black and white serpents within uncoiled, and then Reynard realized that they belonged to the same creature: a mutant naga with an emaciated female torso growing from each end of its long scaled body, its conjoined tail both black and white scales blended together. With a delighted cry both ends of this amphisbaena snatched up the scraps of human flesh and devoured them, the fresh gore running down both their chins until they dripped over their scale covered breasts.

All this Reynard watched with sick horror as the armored things left as swiftly as they had come, and the yellow robed figure . . . laughed.

"Come again soon," it said to them all. "Bring more of the same and you will have more seeds- or gold, if that is what you desire. But come again soon and bring more of the same . . ."

Roenel nodded, and then they left that terrible place without one look behind them.

* * * * * * *

"What was in the box?" Tybalt asked when they had finally returned to the ship with the Lotos seeds and had cast off from the dock.

"You are better off not knowing," Roenel answered, and then he took the helm, his face pale and coated with sweat. He did not speak again until they had left the ruins of Carcosa far behind them.

"I pray that I never have cause to return there," the Captain said, gazing back at the place as night fell and the pale lights of Carcosa burst into abysmal life.

"Was it so dreadful, Captain?" the first mate asked.

"Forgive me, Pelez," Roenel said, relinquishing control of the wheel to Espinarz. "I saw something today that I hoped I would never see again."

"What's that, sir?"

Captain Roenel continued to stare at the lights of Carcosa as he spoke:

"When I first set eyes on this place I was still a young man, not much older than Cointereau."

The Captain seemed to have forgotten that the young deckhand was dead, Reynard noticed.

"The city was different then: I saw wild chimera walking the streets openly, alongside slavers and pirates. But that merchant- that *thing* in yellow- was selling Ambrosia then as now."

"How do you know it was the same merchant?" Bruin asked. "Did he wear that weird mask?"

"That was no mask," the Captain replied. "No mask."

IX

"Tell me of your mother," Isengrim said as they lay in the darkness of their cabin.

Reynard had been expecting questions since they'd returned to the Quicksilver, but Isengrim had said nothing for days. The Captain, too, had not reprimanded him for the incident, and by supper he was sitting again with the men and listening to Grymbart wind his old war stories- but when they thought he was not watching he could see them, whispering to each other, and staring.

He didn't blame them. They had seen his mask slip.

They had seen the real Reynard.

"Is the memory of it so painful?" Isengrim asked, his voice the only sign that another man lay in the darkness of the cabin.

"My mother," he began, finding the words strange to speak aloud, "Was the daughter of a guildsman, a member of the Baker's Guild. She'd been trained to be a chef- to make pastries of all things- and probably would have had a comfortable life, if things had been different."

"What happened?"

"She met my father," he said, his words starting to flow more quickly. "He told her he was the scion of a noble family in Frisia. A petty prince in exile, or some rubbish like that, but a prince just the same. Of course she fell for it. She left her own family for him. Maybe they were even happy, for a while."

"And then, one day, he left. Mother used to tell me that he was on a long voyage, gone back to reclaim his birthright, some half-baked story he fobbed off on her. When I was younger I really thought that he'd come back someday, and I'd be a prince- just like my father."

"Did you ever see him again?"

"No. He'd probably moved on to greener pastures. I suppose he didn't have any interest in us once he'd grown bored of her. It took me a long time to figure that out. Sooner than mother did at any rate," Reynard chuckled to himself darkly. "I think she was still waiting for him, even at the end."

"Did she return to her family?"

"Them?" Reynard scoffed hatefully. "Oh yes, she tried to go back to them. Thought that they would welcome her, let her continue as an apprentice. Ha! They had cut her off like she'd never even existed in the first place. Later, when she was too sick to move, I went to them, told them who I was, and got a good whipping for my troubles. They just couldn't live with the shame of what she'd done, throwing her prospects away and having a bastard with some foreign rake without two bits to his name. Hypocrites, all of them!"

Reynard realized that he was beginning to shout, and calmed himself.

"She couldn't find work- not honest work. Couldn't even get a job with the Renders, boiling dead animals into tallow. Wasn't a part of the guild, right? Landlord wanted her out, and she couldn't pay. Master Pinch, she called him. Don't remember his right name, but he owned the whole block. Told her she could earn her keep in other ways. I was nine summers old then, but even I knew what a pinch-prick was. I tried to stop him, but he just boxed my ears and locked me in a crawlspace until he was finished."

"She became one of Pinch's girls then, the kind of whore that even a roach could afford. It was then that she started taking Ambrosia. Pinch sold that too. Demon's Blood they call it, in the Anthill."

"The Anthill?"

"Old Quarter. That's where we lived, with all the other ants. But it was only for a little while, she always said, just until father came back. But he didn't come back, did he? And so she drank Demon's Blood and dreamt all day, while her son had to scrounge for cast-off bones and rummage through trash to feed her."

"And is that why you became a thief?"

"At first, yes," Reynard replied. "I wanted to save her- to take her away from the Anthill. But it was too late. Her mind went too quickly for me. There were days at a time when she didn't even know who I was."

Reynard swallowed, hard. "And then, one day, she- she wasn't there anymore. And the men kept coming to see her. It- it sickened me, and even then I knew- I knew it had to stop."

"What did you do?"

For a long time Reynard did not answer.

"I played the scared little boy, and did . . . *favors* for Pinch," Reynard finally replied, his voice hollow. "Until he thought he'd gained himself a new little plaything. And then I waited- waited until he and his men were going to spend an evening with my mother and some of his other girls. By then I'd learned a few things about Demon's Blood, like how slow it could make one. I laced their ale with it, just enough to make them sluggish, and then I went downstairs and barricaded all the doors to the upper levels and set the whole building on fire. It went up like a tinderbox. I could hear them, all of them, screaming inside, pounding on the doors, and then I watched Pinch jump out of one of the windows. It was five stories. But he lived long enough to see me."

"I'll never forget his face."

"And the others?" Isengrim asked, and Reynard heard no judgment in his voice.

"Dead, all of them, and they weren't the only ones. The fire spread and burnt down almost a third of the Anthill. I thought about jumping in myself."

"And why did you choose not to?"

"I wanted revenge. On my mother's family, of course, but also all of the rich bastards who had let her die: the guildsmen, the nobles- so fat and comfortable, never stooping to help the bleeding masses that fight their wars and polish their boots. So I became someone else: a priest, a soldier, a merchant, a rake, a servant- whatever it took to make them pay for what they had done."

"You did not seek vengeance on your father?"

"I used to dream that when I was wealthy enough I would hunt my father down. But the older I grew the more I realized how impossible that would prove- I couldn't remember his face, and I knew all too well how easily he could have become someone else. Who knows if the name he gave my mother was even his own? But still, I used to imagine meeting him, in some Frisian dockyard, or along a pier in Calyx. A chance meeting between us, separated for years. Sometimes, in my head, he'd turn and see me, and he would recognize me, and say my name- my true name- and I would forgive him. We'd make a new life together, and he'd take me with him to wherever it was he was going. Father and son, against the world."

Reynard shifted on his bunk and rested his head in the cradle of one of his arms. "Other times he wouldn't see me, and I'd stab him in the heart and whisper my name into his ear as he died."

"I too used to have such thoughts," Isengrim said. "When I was young."

"Did you ever come to know your parents?"

"No. It is forbidden for a blood-guard to know his true family, for he may be forced to judge them one day. My order was the only family I ever knew . . . and now of course I do not have them either."

"So we are orphans, the both of us," Reynard said, and sighed. "It-it is good to speak of it, after all these years."

"Fox," Isengrim said softly, "Do you know why you killed that old woman in the market?"

"Yes," he replied. "I do."

"Your mother is dead, Fox. She cannot hurt you anymore."

Isengrim said nothing more, and for the first time in many years, Reynard felt the sting of tears in his eyes as he silently cried himself to sleep.

* * * * * *

The sound of knocking awoke Reynard, and though it was impossible to tell in the windowless cabin, it felt as if only a few hours had passed since he'd fallen asleep. He assumed the worst as he reached for the dagger he kept underneath his pillow.

Isengrim threw wide the door to reveal Grymbart, who had a worried look in his eye.

"There's something you should see," the grizzled mercenary said without explanation, beckoning both of them to follow.

Grymbart led them to the lower cargo hold, where Baucent and Bruin were huddled around a beer barrel that had apparently tipped over and shattered.

Inside the barrel was a rotting corpse. The thing had bloated hideously, but its golden skin was covered by the same tattoos that all of them recognized as belonging to Dolphin. It was Dolphin, Reynard realized. His neck had been slashed.

This in itself would have been disconcerting to him, but the real horror of it was further compounded by the fact that he knew that Dolphin was currently up on deck with the others.

"Well, this is odd, isn't it?" Reynard said.

"Found this barrel, hidden amongst the sundries," Baucent said. "I was startled and tipped it over, but I don't think anyone heard it. Up on deck I mean."

"Is there something about Telchines that makes people want to stuff them into barrels?" Reynard muttered.

"I do not understand," Isengrim said flatly.

"I'll explain it to you later- Baucent, do you really think this is him?"

"I've known Dolphin for years!" the pig-eyed cook replied in a hushed shout. "This is definitely 'im, right down to the tattoos."

"Then- what's that up on deck?" Grymbart asked, his hand working over his beard furiously. "Who've we been playing cards with the last couple weeks?"

The five men's heads craned upwards, as if they might peer surreptitiously through the planks of the two decks between them and the thing that wore Dolphin's shape.

"Whatever it is," Reynard said, "It killed Dolphin."

"Why did it not dispose of the corpse?" Isengrim asked. "It must have known that we would find the body eventually."

"Maybe it thought that we wouldn't get a chance, what with everyone on deck day and night," Reynard replied. "Maybe it didn't figure that we'd come across this barrel so soon."

"How long do you think it's been on board?" Grymbart asked. "Dolphin looks like he's been dead for some time."

"I've got a better question," Reynard said as Baucent dragged a tarp over Dolphin's rotting corpse. "What are we going to do about it?"

"Well," Grymbart said, reaching for his sword. "I can think of one thing to do."

"As can I," Reynard nodded. "But seeing as we have no idea what that thing is capable of, I suggest we play it quiet. Agreed?"

"Agreed," the other men grunted.

"Then keep your weapons sheathed, and follow my lead."

Reynard and Isengrim exited the hold, and made their way over to the cheerfully whistling figure that looked, sounded, and moved like the golden skinned Telchine.

"What sort of beating do you have in store for me today, *laruwa?*" Reynard asked casually as Grymbart joined them. "Some more swordplay, perhaps?"

"If you wish," Isengrim said, unsheathing his own blade.

"Another fight, boys," Bruin called out as he and the cook approached, "Dolphin, make some room there! I gotta see this!"

You're laying it on a bit thick, Bruin, Reynard cringed inwardly as he drew his rapier.

Despite its outwardly calm demeanor, the false-Dolphin must have suspected that something was wrong, for just as Baucent was getting into position it hurled itself towards the edge of the ship.

So fast! Reynard marveled as his rapier cut through the air where the thing had been just a moment before.

Isengrim was faster and sliced into the imposter as he leapt- but his keen edged weapon merely slashed through a flimsy husk of loose skin that the aberration had shrugged off in order to save itself from death.

Now that its disguise had been cast aside, the thing appeared to be a pale thing of vaguely humanoid form. Its smooth and hairless body was completely featureless- its head devoid of eyes, ears, or nose- and underneath its skin pulsed a rainbow of vivid colors that Reynard could only guess was its blood.

Grymbart rushed the thing before it could throw itself overboard, but as the mercenary lunged forward its left arm extended weirdly to strike him just beneath the jaw, sending the doughty fellow crashing to the deck. Without missing a beat, its right arm wrapped around Grymbart's sword, ripped the blade out of his loosening grip, and bent backwards to turn aside Bruin's axe. As the huge man recovered for another swing, the thing dropped onto the palm of its free hand and pummeled Bruin repeatedly with its legs.

As Bruin went down, one of Tiecelin's arrow shafts sunk into the square of the shapeshifter's back. In response the thing's sword arm uncoiled like a snake and sent Grymbart's sword hurtling towards the Luxian. The blade missed its mark, and buried itself point first into the side of the crow's nest, but it caused the sharpshooter's next shot to go wild as the creature ducked for cover.

The thing made another dive for the gunwale, only to find Isengrim standing in its path, and as it changed its course wildly the Northerner slashed open its chest. The wound oozed a thick opaque slime, but if the thing had any vital organs it obviously did not house them in its upper torso.

It made no noise to indicate that it had been injured, and threw Baucent aside with a wet smack as it made for the other side of the ship.

And ran straight into Reynard.

He managed to cut open one of the thing's forearms before it bowled him over, and then they were tumbling together over the deck- the creature's slippery skin hardening considerably as they struck one of the skiffs.

Scrambling to his feet, Reynard raised his rapier to strike and found that he was looking at . . . himself. Even his clothes and armor looked real.

His double also had his dagger.

"What are you?" Reynard asked. "What do you want?"

"You're the imposter here," the thing scoffed in his own voice as it advanced on at him. "You tell me."

The thing was still frightfully quick, but it was obviously restraining itself in order to pass itself off as human.

"Gods," Reynard swore loudly as his double nearly slashed open his throat. "Do I really sound like that?"

"I'm afraid so," it replied. "Sorry to disappoint."

"Well, you've got my snide remarks down, I see."

"As have you," it shot back, feigning to stumble as it dodged one of his own blows. "Will someone please kill this thing?"

"Drop your weapons!" Captain Roenel screamed at them as the crew surrounded them. "Both of you!"

Reynard and his double eyed each other and laid down sword and dagger.

"Keep your distance," Roenel said as Reynard's double took a few steps towards the Captain.

"Which one's the real Fox?" Pelez said, his cutlass wavering in the air.

"We could just kill one of 'em," Tybalt suggested.

"No," Isengrim said, stepping forward. "I need him alive, remember?"

"Oh- right."

"*I can speak Calvarian,*" Reynard offered in the Northern tongue.

"*So can I,*" the thing said.

"Ah, but do you know how to bow properly?" Reynard shot back.

"Of course I do," the thing smirked.

"Very well," Isengrim said, "If you are the real Fox, show me the respect that I am due."

"Say 'please,'" said Reynard.

Isengrim's sword severed the shapeshifter's neck neatly, sending both its head and torso splashing wetly to the deck. It twitched spasmodically as Tybalt and Ghul hacked at it, displaying a remarkable vitality until its shudders finally came to an end.

Whatever membrane held the thing together collapsed, and soon the creature was nothing but a rapidly dissolving puddle of ooze.

"Anyone care to explain what I'm looking at?" Tybalt said, cleaning his slime encrusted sword with obvious distaste.

"The cook found Dolphin's body down below," Reynard replied. "This thing was masquerading as him."

"Dolphin is dead?" Espinarz asked, staring at the greasy stain on the deck that had resembled his friend.

"For at least a week," Reynard added. "Maybe even longer."

"But," Tybalt reasoned, taking a few steps back from the others, "That might mean that any one of us might be one of these- things."

"He's right," the deckhand named Condylure said nervously. "How do we know there isn't another one on board?"

"That's enough of that talk," Roenel said. "We'll search the entire ship and see if anyone else turns up dead."

"And we will do it together," the Captain added, cutting off another of Tybalt's famous gripes. "But first I want that foul thing washed off of my deck."

* * * * * *

"Well, no more corpses at least," Grymbart said as they finished their third sweep of the ship. Reynard had found the trip quite educational, as he'd briefly been granted access to the Captain's cabin, as well as the tiny room where Ghul had been quartered.

"Of course," Reynard said, glancing towards the crow's nest. "There is one place we haven't searched yet."

"I hardly think there's enough room for a body up there," Grymbart said. "Though Tiecelin's the only one that's been up there since Foinez died . . . and I suppose I need to get my sword back anyway."

As Reynard and Grymbart began to clamber up the rigging, he thought he could hear the chirping of birds- a strange sound considering the desolation of the Waste.

"Your sword," Tiecelin said, holding out the weapon so that Grymbart could see it. "I can bring it down to you."

"That's alright," the grizzled mercenary replied. "We're halfway there already."

"Don't," the scout begged suddenly. "I beg you."

Grymbart shot a look at Reynard.

"Are you going to shoot us, Tiecelin?" Reynard asked the Luxian. Tiecelin shook his head. "No."

"If he's hiding something," Reynard heard Tybalt mutter below them, "I hope it's a woman."

"I'd prefer booze," Bruin said.

"What a surprise."

Reynard reached the crow's nest before Grymbart. Keeping one eye on Tiecelin he peered down into the crow's nest.

At the bottom of the nest was a bed of peat and twine, and nestled within it was a trio of baby shrikes.

They were naked and smooth, save for a bit of soft gray down, and they were begging for food the way that baby chicks did. The littlest one had a beaked mouth. Their father, whoever he had been, must have been less human than their scarlet plumed mother.

"You took the eggs," Reynard said.

"Yes," Tiecelin said to Reynard. "Please, don't kill them."

"Wulf," Grymbart groaned as he pulled himself up the last couple of rungs. "What in the world is that smell?"

Then the mercenary saw the shrikes, and was silent.

"What is it?" Roenel shouted at them.

"I think you should see for yourself," Reynard replied, and turned back towards the dark-eyed scout. "Will you bring them down?"

"I will," he answered, "If you promise they won't be hurt."

"I cannot promise that," Reynard said firmly. "But I will do my best to save them."

Tiecelin stared into his eyes, and nodded. Removing his weather-beaten coat he scooped each of the chicks up and nestled them under his arm, and then the Luxian was gingerly making his way down from the rigging.

"Gods," Roenel said when Tiecelin showed him what was inside of his coat.

"They aren't doing anyone any harm," Tiecelin said.

"Not yet," Tybalt said pointedly.

"They're monsters!" Moire snarled- the first words Reynard had heard her speak since her ordeal with the chimera. "They should all be destroyed!"

"She's right, Captain," Musard agreed. "You saw what stock these things came from. They deserve to die!"

The crewmen muttered their agreement. They had little love for the spawn of the chimera that had slain Cointereau, Foinez, and Tardis.

"I ought to wring their foul necks myself!" Moire shouted. "Give them here!"

Lady Moire snatched at the chicks, her hand shaking with rage, but Tiecelin wrenched away from her, clutching the bundle in his arms like a mother hen.

"Captain," Reynard said, "May I offer a counter argument?"

"I don't rightly see how this is any of your business, Master Fox, but go on and say your piece."

"Shrikes can be tamed," Reynard said smoothly. "The Duke himself has one, and may be interested in adding these chicks to his menagerie- especially if they grow up to look anything like their mother. There could be a healthy bonus in it for yourself and your crew, on top of the coin he'll pay for the Lotos seeds."

Roenel considered this for a moment, and then turned to Tiecelin.

"Can you keep them alive until we return, Master Tiecelin?"

"Yes, Captain."

"Then I put you in charge of their care- and since he is so interested in their welfare, Master Fox will help build a cage to hold these . . . things. They must always stay below deck, do you understand?"

"Yes, Captain," Reynard answered.

"You twist!" Lady Moire shrieked. "Does what happened to me- and Cointereau- mean nothing to you?"

"Master Pelez!" Roenel barked. "Escort the second mate to her quarters, and confine her there until further notice!"

"Yes, Captain," Pelez grumbled, and led a furiously cursing Moire off by the arm.

"Espinarz," Roenel said when they'd gone, "Full sail."

* * * * * * *

It took Reynard and Tiecelin an hour or so to construct a cage out of several cannibalized crates. When they were finished the Luxian gently placed the shrikes inside and repacked the peat around them, wetting it slightly and padding it with packing material. The chicks snapped at his fingers as he constructed their nest, but they had grown no teeth, and the usually dour man chuckled pleasantly at their bites.

"That will keep them warm?" Reynard asked the Luxian.

"There are birds in Luxia that do the same with their young. I am glad, too, that I can keep them below deck. I was afraid that the chill in the North might kill them."

"Have you always loved birds?" Reynard prodded, wondering at the man's strange fascination for them.

"Since I was little. My father bred falcons for the Baron of Riva."

"And now you raise shrikes for the Duke of Arcas?"

"I suppose so," the Luxian said somewhat morosely, and began to feed the chicks partially chewed up bits of meat. "Do think the Duke will treat them well?"

"I suppose he may," Reynard answered. "But until then they are yours to train as you will. And who knows? Perhaps he may let you keep one."

"Aye- that is what I hope." Tiecelin took Reynard's hand and squeezed it. "You are a good man, Master Fox. Thank you."

Reynard did not agree with Tiecelin's assessment of his character, but he did not contradict him either.

* * * * * * *

For near on to a week the Quicksilver traveled north, and with each passing day the landscape looked more and more normal to Reynard's eyes. The river cut through a hilly region, and then a vast plain whose eastern edge was punctuated by snow capped mountains.

The temperature too was changing rapidly, and one chilly morning Reynard awoke to find that the ship was coated with a thin blanket of snow.

"Here," Isengrim said, handing him a long coat whose interior had been lined with soft fur. Gratefully, Reynard put it on over his brigandine.

"Aren't you cold?" Reynard asked Isengrim, still shivering despite the coat.

"I am more than used to it," Isengrim replied. "It is but Darkmonth, and we are not in Calvaria yet- this is but a mere shadow of the ill weather we will have to endure."

"I can hardly wait."

"In any case, the chill in the air confirms one thing: the time to accomplish that which is required of us by the Duke is nearly upon us, and we must resume your training immediately."

"Well, at least the beatings will help keep me warm," Reynard replied, his levity echoing the relief that he felt at the prospect of leaving the horrors of Vulp Vora behind him.

But the land of demons had one last surprise in store for them all.

It came at midday, when the watch on the ship was changed. Reynard had been chewing on a particularly tough piece of jerky when a great sobbing cry rose from the planks below his feet.

"Wulf," he swore as he spat out his meal and drew his sword, "What now?"

By the time he'd climbed down into the hold a crowd had gathered around the door to the forward cabin, where Lady Moire had been sequestered, and as he approached he could see that Baucent and Pelez were in the process of cutting her down from one of the rafters above.

She had hanged herself.

"Why?" Reynard asked the first mate once they had cut Moire down.

"She told me-" Pelez paused, choking on his own words for a moment, "She told me that she hadn't had the Watcher's Curse since- since the night she was taken by the- by those beasts-"

Pelez tore off his wig and used it to cover his face as he wept.

"I never thought she would- she was always so strong! But I guess she couldn't bear to have one of 'em in her belly."

"Frankly, I'm impressed," Tybalt remarked, "I would have thought that bitch would have dried out by now."

Pelez struck Tybalt then, hard. The former brigand stumbled backwards, and then the first mate was striking blindly at him as he howled for his blood. Tybalt fought back, kicking at Pelez viciously as he desperately tried to draw one of his daggers.

"That's enough!" Captain Roenel bellowed when Bruin and Grymbart finally managed to separate the two. "There's been more than enough death on this ship without us tearing each other apart!"

Pelez was not satisfied. "Aren't these men supposed to be protecting us, Captain? If so, they're not very good at it! I say it's about time one of them met the Watcher!"

"Tybalt didn't kill Moire, Pelez! Now control yourself, sir, or I'll throw you off this ship myself!"

This seemed to sober the first mate somewhat, and he replaced his wig and backed off.

"Thank you, Captain," Tybalt said, getting to his feet.

"*You* keep your filthy mouth shut," Roenel snapped. "And if I ever hear you speak that way about one of my crewmen again, alive or dead, I will personally flay the skin from your back. Do you understand?"

Tybalt's mouth opened, and then closed.

"Good."

* * * * * * *

Reynard helped carry Moire onto the deck, and then watched silently as Espinarz began sewing her into a bit of spare canvas. When the helmsman was done, Musard and Condylure hefted the dead woman between them and hurled her into the river.

"I do not understand," Isengrim commented to Reynard as the crew dispersed around them. "Why did they not burn her?"

"She was a suicide," Reynard replied, watching as Moire was rapidly carried far downstream. "She must find her own way to the Firebird- at least, that's what the priests of Fenix would tell you."

"Ah, yes," Isengrim said. "I sometimes forget that your people's ways are so much different from my own. In Calvaria, to choose to end one's own life is usually seen as an honorable thing. Death is often preferable to dishonor."

"But not always?"

Isengrim did not answer.

"Shall we spar, then?" Reynard asked.

"Yes," Isengrim said, drawing his sword.

They had exchanged several blows when Reynard saw a rare opening in the Northerner's defense. He took it boldly, his dagger gliding towards the Northerner's unprotected shoulder, and surprise flashed across Isengrim's face as he whirled away, his sword twisting wildly to parry Reynard's follow up blow.

"You have improved greatly," Isengrim commented as he regained his stance. "Count Bricemer was wise to choose you for this mission."

The Calvarian pressed his own attack now, his blows coming in fast and hard, pushing Reynard backwards until he was pinned against the gunwale, staring into the Northerner's blue eyes over their locked blades.

"Isengrim," Reynard said as he tried to free his left arm, "There is something I would know, before we enter Calvaria."

Isengrim's brow flashed dangerously as he increased the pressure on his own blade. "And that is?"

"Why were you exiled from Calvaria? *Why* are you doing this at all?"

"Why are you?"

"Because Duke Nobel will kill someone whom I love if I do not," Reynard answered, using his opponent's momentary distraction to kick Isengrim back, granting him just enough time to gain some distance.

"Do you truly believe that, Master Fox?"

The Northerner was still, but he had not relaxed his defense.

"What do you mean?" Reynard said, keeping his weapons at the ready.

"What I mean is that a man as resourceful as you could have escaped from this ship long ago," Isengrim answered. "A man like you could have found his woman, could have rescued her, could have hidden where the Duke could not find him. But you did not do any of those things, did you, Master Fox?"

"I suppose I didn't."

"And seeing as that is the case," Isengrim said, "I can only conclude that you are here by choice- as I am."

"That's very clever," Reynard drawled. "I must be rubbing off on you."

Isengrim leapt towards him, blade raised. Reynard parried the incoming thrust, and then went into his riposte. Isengrim countered the strike viciously, knocking Reynard's rapier out of his grip.

There was a whirl of flashing metal as Reynard desperately tried to counter Isengrim's sword with his dagger. But with each skilled deflection the Northerner's blade darted closer and closer to his breast, until its tip was resting comfortably over his heart.

Reynard lowered his dagger, and sheathed it.

"It took me seven thrusts to defeat you," Isengrim said with a hint of approval, "Even when you had only your shorter blade to defend yourself with. You may not be the equal of a blood-guard, but you should prove to be more than a match for any common Calvarian soldier."

"You still haven't answered my question," said Reynard.

"What makes you believe that you are entitled to an answer?"

"I have told you of my own past," Reynard replied as he retrieved his rapier, frowning at a visible nick in the blade. "Will you not do the same?"

"I do not see how that is relevant," Isengrim said as he applied a little oil to his own sword.

"You know, Isengrim," Reynard said, "It's a wonder you were never a thief."

"Why do you say that?"

"Because I'm not the only one who's good at hiding," he answered, and went to retrieve his whetstone.

X

The next day the river met the gray Northern sea. The waves crested white and brilliant, and the sky was rife with gulls.

"May the sea bitch rise up to smother you," Pelez cursed at the receding shoreline, spitting for emphasis. "And may you rot in her coils!"

The other crewmen spat as well, and laughed, but it was plain to Reynard that this show of bravado was only half-hearted: of the eleven sailors under Roenel's command, only five were left.

"This voyage was doomed from the start," Reynard heard Condylure mutter to Espinarz as he helped them tack the sails. "We ought to turn back before it gets any worse."

"And go back through that land of nightmares?" the helmsman replied, silencing any further mutinous talk- though the grizzled old salt did not sound entirely convinced of his own words.

That night they dropped anchor, and Roenel allowed a small celebration to be held below deck. The sailors sang bawdy sea shanties, and gamed, and even Bruin was allowed to partake of an extra ration of Frisian rum that the Captain had stowed away for just such an occasion.

Reynard would have joined them, were it not his turn to stand watch on deck with Isengrim and Ghul, though he suspected that a bit of drink and song would hardly serve to erase the memories of what he had witnessed in Vulp Vora.

Captain Roenel too did not partake in the festivities, and stood watch near the prow.

"The Captain is looking rather grim tonight," Reynard commented softly to Isengrim. "At least, more so than usual."

"Perhaps that is because the Quicksilver must travel back through Vulp Vora to return the gem to Arcasia," the Northerner replied. "And he does not know yet how to tell the men."

"*Back* through Vulp Vora?" Reynard said. "That is his plan?"

"Indeed it is. Are you aware of a safer route?"

"I understand the perils of sailing north," Reynard replied, "But I have doubts that we will survive a second trip through that place."

"The men now comprehend its dangers. They are well suited to make the return journey."

"They also might mutiny," Reynard pointed out.

"That would be unlikely, given that the men in Bricemer's employ now outnumber them entirely."

"And what if the Count's men mutiny?"

"They have nothing to gain from doing so, for without the safe return of the gem, their individual bargains with Count Bricemer will be forfeit."

"True," Reynard said, "But they would still have their lives. If we are killed in Vulp Vora all the promises in the world will be of little use to us."

"The time to have considered that is long since past, Master Fox. Besides, there is no safe route out of these seas- farther north great blocks of ice drift in the water, and to the east is Brobdingnag, a realm of giants. The only other choice would be to travel through the *Nio-geat*, though I would not take that route even if the whole of Calvaria were in pursuit."

"'The Gate of Tears?'" Reynard translated the words aloud.

"Yes. It is a narrow man-made channel that runs through a series of natural caverns, and it once provided access between the eastern and western coasts of Greater Calvaria. It is near the mouth of this place where the Quicksilver will drop its anchor until you and I return from Dis."

"And, I suppose there is a reason it is not named 'The Gate of Mirth?'"

"Joke if you must," Isengrim replied without humor. "But thousands of my people have met their end there trying to purge it of its denizens."

"These would be the naga you spoke of earlier?"

"Yes, naga lair in a nearby reef, and use the channel freely . . . but they are but a mere nuisance compared to the thing that dwells there."

"Please, do go on," Reynard drawled. "Your stories are always so cheerful."

"There are very few men who have braved the *Nio-geat* and have lived to tell of it, but those who have claim that it is the lair of a sea monster: some dark thing from the deep ocean. They say it dwells in a sea cave on one side of the channel, dangerously near a gauntlet of jagged rocks. The naga worship it, and perhaps they are not wrong to do so, for it has dwelled in the *Nio-geat* for over two hundred years. No Calvarian fleet has ever succeeded in destroying it."

"What do you imagine that it is?" Reynard mulled. "The waters of Calvaria are too cold for dragons."

"There are some old legends that tell of the great sea naga, some of whom have been known to grow as long as small sailing ships from head to tail. Or perhaps it is some abomination that has been loosed from the depths to trouble the world of men. There are said to be worse things beneath the waves than the monsters of Vulp Vora."

"I find that difficult to believe," Reynard said. "But I will take your word for it."

"That is good."

"So," Reynard said at last, "It is back through Vulp Vora then?"

Isengrim nodded and added, "When we have the gem."

* * * * * * *

Three days later Reynard could see for himself the entrance to the Gate of Tears: a great arch that cut directly into a gray cliff, its curves too perfect to be natural.

They had avoided the coast entirely, and had sailed instead through waters that Isengrim informed Reynard would prove the most dangerous of all, since their presence here would not be tolerated if they were discovered, even if he managed to repeat the performance that had saved their skins the last time they had been boarded by a Calvarian vessel.

From the forecastle Reynard gazed at the forbidding eastern edge of the Calvarian peninsula. On occasion the overcast sky would break open and the sea would be clear enough for him to make out the dim shape of the mountainous island of Thule. It rose blackly out of the sea, dark clouds enshrouding jagged peaks that stabbed upwards like knives, and then the gray haze would return, and the spray of the white waves seemed to swallow the island from sight.

Despite their proximity to Thule, they encountered no patrolling Calvarian vessels. Isengrim explained that the navy made regular patrols of the coastline to the south and east, slaying chimeras, mutants, or giants as they found them, and burning any permanent settlement that they came across. They had long since given up trying to tame the land of the demons.

When they had sighted the great reef that Isengrim had spoken of, Espinarz turned the ship north and skirted around the hazard, Musard and Condylure using sounding lines to ensure that they did not accidentally run aground. The great danger that this would present to them all was highlighted to Reynard by the sight of silvery salt-water naga disengaging from the rocky outcroppings of the reef, where the things had apparently been sunning themselves, or perhaps hunting for gulls amongst the rocks.

It was not long before Musard's sounding line was nearly wrenched out of his hands by a sharp tug from below. The sailor released the line immediately, rather than be dragged over the side to be consumed by the things now circling the vessel like hungry sharks.

Unlike the naga of Vulp Vora, these things did not appear to be capable of speech, and they merely gazed up eerily from the water with their unblinking fish eyes. A few of them leapt through the icy waves playfully, as if inviting the sailors to join them as they flipped across the water. Tiecelin loosed a few warning shots at them from the crow's nest, and soon the naga appeared to give up their chase, though they trailed in the wake of the ship for some time before disappearing completely beneath the waves.

Again and again Reynard helped to tack the Quicksilver's sails as they slowly glided into a large cove that was concealed from the sea by great chunks of blackened basalt stones. The wind was rising, growing wild, and by the time they had moored the boat all the men's faces were red with windburn.

"Well, we did it boys," Grymbart said with gusto as the ship's anchor struck bottom, the snow in his beard making him look like a wizened geezer. "We made it through Vulp Vora alive."

"Barely," Tybalt added.

"Master Isengrim," the Captain said, ignoring Tybalt's comment, "The Quicksilver will moor here for nine days, and nine days only. Then we depart, with or without you. It is up to both you and Master Fox now to do what the Duke expects of you."

"We will leave within the hour," Isengrim informed Captain Roenel before retiring to his cabin, Reynard following close behind him.

"It is already growing dark," Reynard said as the Northerner began unbuttoning his coat. "Should we not wait for dawn?"

"We are already a day behind schedule," Isengrim replied, throwing off his coat and beginning to slip off his boots. "And it will be safer for us to travel at night, at least until we reach the road that leads to Dis."

"A day behind schedule?" Reynard repeated quizzically. "Do you have an appointment to keep?"

"Just get dressed," Isengrim replied, adding, "Please."

As Reynard slipped into his dun colored servant's ensemble, the Northerner dressed himself in the dusky gray uniform that would serve to identify him as a *heafodcarl*, a mid-ranking officer of some kind or another. Reynard had found learning the complex Calvarian hierarchy far more difficult than their language, but Isengrim assured him that the uniform's color and insignia alone would allow them considerable freedom to move about the Calvarian city . . . unless they were discovered.

When they'd finished dressing, Isengrim added one last item to Reynard's ensemble: a matching conical cap with flaps that could be affixed to cover his ears.

"What's the point of the cone?" Reynard asked as he placed the tall cap on his head.

"It is meant to demean you," Isengrim said, grinning thinly. "It is traditional."

"You know, sometimes I suspect you are making this all up as we go along," Reynard grumbled as he tied the straps of the hat tightly under his chin. He could already imagine the level of respect that the uniform would garner him.

Isengrim had already stowed his personal effects within a handsome leather rucksack, which he'd filled with books and maps written in the strange Calvarian script, as well as a writing kit complete with quills, ink jars, and sealing wax. Reynard had been taught the proper order in which it should be packed and unpacked, and how to carry it on his back without slouching, but it was terrifically heavy all the same- especially considering that he would also be burdened with a pair of bedrolls, along with his own belongings.

"Should I pack my fiddle, *laruwa?*" Reynard asked once he'd finished stowing his thieves' kit in between the lining of his own pack. "So that I may entertain the sweet maidens of your homeland?"

"Unless you look forward to having a longsword protruding from your ribs," Isengrim said briskly, "I would not recommend it."

"Is music forbidden in your country as well as drink?"

"Only that of your churlish country. If we had the time, I would take you to see a traditional Calvarian concert, and you could hear some real music."

"Are they very long?" Reynard grunted as he hefted Isengrim's pack onto his back. "I do hate long concerts."

"The best ones do often stretch over several nights."

"Perhaps it's for the best, then," Reynard said with mock disappointment. "Since we are apparently on something of a tight schedule."

"Yes, we are." Isengrim said, and then strapped on his sword and threw on his own fur-lined overcoat. "Now get moving before I whip your hide."

"Gea, laruwa," Reynard said and as they left their cabin he walked tall and correct, with the air of general distain that Isengrim had drilled into him for the past months.

The others, just finishing their evening supper, looked up as he and Isengrim passed by.

"Be back soon," Grymbart said to the pair as he lit up his pipe for an after supper smoke. "And keep safe."

"Thank you," Reynard replied. "I didn't realize you cared."

"I don't really. I just don't get paid if you die."

The big man laughed then, and slapped Reynard on the arm.

"I'm just pulling your leg, Master Fox. Come back with the gem . . . and watch your back."

"And you as well," Reynard replied, giving the man his hand. "I wouldn't want to go through all this trouble only to find you dead."

Grymbart laughed. "That's the spirit, Master Fox. That's the spirit!"

The others made their goodbyes as well: Bruin wrapped Reynard in a giant bear hug, nearly squeezing the breath from him before Grymbart made him stop. Tiecelin pecked him lightly on the cheeks- a traditional Luxian farewell.

Captain Roenel was waiting for them on deck.

"Espinarz will row you to shore," he said, indicating the skiff that Musard and Condylure were readying to lower into the frothy waves below. "Then you are on your own."

Isengrim nodded, and bowed ever so slightly. In return, the Captain removed his hat and returned the gesture, an act that prompted his men to uncover and do the same.

"Hey," Tybalt shouted at them from the crow's nest, where he had been put on watch. "Fox!"

"Yes, Tybalt?"

"Don't foul it up, alright?"

Reynard smiled. "I'll try not to."

Then he and Isengrim climbed into the skiff, and Espinarz rowed them to the Calvarian shore: a beach that had been strewn with thousands of smooth round stones.

As they landed Isengrim stepped off of the prow of the boat and took a few steps onto his native soil. The wind whipped wildly around him, stirring up his cloak and tussling his platinum locks.

"I am home," the Calvarian said in his native tongue. "You are prepared, Fox?"

"I am," Reynard replied, shifting his balance to remain upright as he stepped out of the boat.

"Then let us be off. We must travel many leagues to reach Dis. If we walk all night we can probably cover ten before dawn."

Isengrim did not wait for Reynard to respond, and began to trudge up the coast, his long legs carrying him quickly over the beach. Reynard took one last look back at the ship, and at the skiff quickly retreating from the shore, and then he followed.

* * * * * * *

By the time that the eastern sky began to turn gray with the coming of the dawn Reynard was nearly stumbling from exhaustion. His legs were certainly agile and strong from the many years that he had spent as a cat burglar, but they were unused to the rigors of a forced march, and Reynard had certainly never had to match as relentless a pace as Isengrim set.

And, Reynard grumbled inwardly as he trudged through the snow, *Isengrim does not have to haul a pack full of gear like a mule.*

By morning Reynard was so tired that he almost ran straight into his lanky companion, who had come to a sudden stop and was standing with his head crooked to one side, listening.

"This will make a suitable camp," Isengrim said. "Wait here."

Reynard nodded, panting.

The Northerner did not look at all fatigued, and Reynard could not help but resent the ease with which he navigated the nearby rocks. Did the man never tire?

Isengrim disappeared for a time, leaving Reynard alone with only the sound of the breaking surf to keep him company. He turned to look back down the coast, and could see their trail marked out clearly in the snow- but he surmised that they were still too distant from Calvarian habitation to fear discovery.

When Isengrim returned he led Reynard through a series of black basalt rocks before stopping at an escarpment that formed a convenient hollow underneath it. It was generally free of snow and, though the ground was frozen solid, it was fairly level.

Isengrim gestured towards the hollow. "Get some rest. I will keep watch until she is at her zenith."

Reynard didn't argue and, laying out his own bedroll, he nestled under the hollow, wrapping his cloak about him for warmth.

He'd hardly closed his eyes when he fell into the kind of fitful slumber that he'd grown used to as a boy. The presence of Isengrim comforted him somewhat, but it had been a long time since he'd slept out in the open, and his vague dreams were full of pursuits and captures, and the long tortures that seemed to drag on insufferably. His tormentors' faces were like the masks that the lifeless things in Carcosa had worn, but horribly familiar. Cointereau, Dolphin, Lady Moire, and in the back, behind them, the weathered face of an old woman, her eyes hollow save for the flames that burned distantly within them.

When he awoke the sky was much lighter. The Northerner had made a very small fire, and handed Reynard a piece of hardtack and a cup of boiling water.

"You made sounds in your sleep," Isengrim commented in the Southern tongue as Reynard dipped his biscuit in the steaming cup.

"Only a nightmare- nothing serious."

Isengrim moved over to the hollow himself and said, "I must sleep now. Wake me at dusk, or if you see anything unusual."

Reynard nodded and, stretching his throbbing muscles, took up a position amongst some of the rocks that afforded him a clear view of the lonely shoreline. The snowfall had ceased but the chill wind still whipped at his exposed skin as he sat through his long watch.

In the end, Isengrim awoke before the time he had appointed, and silently went about his daily ritual of shaving, and greasing his hair and face. He ate sparingly and, after relieving himself behind a rock, helped Reynard sweep away any obvious signs that the two of them had made camp there.

"Let us be off," Isengrim said when they'd finished, and though Reynard's feet ached already he did not complain as they continued their inexorable march north.

So they walked, stopping briefly now and then to reapply the thick oil to their exposed faces so that the biting wind did not crack and blister them. The tender muscles of Reynard's legs bore the dull trudge across the icy landscape better than they had the day before.

They did not keep to the rocky beach for long, and soon Isengrim led him over a barren heath whose low-growing scrub was wreathed with ice. Despite the starkness of the terrain, Reynard was glad to be rid of the sea. Too long had he been listening to the wet lap of waves from the deck of the Quicksilver, and the solid ground felt good under his feet. He also felt a good deal safer, for while their progress was slowed, they would be harder to spot here than near the roiling ocean, where he imagined they cut a stark relief against the white foam.

When the second morning came the two of them made camp again, this time in the hollow of a sparsely wooded dell that would protect them somewhat from the worst of the constantly gusting wind. Reynard was not as fatigued as he had been on the previous morn, and so he sat for a while as Isengrim set about making another small brush fire.

He could not help but observe that the tall man's normally sure hands shook somewhat as he unsuccessfully attempted to light his gathered kindling.

"Something troubling you?" Reynard asked, after Isengrim's third failed attempt.

"I am . . . nervous," Isengrim admitted, something that Reynard did not find terribly reassuring.

"Are we entering dangerous land?"

"All of Calvaria will be dangerous for us, Master Fox," Isengrim replied, "But that is not what troubles me."

"What then?"

Isengrim paused, considering. When he spoke again his voice was soft- almost vulnerable, Reynard thought.

"I have planned to return to Dis for many years now. But it is one thing to plan a thing and another to do it. Now . . . I will see her again."

Reynard thought there was something strange about the words that Isengrim had used: it seemed overly romantic for someone was normally so reserved.

"Have you missed it?" Reynard asked. "Your home?"

"No," Isengrim answered flatly, and then murmured something else in his native tongue: *"Yes."*

The fire caught then, and the two of them warmed themselves as best they could.

* * * * * * *

The third night was free of snow, and the sky was clear. When the Watcher rose Reynard found that the skull-moon's reflection off of the glistening landscape made the night seem as clear as the day, and he wondered if they might be seen as they crested dune after dune of snowcapped hillocks.

But seen by whom? He had seen no lights of any kind piercing the horizon for miles about, a fact that he found strange given their proximity to the Calvarian capital.

He prepared to ask his companion about this oddity, but stopped himself short. Isengrim had come to a halt ahead of him, and had drawn his sword. His other hand was held up in a gesture that Reynard understood demanded absolute silence.

Beyond Isengrim, just at the base of another hillock, was a small copse of conifer trees. It was towards this thicket that the Northerner was bending his gaze, though at first Reynard could make out nothing amidst the low hanging branches.

Then the wind picked up, and as it rustled the firs Reynard could make out the outline of several dark shapes, crouching in wait. They were four legged, and looked very much like dogs, except that they were far bigger than any Reynard had ever seen.

Wolves, Reynard thought at first, and then remembered every story that he had heard as a child of wargs, the most deadly of all the breeds of chimera, and his hand reached instinctively for his rapier, having momentarily forgotten that he had left it back in their cabin.

Isengrim gestured for Reynard to come to his side, and he began to creep forward.

No sooner had Reynard moved his foot then the pack began to move, several of them loping to the left and right in order to surround the two travelers.

"Remain calm," the Northerner said in a hushed voice.

"Are they wargs?" Reynard asked as Isengrim handed him his own belt knife.

"No, and they may not attack, if they have fed recently. All the same, keep your guard up, and stand your ground."

Reynard readied the Calvarian's knife, and tried to shake the feeling that it would be useless against the biting jaws of these beasts.

A large wolf padded out of the trees then, its ears flat against its head and its tail erect behind it. Its golden eyes locked with Isengrim's, as if sizing up the Northerner. Its brethren, having surrounded the two men by now, appeared to be waiting to see how their chieftain would handle these intruders.

The wolf came closer, sniffing experimentally with its keen nostrils. Isengrim kept his head level, and did not back away as the beast approached. To Reynard it briefly seemed as though two wolves faced each other, and he was comforted that he was a member of Isengrim's pack.

The wolf gave first, and its tail relaxed. It turned then, with what Reynard could have sworn was an air of indifference, and sauntered around the two men. The rest of the pack moved to follow suit, until the last of them had disappeared over the rise of a neighboring hillock.

"We are fortunate," Isengrim said, sheathing his sword.

"Surely," Reynard said as he returned Isengrim's knife. "We could have handled them. You bested that bull-headed faun without too much trouble."

"The chimeras that we faced in Vulp Vora were drugged and complacent. I would fight a hundred of them over a single Calvarian wolf any day. I have read that a hungry pack can bring down even an *auroch* when need drives them."

"What is an *auroch*?"

"A breed of cattle that roams our southern wilderness. They are far larger than the domesticated cows your people keep, and far more temperamental. But come," Isengrim said and resumed his steady pace. "I can tell you more of my homeland while we walk."

They passed through the scattered woodland in which the wolves had been lurking, shaking loose snow free from the trees' spiny branches as they brushed against them.

"I have seen no lights since we landed," Reynard said, remembering the question that had died on his lips earlier. "Is your homeland as barren as the northern shores of Solothurn?"

"All Calvarians build their homes at least partially under the earth to protect themselves from the worst of the winter's killing chill. The largest of our cities are housed entirely underground. You would have to be able to see through solid stone to catch a glimpse of the lanterns of that place."

"So, you live in caves?"

"'Cave' is far too crude a term. When you see the majesty of Dis, you will understand."

"It is no wonder that your kind are so frightfully pale," Reynard said, drawing an unamused look from Isengrim. "But how do you see without the Firebird to light the day?"

"We have our ways, Master Fox, and you will see them soon enough."

"You know," Reynard huffed, fed up with being left in the dark, "If you expect me to be of any help on this excursion *beyond* the incredibly important task of polishing your boots, you might consider being more forthcoming with information."

"What would you know?"

"Well, for one thing, you could tell me where the gem is kept. Is it locked in some deep vault, guarded by strong wards and soldiers trained to kill on sight? Or does one of your people's judges keep it in an iron crown, as they say the Demon King did?"

Isengrim twisted his head to stare at him, and laughed.

"Master Fox, the gem is kept in plain sight, unguarded, in the courtyard of the- ah, there is no name for it in your tongue, but it is a repository for art, literature, and artifacts from across the known world . . . the Hall of Knowledge, let us call it. The day that we arrive in Dis I could take you to it, and you would no doubt devise a way to remove it without much difficulty."

Reynard halted, and felt his cheeks growing suddenly hot with anger.

"Then, by the beard of Wulf," Reynard cursed, "Why am I lugging this blasted pack through the wind and snow? Why am I here at all?"

Isengrim put up both of his hands and motioned for Reynard to calm himself.

"Do not fear, Master Fox. If it were that simple a matter the Duke would not have bothered to deal with the likes of you to recover the gem he so covets."

"Go on," Reynard said.

"I am confident that stealing the gem will be a simple matter for a master burglar such as yourself . . . But once you have stolen it, my people will know that there is a thief within their midst, and every exit out of the city will be barred and watched. Then, when there is no escape, Dis itself will be searched, and every pair of eyes and ears will be our enemy."

"I can lead you into Dis, Reynard," Isengrim said as he crested a hill. "But it is you that must find a way out."

"Well, that is more like it," Reynard said, and resumed walking. "I was worried for a moment that it would be too easy."

XI

On the fourth night of their journey the moorland finally broke, and for a time they crossed a stretch of farmland divided by frozen hedgerows.

"Prepare yourself," Isengrim said. "For within a league we should come across a road that will lead us straight to Dis. Once on it we can no longer risk speaking openly, at least not until we are somewhere safe within the city. I assume my lessons have not been in vain?"

"They have not, laurwa," Reynard said in the Northern tongue.

"Then let me give you one final warning, Master Fox. Be cautious, courteous, and above all else, obedient, for though it is not unheard of for a Calvarian to keep a dark-skinned servant, there are many Calvarians who believe that even the most subservient of Southerners are not fit to live. They will look for a chance to kill you out of hand, as you might kill a dog that has gone mad. Be certain that you provide no one with the opportunity to do so."

"I will not fail you, laruwa."

Isengrim nodded, satisfied, and they pressed on.

They had only gone a little ways when Isengrim stopped and gestured silently to a point between two of the western mountain peaks, where Reynard could see what appeared to be a river winding back and forth from one crag to the next. Then Isengrim traced it farther, and Reynard realized that it was no river at all, but an elevated road that made travel through the mountains possible. It stretched across the horizon, east to west, and Reynard marveled at the time and manpower that it must have taken to construct such a thing.

They walked on until they reached this engineering marvel, and traveled within its shadow for a while. Once or twice Reynard could hear the steady clip of horses passing overhead, accompanied by a bright jingling noise that seemed oddly merry for this dark land. And, despite the many years that he had practiced deception, Reynard found himself to be nervous. Always in the past he had been able to blend into the people around him, a more reliable form of stealth than the kind he could find amongst the darkest shadows. But here his accent, his clothes, and his very skin would immediately mark him as an outsider. He did not relish the unwelcome attention that the hue of his face would bring.

It was still dark when a tall snowcapped tor appeared ahead, looming suddenly out of the thick of the blustery night. The road curved around it, but as they drew closer Reynard could see that the hill was actually a partially submerged structure that had been carved out of solid rock. What he had originally taken for the peak was a tower with a sheltered walkway from which a sentry might gaze upon the countryside for miles around.

Creeping up a snowy embankment, Reynard and Isengrim peered over the low parapet that separated the road from the slope and seeing that there was no traffic on the road they clambered over it and made for the gatehouse of the fortified inn.

Though it was the dead of night, it took Isengrim only a few sharp taps on one of the solid doors to elicit a response from within. A pale face appeared in a small iron barred window above them, and a clear voice sang out a command for the strangers to identify themselves.

Isengrim answered with his usual calm, and while Reynard could not make out all of what he said, he understood that his companion was explaining that they had traveled through the night and sought lodgings until the morning came.

This seemed to satisfy the man, and the face disappeared for a moment before one of the doors opened silently.

They passed into a dark courtyard. On their left Reynard could see the entrance to a roomy stable, while on the right a number of sleighs had been parked near an open forge. Even at this late hour a number of Calvarian men stripped to the waist were stoking hot fires with tongs and bellows.

The night watchman, who had descended to greet the guests from his post above the door, stopped in his tracks when he came close enough to see that one of the travelers was not Calvarian.

Reynard winced inwardly, expecting insults, a beating, or the outraged hue and cry of armed men as the garrison of the inn was turned out against them. Instead the watchman regained his composure and said: *"You may enter, but this black dog must be sheltered in the stable."*

"Who then will polish my boots and clean my uniform?" Isengrim said in a tone that would have read as condescending even to one who could not understand the words. As he did so he undid the clasp of his cloak to reveal the insignia that marked him as the man's superior. *"Surely you will not deny me the aid of my servant?"*

The sentry's manner changed instantly, and he bowed deeply to Isengrim.

"Forgive me, Heafodcarl," he said. *"I meant no disrespect."*

"You need not apologize," Isengrim replied. *"I should have warned you that I was bringing a trained animal with me."*

The sentry straightened, the corners of his mouth curling into a restrained smile.

Isengrim went on: *"But now you must show us to our room. I must be gone in the morning, and this one has work to do."*

The sentry bowed again and led them across the courtyard to another set of doors that were far grander than the ones that guarded the exterior. Figures of men hunting wolves had been carved into the chestnut-colored facing, and the brass door handles had been painstakingly decorated.

As they entered the inn's common room, Reynard recalled Isengrim's words concerning the beauty of his homeland, and now that he could see it for himself he had to admit that the man had spoken truly-even the richly cluttered glut of the Duke's palace paled in comparison. It was not merely that the cozy, fire-warmed chamber was supplied with handsome leather-backed chairs and divans, or that the lack of windows was made up for by beautiful oil lamps that gave off a warm steady glow. Rather, it was that there was a uniformity in design that pervaded every object in the place, from the table on which had been spread the unfolded board and multi-colored pieces of what Reynard guessed was an unfinished game of *campraeden*, to the bell and ledger that sat on the front desk of the small office adjacent to the door. Everything was placed so as to balance the room, and even the clutter of the Calvarian night clerk's records had an order that could not have been accidental.

The night clerk was an auburn-haired woman wearing a chalk white uniform. She wore no makeup on her face, tight fitting trousers instead of a skirt, and her locks were trimmed so short that Reynard had taken her for a man until she spoke.

"Name, and destination?" she asked Isengrim before icily shifting her dark eyes towards Reynard, who was careful to avert his own gaze respectfully.

"Foalan," Isengrim replied, *"Heafodcarl, Third Class. I am expected in the capital for the ae-nemniendlic."*

Reynard did not understand Isengrim's last words, but the clerk seemed satisfied with them, and she scratched a series of notes into her log. She did not seem particularly interested in asking Reynard what his name was, and after a moment she rang the bell that sat at her side.

An older Calvarian man, gray haired and weathered in the face but still spry, appeared within moments of the summons. He had a thick ring of keys hanging from his belt, and held a large oil lantern in one of his gnarled hands.

"Seven," the clerk said, and then the porter led them through the common room and up a dark flight of stairs. They climbed two floors before coming to a door marked with the Calvarian rune for the number seven, and then the porter unlocked the door and motioned for them to enter.

As Isengrim made a show of inspecting the room, a sparsely decorated place with no window, Reynard placed his pack at the foot of the room's single bed. The porter used a wick to light the candelabra that adorned a writing desk, then bowed and left them to settle in, closing the door to their room behind him.

Reynard noted that unlike the inns of Calyx, the door to their room had no lock.

Isengrim brought his finger up to his lips, but he hardly needed to remind Reynard to continue to play his role. Accordingly, Reynard went about the business of cleaning the Northerner's clothes with a brush, and applied black polish to his fine leather boots as Isengrim retired for bed. When he was finally done he leaned himself against the wall and caught what little sleep that he could in a room with no lock on the door.

* * * * * * *

Reynard awoke to the sound of a bell tolling. He was bleary eyed and more tired than he had been before he had gone to sleep, and for a futile moment he pulled his conical cap more tightly over his ears and tried to block out the noise so that he might catch a few more seconds of sleep.

Isengrim was already up, and had lit the room's candles so that he might properly groom himself. Reynard moved to join him, but Isengrim waved him off. Staying true to character, Reynard moved back towards the door and waited for his companion to finish greasing his hair.

"Wait here for me and clean yourself," the Northerner said with authority as he dressed. *"I will have something sent up for you to eat."*

"Yes, laruwa."

Isengrim opened the door. The dim stairwell was already alive with the sound of activity coming from above and below, as the inn's guests and staff began to move about their daily routines.

"Be certain to show the staff the same respect that you show me," Isengrim warned him, and then turned to join the other pale-skinned men and women who were making their way downstairs.

Reynard shut the door and went about his own morning rituals, cleaning his face with cold water and being sure to take extra care to properly trim his goatee and to clean and polish his own uniform.

As he was engaged with these tasks there was a brisk knock at the door that heralded the arrival of a maid: a rather handsome young woman whose skin was nearly as pale as her uniform. In her gloved hands she carried a wooden plate covered with a white cloth that she placed on the writing desk before going about the business of tidying up the room.

Normally, Reynard would have spoken pleasantly with this girl, and might have learned much gossip from her about the inn's other guests, but now he kept his mouth shut and refrained from looking at her as she went about her business. For her part she returned the favor. One might not have guessed that she was aware of his presence at all but for the fact that she appeared to be actively avoiding him.

While the maid worked Reynard ate the fresh bread and strong smelling cheese that had been provided for him, and though it was bland by the standards of his homeland it was certainly far better than the mealy hardtack that he had been subsisting on for the past few weeks. He cleaned his plate and neatly folded the napkin that had been provided for him as Isengrim had shown him.

"I must clean the floor," the Calvarian maid said flatly, a subtle command for him to leave the room.

Reynard stepped into the hall as the woman hauled in a pail of water and a scrub brush, and stood stock still as a young pair of armed Calvarian men in gray army uniforms strode down the stairwell. One of the youths frowned at him as he passed, but did not stop to molest him.

Still, when they had reached the next level down Reynard heard them muttering to each other.

"Who was that black dog?" one of the voices queried, obviously annoyed. Reynard could tell that he would soon grow tired of that particular epithet.

"Did you not recognize him?" the other responded lightly. *"A great aeoeling of the dark lands?"*

"Ah," the first voice purred laughingly. *"My memory must be failing me. But where is his handscolu? Where is his corona?"*

Reynard did not recognize all of the words they used, but he could tell when he was being mocked, and he began to relish the idea of dealing these proud and disdainful people an insult they would not soon forget.

The maid finished her work in the room and left Reynard with the stern admonishment to wait in the hall until the floor had time to dry. So he waited, an hour perhaps, maybe longer, listening to the distant sounds of men and women shouting as the Calvarians went through some sort of intense morning ritual.

At last the shouting stopped. Isengrim returned sometime thereafter, the aroma of savory meats and vegetables clinging faintly to his clothes.

"Ready my pack," he said. *"We are leaving."*

Once he'd finished they returned to the foyer, where Calvarian men and women dressed in various shades of tan and gray were passing the time as the sleds in the courtyard were hitched by white suited grooms. Through one of the other doors Reynard could see the inn's communal dining hall, where a few of the guests still sat, enjoying steaming bowls of broth as they warmed themselves next to an enormous roaring fireplace. Somewhere beyond he could hear the clatter of the kitchen staff as they cleared plates and silverware away for cleaning.

Eventually a large Calvarian wearing a bulky white fur coat entered, a tall shako tucked under one arm and a coiled signal whip clutched in his hand. He strode over to the clerk, bowed slightly, and spoke one succinct word:

"*Dis.*"

The female clerk nodded and immediately began calling out names, thumbing through the log with dexterous fingers. 'Foalan,' Isengrim's false name, was the first one to be called.

Isengrim, and nine others from the foyer gathered in a queue near the door, among them the two soldiers who had openly mocked Reynard on the stairs. Reynard stood to the side, as he was considered a part of Isengrim's luggage.

When all of the passengers had been accounted for by the clerk the large man led the queue through the courtyard and out into the suddenly blinding light of day, where a large and well-polished horse drawn sleigh awaited them. Reynard marveled inwardly at the size and obvious strength of the Calvarian horses, all of which were nearly twice the size of the Southern steeds that he was accustomed to.

One by one the Calvarians climbed into the spacious vehicle, whose seats had been cushioned with leather. A pair of porters loaded the luggage into a compartment in the back of the sleigh, including their own packs.

Reynard was momentarily uncertain of how he should proceed until he saw Isengrim subtly motioning for him to follow. As he approached the sleigh the driver glowered at him, his face an unrestrained mask of distaste. He guessed that this man might be one of the few that longed to see him killed, and he redoubled his caution.

The driver used his coiled whip to indicate the cramped space amongst the baggage where Reynard would have to sit, giving Reynard a hard shove that nearly tripped him. With practiced grace he caught himself in time, and made a small bow that asked forgiveness for his momentary 'clumsiness.'

The driver's eyes narrowed with disappointment, but he relented, and stood by motionless as Reynard stepped up into the back of the sleigh. Once Reynard had settled in, the driver covered most of the baggage compartment with a tarp, leaving a space for Reynard's head and upper shoulders. Then he placed the shako atop his head, vaulted himself into the driver's seat, and with a light crack of his whip he set the team of horses tethered to the sleigh into motion.

It was oddly quiet as they raced eastward along the high road that the Calvarians had built. The only noise came from the jingle of the tear shaped bells that were hung around each horse's thick neck, for the passengers seemed content to sit and gaze at the scenery as they traveled. Reynard welcomed the silence, and closed his weary eyes in order to catch some much-needed sleep.

* * * * * * *

He slept very deeply, and without dreaming, waking with a carefully stifled yawn to find that the Firebird was already nearing the tip of the western mountains and that they had nearly reached their destination.

Ahead of them, a league or two distant, the road was blocked by an imposing fortress that stood astride a series of triangular outworks, so that each section of the wall was overlooked by another, higher wall. Reynard admired the design: an invader that managed to breach the first layer could be pelted with arrows from the next, and so on. It would take quite the host to conquer this place.

The elevated road forked repeatedly as they approached these defensive ramparts, and the road traffic along those causeways increased with every passing moment that they raced along, but the driver kept their sleigh on the straight path that led to the main gates.

Beyond the high walls Reynard could see again the jagged peaks of the mountainous island of Thule and, though he could not see it, he knew that they had reached the sea, and the crossing to Dis.

As they approached the massive outer gatehouse the driver of their sleigh reined in his team, slowing them to a near crawl. Two dozen Calvarians stood at attention both above and below as each vehicle that entered the city was brought to a halt and examined by a third squad of soldiers.

After an interminable wait, during which the Firebird sank behind the western mountains, it was at last their turn to be admitted to the city. A quartet of soldiers stalked around the sleigh, while an officer asked their driver a short series of questions.

At the sight of him one of the soldiers called out for his superior, who strode around the sleigh to frown at Reynard.

"Whose servant is this?"

"*He is mine, præfost,*" Isengrim replied, having turned slightly to face the Calvarian officer. "*I have all of the proper papers for him if you would like to see them.*"

The officer held out his hand to accept the forged documents that Isengrim had pulled out of his inner coat pocket. He examined them, looking back and forth between the documents and Reynard.

"*Tell me . . .* Fox," the officer said, saying his name as if it left a bad taste in his mouth, "*Do you serve your master well?*"

Reynard's head bowed very deeply, and he called up one of the stock phrases that Isengrim had taught him. "*I do as my master commands me, liffrea,*" Reynard said, using the Calvarian word that meant 'lord-of-life.' "*And may he slay me if I do less.*"

The officer nodded, satisfied. "*Move along!*" he barked to the driver, and the soldiers split their ranks to admit them into the fortress.

* * * * * * *

Once they had passed beneath the main gates the sleigh came to a halt in front of a cavernous archway. Through this portal Reynard could see a hand-worked avenue wide enough for six carriages abreast to travel in comfort along a lantern lit road that plunged straight into the earth.

Reynard was so taken aback by the engineering skill that must have been necessary to construct such a marvel that he almost failed to notice the thing that was chained to the side of the shaft's entrance. He had at first taken it to be a statue that had been built into the second layer of fortifications, a grotesque decoration of some kind meant to intimidate, but then one of its two heads moved to follow him as he climbed out of the sleigh, and he realized that it was most certainly alive.

It was a warg: a mutant that the Calvarians must have captured in Vulp Vora, and Reynard thought it likely that it might be the largest of its kind in the known world, as it dwarfed even the powerful steeds that had drawn their sleigh. Two jackal-like heads sprung from its torso, the hindquarters of which were covered in reptilian scales. Bony spines protruded from its powerful back, and the end of its sinuous tail was decorated by a row of murderous looking spikes.

Worst, though, were its eyes, which displayed a clear and openly hostile intelligence.

Reynard could not venture to guess why the Calvarians kept such a monster imprisoned here, and he burned to ask someone to explain this bizarre scene to him. The beast certainly looked uncomfortable lying in the cold air, despite the great braziers that had been lit around it. A great chain restricted its movement to a semicircular stone platform, but the padlock that hung from its neck suggested that the beast could be freed to terrorize the entire courtyard. For now though it appeared content to lie with its lizard-like hindquarters nestled near one of the blazing fires, and to watch the passengers of the sleigh disembark.

Another series of white-clothed porters rushed to unload the sleigh, and at Isengrim's command one of them picked up his pack and hauled it over to one of the dozen or so horse drawn coaches that were arrayed just within the shelter of the tunnel. As before, Reynard was made to sit with the luggage, only now he found himself sitting on top of the coach, just behind the coachman. Isengrim and most of the passengers of the sleigh climbed inside the spacious covered compartment, the interior of which had been done over in red velvet cloth. When all were safely aboard the driver clicked his tongue, lightly whipped the horses' reins, and they were off, speeding down the tunnel at a considerable pace.

Reynard took one last look at the mutant warg, whose heads had sunk down to rest on the cold cobblestones of its cramped quarters, and then the sight of the chained monster was dwarfed by the wonders of the Calvarian tunnel. Great murals covered the marble and limestone walls, scenes of conquests and battles, dying generals held by tearful attendants, and Calvarian maidens whose ivory skin gleamed starkly against the blackness of the underworld.

And as they descended Reynard saw that the great passage was honeycombed with as many smaller thoroughfares and walkways as a proper city. Through yawning portals Reynard could make out vast granaries and storerooms, gore soaked butcheries and vast rooms whose stalls were host to entire herds of cattle and swine.

Nor were they the only vehicle speeding along this steadily descending passageway. Other covered coaches carried passengers up towards the surface, and wagons nearly overflowing with crates, barrels, burlap sacks, freshly slaughtered meat, and other sundry goods were in the process of being dragged by teams of great black bulls down into the depths.

Down and down they went, until Reynard was certain that they might be a league or two under the earth. He was acutely aware of the massive weight of the rock above them, and even the enormous pillars that lined the subterranean road seemed paltry by comparison. Then the passage leveled out, and they sped for a time along an ominous stretch of a great, pillared hall. With a thrill he realized that they were most likely under the sea floor itself.

At the end of the hall the carriage passed through another open gate, and then the passage began to widen, before suddenly opening onto the vast cavern that was home to the city of Dis.

Of all the terrible wonders that Reynard had seen on this journey, this was by far the most magnificent, and he realized why Isengrim had taken some offense to his use of the word 'cave' when describing his homeland.

Dis had the appearance of having been carved out of a single piece of bone-white marble, its skyline dominated by a great central spire whose spiked crenellations shone like silver. Off of this citadel thrust a series of buttresses that connected it to both the great walls that ringed the city and to each of the six smaller spires that stood sentinel over the dark water of the lake. Seen from the yawning darkness directly above them, Reynard guessed that the city might resemble a snowflake, albeit one of pale stone and gleaming steel.

The city had been built atop a manmade lake, and the reflection from the innumerable lamps of the place made it seem as though Dis had a darker twin that lay sleeping under black waters. The lake itself was fed from spillways that had been cut into the cavern's walls, and it was contained by a colossal dam that stretched across the far side of the cavern. Beyond loomed a dark gulf, and Reynard was awed by the suggestion of the unseen depths beyond.

Sleek ships plied the lake's calm surface, ferrying men and materiel back and forth from a series of wharfs that stretched towards the city like grasping fingers. The carriage made its way swiftly towards one of these many wharfs, coming to a stop alongside an elaborate slip that housed a ferry equipped with a pair of massive water wheels.

As they came to a halt a number of white uniformed stevedores began to assemble to load the carriage's luggage onto the ship. Their mechanical precision distantly reminded Reynard of the horrible, empty guardians of Carcosa, and for a moment he did not know which of the two he found more chilling.

Isengrim stepped out of the carriage first and with a subtle gesture he motioned for Reynard to disembark as well. He did so gladly, his arm muscles having grown quite sore from having spent so long clutching onto the railing of the carriage top. Here, at least, the Calvarian city seemed alive, for the air was full of the murmur of voices and cobblestones rang with the almost constant clatter of hooves and booted feet.

Isengrim led them to one of the gangplanks that allowed access to the lower deck of the ship, where they waited to board. Isengrim's rank seemed to have little influence here, for they stood behind a white haired matron in a dusky tan uniform ushering along a crowd of Calvarian children, the first that Reynard had yet seen.

Much like the lowest members of Calvarian society these youths, who could not have been more than eight or nine summers old, were dressed in white, though their uniforms were unadorned by badge or trim. At the sight of him the children began to murmur, and despite the harsh words of their mistress their volume rose exponentially.

Again and again Reynard could hear the Calvarian word that meant 'Southerner,' and he was interested to note that the children appeared delighted by his presence. *Perhaps*, he thought, *they have never seen a dark skinned man in this sunless place.*

The elderly matron, her patience obviously dwindling, strode over to Isengrim with incredible grace for a woman of her age and asked, with superb politeness, if he might remove his servant from sight until the children were aboard. To Reynard's surprise Isengrim flatly refused, and the matron went back to her duty without a hint of complaint, even going so far as to thank Isengrim for his time.

Such is the power of rank here, Reynard thought. *The Duke himself would envy such unquestioning respect.*

The children's enthusiasm for Reynard waned soon thereafter, for he did little to amuse them besides standing respectfully at Isengrim's side. He wondered bemusedly what they expected him to do- perhaps to leap out at them like some monster out of a Calvarian story, or dance, sing, and make improper advances on any of the older girls present.

Their children at least must be taught to hate us, he thought sadly.

As the youths boarded, their chaperone herded them onto the top tier of the ferry, and then Isengrim strode up the gangplank. Reynard followed him, nearly unable to restrain himself from gaping at the gleaming white city that lay across the water.

The blow that struck him down took him nearly by surprise, and it required all of Isengrim's conditioning for him to not dodge or retaliate in any way. The force of it threw him to the floor of the deck, his head reeling from the injury that had been dealt him.

"This boat is bound for Dis!" a cracked and aged voice shouted at him. *"And it is meant for the true of blood, not dogs such as you!"*

Above, Reynard could hear the Calvarian children shrieking with delight, and the voice of their chaperone shouting for quiet. He scrambled to crouch into a position of incredibly deep submission, a series of apologies ready on his lips, when the man struck him in the square of his back. He collapsed forward, to communicate that he had been bested, and tensed his muscles for the next impact.

It never came. Instead he heard Isengrim's voice, speaking calmly.

"You are damaging my servant, sir," he said. *"It would be most inconvenient if he were permanently injured, as they are very hard to train properly."*

"My apologies," the aged voice replied, gasping now. *"I did not realize that he belonged to you, Heafodcarl. Please forgive me."*

Reynard glanced carefully upwards. His assailant was a narrow-faced old man armed with a thick staff- the ferry master Reynard guessed.

"I do not know that I should, sir," Isengrim went on, *"As it seems that you forget your place. I should hate to think that I would have to bring this before one of the blood-guard."*

"Heafodcarl, please forgive my actions. He is only a Southerner."

"That is true, sir, but he is also my property," Isengrim said with a good deal of irritation. *"Fox, you may rise."*

Reynard picked himself carefully off of the deck of the ferry, ignoring the angry welts that were no doubt rising up on his injured back. Once he had gained his feet he bowed to his attacker, and to Isengrim, and then stepped backwards so that he was effectively out of the way.

"He does not appear to be seriously injured," Isengrim said after taking a few cursory glances at Reynard. *"I think perhaps we can forget this matter. But do not-"*

Isengrim's voice halted in mid sentence, and Reynard felt a chill run up his spine when he saw the source of his companion's sudden silence.

A man had appeared at the bottom of the gangplank, the men and women on the wharf having split ranks to make way for him. He was nearly as tall as Isengrim himself, and his hair was as pale as corn silk. He wore a fine sword at his side, and his uniform was black and trimmed at the collar with red.

A blood-guard.

"What is going on here?" he asked, striding up the gangplank with an almost feline grace. *"Who dares to disturb the peace of Dis?"*

The blood-guard rested his left hand on the hilt of his sword, and glanced from man to man with the same calm intensity that Reynard was used to seeing in Isengrim's eyes. He decided that it must be a common trait amongst these fearsome sentinels.

Isengrim stepped forward slightly and bowed his head. *"Forgive me, sir, but this is only a small matter, and not worthy of your attention."*

At the sound of Isengrim's voice the blood-guard paused. Reynard's heart beat wildly within his chest as he turned to regard both him and his Northern companion.

At least he is young, Reynard noted with some relief, seeing now that the man's face was smooth and unblemished. He would only have been a child when Isengrim was still one of his order.

The blood-guard directed his attention fully towards Isengrim, lifting his face up with a gloved hand until he was face to face with the blond haired man. His companion kept his focus far from the deep blue eyes dissecting him. Reynard could almost imagine the blood-guard's mind working like clockwork behind his intense stare.

"That is for me to decide," the blood-guard said at last, releasing Isengrim's face. *"Tell me, Heafodcarl, what happened here?"*

Isengrim, acting appropriately chastised, replied honestly, *"This naca-larow found my servant had done him offense, and struck him."*

"Is this true?" the blood-guard said, directing his comment to the old ferry master, who bowed to the man so deeply that Reynard half expected him to fall over. *"Did you harm this man's servant?"*

"Yes, sir," the old man said, his voice quavering now. *"But I did not know that he belonged to the-"*

"And did anyone else see this happen?" the blood-guard asked the crowd, cutting the ferry master off in mid-sentence.

"Yes, sir," answered another passenger, a laborer with a leather satchel. *"I saw it all from here."*

"Very well," the blood-guard said, reaching into his coat and pulling out a leather bound booklet and a short black instrument tipped with a metal quill. *"What is your name, naca-larow?"*

"Vargan, naca-larow forty four," the ferry master answered with resignation.

The blood-guard scratched out this information into his booklet with his odd writing utensil, speaking as he did so, *"Then, Vargan, naca-larow forty four, I will expect you tomorrow at the sixth bell. Am I understood?"*

"Yes, sir."

"Then return to your duties." With that the blood-guard dismissed the ferry master and turned to Isengrim, moving so that he no longer impeded access to the ship's gangplank. The bustle of the boarding passengers attempting to make up for lost time erupted around them. Reynard hardly noticed, for each moment that they spent with the blond man made him feel more certain that they had been caught.

"Your name?" the blood-guard asked Isengrim, his writing utensil ready in his hand.

"Foalan, sir," Isengrim answered. *"Heafodcarl, third class."*

The blood-guard did not record Isengrim's name, a fact that made Reynard slightly uncomfortable. *"And what business do you have in Dis?"*

"I am under orders to arrive at the inburg-campraeden, where I will deliver a full report concerning the Southern Kingdoms."

"May I see your orders?"

Isengrim produced his forged documents, which the blood-guard thumbed through leisurely.

"I see you serve under Latteowa Skoll," the blood-guard said when he had finished. *"An excellent man, by all accounts."*

"Yes, sir."

"And yet I seem to recall that he forbids his men from the practice of keeping the niderlic men of the South as servants. Is this not the case?"

"That is true, sir," Isengrim replied without missing a beat. *"Though exceptions are sometimes made. Due to my own duties I have had constant need of a cierran-notere, and our own resources have been stretched to the limit."*

"A cierran-notere?" the blood-guard mused, and turned to Reynard. *"So you can speak our language?"*

"Yes, liffrea," Reynard said and bowed properly.

"What is your name?"

"My name is Fox, liffrea."

"'Fox' ... ah. A foa, no?" The blood-guard smiled faintly. *"And how did you enter your master's service, 'Fox?'"*

"I am an exile, liffrea," As Reynard spoke the words he saw Isengrim's brow raise considerably. *"My own people cast me out, liffrea."*

"And now you serve their enemies?" the blood-guard asked, his eyes flicking momentarily towards Isengrim.

"That is correct, sir."

"Then you are indeed the lowest of a low people, 'Fox.' A man should stand by his own kind . . . even if he is only a breed of dog."

The blood-guard's reprimand had been delivered without a hint of passion, but Reynard noticed that the muscles at the corner of the blood-guard's face were twitching involuntarily.

He is holding something back, Reynard decided. *But what? Rage at the sight of an 'inferior?' Or something else?*

"See to it that your servant causes no further disturbances, Heafodcarl Third Class Foalan," the blood-guard said to Isengrim as he put his book away. *"It would be a shame to have to kill such a well trained 'Fox.'"*

"Indeed, sir," Isengrim replied briefly, bowing as the blond man dismissed him.

The blood-guard had just reached the gangplank once again when he turned back to Isengrim and cleared his throat.

"I think, Heafodcarl, that I might enjoy attending your lecture at the inburg-campraeden. When do you expect to deliver your report?"

"In three days," Isengrim answered with another bow. *"After the ae-nemniendlic has ended."*

"I look forward to it," the blood-guard said, and then he descended down the gangplank. As he did so the ferry cast off from the wharf and began to make its way across the lake, towards the rapidly approaching splendor of Dis.

XII

The ferry glided through an arched gateway that had been cut into the city's wall, and entered a subterranean dockyard that was crawling with white uniformed men and women unloading barges laden with cuts of butchered meat, sacks of meal, and great wheels of cheese. Gantries hung from the ceiling, allowing access to cranes that had been installed along the interior walls.

Reynard, who had worked on Calyx's docks as Rovel, had to admire the Calvarians' eye for efficiency, noting the speed with which incoming foodstuffs were placed onto a waiting line of handcarts and rolled away. Also close at hand were carts carrying sacks, barrels, jugs, and even heaped up piles of freshly cleaned animal bones that Reynard assumed would be loaded onto the empty vessels and shipped back to the dockyard on the opposite shore.

The ferry slid into the empty dock that awaited it, emptying quickly once the gangplanks had been secured into place. As Reynard stepped off the boat he caught the old ferry master glowering at him, but the Calvarian did not raise his cane to strike again.

There were no coaches waiting for them here, nor were they greeted by any porters, so Reynard took up their luggage, and followed Isengrim up a wide ramp that brought them to the city's first ward.

At once Reynard was struck by the vast differences between Dis and Calyx. His city had been cobbled together over centuries, each district overlapping or replacing another as each reigning Duke had seen fit, so that its avenues and wards were riddled with smaller streets and newer districts were often bisected by claustrophobic alleyways that opened onto ancient squares from the days of the kings of Aquilia. Strangers in Calyx could easily lose themselves within this maze, easy prey for the footpads that lurked there.

Dis, however, had clearly been meticulously planned, and if indeed any alterations had been made to the city over the years, they had been blended into the work as a whole so that nothing looked odd or out of place. Each building and thoroughfare appeared to have been placed so as to maximize efficiency without sacrificing style and comfort. No trees grew here nor any flower, for want of the light of the Firebird, but in their place the Calvarians had set graceful posts that had been expertly carved out of wood and stone so that they resembled trees, and from their boughs hung the pearly lanterns that lit the city, hissing softly as whatever strange fire that was held within them burned.

But despite its beauty Dis had a lonely, deserted quality to it. Each side street Reynard passed was empty of traffic, and there was none of the ordinary hue and cry that he had grown used to as a child: no fishwife or merchant hawked their wares, no children played in the back alleys, and the corners were free of beggars and priestesses. The only signs of life were the silent figures that rushed from place to place on whatever errand had brought them out of doors, and the fragrant smoke that rose from the wide chimneys that graced each and every structure.

Eventually they reached a fortified gate that led to the city's second ward. As Isengrim stopped to deal with the sentinels Reynard admired the banner that hung over the central archway, an intricate thing that bore the emblem of an iron chalice ringed with rubies.

Reynard found that there was something curious in the way that the Calvarians stared at him when they thought he was not looking, almost as if they expected him to drop his act and walk on all fours, and Reynard noticed that none of the other Calvarians that walked the streets were subjected to any such questions as the ones that were directed at Isengrim. But of course, he knew that it was not Isengrim who was under scrutiny at all, but himself.

I terrify them! he realized, remembering for a moment the maid that had cleaned their room that morning. *A single Southerner walks amongst them, but you would think I was a chimera from the way they react . . .*

When they were admitted to the second ward Reynard surmised that it must serve as the workspace and living quarters of the engineers, for almost every adult Calvarian they encountered wore tan, and many were busy at work at open-air forges or bent over woodwork with sets of fine tools. Some of the workshops they passed were full of white-clothed children, most of whom were diligently sketching out chalk-lined schematics on tablets made out of slate as gray haired men and women walked amongst them, inspecting their work with a calculating eye.

Soon they neared the gate to the inner ward of the city, a place apparently set aside for recreation judging from the number of increasingly elaborate courts that were overlooked by rows of marble seating.

As they passed a pavilion-like structure in which tables had been placed around a stone fire pit, Isengrim made a sudden turn that led them away from the main road and onto one of the currently unoccupied side streets.

After traveling several blocks he turned again, this time into an even smaller connecting passage that looked as if it were seldom used. A stairway cut into the pavement there, nestled alongside the blank face of a rectangular building and protected by stone guardrails.

Without hesitation Isengrim descended, and Reynard found himself nearly jogging as he tried to keep up with the man.

The stair wound back on itself several times, opening at one point onto an underground kitchen that was a beehive of activity. Isengrim continued down however, and Reynard found himself wondering just how far the Calvarians had bored into the earth, and whether they would go on descending until they reached the secret fire of creation that Sphinx carried within her womb.

The stairs did not lead anywhere so spectacular, however, and instead brought them to a bare stone passageway that appeared to stretch endlessly in either direction, its length broken occasionally by intersecting passages. Hissing lamps sprouted from the walls every few yards, but their light was dim.

Isengrim stood for a moment and seemed to consider their options before going down the right hand passage. After they had passed three passages he turned right again, and then the first possible left.

They followed this corridor for some time, until coming to an intersection where one of the passages was blocked by a gate. Beyond the portal's ironwork Reynard could see little, for the lamps beyond had not been lit.

Isengrim turned to Reynard, looking him in the eye for the first time since they had scrambled up the embankment and onto the Calvarian's high road. The Northerner traced a finger around the sturdy padlock that held the gate closed, then handed him his knife.

Reynard nodded and removed both of the packs he carried, painfully aware of the way that the noise of tearing seams echoed off of the walls as he cut them open.

When he had at last freed his set of lock picks he went to work, marveling at the detail that had been set into a padlock that he doubted many of the citizens of Dis would ever see. He soon found that it was as excellently functional as it was beautiful, possessing numerous tumblers that had him retrying pick after pick before it finally sprang open.

Reynard had just finished removing the last of his tools from the lock when he heard footsteps approaching from somewhere nearby.

"Hide," Isengrim whispered to him, closing the trunk smoothly.

The half dozen men who appeared around the corner wore military gray, and when they saw a strange man standing in the shadowy hallway they flinched.

"*Halt,*" Isengrim said, taking the initiative. The Calvarian soldiers stiffened at the sound of a voice of authority, and when they saw Isengrim's uniform they saluted smartly.

Isengrim spoke quickly, so fast that Reynard could barely make out what was said, but he could tell that his companion was barraging the men with questions concerning patrol schedules, names of their commanding officers, and possibly even the poor quality of light in the tunnels. As he did so he occasionally motioned towards the unlocked gate and the dark passage beyond.

"*Look at this,*" Isengrim said and walked over to the gate, snatching up the open padlock and showing it to one of the men, a junior officer of some kind. "*This padlock was loose when I found it. Does your patrol take you through this gate?*"

"*No, sir,*" the soldier replied nervously. "*That is prafost Tunstall's watch.*"

Isengrim's eyes narrowed as though he was weighing the soldier's words.

"*Very well. You are dismissed, prafost.*"

The soldiers saluted again, clearly relieved, and continued on their patrol. As they passed, Isengrim replaced the padlock on the gate and snapped it shut.

When he could no longer hear the footsteps, Isengrim looked up at Reynard, who was pressed against the ceiling of the passage, lodged directly between two large support beams.

"Did you have to relock the gate?" Reynard whispered softly as Isengrim helped him down.

Isengrim nodded. "It would have looked suspicious if I had not done so."

Reynard nodded and retrieved his pick set from the front of his uniform, going back to work on the padlock. As he worked he smiled. It felt good to talk openly, if only briefly. The silence he was forced to maintain had been harder to bear than he had expected, especially when he had so many questions. He admitted that he might have even welcomed Tybalt's company, if only to hear insults that were in his own language.

* * * * * * *

Reynard felt rather at home in the absolute darkness of the undercity, for it reminded him of the maze of storm sewers that he had once used to cover his tracks before the Duke had caught him, and for a while he daydreamed that he was returning to his well-guarded apartment above the warehouse in Calyx. Perhaps out of habit Reynard ran his fingers along the wall as they walked, silently counting the number of passages.

After they had traveled a fair distance, Isengrim stopped and fumbled for a moment in the dark. Reynard heard a dull hiss and then a series of clicks, like those of an insect.

A flame erupted to life, blinding Reynard for a moment. When his eyes had adjusted he saw that Isengrim had somehow lit one of the lamps, which now sputtered faintly. They were at another intersection of corridors, each of which looked identical.

"My apologies," Isengrim whispered. "I need to catch my bearings."

"What is this place?" Reynard asked as Isengrim gazed for a moment down each corridor. "A maze?"

"It is one part of the barracks of the city's garrison. And judging by its lack of traffic I would say that things have not changed very much since my days in the blood-guard."

"How so?"

"Dis was built to house and feed six whole regiments: some sixty thousand troops, not including officers. But it has been many centuries since the city has come under direct attack by any outside threat, and its garrison is kept at a mere fraction of that number."

Isengrim returned to the lamp and twisted a leaf shaped knob that somehow snuffed out the flame.

"There should be a sleeping quarter just along this corridor," Isengrim said as he resumed walking. "With an attached bathing chamber, and armory. We should be safe there for awhile."

Isengrim was not mistaken, for a few moments later Reynard heard the noise of his guide operating a latch, and then felt a disturbance in the air as a door swung open. They passed through the opening and Isengrim shut the door softly.

When the first of the old lamps flickered to life Reynard saw that they were in a rather austere room lined with three tiers of stone bunks. The place was equipped with tables and chairs, and one wall had a series of cupboards and cabinets built into it. A large mosaic made up of interlocking circular geometric shapes decorated the floor, and through arched openings in the walls Reynard could see another chamber dominated by a recessed section of the floor intended for bathing.

Isengrim sat down on one of the bunks, and swiped at his eyes tiredly.

Reynard felt the weariness of the day as well. It wasn't only his arms that were tired: his entire body ached. How hard it was to simply walk and stand without a moment to relax his muscles! Still, he was alive, and that was enough for now.

"We have done well," Isengrim said as he stripped off his traveling coat. "So far."

"How long do we rest?" Reynard asked, setting down their packs.

"Until dawn."

"And how will you know when the morrow comes in this lightless place?" Reynard said as he began to strip off the outer layers of his clothes, which had become stifling now that they were far underground.

"I will know," Isengrim said, and tossed Reynard his bedroll.

"These lamps," Renyard said, inspecting the flame that hissed weirdly within the glass bulb. "How do they work?"

"My people have long been miners," Isengrim replied, and began to polish his boots. "There are certain vapors, stones, and even oils found under the earth that burn when lit. These lamps are attached to tubes that run down to a large workshop that produces all of the light for the city."

Reynard stretched himself out on a bunk opposite Isengrim, the bedroll serving as a cushion for his head.

"Do these passages run underneath the entire city?" Reynard asked.

"They do," Isengrim replied. "And I used to know them quite well. But if you are thinking of using them as an escape route I would advise against it. All of the sections on the outer ring are occupied night and day."

"But what was the point of building those city walls above if an enemy could just slip underneath them?" Reynard asked. "Or are those only for show?"

"If the city ever came under direct attack, the different wards of the undercity would be isolated from one another in order to force intruders onto the streets."

"Isolated," Reynard said skeptically. "By locked gates?"

Isengrim shook his head. "Those are merely meant to help contain the work crews that clean the barracks and service tunnels. The real barriers are made of solid blocks of stone, and can be dropped into place from above. You couldn't see it in the dark, but we passed underneath one when we entered this part of the undercity."

"And I take it that the gem is somewhere in the innermost ward?"

"Correct."

Reynard stood up and began to pace around the room. Isengrim looked up from his work and watched his companion circle the chamber, his mouth moving slightly as he whispered to himself.

"So, if I understand everything correctly," Reynard said as he came to a halt, "After we steal the gem we need to sneak our way past three heavily defended city wards full of enemies, commandeer a boat and cross a lake without being seen, get back to the surface and bypass another fortified gate, and hope that we do so before they release that two-headed warg they have. And all of this we must do before the Quicksilver is discovered, or the crew gives us up for dead and abandons us here."

"Yes," Isengrim said. "That is all."

Reynard sat down heavily and began to rub his temples. "I could use a drink."

"I'm afraid I cannot oblige you," Isengrim said. "But I can offer you some good news."

"And that is?"

"We can safely abandon the heavier of the two packs. It has served its purpose."

"Oh," Reynard said under his breath as the Northerner rummaged through his rucksack, retrieving only their essential gear. "That *is* a relief, isn't it?"

"You are beginning to sound like Tybalt," Isengrim said without humor. "It does not suit you."

"Sorry," Reynard said, "But you might have told me more about the city before we had only a single day to steal the gem."

"There was no way for me to be certain that Dis hadn't changed since I had seen it last. And- I thought that it might be best for you to see it with fresh eyes."

"You might have warned me about the warg at the entrance at the very least."

"Ah, but that was a surprise for me as well," Isengrim replied. "When I still served Calvaria there was merely a trio of wolves chained to the gate of Dis. It must have cost many lives to transport that monster back from the southern coast."

"But why keep it there at all?" Reynard asked.

"It is a reminder of the days when Calvarians ran with wargs, drank honey wine, and worshipped the Watcher. There is perhaps a little warg blood in every Calvarian still, and we spend our lives keeping that beast tightly chained."

"Your people never do anything the easy way, do they?"

"No," Isengrim said and moved over to the door. "Now try to get some sleep. You can plan your escape when it is your turn on watch."

* * * * * * *

As tired as he was, Reynard could not fall asleep, even after Isengrim had put out the lights. He never slept well before a job, and the next day he would steal one of the world's greatest treasures. His heart beat hard in his chest as it pulsed with excitement, and he found himself running escape possibilities over and over in his head.

It was for this reason that he was still awake when Isengrim got up from his bunk and left the room. The Northerner moved quietly, but to Reynard's keen ears he might as well have been wearing hobnailed shoes.

Perhaps he is merely relieving himself? Reynard thought, but his intuition told him otherwise. After months spent living in a small cabin with the man, he thought that he knew the man's personal habits fairly well.

After he heard the door click shut, Reynard sat up. He didn't dare turn on the light, so he crept carefully up to the door through the darkness, using his hand to trace his path as he had done back in the storm sewers under Calyx.

He opened the door slowly, and could still make out the distant click of Isengrim's boots on the stone floor of the hallway.

Reynard paused. If he was going to follow his companion he would have to do so now, while he was still within earshot . . . yet he did not know where Isengrim might lead him, and without his guidance he could become hopelessly lost within this underground labyrinth.

As it often had before, his curiosity won out. He buckled on his overcoat, and then padded into the hallway and began to follow his companion as silently as a cat.

Despite the darkness, Reynard's sense of direction was good enough for him to realize that they were not traveling the way they had come, but whether they were moving deeper into the city or not he could only guess.

Wherever he's going, Reynard thought to himself as they walked, *he's doing it in a hurry.*

Then Isengrim's steps came to a halt and Reynard heard the telltale clicking that meant that one of the gas lamps was about to flicker into life. He back-peddled as quickly as he was able to, and averted his eyes so he wouldn't be blinded.

They were in a similar juncture to the one they had been in previously, and after a quick glance down each passage Isengrim shut the lamp off and continued. If he knew that he was being followed he showed no sign.

Isengrim and Reynard turned a sharp corner and a speck of light appeared in the distance, and as they went on Reynard could make out

Isengrim's tall form ahead of him. He let the Northerner gain some distance on him, and resumed his pursuit.

When Reynard came to the intersection of the lit corridor and the dark one he had been following he saw with his own eyes one of the rigged defenses that Isengrim had spoken of earlier: a recessed part of the wall above that housed a huge stone block. A pair of thick chains attached to separate winches apparently held the thing in place, and Reynard noted the catch that would release the block from its housing and cause it to fall into place, effectively blocking the passage entirely.

In the lit passage Reynard came across one of the access stairways to the upper city, which he could hear Isengrim already climbing. He slipped up the stairs after him, and hoped that the upper levels were not occupied.

At the top of the stairwell Reynard saw that they had come to the top of one of the city's outermost walls, which he quickly realized was a part of the enormous dam that he had seen only distantly from the western shore of the Calvarians' man-made lake.

Isengrim was standing some distance from him, gazing over the edge of the dam and into the black abyss beyond, his gloved hands resting on a stone rail that prevented one from falling.

At his back, rising up from the heart of the city, Reynard could hear the roar of thousands of cheering voices, and the harsh blare of trumpets, and he imagined that the Calvarians were no doubt amusing themselves in some form of bloody sport or mock battle. Perhaps that was the reason that he saw no others walking the walls, save for the distant figures that he could spy standing statue-like atop the city's towers.

For a long while nothing happened. And then, distantly, Reynard spied another figure walking towards them. As it drew closer he saw that it was a white uniformed member of the service class.

A woman.

She was clearly quite athletic, her tight-fitting breeches revealing legs as lithe as a Tyrian jungle cat's- yet there was something undeniably delicate about her that was hard to define. Her face was so pale that it might have been carved out of marble and, like most of the Calvarian women he had seen, she kept her hair neatly trimmed in a straight slash just above her brow.

The eyes beneath those sandy locks were blue, and deep as the sea.

Isengrim was staring at the approaching woman as well, and Reynard saw that his right hand was nervously clenching and unclenching.

Whoever this woman was, she had not seen Isengrim yet, for the solitary lamp overhead cast harsh shadows over his face. But as she drew nearer the tall Northerner stepped forward, and she saw him then, clearly.

She halted, and opened her mouth as if to say something- then shut it firmly. The two of them stood there for a long while, staring at each other, and Reynard could see that the woman had begun to silently shed tears.

"I-" Isengrim said, *"I wondered if you would come."*

The woman approached him then, slowly, and reached out to touch him, her slender hands wrapping around his own and lifting them up to her face.

"I am real," Isengrim said softly.

"I had thought-" she began to say, barely choking out the words. *"I thought that you-"*

"I know," Isengrim said, hushing her. *"I would have thought the same, if I had been you."*

"But how? I saw you- saw you fall," she said, and turned towards the far edge of the dam.

"The pynding," Isengrim said, using an unfamiliar word. *"It broke my fall, but it carried me far, far away, far outside the city."*

The woman looked up at him then, her brows furrowed in anger. *"Then why did you not come back? Why did you abandon me?"*

"I- I am here with you now, Hirsent," Isengrim said at last.

She struck him across the face. He did not lift a hand to defend himself. She raised her palm to strike him again, and then lowered it.

"Did they hurt you?" Isengrim asked softly.

"Yes."

"And- the child?"

"He is dead, Isengrim. They killed him after he-"

She could not go on.

"A son?" Isengrim said, his normally sure voice cracking. *"I had a son?"*

Since she could not answer with words, she nodded, her face wet with tears. Isengrim walked slowly over to the battlement and clutched at it as his shoulders shook with grief.

"I had a son," he said again, fiercely.

The woman placed her hand on his back, and spoke soft words to him then that Reynard could not hear.

"Oh, my lufestre," Isengrim said, turning around and enfolding her in his arms. *"I never thought that I would hold you again."*

"You must swear to me," she said as she began to kiss his tear-streaked face, *"That this time you will not let go of me."*

"I promise," Isengrim swore, and kissed her.

"Ahem," Reynard said then, clearing his throat loudly as he stepped out of the stairwell.

Startled, the two Northerners split from each other, and Isengrim's magnificent sword flew from its sheath, the point of his blade coming to rest directly beneath Reynard's jaw.

"Right on schedule, eh, Isengrim?" Reynard said glibly, unfazed by the sword at his throat.

"Fox!" Isengrim said, angrily returning his blade to its sheath. "This is none of your affair!"

"At least I know now why you came back here," Reynard said. "I suppose I should have guessed that it would have been for a woman."

Hirsent looked back and forth between her lover and the dark skinned man who wore the trappings of a servant, a confused look etched across her face.

"Isengrim," she said. *"Who is this Southerner? You speak his tongue?"*

"My name is 'Fox,'" Reynard said, removing his cap and bending into an overly exaggerated Calvarian bow. *"And I do as my master commands, may he slay me if I do less."*

"He is very rude," Hirsent commented.

"Yes," Isengrim said brusquely. *"I will speak with him."*

"So," Reynard said as Isengrim took him aside. "Who's the lovely lady?"

"Her name is Hirsent, and she was once my lover."

"Yes, I gathered that," Reynard said. "And from what I heard I also suspect that you never intended to escape from Dis, did you?"

"No," Isengrim said, the anger draining from his voice. "But you were not meant to find out this way."

"Feel free to elaborate."

"When I first came to your lands," Isengrim went on, "I fell into the service of Count Bricemer. I told him much of my people, and I killed many of his enemies for him. Then, one day he came to me with a question: could a skilled thief steal the gem of Zosia from Dis and return with it to Arcas?"

"Apparently, you told him 'yes'."

"I did- but in my heart I thought it impossible. After all, I served as a blood-guard in Dis for fifteen years, and that did not aid me when we tried to escape."

"Then you aren't an exile at all," Reynard said.

"No. I-" Isengrim glanced over at the beautiful woman who stood at his side, "*We* chose to be exiles, even at the risk of our own lives. We could not go on living otherwise."

"But you were caught."

"Yes, only I-" Isengrim's gaze flicked towards the edge of the dam.

"I see," Reynard said. "And she was left behind."

"Yes."

"So," Reynard said, chewing on his bottom lip. "You came back here just so you could die with her."

"Yes."

"And you brought me with you?"

"Not to die, Master Fox," Isengrim said. "Not to die. I was wrong, you see. Wrong about you. You can do what the Duke desires of you, and you must, for it will hurt them where it will hurt them most: their pride."

"Then why didn't you just tell me?"

"I did not want to burden you, Master Fox," Isengrim replied. "For only you can escape from Dis."

Reynard was about to respond when he felt the hairs on the back of his neck stiffen. Echoing faintly in the distance, he could hear the unmistakable tramp of booted feet. The noise was growing louder by the second.

"*We must leave, now,*" he said in Calvarian so that Hirsent could understand him. "*Soldiers are coming.*"

"*He is right,*" Hirsent said, pointing towards a walkway that led back to the city. Rushing along it was a squad of gray figures.

"Awyrigung!" Isengrim cursed under his breath as he took Hirsent by the arm and began pulling her in the opposite direction. *"The stair-"*

"Is blocked," Reynard said, and a moment later another half dozen Calvarian soldiers appeared in the stairwell, their blades drawn.

They were trapped.

"You should have listened to your trained foa, Heafodcarl Foalan," a familiar voice said from the darkness beyond the lamplight. *"His ears are apparently keener than your own."*

"What is the meaning of this?" Isengrim asked in an imperious tone, his arms crossed in front of his chest in a feigned sign of impatience.

A man dressed in black stepped into the light. It was the blood-guard that had stopped them on the ferry that afternoon.

"Prafost Fasolt," the blood-guard said to one of the Calvarian soldiers. *"Both this man and woman are hlafordswica. Take them and this Southerner into custody."*

The soldier grunted a command, and several of his fellows maneuvered to apprehend them.

When they had come within five paces, Isengrim struck. He moved so quickly that Reynard did not even see him draw his sword. In the space of a second he had cut two of the men down: neither of them had the time to draw their weapons.

Then Isengrim was weaving a deadly dance amongst the others, whose numbers only served to slow them as Isengrim's blade pierced throat and heart. And after the last man had fallen, clutching desperately at the fatal wound in his neck, Isengrim merely lowered his sword and stood as he had before, his weapon dark with Calvarian blood.

"So it is you," the blood-guard said with an almost satisfied tone. *"Isengrim."*

"Who are you?" Isengrim addressed the man. *"Why do you call me by that name?"*

"It is the name of a dead man," the blood-guard replied coldly. *"A blood-guard who was once thought to be the greatest of the order, until he fell in love with a woman far below his station. He used his influence to hide their affair from his brothers and sisters, and he might have done so forever if she had not become pregnant."*

"I was only a boy then, not a true blood-guard," the man continued, taking a few steps forward. *"But like my brothers and sisters in training I admired this*

man: his skill in battle and his discipline . . . if only I had known then that he was a coward!"

From the look on Isengrim's face, Reynard could tell that these words had cut him deeper than any wound might have.

"He threw himself to his death," the blood-guard spat at Isengrim. "And left his lover and unborn child behind to pay for his crimes!"

"Do not listen to him!" Hirsent said, moving to Isengrim's side.

"Do you deny it?" the blood-guard demanded, ignoring Hirsent's outburst. "Speak!"

"No," Isengrim replied softly, "I do not deny it, and I do not blame you for despising me Filtiarn, for I have done so myself every day since."

The blood-guard smiled. "Then you remember me as well?"

"I remember a boy who went by that name who used to watch me while I trained. He would be your age by now."

"And what else do you remember about him?" the blood-guard asked, his pale eyes glittering. "This boy?"

"I remember- that he was not like the others," Isengrim answered. "That he was kind."

The blood-guard sneered. "That child died the day you betrayed him, Isengrim. He is as dead as your son."

"So is the man that you knew," was Isengrim's only reply.

"Is he?" Filtiarn said, drawing his own exquisite blade, "Show me! Or do you fear to fight me alone?"

"No," Isengrim replied. "I am no longer afraid to die."

"We shall see."

"Do not interfere," Isengrim said to Reynard as he drew his sword.

Reynard hesitated. He felt a hand tug on his shoulder, and saw that it was Hirsent's. The look in her eyes was hard.

He nodded and joined her by the far edge of the dam. From here he could see the single narrow bridge that connected the city to the eastern side of the cavern, and the dark abyss that lay below.

The two men stood at a distance from each other now, studying each other, their expressions blank. Slowly the blood-guard raised his sword over his head, gripping it with two hands. As if in answer Isengrim lowered his own stance.

A trumpet blared in the city. Somewhere, a crowd roared.

Isengrim lunged forward, his blade meeting the blood-guard's in mid-strike. He did not let up his attack, but forced his opponent backward as their blades clashed together furiously. Then they split, the increased rate of their breath the only sign of their exertion.

The blood-guard circled slowly to the right, stepping gingerly over the one of the dead soldier's corpses before resuming a ready stance. Isengrim shifted to the left.

This time it was the younger man who made the first thrust, and it seemed to Reynard, who had fought Isengrim almost daily since he had begun his training, that he watched two mirror images battling: their fighting styles were so similar as to be identical.

But while Isengrim was physically larger and stronger than his opponent, the younger man had speed on his side. As Isengrim parried a series of low feints the blood-guard redoubled the intensity of his attack and managed to slash open Isengrim's left cheek.

"You fight well," Isengrim said as they parted, wiping absently at the blood that ran from his wound. *"Without passion, and with total control. You are as I was once."*

"I am nothing like you!" Filtiarn said heatedly as he advanced, his blade flashing as he tested the strength of his opponent's defenses.

"You may even kill me," Isengrim went on, deflecting the blood-guard's blows as he was pushed back. *"And for that you have my pity."*

"What do you mean?"

"It has been ten years since I fell from this place," Isengrim said, and as he spoke he did nothing but parry the blood-guard's attacks, which grew more ferocious with each thrust. *"And yet your anger is so fresh, it might have been yesterday. Is it possible that your hatred for me is all that you have to live for?"*

"Be quiet!" the blood-guard shouted, redoubling his efforts, and with each parried strike, Isengrim opened his opponent's defenses wider.

"Will you learn to love, as I did?" Isengrim went on. *"Will you fight for the honor of a father that you will never know? Or for the affections of a lover you can never have? Or will you finally admit the truth: that for all of your laurels, you are no better than a slave."*

"Better that I should die first!" the blood-guard screamed as he brought his sword down in a wild arc.

"So be it," Isengrim said, and drove his blade through the blood-guard's breast.

Filtiarn gasped, the breath knocked from him by the force of the blow. The sword that had been made by the skill of his own hands fell from them, clattering noisily as it struck the cobblestones beneath his feet. He sank to his knees, dark blood spilling freely from his mouth, and reached out to clutch at Isengrim's belt-loop.

His mouth moved, but he did not have the breath to speak, and so his last words went unheard by any save Isengrim, who knelt down to cradle him as the last of his life drained from his breast.

"Be at peace now," Isengrim said, his hand stroking the blood-guard's face as if he were his own son.

When he stood back up there were tears in Isengrim's eyes.

"You should leave now, Master Fox," Isengrim said, wiping his sword clean with a cloth. "When these patrols do not report back to their barracks the entire city will begin to hunt for us."

"It is not deep," Hirsent said, inspecting Isengrim's wound. *"But we should clean it as soon as possible."*

Isengrim nodded, and kissed the woman lightly on the forehead.

"Perhaps we can distract them long enough for you to escape to the surface- but it appears as though the Duke's gem will have to remain in Calvaria. I am . . . sorry."

Isengrim held out his hand, but Reynard did not take it.

"I am not leaving," Reynard said. "Not without you, and not without the gem."

"Master Fox, you do not have to die here with us."

"I have no intention of dying," Reynard said. "In fact, I've already planned my escape. And- if you are quite done acting so tragically noble- you and your Hirsent are more than welcome to come with me."

"But-" Isengrim said, casting Reynard an incredulous look. "How?"

"Well, that all depends," Reynard replied. "Do you think you can find me some bags of flour?"

XIII

As he and Isengrim ascended back into the city proper, Reynard noticed that many of the city's gas lamps had been extinguished, or were burning low, casting ominous shadows over this district's emptied streets.

Isengrim paused for a moment and looked upward, and when Reynard followed his gaze he saw that the darkness of the cavern was broken by light from the world above, gleaming through far distant air vents to illuminate the city below. Even now he could see massive shafts of sunlight creeping down the jagged walls of the cavern, and imagined the moment when they would strike Dis itself, reflecting brilliantly off of every polished stone and gleaming spike, and a small part of him mourned that he would only ever see the beauty of that moment as he left the city behind forever.

"Are you prepared?" Reynard whispered in Calvarian.

"I might ask you the same," Isengrim said, placing a firm hand on his shoulder, and Reynard realized that his face was beaded with sweat, and his breath had become rapid.

"I am always like this- before," Reynard replied, dismissing Isengrim's concern with a wave of his hand. *"I will be calm when the time comes."*

"Very well," Isengrim said, and started to lead the way to the gate to the inner ward.

There was little difference between this gate and the one that had separated the first and second circles of the city, though the wall that housed it was appreciably taller, and the banner that hung above it was emblazoned with a grinning skull around which grew a stylized wreath of ivy.

You may have me yet, Wulf, Reynard thought as they passed underneath the banner. *If I am slow.*

The city's innermost ward was a hexagon shaped plaza, the corners of which occupied by edifices that rose nearly as high as the walls that contained them. Upon closer inspection Reynard saw that they appeared to be connected to walls themselves, so that the six towers that ringed the ward were actually the uppermost levels of these impressive structures.

But even these were dwarfed by the central spire, the pinnacle of which nearly disappeared into the gloom of the cavern above it. It was the cold heart of the city, and Reynard could only imagine the view from the upper levels, where the laboring populous below might resemble the miniature soldiers of a *campraeden* board.

Just then a sunbeam struck the topmost spire of the citadel, and bells began to ring throughout the city.

Under the clamor Isengrim said, *"The missing night patrol will be noticed any moment now,"* and he quickened his stride.

Isengrim led them towards the first building on their left. As they approached Reynard saw that a great insignia had been carved into the stone façade of its entranceway: an open book marked with the Calvarian script, bisected by a disembodied hand holding a stylus.

Isengrim had called it the Hall-Of-Knowledge.

The city's bells were slowing now, and as they reached the hall's front entrance, Reynard could see figures entering the square, which was gradually growing lighter as sunbeams struck it from above.

A pair of women in gray uniforms, the first female soldiers Reynard had seen in Dis, brushed past them as they entered. One had apparently lost her left leg, and walked on a rather cunning metal facsimile of a limb that bent correctly as she limped out the door. The other, a woman who might have been a maid or laundress had she been born in Calyx, had apparently been in a fire that had burned nearly half of her face into a patchwork of scar tissue. A leather patch covered her right eye, but her left seemed to wink at Reynard as they passed.

The foyer of the Hall-Of-Knowledge was immense, nearly twice the size of the grand entryway of the Duke's palace. Directly across from the main doors a wide stone stair opened onto a column-lined gallery, while to the right and left were arched doorways that led to the separate wings of the building.

They shared this massive space with only one other figure, a slender Calvarian clerk who stood in front of a reflecting pool that lay at the center of the chamber, his arms held firmly behind his back.

The man bowed neatly before saying, in a rather nasal voice, *"And how might I assist you, Heafodcarl?"*

"Would you direct me to the cafortun?" Isengrim replied after a bow of his own. *"I am early for a geancyme and would like something to drink."*

"It is directly through this hall, sir," the clerk said, his eyes flicking unconsciously towards Reynard as he straightened so that he could indicate their path. *"Just past the stairway and through the weapon-hall."*

Isengrim gave a short nod of his head in thanks and began to circle the pool, Reynard trailing in his wake. As he passed the clerk Reynard allowed his eyes to wander, so that for an instant they locked with that of the officious Calvarian.

The clerk's blue eyes widened, his breath catching short as his mouth opened ever so slightly. Reynard dared not look back as they crossed the foyer, but he could hear the man shuffling in place as both he and Isengrim passed beneath another archway, and could imagine the turmoil that was now roiling within this minor functionary as he weighed the risks of committing a clear breach of etiquette in front of someone of far higher rank.

They passed through a hallway that was broken by another central stairway, this one leading down into the service level of the undercity, and entered a large chamber that was true to the name the clerk had given it, for it had been filled almost entirely by assorted arms and armor. Most of it was Calvarian, such as the elaborate suits of plate that stood at attention along the walls, but Reynard saw swords and shields decorated with the image of the Firebird, and even some of the distinctive double-edged blades that the Glyconese wielded.

Beyond this arsenal was a spacious courtyard where several military types sat at cast-iron tables, sipping some sort of steaming broth or herbal concoction out of fine ceramic saucers. Reynard noted that one of them, a florid faced elder with snow-white hair who seemed entirely engrossed by the leather bound book in his lap, wore the voluminous scarlet robes that marked him as one of the city's judges.

But even the sight of one of Calvaria's rulers could not distract Reynard for long, his gaze being inexorably drawn to the monument that dominated the courtyard.

A life-sized figure that had been carved out of the purest marble stood at its center, his strong frame bedecked in armor. Under his left arm this warrior carried his helmet, so that his sculpted locks streamed from his proud face as if buffeted by the wind, and his mailed foot was planted on the chest of another man, whose exposed flesh had been carved from onyx: a bearded Southern king whose crown had fallen from his brow, and whose own sword lay broken at his side. The king's retainers had apparently fallen defending their vanquished lord, and formed a heap of miserable figures at the feet of whatever Calvarian hero had bested them.

In the ivory statue's right palm, which was raised in an opened faced salute, was a blood-red jewel the size of a man's heart.

Isengrim turned his head and looked over Reynard's shoulder, as if he were looking back down the hall they had just exited, and Reynard gave him the slightest of nods. Then the Northerner turned away from him and took a seat at the nearest table.

Reynard did not follow, and stood at the entrance to the courtyard, scratching idly at his scalp.

It took the white uniformed server who approached Isengrim's table only a few seconds to notice the dark-skinned man standing in the archway. When Reynard was certain that he had the man's full attention he re-straightened his cap and then made his way down the steps that led to the floor of the courtyard.

"Is something the matter?" he heard Isengrim say to the server, who was looking at Reynard as if he were on fire.

Some of the other occupants of the court had noticed Reynard as well, and were lowering their cups as their quiet conversations ground to a halt. By the time he had reached the statuary he was certain that there was not a single man or woman present whose eyes were not locked on him, but as yet the Calvarians seemed to be too stunned to act.

All the while Reynard kept an oblivious look on his face, like that of a simpleton, and allowed his movements to become sloppy.

When it was clear that Reynard was approaching the judge, the old man rose to his feet and opened his mouth to address the courtyard.

"What servant is this?" he said in a somewhat raspy voice. *"Who has brought this Southerner here?"*

When no one replied, the judge slammed shut the volume he had been perusing, and took a few steps towards the approaching foreigner, his pale eyebrows furrowed together in annoyance.

"Servant," the judge said gruffly. *"To whom do you belong?"*

Reynard smiled, and then turned away from the elderly man to inspect one of the stricken onyx figures gracing the monument. The room was abuzz now with whispered voices that were growing louder with every moment.

"*How dare you!*" the judge blustered. "*Turn around! I am speaking to you, you black dog!*"

The judge grabbed him by the shoulder and whipped him around.

It was only then that the Calvarian saw that Reynard held a cruel looking switch made out of birch in his left hand.

Before the judge could defend himself Reynard struck him across the arch of his nose, breaking it neatly. The judge's hands flew to his face as he screamed in agony.

There was a moment of stunned silence from the men and women who had just witnessed a lowly servant strike one of the highest members of their society.

Then, predictably, the shouting began.

"*Kill him!*" a soldier howled.

"*Assassin!*" another cried.

"*Defend Judge Fenris!*" several junior officers bellowed as they jostled to form a human barrier between themselves and Reynard.

"*Ahhh!*" the judge screamed.

Reynard did not wait for further comment on his actions, but began to sprint wildly towards the exit, slowing just long enough to snatch up a metal plate from one of the unoccupied tables and fling it straight into the knee-cap of the white-uniformed steward who was moving to block his escape route.

"*Stop him!*" Reynard heard the judge roar over the chaos behind him as he leapt over the server's tumbling form. "*Call out the guard!*"

Then Reynard was in the weapon hall and as he passed by a suit of plate armor he gave it a shove with his free hand, sending it crashing into a glass covered display table.

With what Reynard considered perfect timing, the clerk from the foyer entered the weapon hall only a second later, his mouth gaping at the sight of the Southerner bearing down on him, and at the weapons that he could now see underneath his billowing cloak.

The clerk's nerve broke, and then he was running, almost as fast as Reynard, back into the foyer and shouting at the top of his lungs that a Southern killer had somehow infiltrated the city.

Laughing, Reynard leapt over the thick stone banister of the stairwell that led to the undercity.

He ran down the steps, and briefly caught a glimpse of the great kitchen that was housed on the service level before continuing his descent. Behind him was a chorus of tramping boots that grew louder as the head start that he had gained due to the element of surprise was rapidly narrowed by his pursuers' incredible speed.

He reached the barracks level. Through an archway he could see the straight passage that led under the wall of the inner ward, and the winch mechanism that would cut off his escape if triggered.

Halfway between him and the exit were two Calvarian soldiers.

"Seal the passage!" one of them shouted as he drew his sword and moved to engage the man who was barreling towards them. The other soldier nodded sharply and turned to release the catch.

As the soldier began his swing Reynard leapt to the side, his foot using the smooth wall of the passage for support as he nimbly dodged around his attacker. His left arm whipped back to strike the man in the back of the head with the switch, sending him directly into the path of his pursuers, who collided into the soldier with an audible crack.

Ahead of him, the soldier had reached the winches and was tugging on the lever that would release the catch. Reynard ran wildly now, his sides throbbing with pain as he pushed himself to the limits of his endurance.

He was only five paces from the exit when the Calvarian soldier finally wrenched the lever down. The chains rattled wildly as the stone block began to descend.

Desperately, Reynard leapt forward . . . and landed in a heap on the other side of the gap as the massive stone block slammed deafeningly into place behind him.

Caught underneath the block was the conical hat that he had been wearing for the past few days. Reynard tugged at it, but only managed to tear off one of its ear-flaps.

"It was a ridiculous hat anyway," Reynard said as he tossed the thing away.

There was the distinct sound of stone grinding against stone as the block lifted an inch or two off of the ground, and then Reynard could hear the groans of several men straining themselves with effort, and the clank of metal as the block moved another couple of inches.

"Faster!" a voice shouted through the gap. *"He cannot have gone far!"*

Reynard paused just long enough to ensure that his legs were still attached to his body, and then broke into a trot down the hall. At the first t-section he turned left, then made a right. As his legs pumped, his mind ran through the list of turns he had spent the last hour memorizing. Sure enough, when he had taken another left he found himself in front of a locked gate that was nearly identical to the one he had picked the day before.

He forced his dexterous fingers to work as fast as they were able as he began to pick the lock, all the while aware of the increasingly close noises of pursuit.

The lock clicked open just as a patrol rounded the corner.

"He is here!" one of the Calvarians called out as he drew his sword and charged down the hall towards Reynard, who stuffed the open padlock into his uniform and ran into the complete darkness beyond the gate.

Reynard thrust out his right hand and found the wall, counting the open passageways as he passed them. When he had gone by four he switched hands, and turned into the first opening on his left.

By now Reynard could hear the peal of alarm bells echoing down every corridor, and knew that in a few moments every way in or out of the undercity would be completely cut off. Then all the Calvarians needed to do would be to systematically hunt through the barracks to find him.

Which was exactly what Reynard had in mind.

* * * * * * *

The Calvarian officer responsible for the defense of the fourth ward was a rather taciturn man named Lycaon.

He was not a particularly imaginative man, and had only risen to his present position through a combination of personal achievement on the battlefield and a habit of following his superior's orders to the letter. When this became clear to his superiors he was transferred to Dis, where he made a particularly efficient garrison commander.

His rank had provided him with the excellent opportunity to find a suitable bed partner from amongst the available females of Dis, and the blood-guard had given him the permission to sire two sons with a female stonemason, both of whom proved to be well suited for military careers themselves. He dined with Latteowa Garm at the end of every month, played an ongoing game of campraeden with his fellow Heafodcarls, and occasionally attended the mock combats that seemed to keep the lower classes entertained.

But despite these comforts and amusements, Heafodcarl Lycaon daily found himself missing the battlefields of his youth: the chance for achievement through strength of arms, the long days spent in hard labor and, perhaps most of all, the bonds between soldiers that were rarely forged outside of battle. Some evenings, after he had retired to his personal quarters, he found himself fondly remembering a particularly brutal campaign against the savage kingdom of Brobdingnag, where more than a few of his closest companions had met their end under the crushing blow of a giant's spiked club.

And so when the alarms began to ring throughout the inner ward, and the garrison of the fourth received the first hazy reports of a crazed Southern assassin that had assaulted Judge Fenris before fleeing into the undercity, Heafodcarl Lycaon was one of the first to enter the dusty tunnels in search of the strange intruder.

"Have your men turn on every single lamp," he ordered one of his prafosts as he and a company of soldiers entered one of the passageways that ran along the breadth of the second ward. *"I don't want to give this Southern dog a single shadow to hide in!"*

So, as the men under Lycaon's command proceeded to fan out, searching each garrison block room by room, they twisted the leaf-shaped knobs that controlled the flow of gas into the lamps and caused the flint and steel lighters within them to strike until flame was produced.

Suddenly there was a startled shout from one of the side tunnels, and then Lycaon and his men could hear the distinctive clash of steel on steel.

"He is here!" a woman cried out. Lycaon did not recognize the voice, but as it belonged to a woman he assumed that it was one of Heafodcarl Thryth's company.

"Hurry!" the voice cried, desperate now. *"He is getting away!"*

Lycaon and his men turned the corner just in time to see a dark figure disappearing into the gloom of an unlit intersection, where a pair of soldiers lay dead.

Enraged at the sight of slain brethren, and ignoring the little voice in the back of his mind that urged him towards caution, the Captain drew his blade and roared for his men to follow him. They responded with a war cry that made his heart soar with joy, and then they were charging blindly into the darkness.

As they ran Lycaon heard an odd sound coming from somewhere ahead of them, much like the tearing of fabric. Then he could feel something odd brushing against his face, like falling snow. With his next breath he inhaled a mouthful of powdery stuff that sent him into a fit of coughing. Soon the passage was full of the noise of men desperately trying to clear their lungs.

Placing his free hand over his nose, Lycaon called out for light. One of the soldiers near him found the switch that would illuminate the hallway they occupied and turned it.

For an instant captain Lycaon saw clearly the sacks that had been hung over the decorative support beams above them, and the deep slashes in them that were rapidly bleeding the fine powder that was hanging densely in the air of the crowded tunnel.

"Turn off the lamps!" Lycaon managed to scream, and had just thrown one of his own soldiers aside in order to do so himself when the flour caught.

To the other Calvarians in the tunnels the explosion sounded like a thunderbolt that had somehow arced through the mountain to strike the city above them. The very floor beneath their feet rumbled ominously, and more than a few of the officers ordered their men to pull back in case the undercity itself were collapsing.

Lycaon's second, a Lyftcarl named Varcolac, was the first to brave the possibility of a cave-in to come to his superior's aid. He and his men soon discovered a grisly scene, lit by numerous jets of open flame that licked the air lasciviously from the shattered remnants of the gas lamps that had once lined the hall. Beneath this hellish light were the burned bodies of the injured, and the dead. Amongst these was Lycaon himself, who could only be identified by the number of pips on his charred epaulettes.

"That Southerner may still be within this block," Varcolac said, loud enough to be heard over the moans of the injured men. *"I want every room off of this corridor searched!"*

Varcolac went on to issue an order to cut the gas lines, for there was still a considerable amount of flour strewn about the hallway that had not been ignited, and he did not want to inadvertently cause another explosion. Soon the men were using only covered lanterns for illumination as they moved from room to room.

Those soldiers who had escaped the worst of the flames were already helping to carry their less fortunate brethren out of the tunnels. Strangely, it appeared to Varcolac that soldiers from several different companies had somehow been caught in the blast, for amongst the dead were men wearing insignia from the sixth ward garrison, and he briefly caught a glimpse of a striking female soldier from that unit shouldering another man whose face was streaked with both flour and blood. As they staggered away from the carnage the man coughed violently into the crook of his right arm.

Varcolac was considering stopping the pair in order to ask them what they had been doing in the fourth ward when one his prafosts reported that the body of the intruder had been discovered dead in one of the rooms off of this hall, apparently having been caught in the explosion before he could seal himself within one of the sleeping-chambers.

The Southerner's features were nearly indistinguishable, his head having been burned so badly that it was a mass of hairless tissue. Varcolac might even have taken him for a Calvarian, for he appeared to have an excellent frame under the dun servant's uniform that he wore, and he was somewhat taller than the initial reports regarding the intruder had suggested.

"This was a cleaner death than this coward deserved," Varcolac said, delivering a sharp kick to the dead man's ribcage. He then sent a prafost to report the news of the man's death to Latteowa Garm, all the while wondering what (and who?) had brought this madman here.

He had to have had help, Varcolac reasoned. It was the only explanation that made sense to him. After all, no Southerner would be able to enter Dis so easily without a Calvarian to-

Varcolac looked back at the dead man that lay on the floor. Every report he had been given had said that the intruder was a smaller man, lean and nimble. But this man dressed in servant's clothes was clearly over six feet, taller even than he was.

His pulse sounding like a drum in his ears, Varcolac ripped open the front of the corpse's uniform.

Bronze buttons that had been molded by priests of the Firebird in the great temple of Calyx bounced musically against the floor, but Lyftcarl Varcolac did not hear them. He could not hear anything over the sound of his own heart beating wildly as he stared at the pale, Calvarian flesh that was underneath his hands.

* * * * * * *

Work had come to an absolute standstill on the fourth quarter dock when the city's alarms had sounded, and within moments the soldiers, engineers, and dockworkers who were stationed in the outer ring of the city had scrambled to their assigned posts.

But when it had become clear that Dis was not under attack, and the alarms had been replaced by an ominous silence, the non-combatants had begun to mutter amongst themselves darkly.

"*I heard the grays talking,*" a dockhand said, casting a glance around to ensure that the soldiers could not hear his words. "*They were saying that a judge was attacked by some Southern assassin. Came this close to slicing his throat before the blood-guard cut him down.*"

"*If the blood-guard caught him,*" another asked skeptically, "*Then why are the grays checking every storeroom and kitchen from here to the tower?*"

"*Perhaps there was more than one,*" a third man offered. "*There could be an army of them down in those tunnels. You ever been down on the third level?*"

"*No, I have not,*" the skeptic hissed, "*And neither have you, so keep your mouth shut.*"

"*There might be something to what he is saying,*" said a female cook who had been ushered out of her kitchen along with the rest of the staff. "*I know some of the maintenance staff that work down there. They say there was an explosion somewhere in the undercity. Sabotage they say.*"

The skeptic was about to reply when the man standing next to him let out a brief whistle. The dockhands immediately knew what was meant and suddenly grew very interested in the stones beneath their feet.

A blood-guard wearing a heavy fur coat had entered the dockyard through one of the entryways to the undercity. He was accompanied by two strange figures, both of which appeared to be caked from head to toe with flour, soot, and blood.

"*Where is the harbormaster?*" the blood-guard called out as he approached the clump of dockworkers and kitchen staff.

"*I am here, sir,*" an older Calvarian said, stepping forward and bowing sharply.

"*How long has it been since the last ferry left port?*" the blood-guard asked.

"*Why, it was just before the alarm,*" the harbormaster said nervously, "*At the first bell.*"

"*Were there any engineers aboard?*" The blood-guard's asked, taking a step forward so that he stood nearly nose-to-nose with the man. "*Think carefully.*"

"*Yes, sir!*" the harbormaster said. "*They left with the first shift.*"

"*We have them,*" the blood-guard said, and turned sharply to the armed woman next to him. "*Soldier, report back to . . . no, there is no time. Harbormaster, I will need to requisition one of these cargo vessels, and a crew to guide it.*"

"*Sir, this is-*"

"*I do not have time to argue!*" the blood-guard said. "*Now find me a boat!*"

The harbormaster did not offer any further argument, and soon the blood-guard and his escort had cast off from the pier in a skiff that had been half-loaded with bones.

"*Send a messenger to the guard post at the first junction on the second level!*" the blood-guard shouted from the aft as the ship cut through the calm of the lake. "*Let them know that the traitors left on the first ferry and that we are in pursuit!*"

"*Yes, sir!*" the harbormaster said with a salute, and began to compose the brief missive that he would send with one of the messengers stationed here.

He was signing the document when female soldiers began to storm out of every entrance to the undercity, pushing the white uniformed Calvarians harshly out of their way as they moved to secure every dock and gantry.

One of the last of the soldiers to enter the dockyard was a coppery-headed Heafodcarl.

"Attention citizens of Dis!" she bellowed. *"Be advised that there is a Southern saboteur somewhere within the city who is being aided by one or more of our own people! These cowards were responsible for the deaths of . . ."*

The Heafodcarl's voice trailed off as one of her prafosts approached with the harbormaster at his side. The gray haired man was clearly agitated, and held a piece of parchment in his hands.

"I'm sorry Heafodcarl Thryth," the prafost said, saluting. *"But the harbormaster demands to see you."*

"Well?" she said, regarding the harbormaster with disdain.

"I'm sorry, sir," the man burbled as he approached, holding the missive out for the Heafodcarl to take. *"I wrote as fast as I was able."*

"What do you mean?" Thryth said, as she took the missive and began to skim its contents. *"What is this nonsense?"*

"The blood-guard told me-"

"A blood-guard?" Thryth repeated, her eyes suddenly fierce. *"Was there a man and a woman with him, covered in flour?"*

"Yes," the harbormaster said, a pit of dread opening in his stomach. *"He said that the traitors were onboard-"*

"Never mind what he said!" she bellowed. *"Where did they go?"*

The harbormaster pointed to one of the open archways, through which the captain could see a lone cargo vessel whose occupants were rowing madly. It was already a quarter of the way across the lake.

"Stop that boat!" the Heafodcarl screamed.

* * * * * * *

"It appears that your message was received, sir." Hirsent said to Isengrim, drawing his attention to the small fleet of vessels that were pouring out of the docks behind them.

"Good," Isengrim said, *"But let us not tarry. More speed!"*

Hirsent and Reynard were sitting at the prow of the boat, so as to be out of the direct sight of the six men straining at the oars. Because of their close proximity to each other Reynard could feel the woman sitting next to him shaking, and without thinking he put his hand on the small of her back to calm her.

Hirsent's head snapped towards him, her eyes full of shock. He opened his mouth to apologize but then she shook her head and took his hand and squeezed it.

Over the heads of the oarsmen Reynard could see Isengrim staring at him rather intensely. A moment later he had disengaged from Hirsent's grip and raised both of his hands into the air so that the Northerner could see them. For the remainder of their journey he kept his hands firmly cupped over his knees, and tried to lean as far away from Hirsent as he could.

The boat had hardly pulled up to one of the piers before the three of them had leapt out of the boat and were racing towards one of the coaching stables that were built into the walls of the cavern, leaving their confused crew behind. As they ran, white and tan uniformed Calvarians scurried out of their way, none of them wishing to slow down a blood-guard on some desperate errand.

Reynard spared a moment to glance over his shoulder. Their pursuers, a hundred or so Calvarian soldiers manning all manner of vessel, were only minutes away from reaching the docks themselves.

"You there!" Isengrim shouted at one of the drivers as they neared the carriage depot. *"I need you to take us to the surface immediately!"*

The driver looked down at them skeptically. *"I'm sorry, sir, but I have orders not to go anywhere until the I receive further instructions from my superiors."*

"This is an emergency!" Isengrim said.

"I am very sorry," the Calvarian replied. *"But I could lose my position if I ignore direct orders."*

"We don't have time for this," Reynard said, watching as the first boats slid into the harbor.

"What was that?" the driver said at the sound of Reynard's unfamiliar words. Suddenly he noticed the blood stained uniform underneath Isengrim's overcoat, and raised his whip to strike.

"You are no blood-guard!" the man cried as he brought his whip down.

"No," Isengrim said as he dodged the blow and caught the man by the leg. *"Not any more."*

With a sharp yank Isengrim threw the driver to the ground, and then they all clambered up into the carriage. Isengrim took the reins and then paused, an odd look on his face.

"What in the world are you waiting for?" Reynard yelled.

Isengrim shot Reynard an almost sheepish look.

"I do not know how to drive a coach."

"Hydra's Teeth!" Reynard cursed as he wrenched the reins out of the Northerner's hands. "Don't you know how to do anything other than kill people?"

"Just drive!" Isengrim said, leaping into the carriage's rumble seat. "I will defend our rear!"

Reynard clicked his tongue and whipped the reins, hoping that the huge Calvarian steeds would behave at least somewhat similarly to the horses he was familiar with.

Snorting and stamping, the horses broke into a canter, slowly picking up speed, until they were thundering across the wharf district at an alarming pace.

"Stop them!" Reynard heard a woman howl as the coach thundered out of the depot. *"They are imposters!"*

Men and women, hand-drawn wagons full of goods, and even other vehicles desperately made way for them as they careened wildly towards the cavern's entrance. A squad of armored soldiers rushed to block the gateway, but even these battle-hardened Calvarians scattered rather than brave the hooves of the beasts that were bearing down on them like an avalanche.

The coach shot through the gates, and then they were racing through the hall of pillars. There was as yet little traffic on the subterranean roadway, and they met no resistance from the few coaches and carts laden with goods that they passed, but before they had gone very far Reynard could hear Isengrim shouting something from the rumble seat, though the mad clatter of the wagon drowned out his words.

Handing Hirsent the reins he turned around to see the Northerner pointing to a dozen or so horse-mounted riders that were rapidly gaining on them, their steeds having been bred for speed rather than power.

Cursing, Reynard turned back to Hirsent, who was griping onto the reins desperately, her fine ivory features somehow even paler than before.

"My apologies," he said in her language as he gently took the reins back. *"Do you think that you can fight?"*

"Better than I can steer," Hirsent said, drawing her sword as she clambered onto the luggage rack.

The first of the riders had caught up with them, but he only managed to trade a few blows with Isengrim before the skilled warrior had cut him down. A second man met a similar fate, tumbling from his horse after receiving a fatal cut to the neck. Then three of the riders were upon the former blood-guard, while a fourth armed with a bow urged his steed to race past the ensuing melee, until he was riding directly alongside the high seat on which Reynard was perched.

The horse-mounted archer skillfully drew an arrow from the quiver on his saddle and prepared to fire. In retaliation Reynard dragged on the reins until the coach lurched violently towards the Calvarian, who did not have time to regain control of his mount before it veered wildly off course to avoid being crushed.

"Are you trying to kill us?" Hirsent screamed.

"Just keep these goons off me!" Reynard said, no longer caring that Hirsent could not understand him.

"Halt!" a Calvarian voice cried to Reynard's right. Another soldier had leapt from his horse and onto the side of the coach, and was now climbing into the driver's seat.

Hirsent kicked him squarely in the face, sending him tumbling underneath the wheels, which caused the entire coach to jump wildly into the air. Hirsent flew backwards, only just managing to catch hold of the railing that held the luggage in place.

Just ahead Reynard could see the tunnel that led to the surface, but as he made for it three of the Calvarian riders shot past the coach and rode into the passage.

"Fox!" Isengrim shouted. He appeared to have dealt with his own assailants "They will cut us off!"

"I know!" Reynard shouted back. "But we can't turn back now!"

They entered the tunnel, the coach slowing somewhat as gravity began to take its course. There were only two riders behind them now, but they used this opportunity to close with their quarry. While one kept Isengrim occupied the other leapt into the rumble seat beside him and began to grapple with the former blood-guard in hand to hand combat.

As they fought, the first rider used the opportunity to vault himself into the coach's cabin, whose open door had been swinging crazily open and shut since they had left the depot.

When a steel-tipped sword thrust up through the cushion directly between Reynard's thighs, he was not amused.

The sword retracted.

"Hirsent!" he shrieked at the woman who was still clutching onto the luggage rack before standing up in his seat and leaning forward as far as he could go. *"He is inside the- the-"*

He did not know the Calvarian word for coach.

The sword point erupted from the seat backing, stopping only an inch from his spine.

"He is INSIDE!" Reynard said as loudly as he was able.

Hirsent nodded and repositioned herself so that she was lying on her back, and could grip the underside of the railing just above the door. Then she took a deep breath and kicked off of the coach violently, swinging in a circular arc feet first into the cabin. Wood and glass shattered as the Calvarian sailed out of the opposite side of the coach, his flight through the air rudely halted by a support pillar.

"Not exactly what I would have done," Reynard muttered. "But thanks."

A moment later Isengrim leapt into the seat next to him, his sword sheathed. "That was the last of the ones behind us."

"It is the ones in front of us that I'm worried about," Reynard shot back, nodding his head towards the bright light that was growing larger with every passing second. "You think you can buy me some time?"

"Compared to what you plan on doing, fighting off a few dozen soldiers hardly seems difficult."

"Right," Reynard said. "I almost forgot about that part of the plan."

"But," Isengrim's brows arched in confusion. "Is it not your plan?"

"It is! Don't remind me!"

"I will check on Hirsent," Isengrim said, climbing out of the seat.

The tunnel's entrance was just ahead of them now, the light that poured from it nearly blinding to eyes that had grown accustomed to the dimness of the Calvarian underworld.

The coach flew into the open. Fresh air, cold and bitter, whipped against Reynard's face.

The main gate was blocked by a portcullis, and directly between them and it stood dozens of armored Calvarians. Unlike the soldiers that they had encountered below, these had enough time to form into a cohesive unit, several ranks deep. Their steel-tipped spears bristled before them like the quills of a porcupine, and they showed absolutely no sign that they would break ranks.

Reynard dragged back on the reins, bringing the coach's team to a clattering halt. As they did, another force rushed out of the tunnel behind them, cutting off their rear. On the walls above, a score of Calvarian archers trained their bows on him and on his left, the two-headed warg paced, obviously agitated by the commotion.

"*Surrender!*" a Calvarian officer shouted. "*You are surrounded, and there is no way out!*"

"No thank you!" Reynard yelled out, diving off the coach as arrows began to rain down around him, their shafts thudding dully into the cushion of the seat where he had been sitting just a moment ago. "I'll take my chances!"

To the Calvarian's astonishment, Reynard ran straight towards the monstrous warg, leaping directly onto the platform with a single bound.

"*Hold your fire!*" the officer ordered his archers. "*You'll damage the beast!*"

The archers complied. All of them were interested to see how long the Southerner would last against the Vulp Voran monster.

"I don't suppose you can understand me," Reynard said as the thing padded forward, its ears flattened against both of its heads and a deep growl rumbling in its chest cavity. "But I think you and I can help one another."

The warg pounced forward, its twin jaws snapping and slavering with anticipation. Reynard threw himself aside, and as the creature's forward momentum carried it past him he caught a fistful of its surprisingly silky fur in his hands. As the warg whipped around to face him, he desperately held on.

The warg's heads both twisted furiously to snap at him, bucking wildly and howling in irritation, but Reynard would not let go, and bit by bit he managed to pull himself up to where the thing's chain was attached to its iron collar.

Unable to throw him, the warg went into a wild roll, crushing Reynard with its weight. When it had finished, the small man lay face down on the stones.

He turned over, groaning, and found the warg looming over him, the jackal-like features of its two heads stretched into an eerie pair of grins. It brought one of its forepaws down on him, effectively immobilizing him, and slowly lowered its right head to squeeze the life out of him with its jaws.

Reynard held something up that he had been clutching against his chest. The warg's eyes narrowed as it examined the thing, its left head looking back over its shoulder suddenly with great interest.

The fangs of the beast's right head parted, and then a forked tongue curled out of it . . . and tickled Reynard's face.

The warg shook its shoulders, shrugging off its collar, which no longer had a padlock keeping it in place. Its chain rattled to the ground and it redirected its gaze on the pale-faced men who were slowly backing away from it.

With a deafening pair of howls it leapt off of the platform that had been its prison, and crashed straight into the thick ranks of the nearest platoon. Those who lost their footing found themselves the victims of the warg's fangs, and soon the beast's jaws were dripping with Calvarian gore, and the white snow of the courtyard was stained red with blood.

"Hold your ground!" the officer cried. *"Stay in formation and-"*

Whatever the man's plan had been his soldiers never discovered, for moments after having uttered those words he- along with those unfortunate enough to be standing too close to him- found themselves impaled on the spikes of the monster's tail, before being thrown haphazardly into the air like rag dolls.

Reynard did not waste any time admiring the warg's gruesome handiwork. He rushed instead towards the gatehouse, which had been abandoned as men rushed to get several feet of stone between them and the rampaging monster that was tearing through anyone caught in the open.

As he'd suspected, the winch to raise the portcullis would take two people to operate.

Reynard scanned the courtyard behind him, praying that Isengrim and Hirsent could make it across without being savaged by the warg.

Behind him, through the gate, he could hear the shouted curses of the white uniformed Calvarians who had been caught outside when the portcullis had been lowered.

Then he saw the pair hustling towards him, Hirsent keeping good pace with her considerably taller lover. When they reached the gatehouse, Isengrim turned to keep watch as Hirsent bent all of her strength towards helping Reynard turn the winch.

Despite the ferocious chimera that was rampaging amongst them, a few Calvarians had managed to keep their wits about them, and they rushed now to stop the three fugitives from escaping. None of them, though, knew the skill of Isengrim, and as they came at him one at a time, or in pairs, he cut them down, until a dozen or so men lay in a heap before the door.

With one last burst of effort, Reynard and Hirsent tugged on the winch, and the portcullis was at last open wide enough for them to slip under. Hirsent went first, then Reynard, and finally Isengrim, who sheathed his sword before sliding underneath the portal on his back.

Reynard took one last look back through the gate, where the warg was still tearing men apart with its jaws and pulverizing others with its bony tail. The archers had begun to fire on the beast now, and he wasn't sure how long the thing could endure such injuries.

"Why isn't it running?" Reynard asked. "Does it want to die?"

"Perhaps," Isengrim replied, unhitching a team of horses from a sleigh whose driver had fled down the road, soothing them as best he could. "It is better to die free than to live as a slave."

"Sounds familiar," Reynard said as the Northerner helped Hirsent climb onto one of the horses. "You do have the gem I trust?"

Isengrim reached into his blood-stained uniform, and pulled out the ruby, which seemed to gleam with a life of its own even underneath the Firebird's dim rays.

"If you plan on stealing a man's coin purse with your right hand," Isengrim said, stuffing the gem back into his inner pocket, "Only let him see your left."

"Just thought that I should check before we leave," Reynard said, and mounted. "I don't plan on coming back."

"Neither do I," Isengrim said.

XIV

Reynard was bitterly cold without the coat that he'd been forced to leave behind, and the two days he'd gone without sleep weighed heavily upon him, but his misery was short lived: traveling by horse, it took a mere day to cover the distance that he and Isengrim had walked on foot.

They followed the beach, only stopping long enough to briefly rest their tiring steeds. Reynard felt pity for the beasts, but every time they slowed he knew that the Calvarians gained on them and, by the time they approached the sheltered cove where the Quicksilver was moored, he could make out the dark smudge of their pursuers across the northern horizon.

They showed no signs of slowing.

As they were passing between the series of basalt outcroppings that hid the ship from sight, an arrow with red fletching thudded into the sand directly ahead of them. Reynard's steed reared wildly, nearly throwing him. When he had gotten the beast under control he saw that a heavily armed figure was now blocking their path.

"Identify yourselves!" a familiar voice boomed. "Or you'll be dead before you can take your next breath!"

"You can put away your crossbow, Grymbart," Reynard said, holding his hands up above his head. "It's us!"

"Hold your fire!" the bearded man yelled, his silver tooth flashing as his mouth curled into a grin. "It's Fox and Isengrim!"

A pair of figures appeared out of the shadows of the basalt stones that surrounded them. It was Tiecelin and Ghul.

"It is good to see you again, Master Fox," the Luxian said, lowering his bow. "And you, Master Isengrim."

"Who's the woman?" Grymbart asked, nodding towards Hirsent.

"I'm afraid introductions will have to wait, Grymbart," Reynard replied. "We need to get out of here, and fast."

"Understood," the mercenary said, breaking into a lumbering trot. "Let's move!"

A few minutes later they had reached the cove, and could see the Quicksilver, her prow and stern shrouded in thick snow.

Reynard had never thought that he would be so glad to see a ship.

One of the Quicksilver's two launches was beached on the rocky shore, and once they had shoved the thing into the icy chop of the bay they leapt aboard and rowed with a speed driven by necessity.

"Fox?" Tybalt said incredulously as he helped pull the exhausted man onto the deck. "Is that really you? You look like shit."

"It's nice to see you too, Tybalt," Reynard managed to say before he found himself locked within Bruin's arms.

"I knew you'd come back to us!" the huge man roared as he released Reynard. "There's no man alive that can outsmart Fox!"

"Wulf's fancy," Tybalt whispered under his breath, his dark eyes flashing with lust as Hirsent swung her shapely legs over the gunwale. "And who, pray tell, is this?"

"Isengrim's woman," Reynard replied.

"Well, then it's an honor to meet you madam," Tybalt greeted Hirsent politely.

Hirsent looked at the former bandit quizzically.

"She doesn't speak our language," Reynard explained.

"Good," Tybalt said through gritted teeth as Isengrim joined them on deck

"Master Isengrim," Captain Roenel said, having come down from the helm to greet them. "Have you the gem?"

"We have," Isengrim replied, fishing the blood-red jewel out of his uniform and placing it into the Captain's open palm.

"It is as beautiful as the legends say," Roenel said, holding the stone aloft and turning it slowly, admiring the way the light of the Firebird glinted off it. "But then, I see you have brought a jewel of your own aboard my ship."

The Captain's gaze shifted to Hirsent who, having perhaps gained the impression that Roenel was a man of authority, bowed to him.

"This lady's name is Hirsent, Captain," Reynard said, stepping forward. "And without her assistance Isengrim and myself could not have escaped from Dis."

"Then let her know that she is welcome amongst us, and that she need not bow- rather, it is I that should do so to her, and to you as well Masters Fox and Isengrim."

With great emotion, Roenel took off his hat and bent into a formal bow.

"Fox and Isengrim!" Pelez shouted. "Hurrah!"

"Hurrah!" the crew of the Quicksilver repeated.

"Now, then," the Captain said as he recovered his head. "Master Pelez, you know what to do."

The first mate saluted sharply and then hollered out, "Hoist anchor and make ready to sail! We're going home boys!"

As the crew eagerly rushed to carry out Pelez's command, Roenel retreated to his cabin with the gem.

They'd hardly glided out of the bay when a company of mounted Calvarian soldiers tore onto the beach, and launched flight after flight of arrows at them from horseback. Some of these missiles struck the Quicksilver's stern, but soon the ship was out in the open ocean, and the crewmen jeered at the Calvarians as they dwindled to mere specks against the stones.

Then Tiecelin's voice cut through their levity like a knife.

"Warships off the port bow! Three vessels and approaching fast!"

The Luxian was not mistaken. A trio of slender Calvarian boats had appeared out of the haze of the blustery snowstorm that blanketed the sea, their prows cutting through the waves like advancing sharks. As Reynard watched with growing dread, the lead vessel changed its course in order to intercept them.

"All hands!" Captain Roenel shouted from the helm. "Prepare to repel boarders!"

"Repel boarders?" Tybalt shouted back as the others scurried to arm themselves. "We'll be slaughtered! We've got to try and make a run for it!"

"Do as the Captain says, Tybalt!" Pelez snarled, giving the man a shove. "We'll never make it!"

"And what about that blasted tunnel?"

Reynard stopped in his tracks, suddenly considering the former bandit's words as the others turned to stare at the passage that cut through the mountains.

"Don't you remember what the Captain told us?" Pelez barked. "Even the Calvarians are afraid of that place!"

"All the better!" Tybalt shot back.

"He's got a point," Grymbart said. "Whatever made its home there might have died years ago for all we know."

"No!" Isengrim's voice cried out. "We cannot go that way! It will mean certain death!"

"And this isn't?" Tybalt screamed, pointing to the spiked prow of the nearest Calvarian ship. "What difference does it make?"

"Tybalt is right, Isengrim," Reynard said, putting a hand on the Northerner's shoulder. "The *Nio-geat* is the only chance we have."

"Wait, you're agreeing with me?" Tybalt said, casting an incredulous glance towards Reynard. "Now I am worried."

Isengrim turned to look at Hirsent, whose fingers were weaving her blond hair into locks that would keep them from whipping around wildly in the wind, calm in the face of almost certain death. With great deliberation he turned back to Reynard and grudgingly nodded his assent.

"Enough talk!" Bruin bellowed. "Let's put it to a vote!"

"No vote!" Pelez barked. "This is for the Captain to decide!"

The men onboard the Quicksilver turned towards Roenel, who was at the helm, his eyes trained on the three ships in the middle distance.

"Well, Captain?" Pelez asked softly.

"Ready the oars," Roenel said at last. "For there'll be no wind in the Gate of Tears."

* * * * * *

The Calvarian vessels showed no sign of giving up their pursuit, and all three ships were now skirting around the coral reef as quickly as they were able. Whether they would brave the passage remained to be seen.

"You really must have pissed them off," Tybalt shouted to Reynard from the other side of the deck, where he and Grymbart were manning one of the oars.

"It's what I do best," Reynard shot back, checking that his weapons were in place as he saw to his own oar.

Schools of silvery naga swam alongside the Quicksilver as they approached the yawning darkness of the tunnel, breaching through the waves and letting out unintelligible cries of protest. Reynard's oar nearly jumped out of his hands as one of the naga grabbed at it from beneath the surface of the water, but together he and Bruin managed to free it.

As the Quicksilver passed through the curved entrance to the Gate of Tears, Tiecelin lit the many torches that the crew had affixed along the ship's length, revealing the cracked and salt encrusted walls of the tunnel. The scream of the wind outside echoed off the walls weirdly, and to Reynard's ears it sounded as if a host of voices wailed piteously at them. Combined with the nagas' high-pitched shrieks, this cacophony did little to inspire confidence.

The tunnel was curved and, as the ship skirted around a particularly sharp corner, darkness enveloped them. They had lost sight of the way ahead.

"Easy now," Roenel said, and the men at the oars slowed their pace. Tiecelin moved to the ship's forecastle, and loosed arrows whose heads had been wrapped in oily rags and set alight into the dark, each one briefly illuminating the passage ahead of them before plunging into the channel.

"Perhaps your woman should get below deck," Bruin said to Isengrim, who was standing watch with Hirsent at the rear of the boat, their steel swords flashing red in the torchlight.

"Hirsent can fight as well as any man here," Isengrim replied coolly. "If not better."

"I can attest to that," Reynard nodded.

Gradually the tunnel widened. The smooth, carved walls gave way to the rugged natural stone of a subterranean cavern. Great shelves of rock thrust from the walls, on top of which the naga had constructed crude cairns made of coral and shell around which were strewn treasures scavenged from the deep: gold there was, and precious stones, and heaps of pearl that the tide had scattered.

But even these treasures were nothing compared to the bones that littered that place. Many were those of fish and other creatures of the sea, but human skulls too could be seen grinning at them from recessed alcoves, and the calcified skeletons of chimera lay heaped within the ribcages of whales.

"Hydra's Teeth!" Tybalt gasped, his awe momentarily overcoming his fear of Ghul, who glared at him hatefully. "What a hoard! We could all live like princes with a trunk or two of this stuff!"

Grymbart laughed.

"Don't even think about it, Tybalt! We don't have time to sightsee."

"Easy for you say," Tybalt grumbled. "You're getting paid!"

Suddenly, a hideous scream rent the air. A gray-skinned naga with a pale white belly and a mouth full of serrated teeth had somehow managed to scale the starboard side of the hull and had thrown itself onto the deck. It landed between Baucent and Ghul, and though apparently unsuited for life out of the water it tore a bloody chunk of flesh from the cook's leg before flopping onto the deck, its gills gasping wildly.

"Ghul!" Baucent screamed through his pain. "Kill it!"

If Ghul had heard the cook's words, he did not show it, and merely watched fascinated as the naga thrashed about violently, its tail sweeping Pelez's legs out from under him as the first mate ran up to aid his companion.

When it was clear that the Glyconese man would not act, Grymbart lumbered forward and severed the naga's head from its shoulders with a powerful swing of his sword. Hirsent rushed to staunch the flow of the cook's grisly wound, wrapping her own belt around the man's thigh and binding it tight.

"What's the matter with you?" Grymbart asked Ghul hotly, but the Glyconese did not answer except to mutter prayers under his breath.

"Forget about him and watch my back!" Pelez said, picking himself up from the deck and taking hold of the oar that Ghul and Baucent had been rowing. "We've got to keep moving!"

Several more of the naga attacked them, throwing away their lives in an attempt to kill these interlopers from the outside world, but now the crew was ready for the grotesque menagerie that was clambering up the side of the ship. While the crewmen rowed, the skilled warriors aboard cut down the things as soon as they came within striking distance, and soon the gunwales were dripping with the naga's milky blood.

Suddenly the attacks stopped. In the water below them the chimera disappeared, swimming rapidly back towards the cave's entrance.

"That wasn't so hard," Tybalt said, retrieving one of his daggers from the jellied eye of a naga that was bristling with spines. "Guess they lost the stomach for a fight."

"I do not think they were running from us," Reynard said, and pointed over the ship's prow. "Look!"

They had reached the far end of the cavern, where the Calvarians had carved another passage through the bones of the earth. On either side of this arch the naga had added their own decorations: bas-relief carvings that all depicted scenes of a great seven-headed dragon, wingless and loathsome, rising from the depths of the sea to crush the Firebird between its fangs. Underneath its talons a wolf and a lion lay bleeding and mutilated.

"The Destroyer . . . " Ghul whispered, falling to his knees and beginning to strip off his leaf-plate armor with violently shaking hands.

"Maybe-" Tybalt began shakily. "Maybe we ought to turn back."

"We cannot," Captain Roenel said firmly. "Look to our rear."

There were lights in the darkness behind them, and faintly in the distance one could hear the steady beat of drums.

"The Calvarians," Grymbart said.

"Shit," Tybalt spat. "Shit, shit, shit."

"I'm with Tybalt on this one," Bruin said.

By now Ghul had stripped himself to the waist, revealing both his ascetically conditioned body and the myriad tattoos that covered it. In a strange voice he began to chant the repetitive mantras of the faithful of Hydra, his thumb delicately tracing the sinuous lines of the curling ouroboros on his chest.

"Shall I get him up, Captain?" Pelez asked, concern etching his face.

Roenel shook his head. "Keep to the oars and leave him be. There's no telling what he'll do in the state he's in."

"Aye, Captain."

They had not gone far down the second passage before it opened onto another natural cavern. The walls were coated by some sort of faintly luminous fungi that served to give Reynard a rough idea of the chamber's shape and size: on their left a series of increasingly jagged stalagmites and rocks formed a virtual gauntlet through which no ship could safely pass, while to their right there loomed a partially submerged entrance to a cave that ancient tides must have created long before the Calvarians had come to this place.

And, on the far side of the cavern, Reynard saw a third carved passage: the one that would lead them home.

"We might find a way through those rocks," Bruin said hopefully.

Reynard turned to the man and shook his head. "It would take too long, and the Calvarians would surely catch us."

"But if we take the channel-"

"Then we must pass the cave," Reynard said.

"'Ride to the left, lose your horse,'" Grymbart said, quoting from an old Solothurnian folk tale. "'Ride to the right, lose your head.'"

"We have come this far, men," Captain Roenel said from the helm. "If these pale-skinned demons want us, let's make them work for it! Master Pelez, pick up the stroke!"

"Aye, Captain!" Pelez replied briskly. "All hands, smartly now!"

At the first mate's words the crewmen doubled the pace of their strokes, and soon they were all groaning with exertion.

Their timing could not have been better, for only a few moments later a Calvarian war galley appeared in the passage behind them. Over a hundred oars bristled from her sides, and as they drove backwards and forwards Reynard was given the impression of a great black centipede scurrying forward on multiple legs. A steel ram fashioned to resemble a ravenous wolf's head tipped the galley's bow, and a ballista had been affixed to its forecastle.

A moment later the crew of the catapult launched a stone projectile at the Quicksilver, which struck the ship's stern with a resounding crash.

"Master Tiecelin!" Captain Roenel shouted. "Put some fire on that ballista!"

The Luxian nodded and scrambled to the rear of the ship, where he began to unleash a withering volley of arrows that felled several of the engineers manning the siege weapon. The Calvarians managed to launch a second shot before fleeing the prow entirely, but the stone went wild and collided into a nearby stalagmite.

The snarling head of the war galley's ram was now directly alongside the main deck. Apparently the Calvarians planned to take the Quicksilver by force of arms rather than sink it- Reynard could see the gray uniformed marines on the war galley's deck readying a pair of spike-tipped boarding ramps, while archers began peppering the Quicksilver with arrows that forced him to drop his oar and take cover behind one of the skiffs.

Isengrim and Hirsent were huddled there as well.

"Master Fox," Isengrim said. "I do not suppose you have any last tricks up your sleeve?"

"Fresh out, I'm afraid," Reynard replied. "But there are probably only a hundred of them. Not bad odds."

Isengrim smiled, and said "At least I can trust the man who will fight at my side."

"I am good then," Reynard said. "For a low Southern dog?"

"You are no dog," the Northerner said quietly, "I can see that now, Fox."

"Reynard," he said. "My true name is Reynard. It is the name my father gave me."

"You do me honor, Reynard," Isengrim replied, and bowed ever so slightly.

"As do you," Reynard replied. "I know that I have been- difficult."

"There is no need for you to apologize," Isengrim replied. "I did not give you any reason to call me a friend."

Reynard smiled wistfully. "It has been a long time since I called any man 'friend.'"

Isengrim held out his hand and after a moment Reynard took it and they clasped each other's wrists.

Then the first boarding ramp slammed down onto the deck, and he and Isengrim were rushing forward to meet the armed figures that were charging onto the Quicksilver.

And though he found himself wishing that he wasn't so tired, and that he had been given a chance to have a proper bath before he died, he thought that it was not a bad thing to die amongst friends.

A moment later he found himself flat on his back, the back of his head throbbing with pain. His hands patted down his brigandine-encased chest, trying to find the arrow that he was certain must have struck him. Then he noticed that he was not alone on the deck. Even Isengrim had been thrown off of his feet.

"What-" Reynard began as he tried to regain his footing, and then he heard the roar of wood splintering, and felt the ship lurch violently away from the Calvarian vessel. Those aboard both ships struggled wildly to keep to their feet, while the unfortunate Calvarian marines on the boarding ramp were thrown helplessly into the water, the weight of their own armor dragging them screaming down into the depths.

Then a dark shape shot up between the ships, its ascent accompanied by a deluge of violently displaced water that stung Reynard's eyes and momentarily obscured whatever unnatural thing the dim and melancholy sea had given birth to.

Even as the mist cleared, Reynard could not fully make out what he saw, for the creature had already latched onto the Calvarian war galley and was in the process of tearing the ship apart. The bulk of it appeared to be a great rubbery stalk or tail, from which jutted a number of slavering canine heads. Above this writhing mass sprouted a surprisingly feminine torso whose great leering head was swathed with hair that gleamed sickly green in the pale light of the cavern. With its monstrously strong humanoid arms it languidly swept up handfuls of soldiers from the war galley's deck, rending men in twain or crushing them into a pulpy mess, all the while letting out what sounded like cries of satisfaction from its fang-lined mouth.

But even these men Reynard considered lucky compared to those unfortunates amongst the Calvarians who dared, hopelessly, to fight. Even the steel swords of the Calvarians seemed to avail them nothing, for the cuts they made were merely superficial wounds compared to the sheer immensity of the leviathan, who swept man after man into the snapping jaws that lay nestled at its waist.

"By the gods," Reynard said in a half-whisper, and stood transfixed by the awesome sight of the beast as it curled around the Calvarian vessel's midsection, the numerous tails of its serpentine lower body wrapping around the hull until, with an awful crack, the war galley split into three separate sections, a shower of splintered wood flying through the air as the demolished ship sank into the murk. The colossal chimera dove into the wreckage with a scream that made Reynard's ears ring, and disappeared, its segmented tail showering the Quicksilver with water that was mixed with Calvarian blood.

"Row!" Captain Roenel yelled. "Get hold of the oars and row! Row for your lives!"

The men did not have time, though, to react to the Captain's frantic commands, for a moment later the ship nearly capsized as several of the sea monster's sharp-taloned fingers crashed down onto the main deck, its black nails cutting through the planks as if they were made of cheese. Then the head rose out of the water, and Reynard could see its eyes through the tangle of its seaweed colored hair: golden, with a great black slit that narrowed in the flickering torchlight.

Reynard knew it was pointless to resist- what could anyone do against such strength?- and so he lowered his weapons and dropped them onto the deck, and stared up into the great sea naga's eyes and thought of Hermeline, and of what Duke Nobel would do to her when he did not return.

Forgive me, Reynard pleaded silently as the first of the snarling dog heads lashed out over the gunwale.

Distantly, Reynard could hear Ghul's voice, and saw that the odd-eyed man was standing now, arms outstretched, his chanting grown frantic with religious ecstasy.

"Glory!" he was crying. "Glory to Hydra the Many-Headed, the Dark Mother, whose coils enfold the universe! Destroyer of Worlds, Redeemer of Man, She who existed before the impurity of light and flesh, forgive your unworthy faithful! Forgive your unworthy children!"

Reynard looked back up at the thing that towered over them. It was not attacking. Its many limbs were frozen in mid-air, and its golden eyes were locked on the tattooed man who was singing out praises to Hydra, the Sea Bitch.

"Forgive us!" Ghul chanted. "Mother of us all, forgive us! Let us be washed clean of our sins!"

"Forgive-" Reynard said haltingly, his arms raising slightly. "Forgive me."

Tybalt, who was poised to hack at one of the dog-like things shot Reynard a sideways glance.

"Fox, what are you-"

"Forgive me!" Reynard repeated, his voice rising to match Ghul's. "Forgive me!"

Ghul threw himself to the deck and began to grovel on his hands and knees, throwing up his head only long enough to let out another wild prayer. "Forgive us our weakness! Forgive us our lust, our hatred, our pride, and our deceit! Forgive us!"

"Forgive me!" Reynard said, his voice cracking. "Forgive me!"

"He's gone crazy!" Tybalt said to Grymbart as Reynard dropped to his own knees.

"Yeah- crazy like a fox!" Grymbart replied, throwing down his own weapon and falling to his knees to begin prayers of his own.

Soon there was not a man or woman aboard the Quicksilver who was not chanting with Ghul and Reynard, even Isengrim and Hirsent, who clutched each other by the hand as they kowtowed. And whether the leviathan could understand their words and was mollified by them, or if it merely found it amusing that its prey should so willingly offer up their own lives, Reynard could not say, but when a pair of Calvarian war galleys entered the cavern, and desperately began to launch projectiles at the monster that they found blocking their path, the sea naga disengaged from the Quicksilver with a fierce cry and dove back into the water to destroy these new interlopers.

As soon as the thing had submerged, Reynard stood up and wiped the commingled tears and salt water from his eyes and screamed for them to row.

They caught up what was left of the oars, or threw new ones into place, and as the terrible thing that guarded the Gate of Tears busied itself with the destruction of the Calvarians at their back, they passed underneath the third arch.

Reynard took one last look behind him as they rowed through the darkness, until the pale light of the cavern was but a speck in the distance.

"Forgive me," he said, and turned his face forward, towards the future.

* * * * * *

Three days later, as the Quicksilver passed through the *Nio-Geat's* final channel and they found themselves once again in the blustery sea that lay north of Solothurn, Reynard could at last feel certain that they had escaped from that dark and terrible place. Now all that was left was to traverse the icy winter sea that lay between them and Arcasia.

Though the crew was tired, and ever fearful that the black sails of a Calvarian vessel would appear on the horizon, there was an air of celebration aboard the Quicksilver that Reynard had not seen since the night they had spent moored at Barca. Partly this was due to the fact that they had managed to escape the horrors that a second voyage through Vulp Vora would have forced them to endure, but Reynard also knew that it was because they would be returning to Calyx victorious.

Only Ghul appeared to have been unmoved, acting as though he had never doubted that they would return safely to familiar water, and coldly turned away any attempt by the crew to thank him for having saved their lives in the Gate of Tears. If anything, Reynard thought that he seemed even more reserved than ever, and wondered if the odd-eyed man had perhaps been insulted by the crew's false show of devotion towards his goddess.

Reynard gave up his bed in the cramped cabin that he had shared with Isengrim for the length of their journey and slept with the others in the main hold, allowing his companion and Hirsent the intimacy that they had so long been denied. The effect that this had on the disciplined Northerner was subtle, but obvious to Reynard: he was certainly more prone to smile.

The crew was quick to accept Hirsent as one of their number, save for Pelez, who obviously felt her to be a poor replacement for tough old Lady Moire. But excluding the first mate, there was not a man aboard who did not fall at least a little bit in love with her. This was not terribly surprising to Reynard, due to her statuesque beauty and the fact that the crew had not seen a young woman in months. The cook in particular fawned on her, as her ministrations had saved his life, and Reynard noticed that his meals had improved noticeably now that he was preparing food that she would eat.

So the days passed, and Reynard spent what time he had practicing on his old fiddle, or playing Spoils and Queens with Tybalt, Bruin and Espinarz. At meals he would listen to Grymbart's colorful war stories and, at least once a day, he would pay a visit to the cargo hold, where Tiecelin cared for his trio of adopted shrikes. They had grown quite large in a short time, and had begun to test their wings. As they grew, their downy brown feathers were replaced by brilliant red, dusky black or, in the case of the female, plum. Tiecelin constructed a larger enclosure for them, and allowed them to fly around the cargo hold when no one but he and Reynard were watching.

One day, while Reynard was on the night watch, Hirsent approached him.

"I- thank you," she said haltingly, and with a heavy Calvarian accent. Isengrim had been painstakingly teaching her how to speak the Southern tongue, but she was far from mastering it. "For- Isengrim."

"You are happy?" Reynard asked, but she did not understand the word. He tried again, in her tongue: *"Ablissian?"*

"Yes," she replied. "Now- am having my *lufiend. Ablissian."*

"Then, I am glad," Reynard said, and smiled wanly.

Hirsent seemed to sense his melancholy and her brows knit with concern.

"You- are having *lufestre?"*

Reynard did not answer immediately. He tried to call up Hermeline in his mind, for whose sake he had traveled into the same peril that Isengrim had braved to retrieve his own love, but found that all he could think of was a pair of sad hazel eyes.

"Yes," he said at last.

"Ablissian," Hirsent said and squeezed Reynard's arm. Then Isengrim came up from the hold below and she went to him and kissed him dearly, an act that caused the serious man to blush furiously.

"Be taking care of Fox, my *lufiend,"* she said. "I am needing to help with- ah, what is word- sail?"

"Sail," Isengrim nodded.

Hirsent smiled prettily, and then strode across the deck and began to help Tybalt hoist one of the sails.

As she chatted with the former bandit in broken Aquilian, Isengrim's mouth curled into a deep frown.

"You needn't worry about her, you know," Reynard said quietly, "She can take care of herself."

"It is not for Hirsent that I worry," Isengrim said. "But men like Tybalt- he little realizes what she is capable of."

"Perhaps," Reynard said, "It would be best to show them?

* * * * * * *

At the next mid-day meal Reynard and Isengrim assembled on the deck, and the men gathered around them, fully expecting to watch another breath-taking duel. But of course it was not the tall Northerner who came out to fight Reynard, but Hirsent, who strode onto the deck dressed down to her ivory uniform's tunic and breeches.

"Now here's someone more fitting for you to fight with, Fox!" Tybalt sneered as the blond woman took her place across from Reynard and saluted him with her longsword. "Try not to overexert yourself!"

Reynard shook his head and returned Hirsent's salute.

He had hardly taken a step before his female opponent rushed forward, launching a series of harrying blows that he only just managed to deflect. Then, with a low sweep of her legs, she knocked him flat onto his back and pinned him to the ground with the pointed edge of her blade.

"Who next?" Hirsent said to the crowd of stunned onlookers.

"Who *is* next," Isengrim said, correcting her grammar.

"You then?" Hirsent replied, turning a somewhat perturbed eye towards her lover and raised her sword in a challenge to him.

Isengrim cocked an eyebrow, but did not back down.

As the two Calvarians took their places the men erupted into a series of petty wagers and predictions.

"Ten crowns says he'll throw the thing," Espinarz said, jostling for a better view of the fight.

"I'll take that wager," Grymbart replied.

"Count me in too," Bruin added. "No one can beat Isengrim- not even Fox."

"What do you think, Master Fox," Tybalt asked Reynard, obviously looking for some leverage. "You think he'll go easy on his she-wolf?"

Reynard shrugged. "I suppose anything is possible, though I've not known Isengrim to go easy on anyone."

"And what are you going to bet with, Tybalt?" Bruin laughed. "You got a stash somewhere back in Engadlin?"

Tybalt's eyes narrowed. "I'll make you eat those words, shit-for-brains. Put me in. Ten crowns on the ice queen."

"Done," Grymbart said. "Now shut your big mouth, they're about to start."

It was the shortest duel that Reynard had ever seen. Both Calvarians studied each other for a moment, changed stances, and then exploded into motion, their swords flashing briefly before coming to rest just short of each other's collarbones. For a moment they stood like that, frozen in an almost identical position, and then they backed away from each other, sheathed their blades, and bowed.

"Shit," Tybalt grumbled. "I should have figured it would be a draw."

"It was no draw," Isengrim said then, regarding Tybalt with his unblinking stare. "Had this been a real fight Hirsent would now be dead."

"But, how can you be certain?"

"Do you doubt my words?" Isengrim asked, and the former bandit lowered his head, unwilling to argue the point further.

There was a communal groan from those who had bet on Isengrim's lover as the men returned to their duties.

"Now who has shit for brains?" Bruin said as he put Tybalt into a headlock and began to rap at his scalp with his knuckles. "Someone owes me a lot of drinks when we get back to Calyx!"

"Let go of me, you dumb brute!" Tybalt howled, twisting and kicking as Bruin dragged him back to work.

"No exception for Hirsent I see," Reynard said to Isengrim once the men had cleared.

"When you fight," Isengrim replied. "Fight to win."

"Even against the ones that you love?"

"Especially them," Isengrim said with a sad smile. "For you will never know a more dangerous foe."

* * * * * * *

By Reynard's estimation it was nearly the end of Pearlmonth by the time that the Quicksilver reached Larsa, and he saw once again ships that flew the standard of the Count of Lothier- but this was not the end of their journey. Instead they sailed west and, having rounded the Cape of Lorn, made for the city of Nemea- where Count Bricemer was apparently awaiting their arrival.

They had nearly reached that ancient port when the Captain ordered the crew to drop anchor near a marsh just north of the city proper.

"Well," Tybalt said, picking at his teeth with a knife. "What do we do now?"

"First, Ghul will inform Count Bricemer that we have returned safely," Roenel answered, producing a sealed document from his coat and handing it to the odd-eyed man. "This pass will gain you admittance to the Count."

Ghul nodded and stood by as Condylure and Musard uncovered one of the skiffs.

"While we wait," Roenel went on, "I thought that perhaps those of you in Bricemer's . . . employ would join me for supper. Espinarz has caught some fine-looking salmon and Baucent has promised not to burn it."

"Sounds delicious," Reynard said. "Will there be wine with dinner?"

"As a matter of fact," Roenel answered. "I've been saving some bottles of Jerriais for this evening."

"How delightful," Reynard said, smiling thinly.

"You may join us as well," Roenel addressed Hirsent. "If you so wish."

Hirsent nodded silently.

"What about the rest of us, Captain?" Pelez asked.

"Stay on deck," Roenel answered. "And keep watch for the Count's men."

"Aye."

As he filed into Roenel's cabin with the others, Reynard saw the captain's quarters had suffered considerable damage during their escape through the *Nio-geat*: the windows that ran along the ship's stern had all been smashed, and there was still a deep gash in the floor where the Calvarian projectile had landed. Still, it was roomy compared to the cramped quarters below deck, and the thought of a meal that did not consist of hardtack infested with weevils made his mouth water.

As they took their places at the table, Roenel poured his Frisian wine into fine crystal goblets that looked rather out of place when one of them was placed into Bruin's meaty fist.

"Wulf's Fancy," Captain Roenel said, raising his glass.

"Wulf's Fancy," Reynard and the others replied and drained their glasses, save for the Calvarians, who each took a polite sip before setting their glasses down.

"No wine for the crew?" Reynard said as Baucent brought in the main course.

"I'll buy them a whole barrel once this matter is done with."

"How long before we can expect Bricemer to arrive?" Grymbart asked the captain as he shoveled cuts of fish onto his plate. "I've got a good wife here in Nemea, and I imagine she'll be better disposed towards me if I come bearing a trunk full of gold."

"It should not be long," Roenel replied.

"Are you planning to retire, Master Grymbart?" Reynard asked.

"Retire?" the bearded man scoffed. "And break my ass on some farm? I could have done that in Mandross."

"Then what are you going to do with the money?" Tybalt asked, his words dripping with envy.

"Oh, I don't know. Could always start up my own company, hire on some likely lads who are good with a blade. There's always plenty of work for sellswords. Any of you boys are interested, you're more than welcome to join me. Might even be a place in there for you, Tybalt- you can work off your considerable gambling debt to me."

Tybalt scowled and poured himself a second glass of wine.

"What about you, Master Fox?" Grymbart asked Reynard. "I could use a quick-witted fellow like yourself, and you're no slouch with a blade."

"If it's all the same, Master Grymbart," Reynard replied coolly, "I think it might be hasty of us to consider the future until after we've delivered the gem to Duke Nobel."

"You know," Bruin said, "There's one thing I don't get."

"Just one thing?" Tybalt snickered.

"Yeah," the big man groused. "How much is that stone worth?"

"It's a gem as big as your fist," said Tybalt. "Use your imagination!"

"You're an idiot, Tybalt," Grymbart laughed, "The Duke didn't send us on this little errand just for some fancy bauble. He's trying to start a war."

"What do you mean, a war?" Tybalt snorted. "War with Calvaria? That's-"

"Exactly what the Duke wants," Reynard interjected. "Or else we would never have gone on this voyage."

Isengrim nodded. "The theft of that gem was a grand insult to Calvaria. The judges will be forced retaliate, for fear of appearing weak in the eyes of a people they have subjugated for centuries."

"But what hope does the Duke have of defeating Calvaria?" Tybalt asked.

"By himself, none," Reynard said. "But a noble of the line of old Aquilia, with the gem of Zosia and the Countess of Luxia in his possession could unite all of greater Arcasia against them."

"You are a clever man, Master Fox," a voice said from the doorway.

It was Count Bricemer.

A pair of men-at-arms carrying crossbows flanked the Duke's seneschal, whose gaze passed briefly over the men who had returned alive from Calvaria.

"Interesting," he hummed, his eyes pausing briefly on Hirsent. "I do not recall that I sent *two* Calvarians to retrieve the Duke's gem."

"Count Bricemer," Isengrim said, rising from his chair. "Allow me to introduce my-"

Isengrim's voice faltered uncharacteristically. It was obvious that he was unsure what he should call her.

"Hirsent," she said firmly, stepping between herself and her lover and bowing. "*Fisicien*, second class."

"It is an honor to make your acquaintance, Madam," the Count said stiffly. "But I'm afraid I must cut short the pleasantries. Captain Roenel, do you have the gem?"

"Yes, Your Excellency," Roenel said, and retrieved a strongbox from amongst his personal possessions. The room was silent as Roenel opened the box and revealed the shining jewel that lay within.

"Well, Captain," Bricemer said as he took possession of the gem, "You and your crew are to be congratulated on a job well done: Masters Fox and Isengrim in especial. The Duke will be very pleased."

"I am at his command, Your Excellency," Roenel said, bowing.

"Indeed," Bricemer said, and turned on his heel to leave.

"Here now, Bricemer," Grymbart blustered. "What about the money you promised me? I went through a lot of trouble for the sake of that rock, and it's only fair that you pay up now."

Bricemer paused in the doorway, turning slightly to regard the mercenary. His brows were arched in amusement. "Very well, Master Grymbart. If you are so impatient, then I suppose I must oblige you."

"Sergeant?" Bricemer said, gesturing to one of the armed men flanking him: a scar-faced individual who raised a loaded crossbow and fired.

XV

Grymbart gasped for breath, his hand clutching at the bolt that protruded from his barrel-shaped chest as he struggled to rise from his seat. Then a second missile struck him, this time in the heart. He collapsed backwards, and the cabin was filled with the clatter of metal plates and the tinkling of glass as Roenel's crystal goblets shattered underneath the bulky man's weight.

"Treachery!" Tybalt cried as he reached for his weapons, only to find Captain Roenel's sword at his throat.

Isengrim had drawn as well, and stood ready to cut down anyone who moved.

"Shall I kill this one now, Your Excellency?" Roenel asked, pressing the tip of his cutlass into Tybalt's neck.

"I wouldn't trouble yourself, Captain," Count Bricemer said languidly as a dozen more soldiers poured into the cabin, their crossbows trained on the men who were now standing around the table. "In fact you and Master Isengrim may lower your swords."

"What- what do you mean?" Roenel stammered, his face growing pale. "You said that my crew would be spared!"

"That was a remote possibility- a fleeting one, I'm afraid."

"What have you done with my men?"

"Come outside and you will see," Bricemer replied. "Gandolin, if any of these men make any sudden movements, the Calvarians in especial, shoot them at once."

"As you command, Your Excellency," the scarred man who had shot Grymbart replied.

One by one they were herded onto the deck, where the other half of the Count's soldiers waited for them: all of them were hard-faced men who were well armed and armored.

Ghul stood with them.

Sprawled across the deck were the bodies of Pelez, Baucent, Condylure, and Musard. They had all been slain by sword strokes. Espinarz was draped over the helm, his stout frame riddled with crossbow bolts.

"So," Reynard said, "We were never meant to return from Calvaria."

Bricemer smiled. "Not alive, Master Fox, no. To be honest, I am impressed that so many of you survived the journey."

"You twist!" Tybalt spat. "We did your dirty work, we got your gem, what more do you want from us?"

"Why, nothing, Tybalt," Bricemer replied, laughing. "The fact that we wish to have nothing to do with you happens to be the crux of this matter."

"But, why?" Bruin said, his huge fists clenching and unclenching. "Why kill us?"

"Well, Master Bruin, I hardly think it appropriate that the great jewel of Zosia should be returned to the Duke's hand by a murderous sot such as yourself. Just as it would appear unseemly for the future King of Arcasia to deal with a group of low brigands, thieves, and pirates."

"Then who did steal the gem," Reynard asked. "If not us?"

"Why, these fine men you see before you," Bricemer said, gesturing to the smirking soldiers that ringed them. "They are some of my best men, and will be well rewarded for their efforts."

"And, what of Isengrim? Was he not a loyal servant?"

"Yes," Bricemer said with mock sympathy. "I do regret having to dispose of so fine a tool, but I'm afraid that Master Isengrim's usefulness has come to an end. We've learned as much as I think we can from him about Calvarian military tactics, and with war brewing it would be dangerous to keep a Northerner so close to the Duke's inner circle. Even a tamed wolf may one day bite the hand that feeds him."

"You should prepare yourself to feel that bite, Bricemer," Isengrim said darkly. "You should have brought more men with you."

"Why bother?" Bricemer asked with a smirk. "When Ghul has killed all of you already."

"What do you mean?" Tybalt said.

"I mean that Ghul has been poisoning all of you since you rounded the Cape of Lorn- that was his mission, you see, and you have Master Fox to thank for his cooperation. The Glyconese find the disturbance of the dead to be a very serious crime, Master Fox, and he could hardly pass up a chance to personally see to the destruction of the one who desecrated a Glyconese graveyard."

"Poisoned?" Tybalt balked. "I feel nothing."

"Neither do I," Roenel added.

"You will," Ghul said. "Very soon."

Ghul began to stalk towards Reynard, and as he talked he fingered a delicate hooked blade of Glyconese make that had been lovingly polished.

"It will start as a tingling in your fingers. Do you feel it, you heathen? Soon, the tingling will become a burning, and the burning will climb into your chest. By then you will be unable to move, paralyzed, but you will still able to feel even the most delicate touch."

"And then, Master Fox," Ghul said, raising the hook for emphasis, "We will begin."

"That certainly does sound unpleasant," Reynard replied. "And what, may I ask, do they call this poison of yours?"

"Redeemer's Kiss," Ghul replied. "It is tasteless and odorless when dissolved into food. The perfect thing to kill a rat with."

"I don't suppose it happens to look anything like this?" Reynard drawled, lightly tossing an object to the deck: a leather pouch that had spilled open to reveal its contents, a chalky powder.

Ghul's almond-and-hazel-colored eyes widened, and then flashed back to meet Reynard's. Then the Glyconese killer raised his own hands and stared at them as they began to twitch.

"No," Ghul hissed.

"Yes," Reynard corrected. "Now, Tiecelin!"

At Reynard's words, the Luxian scout let out a sharp whistle. In response, a trio of winged figures erupted out of the hold, screeching as they launched themselves high above the deck.

"Doom!" the eldest of Tiecelin's shrikes shrieked.

"Doom!" the female cried in agreement as they launched into a perfect dive.

"Doom!" the youngest screamed as his talons tore into the neck of the soldier that he had barreled over with the force of his impact.

"You may have poisoned me," Ghul hissed at Reynard, drawing out his twin swords and lunging towards him with considerable speed for a man who was dying inch by inch. "But I still have time enough to kill you!"

Reynard drew his rapier as he dodged Ghul's opening salvo of strikes, careful to keep the Glyconese assassin between him and the bulk of the crossbow-wielding soldiers, who were still unsure of how to proceed- they might be veterans, but even the canniest among them could not help but be momentarily distracted by the sight of the vibrantly colored creatures swooping amongst them.

Yet, a moment was all the time that Isengrim and Hirsent needed to cut down the two unfortunate soldiers who were within striking distance. Their armored bodies had not even struck the blood stained deck before both Calvarians had felled a second set of adversaries.

"Kill them!" Reynard heard Bricemer scream, his natural calm having completely evaporated in the face of real danger. "Fire!"

A sort of drum-like staccato filled the air as a dozen crossbows released their quarrels. Bolts filled the air, most of the shots going wild as the Count's soldiers were forced to choose between multiple targets: the shrikes circling overhead or the trained killers who were cutting a bloody swath across the deck.

Reynard only barely registered the fight that was erupting around him, for he needed all of his considerable skill to fend off Ghul's ferocious attacks, one of which shattered his parrying dagger.

Casting aside the useless weapon, Reynard danced away from his foe, briefly catching sight of Bruin tossing one of the Count's men over the side of the Quicksilver as he tore at the clasp that held his cloak to his shoulders. Ripping it free he bundled the cloth around his fist and whipped it at Ghul, attempting to entangle one of his opponent's weapons in its folds.

The Glyconese assassin danced backwards, and for a moment they traded cautious blows. Then the Glyconese came in close, his twin blades casting Reynard's rapier aside as he used the force of his own body to knock the smaller man onto his back.

Reynard rolled away just as one of Ghul's swords glanced off of the deck, missing his head by mere inches. With a flick of his wrist he wrapped the tail of his cloak around the assassin's booted foot, and yanked.

As Ghul fell forward, his body twisting wildly to avoid landing on his own swords, Reynard leapt to his feet and gained some distance on the odd-eyed man.

"You haven't been building up an immunity to Redeemer's Kiss, have you?" he asked Ghul as the assassin leapt back onto his feet. "I think it would be only fair for you to tell me if you have."

A fierce growl through clenched teeth was Ghul's only response before he resumed his relentless attack, his armor flying around him as he spun into a whirling series of slashes and kicks.

"You're very good, you know," Reynard managed to quip as he narrowly dodged one of the assassin's strikes. "Have you considered a career as a temple boy?"

"Fight me, curse you!" Ghul snarled.

"It's just that, with your foot-work and those mysterious eyes of yours," Reynard responded, not letting up even as one of Ghul's swords slashed open his arm, "You could have made just as much money as a knifeman does. I know plenty of women, and some men as well, who would have taken to you very much."

"Blasphemer!" Ghul screamed. "Heretic!"

"And what a voice! With a little training I'm sure you'd make quite an impression at one of Lord Chanticleer's concerts. Tell me, do you know any of the words to Lady of Diamonds? I happen to play a rather stirring rendition on fiddle, and if there's still time after the fight-"

Ghul's right foot connected solidly with Reynard's jaw, a blow that sent him crashing against the ship's deckhouse.

"Ah, well," Reynard muttered as he struggled to his feet, "Perhaps another time then."

"Die!" Ghul whispered through chattering teeth as he shakily raised his sword for a killing stroke.

Then Ghul paused, his mismatched eyes widening as the tip of Isengrim's sword erupted from his breast.

For a moment he seemed not to have registered the wound. Then he dropped the short sword that his left arm clutched, and weaved drunkenly back and forth, dark blood washing over the greenish patina of his leaf mail. Finally, with a ragged gasp, he keeled over onto his side.

"Took you long enough," Reynard said to Isengrim.

"Some of them had some skill," Isengrim replied, cleaning the blood off of his blade with a cloth.

The fight on the deck was over, and for a moment there was no sound but the moans of the wounded and the dull lap of the ocean.

"Corbant is dead," Tiecelin stated flatly as he bent over the still form of the youngest of his shrikes, which had landed unceremoniously onto the forecastle after being struck by a crossbow bolt.

Hirsent was leaning against the ship's mast, her ivory uniform stained red with the color of her own blood. Isengrim rushed over to her and began following her instructions in order to dress the wound.

"It is not fatal," Isengrim reassured Reynard as he sewed the wound closed. "A clean cut through the shoulder. She is not accustomed to fighting so many opponents at once-"

Hirsent winced in pain and muttered a harsh Calvarian admonition under her breath that immediately shut Isengrim up.

"Roenel?" Reynard asked Isengrim.

"He went straight for Bricemer," Bruin replied, shaking his head. "The Count's men killed him before I could reach them."

Reynard found the Captain face down in a pool of his own blood. The tip of a crossbow bolt protruded from his back.

"And where is Bricemer?" Reynard asked coldly.

"He is here, Master Fox," Tiecelin replied, pointing a slender finger towards the side of the deck. "I saw him trying to escape so I put an arrow through his kneecap."

Count Bricemer was slumped against the gunwale and moaning loudly, obviously in great pain. He still clutched the strongbox that held the gem, and had drawn his own rapier, which he raised feebly as Tybalt approached him.

"So," the bandit said, kicking Bricemer's weapon aside and gripping the wounded noble by the front of his finely embroidered doublet. "You thought you could just use us and then cast us aside when it suited you, you miserable excuse for a man?"

"Mercy," Bricemer said between pained breaths.

"The same mercy that Grymbart and the others received?" Tybalt asked, pressing a dagger under the Count's neck. "Is that the mercy you mean?"

"No, please-" Bricemer pleaded. "I can pay you!"

"Silence, you slime!" Tybalt said, the tip of his blade drawing blood as he pressed it deeper into the Count's flesh.

"That's enough, Tybalt," Reynard said, placing the tip of his own blade on the back of the hot-headed man's neck.

"You mean we're not going to kill him?" Tybalt snorted, but let go of Bricemer, sending him crashing down to the deck with a howl of pain.

"I'm afraid not," Reynard replied, turning to face Isengrim. "Have Hirsent see to the Count's wound as soon as she is able. We don't want him dying on us after all the trouble we went through to capture him."

"Oh, Fenix's blessings on you, Master Fox-" Bricemer managed to say before Reynard struck him a solid blow across the head with the hilt of his sword.

"You could have at least let me do that," Tybalt pouted sulkily, pulling one of his throwing daggers out of the eye socket of one of the slain. "But tell me, 'Master Fox', just how long have you known that the Count was planning to kill us?"

"Since the beginning."

"You idiot!" Tybalt spat. "You could have gotten me killed! And Grymbart might have lived if you'd bothered to warn us: Espinarz and the others too."

"I couldn't risk telling them," Reynard said, turning to face Tybalt's accusing gaze. "I wasn't certain who I could trust."

"But- if you knew about the poison, then surely that would tell you who the Count had marked for death, right?"

"Not necessarily," Reynard explained. "There might have been an antidote to the Redeemer's Kiss that only the Count's minions knew about. Or perhaps some of you might have been told that they would be spared if they didn't interfere while the others were killed: Roenel was obviously amongst that number. There was also the remote possibility that Ghul had been acting under the orders of another party altogether in order to sabotage the mission. Since I couldn't be sure, the only safe thing to do was to switch the poison for a harmless look-alike and set up an ambush of my own."

"If I were you," Tybalt scoffed. "I would have stolen the gem, jumped overboard during the night, and sold the thing to the highest bidder."

"And that's exactly why I didn't involve you, Tybalt. But don't worry, I don't think you were going to betray us to Count Bricemer either."

"That's right," Bruin said, slapping one of his giant hands onto Tybalt's shoulder. "Fox said that we could trust you."

Tybalt shot Reynard an incredulous look. "You told Bruin, and not me?"

"Bruin was trustworthy."

"Bruin, the drunk? Bruin, who can't write his own name?"

"The very same."

"You told Bruin," Tybalt repeated with astonishment as he stalked off to sulk.

"In any case," Reynard said heavily, "It is growing late. Bruin, I want you and Tybalt to load up whatever supplies you can from below onto the launch. We've got a fortnight's journey ahead of us and I don't like to travel on an empty stomach. Tiecelin, you keep watch while we work, and see to it that Rohart and Sharpebeck do not eat the dead."

Tiecelin nodded and whistled sharply to the two shrikes, both of which were already eyeing the still forms of the bodies. The chimeras chirruped unhappily but obeyed, and flitted up to roost on the cross mast.

"Hey!" Tybalt yelled. "Who put you in charge?"

"Just shut up, and do as the man says," Bruin growled, but the former bandit was not so easily swayed.

"Not until I get an explanation! I'm tired of being left in the dark- where are we going now, Master Fox?"

"Haven't you guessed?" Reynard said blithely as he stooped over to remove his boots. "We are going to Calyx."

"And what about the Lotos?" Tybalt asked Reynard.

"That's right," Bruin said. "That stuff is supposed to be worth a fortune."

"Leave it," Reynard answered. "Let it burn with the ship."

* * * * * *

The fire that lit Duke Nobel's study had nearly died when there was a polite knock on the door.

"Enter," Nobel said, rousing himself with a yawn, and reaching for a wine glass that he had already drained an hour previously. The war manual that he had been perusing lay open at his feet, and he silently berated himself for his carelessness as he stooped over to pick it up.

"What is the hour, Verseau?" Duke Nobel said as his aging steward entered the room.

"It is just past midnight, Your Grace," the steward answered correctly. "You will pardon my intrusion, but a man claiming to be in the employ of His Excellency the Count of Lothier has arrived, and has requested a private audience with Your Grace."

"A private audience?" Duke Nobel said, rubbing his tired eyes.

"I would have refused him, Your Grace, but he carries a letter of passage with the Count's personal seal, and several of the Count's personal guard accompany him."

The Duke drummed his fingers on the table next to him for a moment, contemplating. He had not been expecting to hear word from Bricemer so soon.

"Did he carry a letter?" he asked. "Or perhaps a strongbox?"

"No, Your Grace. He merely said that the Count had entrusted him to deliver a message directly to you, and to you alone."

It was not like Bricemer to contact him through an intermediary, the Duke thought, but then perhaps the Count feared what might be discovered should a message fall into the hands of enemies of the state. Nemea directly bordered Engadlin, and there was always the threat of banditry in that region.

The Duke could think of only one matter that would call for such secrecy, and his greed for news of the gem at last overpowered his caution.

"You may admit him, Verseau."

"Very good, Your Grace," the steward said. "Shall I have the audience chamber prepared?"

"No, I think not," Nobel said, only half feigning the onset of sleep. "I shall receive him here."

"Here, Your Grace?"

"Yes," Nobel replied curtly. "You will, of course, see that he is unarmed?"

"Of course, Your Grace," the steward said, dismissing himself with an obsequious bow.

Nobel did not doubt that his steward would be thorough, but once the man was gone he strapped on his rapier all the same. There was no point in being careless with his safety.

When the steward returned it was with a man dressed in the manner of one of the Count's more expendable minions. Dried mud encrusted his legs and boots, as well as the studded jack that he wore in the style of a common footpad. His dark hair was unkempt and wild, and he had obviously not bathed for some time judging by his considerable reek. His nose was slightly crooked, but his rugged face was handsome.

His most arresting feature, however, was the fact that he had only one almond-colored eye. The other was hidden beneath a thick leather patch.

"Your Grace," the man said, stooping into a refined bow that contrasted oddly with his shabby appearance.

"My steward tells me that you bring a message from the Count of Lothier, Master . . ."

"Rovel, Your Grace," the man said, unbending his knees. "And I am instructed to deliver it to you, and to you alone."

"Leave us," Nobel said, turning an eye towards his steward.

As Verseau retreated from the chamber, the Duke took a few cautious steps towards the man.

"Tell me, Master Rovel, have we met before?" the Duke asked. "Your face seems familiar to me."

"Your Grace honors me. I have been in your presence but twice before, but I would hardly expect you to remember me, low servant that I am."

The Duke could detect an odd hint of mockery in the man's tone, and it unsettled him.

"And what message do you bring me from the Count?"

"I am instructed to inform you that the Quicksilver has returned from Calvaria, and that it bears a certain gem of interest to you."

"Continue," Nobel said, his pulse quickening as he turned to gaze at the last simmering embers of the fire.

"The captain of the Quicksilver and his crew have been disposed of, and the ship itself has been burnt and scuttled."

"And the Count?" Nobel said, turning.

"Held prisoner," Reynard said, lightly pressing the tip of the rapier that was now in his grip against the front of Nobel's doublet. "By the very men that Your Grace had intended to die with the crew."

"Fox!" Nobel gasped, recognizing the cat burglar at last.

The Duke leapt backwards, grasping at the thin air where his scabbard had been only moments previous before realizing that the one-eyed man was wielding his own rapier. He could not help but feel rather irritated by the irony of the situation as he reached for the bell pull that would summon his guards.

"I would not do that if I were you," Reynard said sharply, punctuating his point by resting his blade on the nape of the Duke's neck. "I have no desire to kill you, but I will if I must."

"You may slay me," the Duke said with somewhat admirable lack of fear. "But you will most certainly die with me, and your Temple whore as well. My men will see to that."

"By the same token," Reynard said, "I feel it is only fair to mention that if I do not contact certain parties by the morning my compatriots are under orders to ensure that both Count Bricemer and the gem of Zosia will conveniently wind up in the hands of the Calvarians, and Arcas will face a war it cannot possibly hope to win."

The Duke's teeth ground against each other noisily for a moment as he digested this.

"Yes," Reynard went on, "It is quite a dilemma: I cannot safely kill you, and you cannot safely kill me. Therefore, I suggest that you lower your arm, and I will lower your sword, and then we may both sit down so that we may have a proper chat."

Slowly, the Duke lowered his arm.

"Thank you for being reasonable," Reynard said, and sheathed the Duke's rapier. "As I said before, Your Grace, I have no wish to kill you. And I do hope you will forgive me for not being completely honest with your steward, but I'm afraid this is the only way I could be certain to speak openly with you."

"What is it that you want with me?" Nobel croaked as he moved over to his favorite chair and slumped into it heavily. "Revenge, I suppose."

"That had occurred to me, though a lifetime spent revenging myself upon the rich and powerful has left me rather unsatisfied."

The Duke was silent as Reynard peeled off his eye patch.

"Besides, even if I did manage to kill you, I would be depriving myself of a wonderful opportunity to make a little profit. After all, I have something that you want, and you have many, many things that I want."

"Go on, then," the Duke said with resignation. "Name your price."

"First," Reynard said, producing a rolled of piece of parchment, which he then handed to the Duke. "You will concede to the following list of demands that my companions and I have compiled."

The Duke eyes widened considerably as he scanned the document.

"This is preposterous," the Duke blustered aloud as he neared the bottom of the scroll. "Ruinous, even."

"Yes. But it's a small price to pay to be King, don't you agree?"

The Duke simmered for a moment before nodding.

"Then you will honor our requests?"

The Duke rapped his fingers on the armrest and glowered hatefully at Reynard, as if his very gaze might strike the man dead, but his head nodded once again in the affirmative.

"Good," Reynard beamed. "Now all that is left is the simple matter of agreeing on when we will make our exchange. And, of course, as a show of good faith between us, I would think some sort of public display of our new relationship would be most appropriate."

"I believe," The Duke said with a sigh, "That something suitable can be arranged."

* * * * * *

In the days leading up to the coronation of Duke Nobel, which was auspiciously scheduled to occur at the height of the festival of Crowning- the day that marked the end of the Watcher's winter- the broad avenues of Calyx were decorated with hundreds of banners that the Guild of Tailors had provided for the occasion. The members of the powerful Guild of Carpenters, meanwhile, were bending all of their efforts towards constructing an intricate series of platforms in Harbor Square, as well as erecting row after row of tiered seating that would give even the lowliest resident of the Anthill an excellent view of the pageant that would take place there.

The population of Calyx had nearly doubled within this time, and the city was soon filled with landed nobles from across the breadth of Arcasia, as well as the considerable number of servants and house guards that followed in their wake. Many common folk, too, had come from miles around to witness the crowning of their new king, and these country rubes had attracted a small army of curio dealers, con men, Frisian spice merchants, and squadron upon squadron of temple prostitutes.

There were also the foreign emissaries who had come to pay their respects, so that hardly a day passed without the arrival of some oddly titled lord from Solothurn or dense retinue of dark-robed scholars from Mandross. These foreigners were so numerous that the Duke was forced to rely on the city's guilds to house them, with the result that the regular patrons of the Bleeding Hart, the tavern that was run by the Guild of Vintners, found themselves rubbing shoulders with the fancifully dressed representatives from Therimere, or the fearsome Myrmidons that protected the single hooded envoy who had been sent from Glycon.

But even these exotics paled in the collective imagination of the citizens of Calyx when compared to the arrival of Lord Corvino, the self-styled Count of Luxia, uncle of the Countess Persephone and the current head of the rebellious provinces that the Dukes of Arcas had battled for generations. With him came his own court of advisors, servants, and men-at-arms, and in honor of his presence the burgundy standard of Luxia was added to those that flew over the Duke's palace.

Finally, just when it seemed as if the city might burst, the day of Crowning came.

At first light, the wretched prisoners who languished in Westgate were taken from their damp cells and were escorted to the nearest temple of Sphinx, where they were fed, bathed, and clothed before being released into the streets with a freshly minted gold crown pressed into their palms. As these bewildered men and women wandered free, truly flummoxed by their sudden turn of good fortune, the streets began to ring with the shrill voices of the heralds of the Royal Guild of Messengers, who loudly proclaimed that Duke Nobel had decreed that there was to be an abolishment of all outstanding debts owed to the Royal Bank.

Within moments the streets were filled with jubilant men and women, who were greeted by the sight of brightly colored wagons supplied by the Wheel and Wainwrights' Guild, each one heaped with fresh bread, roast poultry, pickled eggs, great wheels of cheese, kegs of beer, jugs of wine, and all of it provided at the Duke's expense.

At midday, just as the revelers had nearly sated their appetites, an odd procession passed through the western gates of the city. At its head was a chorus of lovely young women adorned in the twirling skirts and colorful scarves of priestesses of the Lioness. They tossed scented petals from their hands as they danced the Chozo to the jubilant strains of the skilled musicians who followed them, so that the street itself was soon carpeted with them.

Behind the musicians rode a number of strange figures. At their head was a handsome man, his rich coat cut in the latest style. He had the bearing of a nobleman, but as he passed a group of maids he turned his brilliant eyes to them and flashed a charming smile.

On either side of this dashing figure, as if in escort, were two grim-looking Calvarians. The man, who appeared tall even in the saddle, wore black. The woman, an exotic beauty who wore trousers and boots in the manner of a man, wore white. A pair of finely wrought Calvarian blades rode at their hips, and they kept their heads held high.

"Who're they, then?" a lowly render muttered, his skin raw and stinking from years of working with lye.

"Don't you know?" said one of his similarly disfigured companions as he chomped on a fine bit of fresh cheese. "That's Lord Reynard."

"Who?"

"Haven't you heard the songs them servants of the Watcher been moaning every night at Scorpion House?" the second render said with considerable disdain for his companion. "He's the one what filched the gem o' Zosia from the lowest vault o' Dis."

"That's the draw-latch what lifted Duke Nobel's bauble?"

"Aye."

"Then what's them white demons with 'em for?"

"You shut yer mouth, ya twist," a weathered laundress bawled at the first render. "You want to get us used up? Them's Lord Isengrim and Lady Hirsent, and they'll smooth ya right quick if'n they hear yer prattle."

Indeed, the romance of Isengrim and his lover Hirsent, and their deadly skill with a blade were common knowledge to the simple folk of Calyx, for the servants of the Watcher had been singing of the exploits of wily Lord Reynard and his bold companions, until their names and descriptions were common knowledge from one end of the city to the other. Even their weapons had been given names, so that Bruin's old battle-axe had become Mauler, and Hirsent's stolen sword now wore the fanciful name of Harrower. Only Isengrim's weapon was without a title, until one of the Watcher's servants had been inspired enough to name the blade Right-Hand.

Of course, each servant of the Watcher told these stories differently, and there were none that could agree on who Lord Reynard was, or what lands he had come from. A deposed Frisian noble, some guessed, or perhaps even a distant relation of the Duke himself. There were even some who claimed to have known him when he was just a young man in the Anthill, but no one paid these stories much attention, as they were often told by the wretched men and women who spent their days in the death dream of the Lotos seed.

"Look," said a young boy as a solemn figure wearing a feathered cap with a narrow brim rode past. "Tiecelin the Sure-Shot!"

"And Bruin the Mighty," another boy chimed as the huge man lifted up an offered cup of wine to his mouth. "I bet he could chop a man in two wif' Mauler."

Behind these two legendary figures came a scowling man astride a gelding, his bandolier bristling with knives letting all know that he was Tybalt, the Bandit King. At the sound of his name being cheered he brightened considerably, and by the time that they reached Gin Lane he was laughing merrily, his steed chased by dozens of young maids, several of whom he stooped over in his saddle to honor with a passionate kiss.

Last in the procession was Count Bricemer, who wore a sour expression and did not wave. His mare was surrounded by a strange company of armed men who wore no badge or crest: Mandrossian mercenaries by the looks of them. It did not occur to any of the onlookers that these men were not so much guarding the Count from the crowd as they were preventing him from fleeing.

So it was that, by the time Lord Reynard and his now famous companions reached the largest of the three bridges that hung over the Vinus, nearly the entire population of the Anthill was trailing in their wake, dancing, drinking, and singing raucously. The lavishly dressed Lords and Ladies of Calyx who were seated according to precedence along the edges of Harbor Square were troubled by the sight of this approaching throng, and began to mutter darkly.

For a moment it seemed that the unruly mob that followed Lord Reynard might overrun the highborn nobles and great guildsmen that were assembled, until at last the procession came to a halt, and the company of priests and priestesses that cavorted before Reynard split their ranks, and allowed his steed to canter between them.

As he rode forward, Reynard smiled back at the venomous glares directed towards him. The guildsmen and nobles too had heard the tales of Reynard, and had dismissed them as utter fabrications. The demon-haunted cities, sea monsters, and the endless narrow escapes that filled these stories might make for popular entertainment amongst the lower classes, but they could not seriously be taken at face value. "Where does this 'Lord' Reynard come from?" they twittered to each other as they sat at dinner, assuaging their own pride. "What sort of a lord is he, with no lands or titles to his name?"

Reynard saw many familiar faces amongst the upper class: there sat the ruddy-faced Lord Belin, and closer to the central platform was Lord Chanticleer, pale and sweating in the midday sun. Baroness Gallopin sat with her rakish husband, but even she did not recognize the man who had once stolen her heart under the name of Malbranche.

When Reynard reached the center of the square, just past the gallows where he had once had the singular honor of witnessing his own execution, his eyes met those of a woman who stood prominent amongst the priestesses of the Temple of Sphinx.

It was Hermeline.

He halted his steed. Hermeline took a few steps towards him, her mouth fluttering, and then she fainted away.

The crowd gasped as the priestess fell, but before anyone could reach her Reynard had vaulted off of his horse and was at her side, waving away the younger priestesses who were crowding around them.

"Water!" Reynard shouted, and one of the girls brought him a cup of the stuff, which he slowly dabbed onto Hermeline's brow with a gleaming handkerchief.

"Perhaps you should rest, Madam," he said as Hermeline's eyes fluttered open. "You have been in the sun too long, I think."

"Percehaie?" Hermeline replied. "My love, but you are dead-"

"I'm afraid, Madam, that you have mistaken me for someone else," Reynard said with sympathy. "But whoever this Master Percehaie may have been, I am certain that he was blessed to have had such a lovely woman as you for a lover."

Hermeline looked up at him, unconvinced.

"You sound like my Percehaie . . . and you wear his face, though your chin is covered in whiskers."

"He must have been a terribly handsome chap- perhaps we are related?" Reynard said, "Tell me, what sort of a man was this Percehaie?"

"He was a liar," Hermeline said, her eyes narrowing. "And a thief. And I loved him."

"And did he love you?"

"I thought that he did. I am not so certain now."

"Then be comforted," he said and kissed her lightly on the back of her hand.

"You horrible little man," she fumed then, her head shaking from side to side with mounting disapproval. "I thought you were dead!"

"So did I," Reynard replied as graciously as he was able, and glanced nervously at the crowd of nearby gawkers who were staring at them. He wished that he had the foresight to steal more than one jewel from the underworld.

"You might have left me a letter!" she said and slapped his hand away. "I cried every night for a month!"

"I didn't exactly have time, my dear."

"And now you are back, on your fancy horse, and you expect me to blush and coo like one of your other girls?"

"That's not-"

"Well you can forget it!" she said and jabbed her fingers into his chest. "I'm through with you, Master Fox, or whatever your name is-"

"It is Reynard," he said. "Lord Reynard. Haven't you heard the songs?"

"Reynard?" Hermeline clucked. "That is a stupid name."

"I know," Reynard conceded, adding, "Will you please stop hitting me?"

"No," she replied, and delivered a sharp jab to his triceps that made them sing.

"Isengrim," Reynard squealed. "Get this vixen off me!"

"This is *lufestre* of Reynard?" Hirsent asked the Northerner, who shrugged and did not move a muscle to come to his friend's aid.

The sound of blaring trumpets saved Reynard from certain death at the hands of Hermeline, for they heralded the arrival of the Duke, who was coming down Royal Street with much pomp and ceremony (though not as much ceremony as he might have wished for, having been forced to spend an exorbitant sum of money in order to comply with Reynard's demands.) Reynard used this temporary distraction to scamper back to his horse, blowing Hermeline a kiss as she grouchily joined the other dancers who were already twirling around the edges of the square.

The Duke had come in the company of the priests of Fenix, who were robed in brilliant reds, oranges, and yellows that were the hue of Luxian lemons. They wore dazzling mitres, and carried ceremonial hammers made of silver and gold, save for Petipas, the high priest, who held a silver diadem in his gloved hands.

When the servants of the Firebird were in position, another fanfare sounded, and the various nobles present mounted the platform, arranging themselves by order of importance around the carpeted area where the Duke would be crowned.

"Isengrim," Reynard said to his companion, "Have our Mandrossian friends release Bricemer so that he may take his place at his master's feet."

Isengrim nodded and signaled to the mercenaries guarding the Count. Within seconds they had parted ranks, allowing the stiff-lipped man passage. The Count dismounted awkwardly, and limped across the square to join his peers just below the central dais.

It was at this moment that Reynard caught sight of the Countess Persephone, who had joined a flock of her own countrymen from Luxia and was now standing rigidly at the side of her uncle.

Reynard found her as beautiful as he had remembered her. More so, he thought, for the Persephone that had inhabited his imagination for so long was a pale copy compared to the woman who was standing now with quiet dignity, even as she rubbed shoulders with the man who had sought her death since the passing of her father. She seemed older, her time spent as the Duke's prisoner having perhaps lent her a sense of gravity and bearing that she had lacked previously. He wondered then if the stories of his accomplishments had reached her secluded rooms in the palace, perhaps whispered to her by some maid she had befriended, or scowled upon by the prim Madam Corte, who was even now hovering over her shoulder, her eyes half-closed in the brightness of the day.

He half expected her to turn and see him, to know him, and perhaps to collapse as Hermeline had, or to smile knowingly, or weep tears of relief.

She did, however, none of these things, and kept her gaze level as her uncle spoke to her, and briefly took her gloved hand in his.

Then the Duke himself mounted the platform. He was clothed in rich furs and supple cloth dyed purple, but wore no silk or jewels save the signet ring on his finger. As he took his place atop the dais the square quieted considerably, and each member of the crowd leaned forward expectantly.

"My people!" Nobel began, "Today is a great day! For a hundred years, and more, Arcasia has been a land divided: beset by war, famine, and plague! I have seen the green fields of Engadlin soaked in a sea of blood, while year after year the best of our crops are sent to feed the pale-skinned invaders who hold our northern provinces captive! But no more! This very day we send word to the Calvarians that they will receive no more shipments of grain and cattle: no more tribute! For today Arcasia is a land united!"

The crowd roared with approval.

"And what great lord has done this, you ask?" Nobel said as the din subsided, his gaze lowering so that it encompassed Reynard and his companions. "Why, no lord at all! Indeed, less than ten men have triumphed where entire armies have failed!"

"He has forgotten Roenel," Tybalt said under his breath. "And the others."

"Hush," Reynard said, for all eyes were on them now. "It's artistic license."

"Murder is what it is," Tybalt sniffed, but was quiet.

"Behold!" Nobel continued. "These men have braved the heart of Calvaria and have returned with our greatest treasure! For it is said that no man may rule Arcasia who does not hold the gem of Zosia!" Nobel shifted his gaze to Reynard, and waited expectantly.

Reynard took his cue, and with a touch of solemnity he approached the dais, stepping past rank after rank of petty nobles.

As he passed the delegation from Luxia there was a startled cry, and he turned in time to catch a glimpse of Madam Corte, her right hand held up to conceal the almost comical look of surprise etched across her face.

The Countess Persephone's gaze met his.

"Your Excellence," he said to her, unable to resist. "It is good to see you again."

"And you, Lord Reynard," she replied. "I had not thought to see you again . . . at least not so soon."

A muffled cough interrupted their brief reunion.

"The gem if you please, Master Reynard," Duke Nobel said with delicately concealed contempt.

"But of course, Your Grace," Reynard said, and removed one of his gloves before placing two of his fingers into his mouth in order to let out a piercing whistle.

A moment later the shrikes that Tiecelin had named Sharpebeck and Rohart, who until now had been perched amongst the gargoyles decorating one of the larger buildings that faced Harbor Square, glided down towards the dais, much to the horror of the nobles there assembled.

Sharpebeck, whose plum-colored feathers nearly matched the Duke's own garments, clutched a velvet bag in her clawed feet. When she was low enough she beat her wings rapidly so that she hung hovering above Reynard, who gingerly reached out to catch the treasure that she had been entrusted with.

"Long live the King!" the shrike chirped. Her voice was like that of a young girl.

"Indeed," Reynard said earnestly, handing the heart-sized gem to Duke Nobel before descending several steps and shouting, "Long live the King!"

As the two shrikes swooped away from the dais, Nobel raised his arm, the gem of Zosia in the flat of his palm.

"Long live the King!" the crowd shouted as Petipas stepped forward to place the gilded crown on King Nobel's head.

"Now," King Nobel said, "Let it be known throughout our domain that the civil strife between Arcas and Luxia is over! For, as my first act, I name as my Queen the Countess Persephone of Luxia, and our two houses shall be as one!"

Reynard felt the world slow around him as the crowd erupted into cheers. He turned and saw her walking slowly up the stairs, and at last he knew why her eyes were so sad.

The Countess came to a point just below Nobel, who took a second crown from Petipas and placed it on her brow as she knelt before him. Then he lifted her up onto the dais, and kissed her, and she was the Queen of Arcasia.

"Long live the Queen!" Count Corvino, now the rightful lord of Luxia, shouted above the din.

Reynard felt his lips move, but no words escaped him as the crowd responded in kind. And as Nobel handed Persephone the gem that it had taken all of his wits and skill to steal, he could not help but feel as though he had been outmaneuvered.

When the cheering had abated, King Nobel held up his hand for silence. "And, as it was in the days of the kings of old Aquilia, I shall grant my bride a single boon! What it is in my power to grant, shall be hers."

"You need not name it now, my dear," Nobel said to her in a softer tone that made Reynard sick to hear, "If you have not decided."

Persephone turned away from Nobel, glancing at Reynard, and finally said, "I ask nothing for myself, husband, for already you have done more for my people than I could have dreamt possible . . . but there is one thing that I would ask of you, if you will grant it."

"Name it, then, and it shall be done."

"Very well. This I ask," the Countess said with conviction, and gestured toward Reynard. "Let this common man, who was the architect of our union, be rewarded for his great deed!"

"My Queen," Nobel began to protest, "I have already made arrangements to reward Lord Reynard and his companions: a considerable pension has-"

"If that is the case, then grant him lands and a title, so that he may continue to serve us."

There was a startled gasp from the assembled nobles, and a low murmur arose from the guildsmen beyond. Nobel had already promised many of the Lords and Ladies of Calyx noble titles in order to secure their allegiance, and he could only grant another by depriving one of them.

Reynard watched with considerable relish as Nobel squirmed.

"That is-" he said. "That is, I'm afraid-"

"Yes?" she said, with mock innocence.

"What I mean to say is," Nobel said, perfectly aware of the eyes watching them. "If that is your wish-"

"It is."

"Then," Nobel sighed, "Step forward, Reynard, and receive your just reward."

Reynard approached the royal couple.

"Kneel," Nobel intoned bitterly.

Reynard bent to one knee, and for the first time in his life found the act of bowing a delightful thing.

"Remind me, Count Bricemer," Nobel said then, turning to face his recently returned advisor, "Was this man not recommended to me by your noble personage?"

Bricemer lowered his gaze. "He was, Your Majesty."

"Then I think it is only appropriate that he be your responsibility. Name for me, if you would, one of your baronies."

"My King," Bricemer bristled, "Surely-"

"Name one, Count Bricemer. Or, do you mean to disappoint me a second time?"

"No, Your Majesty."

"Then name one of the baronies of Lothier."

"There is one barony that comes to mind, Your Majesty" Count Bricemer said after a moment. An odd smile had appeared on his face. "Maleperduys."

"Ah," Nobel said, his own face lighting up with humor. "Yes . . . a fine suggestion indeed, Count Bricemer. You remind us of how well you serve us."

With that, Nobel drew his sword, laid it on Reynard's left shoulder and said, "Master Reynard, do you swear by your life's blood that you will be faithful, and bear true allegiance to the King of Arcasia, his heirs and successors, uphold his laws, and bear arms on his behalf?"

"I do, Your Majesty."

"So be it," Nobel said, and lowered his sword so that Reynard might take it in his hands and press his lips to the blade. This he did, and Nobel smirked as he went on to say, "Rise, Baron Reynard, Lord of Maleperduys!"

Reynard unbent his knee, and as he did so the thick crowd of commoners that choked the far end of the square erupted into cheers.

"One last gift I have for you, Baron Reynard," Queen Persephone said, and Reynard saw that she held in her palm the silver necklace with the violet stone that had brought him to the palace. "A token of my own appreciation for what you have done."

"I cannot accept such a gift," Reynard said.

"Do not speak nonsense," she said, and took a delicate step forward. "You have brought me a far finer gem with which to adorn ourselves, and . . . there is nothing else that I can give you."

Her lips were curled into a sad smile.

"You honor me, Your Highness," Reynard said, and bent his head so that the Queen could slip the silver chain over his head, her fingers lightly brushing against him.

"And now, *Baron* Reynard," Nobel said, "I ask that you join your peers below, for there are many assembled here who must do me homage before the day is done."

"With your permission, my King, I think that I might do best to retire from these proceedings, for I have a long journey ahead of me now, and I do not believe I can afford to tarry."

"Such insolence from one so low," one of the nobles whispered somewhere behind Reynard.

"A long journey?" Nobel said, his lips pursing angrily. "Do explain yourself."

"I am Baron of Maleperduys, am I not Your Majesty?" Reynard quipped. "Surely, I must see to the state of my domain."

"No-" Persephone said softly, the word slipping out of her mouth before she could stop it.

Nobel ignored his wife's outburst, and arched one of his eyebrows as he regarded the figure that stood below him with barely concealed disbelief.

"Baron Reynard," said Nobel. "Surely you must know that Maleperduys, as well as the rest of Lothier, is currently under the control of the Calvarians."

"All the more reason for a hasty departure, Your Majesty."

"I see," Nobel said, and smiled cruelly. "Very well. I will relieve you of your duties here at court, but do not forget, Baron Reynard, that war is coming and, should you survive your journey, I will expect you to fight in the defense of the kingdom."

Reynard bowed. "I am at Your Majesty's command."

"See to it that you do not forget that," Nobel said, and then dismissed Reynard with a wave of his hand.

EPILOGUE

"What are you thinking?" Hermeline asked Reynard, who was standing amidst the wreckage of the warehouse where he had once made his home, back when he was the best thief in Calyx. Vandals and derelicts had moved into it once Nobel's agents had finished with it, and there was hardly a window or crate left unbroken in the place. The little office, and the false bedroom above had been emptied, and the secret door that led to his private quarters had been torn off of its hinges and hacked apart by treasure hunters who had hoped to find some hidden store of the notorious Fox's stolen lucre.

"Hmm?" Reynard hummed.

Hermeline placed her hands on his shoulders and gave them a gentle squeeze. "It's just that you are so quiet."

"Am I?" Reynard said, turning.

"Yes," she said, and smiled. "And it makes me wonder what is going on inside that head of yours."

"I should have brought you here before," Reynard said, climbing the steps to the third floor. "You would have liked it, I think."

His old room was a shambles. Nothing of any value had been left in one piece. Even the roof had not been safe from the scavenger's depredations, so that the beautiful loft had become a roost for the filthy pigeons that inhabited the city.

"Greedy fools," Reynard muttered as he descended the stairs, pausing to smash apart a section of the thick plaster just above the doorframe with a hammer that he had brought for just such a purpose. Once he had made a hole large enough for his hand he reached into a hidden cubby and retrieved his final secret reserve of wealth: a small pouch that was stuffed full of diamonds.

"Are you ready to leave?" he asked her, taking Hermeline by the waist and giving her a little kiss on her forehead.

"No," she pouted.

"Don't sulk," Reynard chided. "You know very well it is for your own safety."

"For safety I must go to some horrid far away place where there are wargs in the forest, and those Northern demons are as thick as flies?"

"The farther away, and the more enemies between us and Nobel the better," Reynard said seriously. "He will kill you for certain if we stay."

Hermeline nodded, and he kissed her again before leading her down the stairs into the ruined office.

"There will be no hot water there," she said suddenly. "And I am leaving so many of my nicest things behind."

"Ah-ha!" Reynard laughed. "Now we see what is really troubling you."

"It will be horrible."

"No it will not," he said, wiping a tear from her eye. "I promise you. Besides, who will take care of me if you do not come?"

"Stupid," she said angrily to herself, wiping her eyes. "Stupid."

"Why are you crying?"

"Because I love you," she said, and laughed.

"Poor Hermeline," he said with sympathy, and held her.

"The others will be waiting," she said after a while, and they parted. She brushed several stray curls out of her face. "How do I look?"

"Like a queen."

She beamed happily and said, "Then it is too bad that Calyx already has one."

"Yes," Reynard replied. "It is."

The others were waiting for them on the street outside, an odd looking group amongst the slovenly porters who inhabited this part of the city.

"How far is it to Maleperduys, Reynard?" Bruin asked gruffly. "And what sort of inns do they have there?"

"Let us hope none at all," Reynard answered, "If they are anything like the ones in Calvaria. As for distance, I cannot say, for we shall not travel by road. Still, I think we will manage somehow." He tossed the pouch of diamonds to Isengrim. "It is not enough to raise an army, but it's a start."

Isengrim shook his head as he deposited the bag of precious stones into his saddlebag. "I still do not understand your people's obsession with shiny rocks."

"They please the eye," Reynard said with a shrug. "And they are rare. What can I say? Ours is a shallow race, that spends its days and nights desiring all of the beautiful things that we cannot have."

"Ah," Isengrim said as he turned his gaze towards Hirsent. "That I *can* understand."

Hirsent clucked her tongue with mock disapproval. "You must be being careful, my *lufiend*, that this land of softness is not making you soft as well."

"Later, perhaps, I will show you how soft I have become," Isengrim growled.

Hirsent blushed and whispered a few protests in Calvarian that only made the others laugh harder.

"Men," Hermeline snorted.

"Let us be off," Reynard said finally, mounting his own steed and helping Hermeline to climb up into the saddle behind him, "In case Nobel decides to ambush us before the day is out."

"If he does," Tiecelin said, pulling on the brim of his feathered cap, "He will not catch us unawares."

Reynard craned his neck and spotted Sharpebeck and Rohart soaring in the skies above, swooping and diving as they played at hunting the way that cats do. During the day, at least, the shrikes would serve as Tiecelin's extended eyes and ears.

Reynard nodded, pleased, and then took one last look at the warehouse that had been the home of Percehaie the foreign spice merchant, Rovel the dockworker, Cuwart the messenger, Malbranche the rake, and one other.

"Reynard the Fox," he chucked to himself, and whipped his reins. Hermeline let out a little cry as the horse began to canter through the streets, and Reynard guessed that she had never ridden one before.

They had just reached Westgate when Tybalt caught up with them, scowling as usual, his fine clothes discarded for his rough leather armor and bandolier full of knives.

"Have you changed your mind, Tybalt?" Reynard asked. "Or have you already run through all the gold that Nobel gave you?"

"Perhaps I just want to be there when you fall from your high perch, *Baron* Reynard," Tybalt replied, flipping one of his knives into the air and catching it in his gloved palm.

"Then I hope you know how to land on your feet," Reynard replied, grinning wickedly.

"We shall see," Tybalt answered, and sheathed his dagger. "Won't we?"

* * * * * *

"Reynard?" Hermeline whispered into his ear when they had left the city, their steeds breaking into a steady canter as they turned onto the road that led north. "Do you love me?"

"You know that I do," he replied, turning in the saddle to kiss her. "Does that make you happy?"

"Yes," she said, and was quiet for a mile or two.

"Do I make you happy?" she asked at last.

"Yes," he said, his fingers slowly encircling the violet ruby that hung round his neck.

Acknowledgements

I would like to thank first and foremost my parents, whose patience and support made the writing of this book possible, as well as the dedicated group of people (Danielle, Ian, Molly, Peter, Phil & Sarah) who provided me with much needed input along the way. I'd also like to thank Lindsay Ribar for her (free!) editorial work, Roy vanNorstrand for encouraging me to start writing back in 2006, and- finally- Bruce Coville, who gave me the best advice one can give to an aspiring author: "Just finish your book. You can worry about the rest later."